Anna K
K
Away

Also by Jenny Lee

Anna
K

JENNY LEE

Anna K
Away

FLATIRON
BOOKS
NEW YORK

This is a work of fiction. All of the characters, organizations, and events portrayed in this novel are either products of the author's imagination or are used fictitiously.

ANNA K AWAY. Copyright © 2021 by Jenny Lee. All rights reserved. Printed in the United States of America. For information, address Flatiron Books, 120 Broadway, New York, NY 10271.

www.flatironbooks.com

Library of Congress Cataloging-in-Publication Data

Names: Lee, Jenny, 1971– author.
Title: Anna K away / Jenny Lee.
Description: First edition. | New York, NY : Flatiron Books, 2021. | Series: Anna K ; 2
Identifiers: LCCN 2020056406 | ISBN 9781250236463 (hardcover) |
    ISBN 9781250798954 (international, sold outside the U.S., subject to rights availability) |
    ISBN 9781250236456 (ebook)
Subjects: CYAC: Dating (Social customs)—Fiction. | Love—Fiction. | Korean Americans—
    Fiction. | Wealth—Fiction. | New York (N.Y.)—Fiction. | Korea—Fiction. | Los Angeles
    (Calif.)—Fiction.
Classification: LCC PZ7.L512533 Anp 2021 | DDC [Fic]—dc23
LC record available at https://lccn.loc.gov/2020056406

Our books may be purchased in bulk for promotional, educational, or business use. Please contact your local bookseller or the Macmillan Corporate and Premium Sales Department at 1-800-221-7945, extension 5442, or by email at MacmillanSpecialMarkets@macmillan.com.

First International Edition: 2021

First Edition: 2021

10 9 8 7 6 5 4 3 2 1

For every teenager who had their school year,
prom, graduation, and summer vacation disrupted
because of the global pandemic

Who's Who in *Anna K Away*

BEATRICE D.
Seventeen, rising senior at Greenwich Academy. Cousin of the late Alexia Vronsky.

CLAUDINE C.
Sixteen, Beatrice's girlfriend or ex-girlfriend (depends on who you ask).

ANNA K.
Seventeen, rising senior at . . . not sure yet. Sister of Steven, love of Alexia V.'s life.

ALEXIA V. (AKA VRONSKY)
Forever sixteen. Dead and buried.

NATALIA T.
Eighteen, high school dropout. Kimmie's best friend, former girlfriend of Dustin's late brother, Nicholas.

DUSTIN L.
Eighteen, graduate of Stuyvesant High School, deferred a year at MIT to stay in the city. Best friend of Steven, boyfriend of Kimmie.

TIARE A.

Nineteen, dropped out her senior year and got a GED. Santa Barbara surfer chick. Love interest of Beatrice.

STEVEN K.

Eighteen, graduate of Collegiate School, soon to take a post-grad year at Deerfield Academy. Anna's older brother, boyfriend of Lolly.

LOLLY S.

Seventeen, rising senior at the Spence School. Girlfriend of Steven, older sister to Kimmie.

KIMMIE S.

Sixteen, rising junior at Eleanor Roosevelt High School. Lolly's younger sister, girlfriend of Dustin.

CHANG-RI P.

Twenty-two, assistant producer on a music show. Anna's new friend in Seoul.

QUENTIN L.

Twenty-one, lead singer of the K-pop group The NowNows.

KIRIL V.

Twenty-one, rising junior at Wesleyan University. Alexia Vronsky's older brother.

DEAN J.

Seventeen, rising senior at South Dillon High in Texas. New kid at Interlochen Arts Camp.

JAMIESON T.

Seventeen, rising senior at Tacoma School of the Arts in Washington. Lolly's theater camp bestie.

Part One

It's a cruel, cruel summer.
Leaving me, leaving me here on my own . . .

—BANANARAMA

I

When Shakespeare wrote *"parting is such sweet sorrow,"* he never had to say *good-bye to a melodramatic French girl in an airport.* This was what Beatrice was thinking as she stood in front of Claudine, who was barely keeping it together. Her pillowy lips quivering as she tried and failed to harness her emotions. "Are you sure you don't want me to come to LA with you?"

"Babe, my internship starts on Monday and I've gotta spend the whole weekend with my Uncle Chadwick at a très boring third wedding of some B-list Hollywood actress." This was the truth, but then Beatrice added a lie. She was so good at lying. Her lies always felt true as soon as she said them. "I tried to get a plus one to bring you, but no dice."

"No dice?" Claudine repeated in her breathy French accent, brow furrowing.

Beatrice leaned forward and kissed Claudine softly. "It's a gambling expression. It means we're out of luck."

"But you never take no for an answer." Claudine pulled her face into a petulant pout, which Beatrice knew was a last-ditch effort to get her to change her mind. Beatrice hated to be told no and would rarely let it stand if she wanted something. But what she truly wanted, no, what she *needed*, was some time alone. And a summer in LA was the exact change of scenery she required. Bringing her "girlfriend" (if that was what they had to call it), no matter how exquisitely sumptuous she happened to be, wasn't the fresh start Beatrice had in mind.

All she knew was that she needed to get away. Everything in Manhattan reminded her of Vronsky. She saw him on street corners, walking away from her before disappearing in a crowd. She heard his laugh coming up through sewer grates. She turned her head at the *vroom-vroom* of every motorcycle. She even listened to his voice mails when she was feeling really desperate—*Yo Bea, Queen Beatrice in the house, Stop screening my calls Bea-yatch!* Her beloved cousin was everywhere around her, as though her memories of him had escaped her mind and now flitted about the city like ghosts.

"Just tell your uncle how sexy I am, and he'll let me come," Claudine pleaded.

Beatrice was moments from bringing out her cat claws. But that was not how she wanted to bid farewell to Claudine. Beatrice knew her fuse was short lately. It was understandable in the wake of her cousin Vronsky's death, but because she cared about Claudine, she was trying to bid farewell on a positive note, even if it was a false one. Claudine was the daughter of her aunt Geneviève's best friend, so she also had filial piety to consider.

Beatrice gave her a deep tongue kiss, pushing her watermelon Trident gum into Claudine's mouth as a parting gift. Claudine had once done the same thing to her, and Beatrice had found it hilarious and strangely hot. Now, she copied it symbolically as a sign of things having come full circle.

Claudine smiled and started chewing the gum. "You'll text," she said, not asked.

They had spent the last five weeks together, rarely if ever apart, and Beatrice knew Claudine was depressed by the idea of being away from each other. "I'll do better than that." *Easier to string her along than get in a fight and have to make up over the phone,* Bea thought. "I'll ravish you tonight in our dreams," she said.

Claudine giggled with delight, her cheeks reddening. Beatrice was the only person who could make Claudine blush. She hooked Claudine's belt with her fingers and pulled her close, giving her a long slow kiss goodbye. *Why did the crazy ones always taste so good?*

Walking away, she could feel Claudine's eyes on her back, willing her to turn around, but Beatrice resisted the impulse to feel anything. Love was a luxury she didn't get to indulge in anymore. Not with Claudine. Not with anyone. Not since Vronsky . . . Beatrice adjusted the monogrammed LV duffel strap on her shoulder as she approached the JFK airport VIP hostess, who had been waiting to walk her through security. Normally Beatrice flew private, but her parents were using the G5 this weekend, so she had to fly commercial like one of the terminal people, as she snobbishly thought of them.

"This way, Ms. D.," the hostess said, taking Bea's bag. Bea put on her Chrome Hearts sunglasses, feeling safe behind the dark tint of the lenses.

Initially Beatrice's mother had refused to pay the extra three thousand for Beatrice to be ushered through security, seated in her own private room, and waited upon until boarding. She had recently read in Oprah's magazine that saying no to your children from time to time would better prepare them for real life, so Beatrice charged it on her own card, knowing full well her mother hadn't looked at a credit card statement in over two decades.

"Is she still back there?" Beatrice asked the hostess, who stared at her blankly. "The hot French chick. Is she still there? Look, just don't be obvi about, it 'kay?"

The host turned and looked at Claudine.

"I just said don't be obvi about it!"

"Sorry, I, uh . . . She is. Yes. Standing there. Still."

"She's not crying, is she?" Bea asked.

"Hard to tell . . . no, yeah . . . she just wiped her nose. Definitely crying."

"Probably because I didn't let her finish when I went down on her in the limo." She glanced at the VIP hostess over her sunglasses. "Always leave them wanting more. Remember that . . ." Beatrice quickly glanced at the woman's name tag. "Dara."

"Excellent advice, ma'am," Dara replied quickly, remembering what she was told when she first started the job a few months ago: the rich weren't as polite as celebrities. Celebrities had a fear of getting exposed as assholes, but rich people, like really rich people . . . well, they didn't call it fuck-you money for nothing.

"Did you just call me ma'am?"

"Yes, ma'am. I'm sorry, I just did it again." Dara turned her attention to Beatrice's boarding pass. "Headed to Los Angeles, I see."

"My uncle's a hotshot manager slash producer out there." Beatrice had a way of sounding flirty even when relaying basic facts. "I'll be in LA for basically the whole summer. It's such a relief, I can't even tell you. . . . I'm so fucking sick of New York."

II

Under normal circumstances, a summer abroad might sound glamorous, adventurous, and luxurious, but for Anna K. there was nothing normal about her current circumstances. When she boarded her father's plane the morning after a long dark night of the soul in the bowels of Grand Central, she sat down in a chair across the aisle from her father and realized something. She had no idea where she was headed, figuratively or literally.

Anna had a hazy recollection of her father sitting on her bed yesterday morning, outlining their travel plans for the summer. He kept saying things like "new school, new start, new beginning." But Anna was barely listening. She was still trying to figure out why she felt so altered. She looked the same, sounded the same, but she had undergone a profound change. She heard from her brother, Steven, that the therapist her parents consulted had told them it was impossible to know how she might react in the aftermath. The boy she loved had been killed by a train. In front of her no less. This wasn't the typical teenage trouble. This was an outlier event, this was . . . unprecedented.

That was how she felt. Reborn into a life without precedent. Ever since Anna was a young girl everything had gone so predictably, so smoothly, so utterly planned out by her strict Korean father and chilly WASP mother. She did as she was told and didn't question them and it never bothered her. Not until she met *him*. He changed everything, first for the better, and then for the worse. She had never soared so high, or fallen this low.

Most people would assume she was in mourning for her once perfect life—a good daughter from a fine family—but that was wrong. What she was mourning right now was a future with Alexia Vronsky. He had been ripped out of the present and relegated to the past so abruptly that her love for him had far outpaced the memories they had created together, which left her feeling shortchanged and grateful at the same time. Miraculously, they had found big love in their teenage years. Their time together was just beginning and then as quickly as it had started, it was over. If offered the chance to go back in time before she had met Alexia, she wouldn't take it. She was done with that so-called charmed life forever.

But what was she supposed to do now? Was she supposed to pick up the pieces of her old life and try to put them back together, or should she start over completely and build a new life from ground zero? She didn't know how to proceed; this was also a new feeling for her.

Before Anna left for the airport, her mother pulled her into her bedroom closet and handed Anna a box wrapped in plain brown paper. "What is it?" Anna asked quietly.

"It's something you should have," Greer told her. "You'll understand when you open it. Don't tell your father."

"When should I open it?" Anna asked. These days decisions were hard for her to make.

Greer sighed, her expression softening for a moment. "Wait until after his memorial."

"His name is Alexia," Anna said with more spark than she had been able to muster in some time. "Was. His name was . . ." Her eye felt twitchy from the strain of trying not to cry in front of her mother.

"Yes." Greer nodded. "May he rest in peace, and once he is, I hope you can find the strength to put all of this behind you. You have your whole life ahead of you, Anna. You need to be wiser with the choices you make. It's the summer. A good time to figure out a way to rein your life in."

Rein in my life? Like it's an unruly horse who broke free and ran away?

You think it's so easy to just gather up the pieces of my heart and put them back together again? So I can be—what? An ice queen like you? Your own marriage is crumbling, your husband is taking leave, and you're telling your daughter to buck up and pull it together? This was what Anna wanted to say, but instead she bit her tongue, took the box with a solemn nod, and tucked it gently into her nylon Prada duffel.

Her father woke her up after they landed and Steven and Lolly had already deboarded. "Anna, we're here."

"Where?" she asked softly.

"Bristol Airport," he said. "We'll spend a week here before heading to Italy for . . ." He didn't finish his sentence. He didn't have to. Anna knew what he was going to say. They were going to drop off the dogs in the Cotswolds, then fly to Italy for Vronsky's memorial service. She nodded to show she understood. She wanted to scream, but all she did was press her lips together and say nothing at all.

"You're going to be okay," her father murmured.

You don't know that, Anna thought. *How can anybody know if anything's going to be okay?*

Outside on the tarmac, there were two black SUVs ready to drive them to their country estate in the rolling hills of the Cotswolds. It was a house that Anna adored, but which they hardly ever stayed in. She asked her father once why they needed such a large house in the English countryside when they never spent much time there, and he told her that one of the best ways to store wealth was in the acquisition of real estate. *At least the dogs will get to enjoy it, they will romp and play,* she thought.

Once they arrived at the house Anna went straight to the boot room, the UK version of a mudroom, and pulled on a pair of wellies. She grabbed a puffy jacket off a hook by the door and headed out the back door with Gemma and Jon Snow, her beloved black Newfoundland show dogs. She had walked barely twenty paces when Lolly's voice rang out behind her. "Anna!" she called. "Wait for me! Steven and your dad are both napping, and I'm bored out of my gourd." She said this last bit in a British accent. "Just trying it out!"

Anna wasn't in the mood for company, but she stopped until Lolly caught up.

"It's so beautiful," Lolly said, looking around at the grounds as they walked the dogs. "I didn't even know your family had a house here."

Anna turned to Lolly and grabbed her hand. "I'm sorry, Lolls. I can't do this right now. I can't make small talk like everything is normal."

"Then don't," Lolly said. "Say whatever you want."

"I don't want to say anything. What I want is . . ." Anna hesitated, unsure what that was anymore.

"What you want is . . . ?" Lolly encouraged her.

"Is to scream." Anna looked down at her feet, feeling weird about admitting such a thing.

"Then let's run and find a good place for you to scream," Lolly said, pulling Anna forward. Anna, not having much choice, started to run alongside Lolly. Gemma and Jon Snow grew excited and started to chase after them, their deep, delighted barks only making the girls run faster. They ran through the gardens bursting with white roses, alliums, and Red Shine tulips, past the koi pond and the little wishing bridge, and past the crumbling stone wall until they were out of breath, hands on their knees.

And then Anna screamed with every square ounce of air in her lungs. Lolly followed suit, shrieking to the sky. It was exactly what both girls needed, Lolly because she had assumed that Anna had read the same article she had in *Vogue* about the positives of primal screaming, and Anna because it seemed the only true way to unleash some of the frustration that was building up within her.

The two girls walked back to the house in silence, but before they entered, Anna stopped. "I don't know who I am anymore, Lolls. I don't know what I want. I don't know anything."

"Anna, you're going to take it one day at a time," Lolly said in a mature, assuring voice. She was pleased that she could be the one to help for a change as opposed to being the girl who needed it. "We're going to get you to Italy. We're going to get you through the funeral in Sicily. I'll be there for you and so will Steven. Then we're all going to get really drunk together in Rome."

"Thank you for calling it what it is," Anna said. "A funeral."

"It's going to be one big blur for you, but you're going to get through it."

"I love you, Lolly." Anna leaned in and put her head on her friend's shoulder.

"Oh, Anna! I love you, too." Lolly cradled Anna's head in her hand.

It was now the afternoon after the service, and looking out at the Italian seascape, Anna didn't feel a dot of closure. It was her second funeral in less than six months. Dustin L., her brother's homework tutor and new best friend who was also dating Lolly's sister, Kimmie, had lost his older brother, Nicholas, to a drug overdose in late March. That was the first one. Vronsky's had just been the second.

And Lolly was right. The whole thing was a big blur.

Anna had watched as Alexia's mother sobbed behind a black lace veil during the brief ceremony. She stared as Alexia's older brother, Kiril, picked up a handful of dirt and dropped it into the grave after the coffin was lowered. Where Alexia had been fair, blond, and blue eyed, his older brother was tan, dark-haired, and had a Bowie-like gaze, one blue eye, one green eye, which Anna found unnerving when he looked directly at her.

Everyone in attendance was then permitted to take a small gardening spade to drop in some dirt and say their farewells. When it was Anna's turn, she grabbed a handful of dirt and tossed it in. Standing there, she tried to open her heart and release all her feelings for him like a flurry of birds. She had fallen in love with him in an instant, as if he had flipped a switch in her. Could she be rid of the pain of his loss just as fast? If there was a switch to flip, would she? Or was the switch once flipped unable to be flipped back? She wanted to whisper a good-bye but she couldn't find the words.

She felt empty when she returned to the hotel, sad and exhausted. Now she sat and stared at the box her mother had given her before she left. She unwrapped it to find a Post-it Note in her mother's cursive: "I hope you understand why we chose not to give these to you then. And why I am giving them to you now."

Lifting the lid, she pulled out the tissue paper and found a stack of letters tied with a black Net-A-Porter ribbon. There were probably more than a dozen envelopes of all shapes and sizes. When she untied the bow, her hands were shaking. The levee of numbness that had been like a fortress for her suddenly gave way to a flood of emotion, and Anna was barely able to keep her head above the rising tide of pain and regret—all because of a box filled with love letters from a beautiful boy who had just been laid to rest in Sicilian soil.

She picked up the envelope on top and turned it over in her hands. Each letter had the date on the back of the envelope, marking the day when he had dropped them off for her during the time they had been forbidden to see each other. The last one was written the day he died. Seeing his handwriting made her heart hurt.

With a parched mouth and trembling hands, Anna opened the first letter.

APRIL 2019

Dearest Anna,

I'm going out of my mind being unable to see you or talk to you so I'm kicking it old school and writing with pen and paper. I doubt your parents will pass these along to you, but I have every intention of bribing your doormen with doughnuts and Yankees tickets. The hope is they will take pity on me and agree to slip this to you while you're walking the pups.

I keep thinking back to our time on the plane and how those will be my last happiest hours until I see you again. My feelings are unchanged and, when the smoke clears, you will see me standing, steadfast and waiting. I'm sure your father probably despises me, but I will do whatever it takes to gain his respect. I can be quite charming when necessary, as you well know.

Hmm. My letter sounds overly formal and whiny . . . am I whiny? You have to tell me if I am; I'm a big boy, I can take it.

I love you so much.

Forever and always yours,
Alexia V.

III

Natalia sat on a bench in the Washington Square dog park, twirling a lock of her bright silver hair as Edgar the pug sniffed around the outer edge of the fence like he was solving little doggie crimes. Edgar had on a white collar with a black tuxedo bow tie that cost five times the amount Natalia made from the dog-walking app service every day. The pay wasn't great, but she loved the freedom of setting her own schedule and the odd cross section of humanity that hired her to walk their dogs at night.

She'd been in New York less than three weeks and had already fallen in love with the city. She loved it best at night, consistently awed by the sheer verticality of lit windows on high-rises towering up toward the stars. It amazed her that in every window someone's life was playing out, every pane a reality show more real than anything on television. She had grown up in Vegas, a city with its fair share of bright night lights, but those were different. Vegas lights were all overindulgence and debauchery, whereas the lights of Manhattan were oddly hopeful.

Another thing she loved about the city was all the foot traffic, everyone walking around. It was like your life could begin as soon as you hit the sidewalk. No more being stuck in cars or buses or having to hide away indoors because of the oppressive and unrelenting desert heat. Granted, New York was hot in the summertime, too, and it took her a few days to get used to the humidity and the warm stink of rotting trash, but when fall showed up, it would be the first time she would see trees actually change color before her eyes.

It was Kimmie who suggested Natalia become a dog walker when she needed to start making money. "You know, 'cause you're already obsessed with walking the streets, might as well get paid while you're at it, right? Manhattan has millions of dogs and plenty of people too busy to walk them."

Kimmie was one smart chick, and Natalia knew she was lucky to count her as a friend. Without her help, Natalia would probably be sleeping on a bench in Tompkins Square Park as opposed to a comfy queen bed on Madison Avenue. For the past week, she'd crashed with Kimmie at her dad's fancy digs, which seemed like a royal palace to Natalia. She had never met anyone as rich as Kimmie before. She could barely comprehend Kimmie's claim that they were "New York City upper-middle class." Kimmie had explained there were so many families like her own in the city that to really call yourself wealthy in the Big Apple, you needed to be a double-digit millionaire at the least. Natalia thought about all the times when her mother couldn't make rent and they had to pack their belongings and sneak out in the middle of the night.

When Natalia and Kimmie first reunited, Kimmie was staying at her mom's place, and there was no way Natalia could crash there because Kimmie's mother kept much closer tabs on her and her older sister, Lolly, than her dad and stepmonster did. So the first week she had to bed-hop a bit, which included two nights on a bench in Grand Central, one night at a youth hostel in Harlem for twenty-two dollars, and a fourth night at her dead boyfriend's dad's place . . . only because Nick's younger brother, Dustin, snuck her in after everyone had gone to bed. In the morning she had hid in his closet until his father, stepmom, and baby stepsister left the apartment. This was all fine with Natalia. All she really required was access to a shower with strong water pressure every now and again.

Meeting Dustin for the first time had been kind of a shock for her. For whatever reason, Kimmie hadn't bothered to explain that Dustin was Black, so Natalia stood there with her mouth agape, her pierced eyebrows arched, and said, "So you're Nick's brother? Cool. Cool. Cool." She racked her brain to remember if Nick had told her that his adopted brother was Black; not that it made any difference, it just surprised her. Dustin told Natalia he was thrilled to finally meet her, and he'd only heard good things about her from Nicholas.

"So bizarre to hear you call Nick that," said Natalia. "He never struck me as a Nicholas."

"I can see that, but old habits die hard," Dustin said.

"Yeah, or they kill you. Like they did him, the dumbass." And just like that she had put her big Doc Marten boot right back in her mouth.

Dustin chuckled, which broke the tension of the bizarre situation of having his new girlfriend and his dead brother's old girlfriend hanging out like besties. He liked that Natalia had absolutely no filter, because his brother had been the same way, and in turn Natalia really liked Dustin, although he couldn't have been more different from Nicholas. Dustin was a total nerd who reminded her of a hot Steve Urkel from *Family Matters*, which was one of her favorite shows to watch in reruns when she was in rehab. Natalia loved all traditional family sitcoms. They were so totally different from her own upbringing that she took comfort in them.

Natalia was staring at Edgar inspecting the fence and ignoring a Chihuahua named Friendly, who followed him around like a faithful sidekick, when her phone buzzed in her pocket. "Yo, y'got Nat," she answered without bothering to see who was calling. She never went by Nat, but she was trying it out for a while to see if it took. She felt like she needed a fresh sobriquet to go with her NYC life.

"Where are you?" It was Dustin on the other end of the phone.

"Washington Square," Natalia answered.

"Wait, now I see you . . . ," Dustin responded, and moments later he appeared in the dog run, carrying two bottles of water. This rendezvous had become a thing, Dustin meeting her at the various dog parks around the city. For some reason, after both losing Nicholas, Dustin and Natalia found comfort sitting side by side on park benches together. They didn't always talk about him, but they always felt the bridge of shared loss between them. Today, however, Dustin was missing his older brother more than usual. He handed Natalia a bottle of water and asked her to tell him about when she met Nicholas in rehab and lived with him in Arizona right before he died.

Natalia stared ahead at Edgar the pug and told Dustin everything she remembered. Even though he'd heard some of the stories before, Natalia could tell Dustin was crying, but she said nothing about it. He clearly missed his older brother tremendously, and from what she gathered, his mother still found it too painful to talk about him. He craved a safe space where he could remember his brother out loud. Natalia understood this need because that was exactly how she felt, too.

She talked about Nick, which was how he introduced himself when they'd first met outside of Desert Vista in the smoking area. If she squeezed her eyes super tight, she could still see Nick lying on his back, his legs dangling off one end of the bench, left arm behind his head, taking a long drag off a cigarette. Sometimes, she liked to pretend he had never OD'd on heroin, instead making up a spectacular fake fight, so she could tell herself that they had only broken up and that Nick was still somewhere out there, not dead and buried in a Jewish cemetery in Queens.

Natalia told Dustin how Nicholas spoke of him often, always bragging about what a genius he was and how proud his parents were of his many accomplishments. *"My brother, Dust, he's a human IMDb. He knows all the shit from every film he's ever watched, all cataloged away in that genius brain of his. His movie knowledge is motherfuckin' encyclopedic."* Natalia mimicked Nicholas's speech patterns so well it sent shivers up Dustin's spine. Dustin asked her if his brother seemed bitter about Dustin taking up so much of his parents' affection, but she said the opposite was true.

"He was happy they adopted you. He said it was like you lightened the load of your mom and dad's disappointment about how he turned out," Natalia answered.

"They weren't disappointed. They loved him," Dustin said, his voice thick with emotion.

"Dude," Natalia replied. "He knew they loved him the same way he knew they were disappointed. Rehab factoid number four hundred and twenty-one: It's okay to be more than one thing to somebody. He was smart, too, your brother. He knew the score and he wasn't a bullshitter, which is why I loved him. He always spoke his truth and I have mad respect for people who don't sling bullshit, and he was top of the heap in my heart. Though I don't know if I'll ever forgive him for checking out without me and leaving me behind, y'know?"

"Yeah, I know," Dustin said quietly. "I gotta tell you, I thank god every day that he fell in love with you before he died. You made him really happy."

"I did and I didn't," she said. "I haven't said this out loud to anyone, not the cops or even Kimmie. But I chickened out. That last time we were gonna do it together, my first time and his last, but I couldn't. I was scared and he didn't pressure me. Why didn't I tell him not to do it? I had been to rehab two times for meth before we met. I knew he shouldn't use again. I knew better. I'll never forgive myself for it."

Dustin took in her painful confession with a grace way beyond his years. "Like I said, you brought him the love I think he had been chasing his whole life, unconditional love. He knew it and now so do I. It's not your fault that it was such a brief time. Better that than nothing."

"Yeah, man, tell me about it." Natalia stood up and wiped the tears off her cheeks. It was time to get Edgar the pug home. "I know all too well that when the good times roll toward you, you gotta grab on to them and hold tight because it never lasts as long as you want it to. Not ever. Well, at least that's the way it's always been for me."

IV

San Ysidro Ranch was a luxury hotel in the foothills of Montecito, California, and was known for its long history of famous guests. It was where Vivien Leigh and Laurence Olivier married, John F. Kennedy and Jackie Kennedy honeymooned, and Winston Churchill stayed with his family to escape the miserable winters of England. The property had been purchased in the early aughts by the billionaire creator of Beanie Babies, who lovingly restored it to its former glory. Now if you were a wealthy West Coast socialite, one way to show off to your friends who had known your first two husbands was to marry the third at San Ysidro, all expenses paid. Because Beatrice's uncle Chadwick had attended the bride-to-be's first two weddings, they had scored the Winston Churchill cottage, which had a private hot tub and outdoor shower, and there were two perfectly manicured putting greens at the end of a flower garden that served as their backyard. But there was only one bedroom, and Beatrice would have to sleep on a rollaway bed for the duration of the wedding weekend.

Honestly, Beatrice found weddings painfully boring, and as this was the bride's third time at the altar, there was a whole been-there-done-that vibe, so Beatrice promised herself that after she heard five guests make the "third time's a charm" joke, she could bail. The fifth mention was by the groom himself as he toasted his much older but also much wealthier bride. Bea leaned over and whispered to her uncle, "I'm outta here. . . . Don't do anything or anyone I wouldn't do."

"So that would be exactly nothing and no one?" he asked with a sly smile.

"Actually there's plenty of D and P here I'd take a hard pass on. I'm already rich. I don't have to be anyone's sugar baby."

Chadwick had forgotten how amusing his niece was, and it gave him hope that Manny, Chadwick's younger trophy husband, would get along with her once they spent some time together. Manny was not happy when he heard the news that Beatrice would fly out for the wedding and then return with Chadwick to their home in Brentwood for the rest of the summer. Since Chadwick was the one who paid for their high-end lifestyle, Manny had little recourse to stop his rich hubby's lugubrious niece from coming. Chadwick was himself a bit concerned with his niece's current state.

Earlier in the evening he had tried to bring up the subject of Vronsky, whom he had only met a handful of times as he was not technically the boy's uncle. "I was so sorry to hear about your cousin," was all he managed to get out before Beatrice cut him off sharply.

"That subject's off limits unless you want me to flip over this fucking table right now." Her father had been correct when he told Chadwick that she was not processing her grief well.

"Want me to bring you back a piece of cake number three?" Chadwick asked.

Beatrice shook her head and stood. "Nopes. I'm on the prowl for a different sort of treat. Don't worry, you won't come back to find a necktie or a thong on the doorknob. Scout's honor." She threw up a peace sign and strutted away from the reception.

As Beatrice walked down the hill, she used her room key equipped with a mini flashlight to illuminate her path back to the cottage. She could hear "Lady in Red" playing in the distance and she pictured all the boomers and aging Gen-Xers slow dancing to it, glad she had left. She was on a mission for a palate cleanser, something to get the lingering flavor of Claudine's neediness out of her mouth. Claudine had already texted her a million times and it hadn't even been forty-eight hours. When Beatrice checked in earlier, she had noticed a girl behind the front desk who looked far too cool to be wearing a polo shirt with the hotel name monogrammed on the collar. She took off her Louboutin slingbacks and skipped up the stone steps of the front office, under the archway of magenta bougainvillea.

When she entered, the girl was alone at the registration desk. She had tawny brown skin and a shock of spiraling curls that were an inch too short to tuck behind her ears. "Good evening, Miss D., how may I assist you this evening?"

Normally Beatrice would have said something shocking, but she was momentarily stunned by the girl's wide-set hazel eyes dazzling her with tiny flecks of iridescent green and silver. "Um, yeah, I heard something about fresh-baked cookies; the wedding cake was not my thing. If you're gonna screw up a cake by putting fruit in it, the least you can do is spend a bit more and get the seedless raspberry jam."

The girl gestured toward the counter, where an Italian ceramic platter displayed neat rows of tiny oatmeal raisin, chocolate chip, double chocolate chip, and sugar cookies. "Please help yourself."

Beatrice walked over and inspected the tray. She had been lying about the cake. It was delicious, and she'd had her piece as well as her uncle's, who was currently doing an intermittent fasting/keto combo diet. The last thing she needed was more sweets, but she did need an opening salvo.

"Which one's your favorite?" Beatrice asked.

"They're all good, but personally, I like the dog cookies."

Beatrice's eyebrows lifted. "Say what now?"

The girl let out a robust throaty laugh. She pointed to an iron statue of a cat in a top hat carrying a tray of bone-shaped cookies. "We're dog friendly here, and our pastry chef makes homemade dog biscuits for our four-legged guests. They're less sweet, and crunchier. I don't have much of a sweet tooth." In a show of good faith, the girl grabbed a dog treat, snapped it in half, and popped a piece in her mouth.

Beatrice leaned over the counter, opened her mouth, and stuck out her tongue for the other half. The girl hesitated for only a moment before placing the cookie on Beatrice's tongue. She chewed thoughtfully. "Not bad. They kinda taste like . . ."

"Graham crackers!" the two girls said in unison.

Normally, Bea would gag over such a corny Disney Channel moment, as if actual people ever jinxed each other in meet-cute fashion. But since it had just happened to her, she dropped her cynicism and chose to find it adorable. "Bet you could make a mean s'more with these," Beatrice said. She and Vronsky used to make them in the fire pit at the country house, the recollection flashing in her mind involuntarily. She scowled at the memory.

The girl noticed Bea's expression change. "Something wrong?"

"Not at all," Bea replied, forcing her memory to go blank. "So, what's your name and when do you get off tonight?"

"My name is Tiare. Well it's actually Vaitiare, but I go by Tiare. It's Tahitian for . . ."

"For 'flower.' I've been twice."

The girl looked at her in surprise. "I was born there. But moved here in sixth grade. My mom moved back a few years ago."

"That's cool," Beatrice said. "Must be fun to go visit."

"My mom and I don't really get along. My dad was some white dude who wined and dined her but didn't give his real name. After I was born she tried to track him down, but she never found him. It kinda ruined her life." Tiare had no idea why she was sharing such personal information, but she thought she knew what this guest was after, and she needed to shut it down fast. The hotel had a strict policy about fraternizing with guests. She couldn't afford to lose this job, not for some fancy rich girl.

"Look, I'm sure there's some policy about you not hanging with guests, I get it. But I'll never tell. I couldn't be more bored, and I just thought . . ."

Tiare hesitated, biting her lip, which only made her look that much sexier to Beatrice.

Right then, a man entered through a back door behind the desk, wearing a perfunctory smile. "Good evening, Miss D. Are you enjoying your stay with us?"

Beatrice could tell he was Tiare's boss by the way she stood up straighter in his presence. Bea smiled back brightly. "Oh yes, any place that serves such yummy-looking morsels at the front desk is all right with me." She stared at Tiare and Tiare's nostrils flared.

"Please, help yourself. Would you like a plate so you can take some cookies back to your cottage?"

"Is room service closed for the night?" Beatrice asked, knowing full well that service had stopped fifteen minutes ago at 10 P.M.

"It is, but I'm sure we can accommodate you if you had a particular request."

"I'd love some milk. You know, for . . . getting my cookies good and wet?" She mimed dunking a cookie and saw that Tiare was working overtime to keep a straight face.

"Tiare would be happy to look into getting you some milk for your cookies," her boss said.

"Technically, I'm off the clock," Tiare said. "William's running late and he asked me to cover the desk until he shows up."

"I'll cover the desk and wait for William; I'm sure he'll be here momentarily. You can leave right after you assist Miss D."

"That would be amazing, Mr. . . . ?"

"Foster. I'm the night manager here at the Ranch. I know your uncle well and we've been fortunate to have him refer many guests to us."

"Well, thank you, Mr. Foster. I'll be sure to tell my uncle how accommodating you have been." Beatrice turned to Tiare. "Shall we?"

Having no other choice, Tiare forced a phony smile. "Certainly, Miss D. Let me grab my bag. Here's a plate for your cookies." She handed Bea a small white dessert plate with the hotel logo on it.

Bea made a big show of picking out a few cookies and even snagged a few more dog biscuits as well. "For my uncle's pup back home," she said, enjoying the little white lie as her uncle was a cat person and had two gray Persians that were as cold as they were fluffy. "I'll wait outside. It's such a beautiful night."

"I wish you a wonderful rest of your evening," Mr. Foster said, oblivious to his role in assisting Beatrice on her quest to make her night wonderful indeed.

Tiare didn't say a word after they left the registration office. It was so dark that Beatrice couldn't see Tiare's face, so she had no idea if she was annoyed or amused. She realized she had put Tiare in an awkward position with her boss, but Bea knew he was totally clueless about what was really going on. How could she not go for it? That was basically how she'd led her entire life thus far: just going for it, whatever it was, like the reigning princess of pop, Ariana: "I want it, I got it. I want it, I got it . . ." Bea's mother would tell her she was selfish, and Bea would just shrug and retort, "I'm a teenager; we're supposed to only think of ourselves."

When they entered the room-service kitchen, a man in overalls was cleaning up. He had headphones on and didn't bother taking them off. He nodded at Tiare, who nodded back. Tiare threw open a large industrial fridge, and in the cool yellow light Beatrice once again marveled at her beauty. She had no makeup on, maybe the tiniest hint of gloss, and wore simple gold studs in her ears. Her eyelashes were extraordinarily long, and Beatrice could tell they were natural, unlike her own Barbie-Gone-Bad fake ones she was wearing on top of her lash extensions.

"What's your preference? This is California luxe, so we have everything: whole milk, two percent, one percent, skim, almond, hemp, coconut milk, soy, cashew, oat, raw, and even pea. Milk from peas. Not actual pee . . ." Tiare asked, a forced politeness to her voice.

"What are you drinking?" Beatrice asked back.

"I'm not."

"You don't like milk and cookies?"

"Like I said, I'm not that into sweets."

"But are you into me?" Bea asked, not caring that the guy was still mopping the floor five feet away from them. "I promise I'm more salty than sweet."

"Skim milk it is," Tiare said grabbing the jug out of the fridge and letting the heavy door slam shut. Tiare opened cabinets at random until she found the glasses and took out two, which gave Bea a little hope that she was making progress.

They headed back toward the Churchill cottage, Bea trailing slightly behind Tiare, evaluating her frame. Tiare was at least four inches taller than she was, and had a sturdy athletic limberness to her lanky gait. Tiare stopped walking and waved for Bea to catch up. She held her finger to her lips, Beatrice sidled next to her. They stared out into the darkness and Beatrice saw two sets of glowing yellow eyes ten feet away.

"Coyotes?" Bea whispered.

"Foxes," Tiare said, and as if on cue, two tiny red foxes scampered across the path and ran into a field of flowers.

"Did you watch season two of *Fleabag?*"

Tiare turned toward Bea quizzically. "I don't even know what that is."

"It's a TV show. Phoebe Waller-Bridge? British chick? Hot priest? The mean stepmom's the same actor who played Queen Anne in that movie *The Favourite* . . ."

"I don't remember the last movie I went to, and I don't watch TV," Tiare said.

"Like, at all?"

Tiare finally smiled. "Like, not even a little bit."

Normally Beatrice would have mocked her, but since this girl was different from anyone she had ever met, she refrained. Tiare had an air of mystery, yes, but what Beatrice really liked was her confidence. Beatrice hated weakness in others, in herself, and most of all in potential lovers.

Beatrice hadn't even noticed when they stopped walking, but they were now standing outside the Churchill cottage. She could tell her uncle wasn't back from the wedding yet, since the cabin lights were dark.

"You're coming in, right?" Bea asked.

"Not even a little bit," Tiare repeated.

"Oh, so are you expecting me to beg? Because I will, but my already high expectations for you will only get higher."

Tiare smirked and shook her head. "You're too much."

"You're not the first to say so."

"I'm sure I won't be the last," she said. "Do you want me to pour you a glass of milk or should I leave the jug?"

It was then that Beatrice knew Tiare was serious about not coming in, and the thought of watching her walk away made her feel frantic. "Fine, forget it. Can we just hang out somewhere else?"

"Miss D.—"

"Beatrice. Bea for my friends."

"Miss D., please don't think I'm rude. I really need this summer job. My aunt is the one who hooked it all up. The owner took a chance on me, and I'm not gonna screw it up. My aunt would have my head."

"Whatever you make, I'll double it and Venmo you."

Tiare's nostrils flared. "Who do you think you are? I am not for sale!"

"Think of it more like a rental?" Bea awaited Tiare's response, unsure how she would react to her brand of brash humor after being insulted. Sometimes Bea's crass, devil-may-care attitude went over well, and sometimes it backfired. Though when her manner offended someone, Beatrice was known to double down on her snark, as opposed to backing off. She believed the best defense was to be on the offensive, intimidation as protection.

Without another word, Tiare set the two glasses and the jug of milk on the driveway and walked back down the hill.

"Oh my god! I was kidding. Sheesh, can't you take a joke?" Beatrice's voice was shrill. She flung her shoes off and ran after Tiare barefoot. "Wait. Stop! Please." But Tiare was on the move. "I'm sorry. I'm a fucking bitch. Please, stop?" When that didn't work, Bea bent her neck back and let out a wild coyote howl into the starry night.

At the howl, Tiare stopped and turned, looking back at Beatrice, whose sequined dress shimmered in the moonglow. Tiare wasn't usually quick to forgive when she was pissed, and she was righteously pissed at the moment, but the howl caught her off guard. Also, there was something in the girl's voice, a quality she recognized but couldn't name. "You're forgiven. But really, I should go."

"Can I go with you . . . please?" Beatrice had never sounded so desperate.

"Why? You want to slum it with the ninety-nine percent for a thrill? See how the majority of the world lives? Play the part of lonely unloved rich girl?"

Beatrice basked in Tiare's wrathful sneer. "Totally fair. I deserve that. Actually, if you knew me better, you'd know I deserve so much worse. But today's only my second day in California, and I don't know anyone, I mean, anyone who isn't related to me and like a thousand years old. I don't want to be alone."

"You should change then."

"I think it's a little late for that. Being like this is all I know."

"I meant your clothes, rich girl," Tiare said. "Wear something you don't mind getting dirty, and Uber to the zoo. I'll meet you there in an hour. I can't drive you, because we'd pass the guard gate."

"The zoo?"

"I have a second job at the Santa Barbara Zoo. The late shift. You do know what a job is, right?"

"You want me to meet you at the zoo?" Just hearing the words come out of her mouth, they sounded absurd, and yet Beatrice grew instantly excited by them.

"If you want. If you don't want, all good."

Beatrice watched Tiare continue down the hill, just a shadowy figure growing smaller in the darkness. She wanted her to turn around like they did in the movies, and give her the lookback with that playful smile, but Tiare didn't do it.

Or maybe, it was just too dark to tell.

VI

My love,
Last night Bea dragged me out clubbing with her and Claudine. I
wasn't in the mood, but you know how she is, so it was easier just to
indulge her.

  You were all I thought of on the dance floor (dancing by myself like
that old song). I was reminded of our first night of dancing at Jaylen's
party when hours felt like minutes and seconds felt like hours. I can
still smell how you smelled. If you write me back, please tell me the
name of your perfume. I will buy it and spray it on my pillow so I can
dream of you at night, of your gorgeous face, the curve of your lips, the
way you throw your head back and put your hands over your mouth
when you laugh.

  I especially miss your big vocabulary, because of you I now know
the word "apotheosis." But I just have one question, one lingering
question that I can't find the answer to . . .

  Now that we found love, what are we gonna do with it? If you
know, tell me because I will admit this is my first grand adventure
with dropping L-bombs.

Devoted and desperate,
V.

Anna put down the second letter after reading it twice straight through.
It gave her goose bumps to read his words. Not only did he feel close, it
felt like he was still alive. If she didn't know better, he could have written
these words yesterday to say how much he missed her for being away for
the summer.

If only.

A wave of melancholy swept over her. If she read another letter, she
would have to read them all. And as much as she wanted to rip them
open and race through his words, devouring his love . . . she knew she

should wait. These were his last private thoughts, and they were just for her. She needed to treasure them and decided that she'd only read them when she needed them the most.

Anna was no longer in the mood to mope, which was all she had been doing lately. The way she figured it, she was going to be immensely sad for a long time, so what did it matter whether she did it sulking or while she was trying to live her life? Easier said than done. She tried to hide her mood in front of her family or when she was out sightseeing with Lolly and Steven, but she knew she wasn't doing a very good job of keeping up the façade. She was pretending to be fine, and everyone else was pretending not to notice. It was a sorry state of affairs, but there was no survival guide for dealing with a broken heart and she no longer had access to acres of land to scream out her frustrations. She had hoped that the "fake it 'til you make it" method would work, but so far slapping a half smile on her face and trying to sound cheerful only made her feel more depressed and caused those around her to bombard her with their maladroit sympathy.

Neither her father nor Steven—nor for that matter Lolly—were good at concealing their genuine concern and it seemed like every time Anna entered a room, she walked into the clipped silence of a conversation cut short by her presence, as if everyone were talking about her right up until her entrance. The awkward changing of subjects was always excruciating. Once she tried calling them out on it, but they all denied that they had been talking about her while at the same time asking her if she'd like to talk to them about anything, anything at all. *Really, Anna. Seriously!* So just as they denied talking about her, Anna denied having anything she wanted to talk about with them, even though she did. Her whole identity was wrapped up in being such a paragon of togetherness and perfection—the good daughter, the patient sister, the exceptional student, the wise friend—it seemed surreal to be the one in need of help. If only she were better at sharing her grief maybe she wouldn't feel like she was walking around with an anchor weighing her down. She was so good at empathizing with others, she wondered why she couldn't be better at accepting it from those who loved her.

Anna had been letting herself go numb and trying to get through each day so she could retire to her bedroom at night only to lie awake for hours on end. It was torture, and yet it felt good to suffer because she felt like she deserved it. If only she had done things differently on the night of his death. If only she had reacted in any other way. The what-ifs were overwhelming. Rationally, she knew that her regrets were a waste of emotional energy because she knew no amount of wishing could change the fact that Alexia was gone forever. Sometimes she wondered if she secretly enjoyed the sadness, the merciless torture of loss reminding her of the grandeur of their love.

Perhaps she should see his love letters as a reprieve from her sorrow. Yes, he was gone, but he still had things to say and maybe it would be wise of her to listen. If Alexia had missed her less when he went out dancing, then perhaps she should follow his lead.

"I want to go dancing," she blurted out to Steven and Lolly that night in Italy after Edward had gone to bed.

"It's after midnight."

"And your point would be what, Cinderella?" Anna asked playfully.

"Dad's going to nix it," Steven said.

"Dad's asleep," Anna said. "Can't nix something if you're asleep."

"Anna, are you okay?" Lolly piped in, but Anna did not respond.

Steven stared at Anna and sighed, the wheels in his head already turning. "Fine, but if we're doing this then we're doing it my way, because if we get caught, I'm the one who's going to pay for it."

"When in Rome, do whatever Steven says," Anna told him, and Lolly let out a loud goofy laugh, the weed gummy she had taken an hour ago now fully kicked in.

"Get it, we're like actually in Rome, right now! The city of lights!"

"That's Paris, but close enough," Anna responded. "Rome is known as the eternal city, or is it something else?"

"Who cares?" said Steven. "I'd rather go out than debate city nicknames. By the end of the night, we're gonna have a new nickname for Rome."

"Not this one," Lolly said, pointing to herself. "I'm way too high and paranoid to sneak out."

"Such a lightweight," Steven said. He agreed to take Anna to Raspou-
tine, a popular Italian nightclub, and told Lolly that in the event Edward
woke up and noticed they were gone, she should play dumb or just pretend to sleep. "Do not say anything. Just squint your eyes and shrug your
shoulders and make a sleepy noise."

"I can do all of those things." Lolly gave a thumbs-up. Anna didn't care
that Lolly was too paranoid to sneak out. She knew that Lolly was scared
of her father, who she still called Mr. K.

Anna appreciated Steven taking her out. She knew it was risky, but
he was doing it for her anyway. They got in easily even though she
was under eighteen. When Steven fetched the drinks from the bar
Anna went directly to the dance floor. Being out there made her feel
better, like she was a depleted vampire feeding off the energy of the
crowd. The cocktails Steven kept bringing her didn't hurt, either, and
before she knew it, Anna and her brother had gone from buzzed to
drunk, doing silly dance moves, belting out lyrics even though neither
of them spoke Italian, and making goofy vogue faces in the middle of
the packed dance floor.

For the first time since Vronsky died, the smile on Anna's face
wasn't forced, and she could tell her brother was thrilled to be doing
something to help her. Anna didn't care that she was using alcohol
to mask the anguish she had been feeling. The headache tomorrow
morning would be a small price to pay for the carefree joy she felt goof-
ing around with her brother. It was exactly what she needed to shake
her out of her slump.

On their way back to the hotel, in the dark backseat of the taxi, Anna
thanked Steven for going out with her. She knew he was trying to be better and not party as much this summer, so she felt bad making him sneak
out and get drunk with her because she was such a mess.

Steven waved his hand at her, as if to say, *don't give it another thought.*
"Though I will admit clubbing is much less fun without a little cocaine in
my membrane," Steven confessed. "But I promised Lolls no hard drugs

this summer." A kid they knew of from Horace Mann had died at his own graduation party and rumor had it that he'd gotten an eight ball tainted with fentanyl. The story so terrified Lolly that she immediately proposed a drug-free summer (not including pot, of course) and, surprisingly, Steven had agreed. He wanted the summer to be mellow and relaxing. The end-of-the-school-year drama had taken its toll on everyone, himself included.

"I think that's great," Anna said, her cheeks still flushed from the booze. "The no-drug thing, not the part where you didn't have any fun tonight."

"I had fun with you," he said. "It was just different. Besides, I only care if you had a good time." He paused. "Dad's not the only one who's worried about you."

Yeah, she thought. *I'm worried about me, too.*

On the top floor of the hotel, the two of them tried to stifle their drunken giggling the best they could as they pushed quietly through the door to their penthouse suite. Shushing each other while bumping accidentally into walls, they tiptoed down the entryway hall. But Edward was already standing in the great room, arms crossed, a stoic look etched over his tired face. Anna gasped and Steven froze, both holding their breath before exploding with laughter. Edward endured his children's outburst gracefully, giving it about as much notice as he would a drizzle of rain, a slight annoyance that would ultimately leave him unperturbed.

"We're in so much trouble!" Anna whispered loudly with a big smile on her face.

"I'm in so much trouble," Steven whispered back. "You're going to have a bitch of a headache tomorrow, though."

"I can hear you both quite clearly," said Edward.

Anna looked at her brother with sad drunk eyes. "Sowee, Steven . . . I guess we can call Rome the city of Oopsie We Got Busted!"

"Anna, go to bed," Edward said, his voice sharp. "I need a word with your brother."

And as Anna stumbled to her room and flopped on her bed, Steven stood strong in the face of their father's anger and took one for the team.

VII

This was the first summer of her life Kimmie could remember not being stressed out. When she was an Olympic hopeful, summers meant long days of uninterrupted workouts on the ice. But now waking up late, an entire summer day stretched out before her, was a brand-new sensation, and she loved it. Finally, she felt like a normal teenager.

When she stayed at her mom's apartment, it was especially enjoyable. With her sister, Lolly, abroad and their mom's morning workout classes, Kimmie had the entire place to herself. Sleeping late at her dad's wasn't as easy. The stepmonster had a voice that Kimmie likened to the screech of car brakes right before a catastrophic traffic accident.

"What the holy hell?" Natalia's sleepy voice came out muffled from under the covers. "Is that her squawking or those awful parrots?"

"It's her. And they're lovebirds, not parrots," Kimmie replied.

"Fine. So is that why those dumb assholes never talk back to me? I was starting to take it personally."

"She got them for my dad for one of their anniversaries," Kimmie told her. "He hates them, but of course he can't tell her that."

Natalia stretched her arms over her head and yawned. "So, what trouble should we get into today?"

"I'm supposed to see a movie with Dustin, but you're welcome to come along if you want."

"Subtitles?"

"Prolly, but I'm not sure. I'll text him." Kimmie grabbed her phone off the bedside table, but Natalia snatched it away from her.

"No, don't. I can't always be the third wheel. You two should go spend some time together. Alone. If it's a boring foreign flick you can give him a hand job to pass the time."

"Oh my god, have you ever done that?" Kimmie asked.

"A movie theater handy? So many times," Natalia said proudly. "Once

I even gave a BJ . . . and his name might have actually been BJ. Or maybe it was JT?"

"It would blow Dustin's mind if I did that." Kimmie smiled at the thought.

"Yeah, that's not the part you're supposed to blow. But isn't that what you want? To be mind-blowing? Though with a mind like his, it may take extra work. Speaking of, is his brain the only thing that's . . . big? Do tell, do tell!"

Kimmie squealed at the suggestion and then covered her face with her pillow with embarrassment. "It seems big."

"Seems? You don't know?"

"Like through his jeans," Kimmie whispered. The truth was Kimmie didn't know. She and Dustin had been taking things slow, which she appreciated in the beginning. But she was wondering lately if this slowness was less out of chivalry and more because of something going on with him. "We haven't done it yet. Honestly, we haven't done much of anything except kiss. When should I start to take it personally?"

"Now, you should be taking it personally right now. Shit, I'm taking it personally and I'm not even you!" Natalia responded.

"He's a good kisser. Like really good," Kimmie added, feeling a bit guilty talking about her boyfriend behind his back.

"Nick was just so-so at smooching in the beginning, but he got better. After I gave him instructions, of course."

"You gave him actual instructions on how to kiss better?"

"Not with words, but by guiding him along . . . with my tongue." Natalia undulated her tongue at Kimmie. "He used to kiss so aggressively, with his mouth so wide I'd end up with spit all over my chin." Natalia demonstrated on Mr. Bearbear, Kimmie's favorite stuffed teddy, practically stuffing his whole snout in her mouth. "So, I started kissing him slowly, all sexy-like, and he eventually figured it out. Why all guys think fast is better than slow is beyond me. Like, how dumb are they? Spending all their time thinking about it, obsessing over sex, and once they're finally getting it they hurry their way through it? Boys. Are. Stupid. Even the smart ones."

"Did you just learn this stuff on your own?" she asked Natalia. She wanted to know more. She wanted to be good. Kimmie was a girl who had spent the last ten years of her life trying to be the best ice dancer on the planet before she tore her knee to shreds, so her winner-take-all competitive energy had to go somewhere.

"My mom's mothering skills sucked, but she was useful in teaching me how to control men. It's dumb of us to expect boys to be mind readers about what we want, so the key is to trick them into letting us let them know what we want without bruising their fragile male egos."

Kimmie hung on Natalia's every word, enraptured. Sure, Lolly was her big sister, but she wasn't much use in advising her on these kinds of things. Technically, Kimmie had lost her virginity before Lolly did, so their experience level was about the same. Plus, her sister's relationship with Steven couldn't be more different from her relationship with Dustin. Lolly and Steven were very physical around each other, but she and Dustin were shyer with PDA.

Kimmie threw her arms around Natalia. "You're the best. I was trying to learn stuff online by checking out porn, but it grossed me out. I did not find it sexy at all."

"Happy to help. If you need to know how to get a blackout drunk dude to cum faster because he's taking too long, I'm your girl."

"God, I hope I don't ever need to know that," Kimmie said, then paused. "Actually, tell me . . ."

Natalia flipped over and got on her hands and knees. She stuck her butt in the air and barked. "Doggy style delivers every time! Woof! Woof!"

Kimmie burst out laughing, even though she didn't quite understand why doggy style would be effective. The only time she had sex was with Vronsky and he had been on top. Kimmie missed feeling a sense of power and strength from her body and had high hopes that her second time having sex would not only help erase her first time, but also show her what all the fuss was about.

She had told Natalia about losing her virginity to Vronsky back when they first met at Desert Vista. Natalia was in an outpatient rehab program for meth addiction, and Kimmie was working through her depression. What she hadn't told Natalia was that Vronsky was the same boy who had died in a horrific train accident, saving the life of the girl he truly loved, Anna K. When Kimmie first heard about Vronsky's fatal accident, she was just as shocked as everyone else. She couldn't help thinking about her visit to his apartment a month before his death when she told him how much he'd hurt her feelings and that she didn't think he was a good person. She didn't regret anything she'd said because, in doing so, she felt a sense of closure on that particular chapter of her life. But she sometimes felt pangs of guilt that he was no longer alive while she was in a happy relationship with the boy she should have chosen from the start. She had met Dustin and Vronsky on the very same night, like in that Robert Frost poem about the two roads. Oh, how she wished she had picked the one less traveled right from the start—it would have saved her so much grief. And if she had, Vronsky might still be alive. . . .

VIII

It was a little before eleven when Beatrice exited the cottage wearing her best bra, a pair of R13 boyfriend jeans, a Bella Freud tee, her black Coachella hoodie, and Vetements Doc Martens. She almost ran into her uncle, who was coming back from the wedding reception, holding a table arrangement of flowers. He jumped back in surprise and dropped them, the glass vase smashing at his feet. "Dammit!" he yelled at no one in particular, not upset about the flowers but at the water droplets on his new suede loafers.

"That sucks," she replied, not thinking to apologize for her part in it.

"Ugh, what do I do about this?" he said.

"Umm . . . you call the front desk and let one of the peoples deal with it." As the words left her mouth, she realized one of the "peoples" could have been Tiare, though technically she didn't work in house-keeping.

"Eh, whatever. I didn't even want them. Some drunk old bat at my table was going around, grabbing them off every table, and forcing them into the hands of anyone standing near her, fussing about not letting them go to waste. I took one just to shut her up."

Beatrice wasn't listening but was instead looking up the address of the zoo, hoping she wasn't about to get punk'd by some townie for hitting on her while she was at work. She didn't think that was the case, but who worked at the zoo after midnight?

"Where are you off to?" Chadwick asked.

"Just a little off-campus rendezvous."

"What's his name?"

"Not very woke of you to assume it's a guy," she challenged.

Chadwick laughed at his lightning-quick niece and wondered if she'd ever consider a Hollywood career. She'd make one helluva agent. "I beg your pardon. I guess in these modern times I shouldn't assume anything. Well, be careful, okay? You're my responsibility now and I don't need your parents breathing down my beautifully tanned neck all summer."

"I'm a big girl, I can take care of myself. I'm always careful," Beatrice said and ordered herself a black car. She blew her uncle a kiss as she stepped over the peonies and broken glass.

"Will you be sleeping out?"

"Not sure yet," she said. "Hopefully." Beatrice winked and waved night-night while Chadwick watched his niece head down the hill.

Beatrice wouldn't admit this to anyone, but she was nervous. She was no stranger to random one-night hookups, but there was some-thing about this girl that had upset her balance. She wasn't used to be-ing the one in pursuit. She gave herself a private pep talk, telling herself she needed to toughen up and stop being such a pushover. Tiare wasn't *that* hot. Well, that was a lie; Bea couldn't remember ever craving anyone more, not even Claudine.

As if divining her naughty thoughts, her phone dinged and she received a pic of Claudine, just a shot of her gorgeous tits and her painted red lips. Claudine texted that she was thinking of Bea and hoped she'd had fun at the wedding. Bea left her hanging and instead turned her thoughts to Tiare and the last time she had been to Tahiti, a trip with Aunt Geneviève, Vronsky, and his brother, Kiril, a few years ago. It was a gorgeous island, but there wasn't much to do. Kiril had gone into town and managed to score some hash from some locals, and the three of them got lit on the beach. They built a bonfire with driftwood Vronsky had combed the beach for and made s'mores. When Bea roasted marshmallows, she had no patience and they always caught on fire, but Vronsky held his marshmallow high above the flame and slowly turned it until it sizzled with a perfect golden-brown crust and was totally gooey all the way through. She would pretend she liked her marshmallows burnt even though it wasn't true, and V would without fail offer up his first perfect marshmallow, bowing dramatically, his golden curls shimmering in the moonlight. "A sweet treat for the sweetest treat in all the kingdom."

By the time she pulled up to the zoo entrance, Beatrice was on the verge of tears.

"Shit!" she said, angrily blotting her eyes and leaning forward to check her mascara in the driver's rearview mirror.

"The zoo's closed right now," the Uber driver told her.

"Thanks for the info, Captain Obvious . . ."

"Screw you, princess," the driver muttered.

Bea clenched her fists. She had a high Uber rating and wanted to keep it that way. "Hey, look . . . I didn't mean to be a smart-ass. Don't ding me on the rating and I'll give you a twenty-dollar tip, okay?"

"Yeah, sure thing. Five stars for you, pumpkin."

"Don't fucking call me pumpkin. Ugh. Sorry! Here." Bea waved a fifty-dollar bill at the guy. "Now let me see you rate me." She watched him do as she commanded then handed him his bribe and got out of the car. She flipped him off as he drove away and promptly gave him a one-star rating in retribution.

It was then that she realized she'd never gotten Tiare's number. She looked around the deserted entrance, all alone, before she heard what sounded like a bird call. She squinted through the darkness. In the shadows she could see Tiare leaning against the wall by the ticket windows. Instantly relieved, Bea licked her lips and hurried over.

"Hey," Tiare said, taking a drag of her cigarette.

Bea reached out and grabbed the half-smoked cigarette from the girl's slender fingers.

"So you actually came," Tiare said.

"Not yet, but I'm looking forward to it."

Tiare snorted a laugh. "Man, do you make everything about sex?"

"Depends on who I'm with. Why, does my sexual confidence offend you?"

"Nah, just curious. So, I hope you like animals, because if you don't that's a deal breaker for me."

"I don't have pets because my mom's allergic to everything, but I like anything soft and furry . . ." Bea giggled. "Maybe I do make everything about sex. I'll try to contain myself if it scares you."

Tiare scoffed and flicked the butt of her cigarette. "I'm not promising you sex, but I am curious to see how well you cuddle. Come on."

Ten minutes later, Beatrice was sitting cross-legged on the floor snuggling a small clawed otter pup named Walter to her chest while Tiare gave a bottle to a much tinier pup named Jesse. Tiare explained how the pups were born prematurely and needed to be bottle-fed around the clock with a special formula developed by the zoo's veterinarian nutritionist to get their weight up. Bea had never held a baby anything before, but after Tiare explained that the pups needed to be cuddled to stay stimulated, Beatrice was obsessed. She cooed at Walter and told him he was the most handsome baby otter she had ever seen.

"Why's Jesse so much smaller than Walter?" Bea asked.

"He's the runt, I guess. When they were born, I was told they didn't think Jesse would make it, because he was so small. But he's a fighter and I think he's gonna pull through. Isn't that right, Jesse, my handsome boy."

Tiare explained to Bea that her mom's brother was a zookeeper in San Diego and he's the one who helped get her the job. "The zoo community is very tight-knit."

"So, you work two jobs?"

"Three actually. Sometimes I drive under a cousin's Uber account. But not so much lately, she got freaked out about getting busted since they've been cracking down. I'd do it myself but I'm too young."

"Three jobs is . . . a lot. I guess you don't go to school?"

"Nah, school was never my thing. I dropped out my senior year and got my GED. Summers are great for part-time work, and if I kill myself, I usually make enough to live on for the whole year. The rest of the time I surf."

"Surf? Like . . . surf-surf?" Bea asked. She wasn't sure what she was expecting, but for some reason, surfing was not it.

"Yeah. Most of the year I live in Costa Rica where it's super cheap. I hit the waves in the morning and then work part time at a hotel teaching little kids to surf."

Tiare told her that surfing a big wave was such a high for her that no drugs ever matched it, so she pretty much only dabbled in a little bit of weed here and there, which was now legal in California. Tiare didn't even drink alcohol, saying it messed with her training schedule. Even though she worked all summer, it was important to keep in shape: she swam laps at the Y and jogged on the beach most days.

After they finished feeding the otter pups, they moved on to the slender loris, the western woolly lemur, and two honey badgers named Henry and Thoreau. As Tiare worked, they whiled away the hours of her shift talking. Beatrice couldn't believe it when she checked her phone. It was almost 5 A.M. She had never stayed up this late without being high or drunk or having sex.

Their night ended with Tiare calling Bea an Uber, which Bea tried to give her money for, but Tiare refused. "No, you kept me company and I finished an hour faster than normal."

"Please, I feel guilty, you work so hard for your money, and . . ." She trailed off, not wanting to offend her new crush.

"And what?" Tiare asked in a tone that was hard for Bea to read.

"And I'm exactly the ungrateful rich bitch who has no concept of money that you think I am." Tiare was surprised by Bea's candor and cocked her head the same way the capybaras did when Tiare had called out "who wants din-din?"

Bea took advantage of the moment and leaned forward to kiss her, but Tiare leaned her head back. "I don't start things I can't finish," she said, and her phone dinged. She looked down at it. "Your Honda awaits."

Bea didn't want to leave, but she knew that Tiare only had a few hours to sleep before she had to wake up and take her nieces to school for her aunt, who was an ER nurse. Tiare was crashing on a cot in her aunt's garage for the summer. And for once, maybe for the first time in a long time, Bea was thinking of someone else's needs instead of her own. Truthfully, the only person whose happiness she ever thought to put above hers had been Vronsky's.

As the white CR-V pulled up, Tiare grabbed Bea's phone out of her hand, held it up to Bea's face to unlock it, then added herself to her contacts. "Here's my number. I don't have time for chitchat and kitten gifs so none of that shit, okay? But let me know if you're making it up here again in the next few months."

And like that, the night was over.

IX

When Bea walked into the cottage after her adventure with Tiare, she found her uncle Chadwick already awake soaking in the private outdoor hot tub. She should have gone straight to bed, but she was in such a good mood, she ended up tossing on her bikini and joining her uncle in the frothing hundred-and-four-degree water.

"You're up early," she said, lowering herself into the steamy roil of the tub. The hot water felt amazing after a night out, all the pent-up excitement oozing out of her skin. She tried to let her brain relax, as well, but images of Tiare kept creeping into her mind's eye. Even in the blur of memory she was sexy as hell.

"And you're up late," he said. She nodded but didn't say anything more.

"What did you even do all night? I can't even remember the last time I pulled an all-nighter."

"Same, I mean, without the help of drugs, booze, or even Red Bull!" Beatrice marveled. "I was at the zoo all night." Beatrice proceeded to fill her uncle in on every detail of her evening, which was rare for her. She never shared her personal life with adults. Honestly, she rarely shared her true feelings with anyone.

As she gushed about Tiare and her night of cuddling a baby otter named Walter, rattling off the names of all the nocturnal animals she'd encountered, Beatrice was smiling so broadly that the usual hardened edge in her voice disappeared for a while. For once, Bea sounded like a typical seventeen-year-old girl.

It seemed so obvious to her uncle that he just blurted it out, interrupting her midsentence. "You're really falling for this girl."

His words stopped Bea cold. Normally she would have slung a comeback right back at him, but instead her shoulders tensed up and her mouth went dry.

When she didn't respond, he continued, "Have you . . . ever been in love?"

It wasn't like Bea had never dropped a few L-bombs before, on Claudine, on Rooster, the Brunswick quarterback she used to hook up with (though she had only meant his sexual prowess, not really him), and once on this Scottish college girl she met at a keg party when she and Vronsky visited Kiril at Wesleyan. But she had never said it totally sober, nor had she ever really meant it. With one exception. Vronsky, who had always been like a brother to her. She had told him that she loved him, and meant it. But had she ever said it romantically, like in a passionate way?

Beatrice had always lied a lot, mostly by omission and usually to maintain the aura of mystique she always liked to cultivate. But now she was beginning to see the power of truly knowing herself, of facing the hard truths, even if it meant getting hurt. She'd felt so numb lately. "Never. I mean, I would know, right?"

Her uncle gave a half shrug, suddenly aware that he might be witnessing something big and important in his niece's life, not just witnessing but participating in a conversation she was going to remember forever. "You would probably know if you'd been in love before. But romantic love is a tricky mistress, like you, dearest niece. It's different than lust or infatuation. The flood of emotions is like a physical rush . . . it's like being on a drug but without the drugs, kinda like how you are now. You're practically glowing talking about her. And, before you get all embarrassed, I'll shut up. But I want you to know that if you are in love, then I'm happy for you. You've had a rough go lately, and if anyone deserves a summer romance, it's you."

Beatrice's heart started beating fast. It'd been too long since she had slept or eaten. She felt like she might cry and that was something she just could not do in front of another person. Not even her uncle. She sank down into the hot tub, fully below the surface, which her colorist had strictly forbidden after dying her hair a fresh platinum blond only a week ago . . . but she didn't care. This was big. This was epic. Beatrice was falling in love.

What a crock of shit, she thought as she ducked under the bubbling water and let out an unheard scream.

Dustin couldn't have been happier that Steven and Lolly were finally coming back to New York, Steven especially. He had come to enjoy hearing about Steven's jet-set lifestyle since they had become tighter friends, but Dustin had come to rely on Steven's advice. Though he didn't always agree with his friend's impulsive choices or recreational drug use, Dustin admired Steven's acuity and perspicacity when it came to dealing with the opposite sex. In fact, Steven had become something of a tutor with regards to Dustin's social life as well as his love life. And that was precisely what he needed help with today.

Kimmie was barely his second official girlfriend. The first was a strawberry blonde he'd dated for two weeks during a summer STEM camp, which in hindsight may not have actually counted. Never in his life had he felt anywhere near what he felt for Kimmie. For him it was "love at first sight" at Steven's New Year's Eve party, no matter that his initial slack-jawed infatuation wasn't reciprocated. She was no longer his fantasy dream girl but his real, actual, non-catfish girlfriend, and she was almost all he thought about. He now understood all those cheesy euphemisms about love, how it was like walking on air, but for him it was even more than that. For him it was a soaring sense of elation so intense that his scientific brain could only conclude that love must have similar properties to helium, the gas that actually *was* lighter than air. Also, he noticed, they both made you sound funny when you talk.

Dustin had been an anxious kid. His adoptive mother said his propensity for worrying about everything was how she knew she had raised him to be a good Jewish boy. "It's our culture . . . you're welcome." He knew she was teasing him when she said things like that, but she wasn't exaggerating. Even as a small child, well before he had any inkling of how the world worked, he felt a constant nagging buzz in his head. *Careful, oh no, that could be bad, watch out, don't do that, uh-oh.* He often wished he could be different and wondered what it would be like to wake up and feel calm and ready to face a new day. Instead, his eyes would pop open in the morning and he'd think: *What fresh nightmare of drug epidemic, flu pandemic, climate crisis, or geopolitical strife will I wake up to today?*

The only reason people didn't know about Dustin's crippling anxiety was that he'd been in therapy since he wandered into the kitchen one Sunday morning, a six-year-old with tears in his eyes, and asked his parents what was going to happen to the polar bears now that the ice caps were melting. When they couldn't supply him with a sufficient answer as to why no one was doing anything about it, he had a near-breakdown for the entire school week.

Over a decade (and countless hours of therapy) later, Dustin still experienced the world through the lens of impending catastrophe. But, as of late, he'd started to feel differently. He would wake up and think: *Yes, it's a new day. Another day to see her. Another day to think about her. Another day of blue skies and sunny days, even if the climate crisis is causing it to be the hottest New York summer on record.* And it was all because he loved a girl named Kimmie, who incredibly, remarkably, fantastically loved him back.

Every time they were supposed to meet, he'd get this crazy panicked feeling that she'd tell him she didn't think they should date anymore. So far it hadn't happened, but lately when he saw her, he'd have a split second of fear that his time as Kimmie's boyfriend had run its course, and then she'd just give him one of her smiles, that smile that ripped him in two every time. Her beauty contrived to stop him in his tracks. She was the most beautiful girl he had ever seen, usurping the top spot he had always reserved for Zoë Kravitz. For the first time in his life, his reality was better than his fantasy.

But what he and his therapist had been talking about nonstop for the last few weeks was an entirely new beast, a worry that was so large and terrifying he wasn't sure what to do with it. Dr. Cohen hadn't figured out how to advise him, which was why he knew it was time to bring in the big guns. He had to talk to Steven. He was the only person Dustin felt he could trust with his most anxiety-inducing ordeal to date: Dustin was a virgin and he had a girlfriend who'd already lost her V-card.

It wasn't that she was so much more experienced than him, although that was a factor. Dustin always assumed he'd be one of those guys who would have his first sexual experience at college with a girl his own age who was as inexperienced and awkward as he was, and they'd fritter away their virginities unceremoniously after some keg party or something. But now he had Kimmie, and he knew she wasn't a virgin because she had blurted it out once. She then followed it up by saying she was not ready to discuss it with him but needed him to know.

He assumed it was Vronsky, and Steven had confirmed that it was. And since it was Dustin's ambition to be the best boyfriend the world had ever known, he had to respect her wishes and say nothing except "That's cool. We can discuss it whenever you are ready." Secretly, however, he was hoping they didn't ever have to speak of it again. He had no desire to discuss his inexperience with her anyway. What girl would want to deal with a guy's hang-ups about sex?

He had almost been desperate enough to talk to his dad about it, but when push came to shove, he just couldn't bring up the subject. He was truly frightened to have sex. *What if he messed up their first time? When does a fantasy every match up with reality? Almost never!* So when his dad showed up in his room after he mentioned he wanted to talk, Dustin quickly told him that Nicholas's girlfriend, Natalia, was in town and that Mom had found out about it and wanted to meet her. "Do you think that's a good idea?"

"I don't really have a say in your mom's life right now, you know, I sorta gave up that right when we got divorced. I'm lucky because I have Marcy to talk to about my regrets over Nicholas's death, but your mom doesn't have anyone."

"I know she's been talking to the rabbi," Dustin said. "Should I be trying to get her to talk about it more? It's just so . . . painful. I think she feels guilty, like she gave up on him right before he died, and that maybe if she hadn't, then . . ." Dustin couldn't go on.

"She and I both have reasons to feel guilty. These feelings aren't going to go away easily, if at all. I probably haven't done the best job checking in with you about how you're doing."

"I'm okay. Not great, but I have someone to talk to, too."

"Kimmie?"

"Actually, no. Not that she wouldn't be a good listener, or she doesn't ask about him. I just don't really want to be the boyfriend who can't get over his dead brother, you know? I've been talking to Natalia. She really loved him, and she knew him really well."

His father had told him that perhaps learning about Nicholas and Natalia's relationship would be beneficial for his mother to hear, too.

"And I know you may be smarter than me and your mom combined, but we *are* the adults, so if she wants to meet Natalia, then you should trust her to know what's best for herself the same way we trust you."

His dad's advice was so sound and thoughtful. Dustin thought again about soliciting his father's take on his sex life, but at that exact moment, his phone vibrated with a message from Steven K.: Dude. Me and you. Big slabs of meat. Tonight!

#

When Dustin walked into the restaurant Steven had chosen on the Lower East Side, he assumed there must have been a mistake. This was not the usual high-end establishment Steven normally liked to frequent. There wasn't a single fashion model or designer-wearing rich person in the entire place. Dustin went outside to call, having recently decided that texting was not good for building lasting relationships. As the phone rang, he spotted Steven stepping out of a black SUV wearing mirrored aviator sunglasses, in spite of the late hour.

The two boys embraced on the sidewalk, and Dustin was happy to hear Steven say he had missed him while he'd been away. He hadn't looked Dustin directly in the eye when he'd said it, but merely expressing how he felt was progress for Steven. "Here," he said and handed Dustin a shopping bag.

Dustin looked in the bag and pulled out a Gucci shoebox. "There better be a snow globe with the Trevi Fountain in here." Dustin opened the box and found a pair of black Gucci sneakers with little tigers printed on them. "Bruh, these are incredible, but I can't accept them. I can't walk around wearing five-hundred-dollar kicks. My mother would disown me."

"It's all good, man," Steven told him. "It's a summertime funtime present."

"What's a summertime funtime present?" Dustin asked. "Is that a real thing, like Sunday Funday?"

"No . . . summertime funtime isn't a real thing, well, not to the world at large. But it's my thing. I invented it. I mean, Anna and I both came up with it when we were little kids. It was summer and we were bored, and we asked our dad if we could throw a party and he was all like, 'For what?' And Anna said, 'Because this summertime is no funtime,' to which my dad replied that summer had only started two days ago and to give it a chance. But then we started whining, you know, to get what we wanted, and he caved and agreed to let us throw a party . . . and henceforth the Summertime Funtime party was born! It's not the same as my New Year's Eve bash. We mix it up every time. Sometimes it's in the Hamptons. We did Hawaii once. Last year it was after the Hampton Classic, which I thought was lame because summer was over . . . so that would technically be a good-bye-summertime-no-more-funtime party . . . I don't even know if I should bother this year with Lolly going to theater camp and Anna being away."

Dustin shook his head and chuckled. "Wow, just when I think you couldn't possibly top yourself in 'the lifestyles of the ridiculous and enti-tled' you somehow pull it off with grace and aplomb."

"Which is why you missed me so much when I was gone."

He could sense Steven was in a particularly high-key mood so there was no point in arguing about the shoes. Dustin decided it was easier to accept them, though his plan was to sell them later and use the money in a more responsible way. Like buying one hundred pairs of shoes and donating them to a homeless shelter.

Steven put his arm around Dustin's shoulder. "You ready to get your drink on? I know one of the waiters here and you can order a bottle of vodka that's served frozen in a block of ice!"

Now Dustin understood why they were there. "I wasn't really plan-ning on drinking—"

Steven clapped Dustin on the back and ushered him through the door. "Dust, my friend, plans change all the time . . . we're gonna have ourselves a time and close this bad boy down tonight."

As soon as they sat down, Steven told him the story of taking Anna out to a nightclub in Italy and how when they came back shit-faced and laughing, he and his dad had gotten into an epic fight. Now they weren't speaking. They weren't even texting. "But what else is new?"

Because Dustin had always had closer than normal relationships with both his parents, it disturbed him to hear how at odds Steven was with his father. "Perhaps your dad is still trying to reconcile the fiction of Anna as paragon of chastity and virtue he has in his head with the reality of her sexual actualization."

"No therapy speak," said Steven. "And also, let's remember that I'm Anna's brother, so no sex talk, either, please and thank you."

Dustin nodded and elaborated that it seemed Edward tended to see things in black-and-white and that he had categorized Anna as "good" and put Steven in the "bad" category by default. When Anna started breaking free from their father's expectations and making choices for herself, Edward was unwilling to accept that he had lost control of his daughter. It was easier for him to blame Steven, the habitually out-of-control one. "It's basically a form of denial. People are often willfully ignorant when it comes to the ones they love."

"I get what you're saying. He can't deal with his perfect daughter sullying the family name, so he's gotta take me down because I'm the screwup."

"Yeah, basically," Dustin said. "Maybe after your dad thinks it over he'll apologize."

Steven almost did a spit take with his vodka tonic. "Fat fucking chance. But I will say one big fight over three weeks together is definitely a record for us, so whatever. I guess I was lured into a false sense of security thinking that we were getting past some of our old bullshit."

"One fight doesn't erase all progress. He just overreacted. He's clearly on edge when it comes to Anna," Dustin said.

Steven stared at his friend with a mix of admiration and awe. "Dude, I feel like you're my brother-in-law or some shit."

"Well, we are, kinda," said Dustin. "But like the boyfriend-girlfriend version."

They then moved onto other topics, chowing down on the fattest steaks Dustin had ever seen, bigger than the plates they were served on. Steven told Dustin about the pizza in Italy (dope), Vronksy's memorial service (sad and not dope), the day Lolly insisted on flying to Lake Como to figure out where George and Amal Clooney lived (sorta dope), and how he was worried about Anna but he didn't know how to help her (most undope). He also shared his newest dilemma: on the plane trip home, Lolly had a total meltdown about how she was paranoid he was going to cheat on her again when she left for theater camp in a few weeks.

"I told her if I could detach my diz-nick and let her take it with her, I'd do it because that's how confident I was about not needing it. Obviously I was kidding, but man, if I didn't see a psycho gleam in her eye over the idea of my detachable penis."

"They do have these chastity belts for men," Dustin said with a grin.

"Don't give her any ideas. Ugh. That's a problem for future Steven, not tonight Steven." He slammed another shot to put his girlfriend's insecurities out of his mind. "What's up with you, what'd I miss?"

For once, Dustin had equally interesting developments to share. He told Steven about Natalia sleeping on his floor and their talks in various dog parks all over the city. He knew Steven was going to find Natalia amusing because she had a wild streak, like him. And Dustin told him he had finally summoned the nerve to tell Kimmie that he loved her, and, to his joy and surprise, she said it back without any hesitation whatsoever.

"Dude! Congrats!" Steven yelled, filling up two shot glasses. "Welcome to the love club! Nostrovia!" He downed his shot but Dustin held off. He had more important things on his mind.

"Actually," Dustin said. "I could use some advice to get into a different sort of club, or it may be more apt to say I'm trying to get out of a certain club, if you know what I mean."

Steven shook his head, his face flushed from the booze. "Bruh, I don't know what you mean at all. Tell it to me straight! Just say it like a man!"

Dustin took a deep breath . . . "I have a paralyzing fear about having sex with Kimmie! And I feel like I'm going to be a virgin forever." The room quieted down a bit, and Dustin regretted his confession instantly. But then a group of millennial men started whooping and congratulating the young man's openness. Steven started to clap, and Dustin's embarrassment diminished. As the old saying went, the first part of solving a problem was admitting that you had one.

XII

Steven and Lolly had been gone less than forty-eight hours, and Anna, still in Italy until tomorrow, was already going mental. After her and Steven's disco sneak out, her mood had buoyed a bit and, since Edward had basically grounded Steven, the three of them ended up spending their last week in Rome in the hotel room, playing Boggle and backgammon, watching movies on the wall with a mini movie projector, and racking up a room-service bill that would make their father do a double take. Sure, it wasn't that glamorous or cool but in a weird way it was exactly what Anna craved, mindless rest and relaxation with her family.

Anna kept trying to clear the air with her father about the night she and Steven went out, but Edward was always dealing with work. Her father was not currently on speaking terms with Steven, and Anna begged her brother to let her tell him the truth: that it was her choice to go to the disco and Steven accompanied her to make sure she was safe and not the other way around. Why didn't her father understand that she was capable of making poor choices? Did he not think she had a mind of her own? *She* made the choice to cheat on Alexander with Vronsky. *She* ended up on a sex tape that her ex-boyfriend's half sister Eleanor sent out to god only knew how many people. *She* jumped onto the subway tracks to save a homeless man's dog.

Anna sat up in bed and switched on the bedside lamp. The clock read 11:35 P.M. She had gone to bed early, but now over an hour had passed and, if anything, she only felt more awake. Without overthinking it, Anna slipped out of bed and started getting dressed. She knew it was a bad idea, especially as a girl alone in a foreign city. But she couldn't lie awake with her thoughts anymore.

When Anna crept through the living room, she saw that the light was still on under her father's bedroom door. She almost turned around, but she couldn't remember her father ever checking on her late at night. As inconceivable as it was for Edward to believe his little girl was responsible for her actions the past few months, she decided he would never suspect her of sneaking out after hours, especially when they were departing in the morning for Seoul to see her grandmother.

She smiled at the guy behind the front desk and went out the revolving door. There—she had done it. She looked at the deserted cobblestone street and then went back through the revolving door into the lobby.

"*Mi scusi*," Anna said, using two of the twenty Italian words she had at her disposal.

"I speak English, Miss K.," the man in the gray blazer answered with a smile. "But I appreciate the effort."

"I was wondering if you knew of a dance club nearby?" She tried to sound as casual as possible.

He told her about a new club called Foresta Proibita, "the forbidden forest." He wrote down the address for her and offered her a ride in the hotel's car. Anna didn't want to leave a trail, nervous that her father would somehow find out. As if sensing her thoughts, the desk clerk leaned forward and told her in a hushed tone that all their guests received equal discretion. He would call ahead; a friend of his worked there, and he'd notify them that she was a VIP guest of the hotel. Grateful for his kindness, Anna tipped him fifty euros.

"*Grazie*," he said. "And give my regards to the Fox King."

Ten minutes later, Anna was the beating heart in the center of the crowded dance floor. She raised her arms over her head and swayed her hips to the beat of an Italian EDM track with the chorus: *Amore! Amore! Amore! Amore!*, everyone jumping up and down and shouting along. Anna screamed so loudly her voice started to become hoarse.

Song after song she danced alone, sometimes joining a pair of girls who beckoned her over to them, or a group of friends in a circle. At one point, a sexy middle-aged couple sandwiched her between them and freaked with her for an entire song. There were a few men who pulled her in a little too tightly, or the ones who came up behind her and got a little too gropey. But in these instances, she had no problem shaking her head and saying, "*No grazie!*" She just danced away, chasing the high of the music, or found another couple of girls to shield her in the hot swampy musk of the outdoor dance club.

Anna was sweating, getting sweated on. She danced to feel close to Vronsky. Once they had spoken a whole language of longing on a dance floor. Once. Her heart didn't ache from missing him, because she knew he would be happy to see her feeling so free, even if it was only for a short while. The boy had loved to dance and as Anna now danced alone, she closed her eyes and imagined him with her, touching her hips and her sides as they writhed rhythmically together.

At two in the morning, Anna noticed a group of girls in fox masks trotting around the open-air discotheque. They wore furry clip-on tails, carrying big baskets through the crowd. Everyone on the dance floor cheered and reached their hands into the baskets. Anna did the same and pulled out a white feathered duck mask. She looked around and saw that everyone around her was excitedly putting on their own animal masks. There were elephants, frogs, cows, ducks, cats, and many foxes.

Anna had no idea what was going on, but she put on her duck mask. She looked around the crowd in wonderment and started laughing: a congregation of wild critters in the forbidden forest.

Soon the DJ played a wildly popular Swedish song about a fox, and everyone started dancing. About half the crowd seemed to know the words but Anna did not. The song was kind of silly, but it didn't matter because everyone was giddy with joy. When the chorus came on, everyone started lining up and doing the same dance: swiveling their hips and putting their arms up like paws while swaying back and forth. It was easy enough, and soon Anna was in line, swinging her hips, flapping her duck wings, and quacking with wild abandon. A chorus of shouts rippled through the crowd, and though Anna couldn't see over people's heads, she knew something unusual was going on.

The mass of revelers parted to reveal someone in a full head-to-toe fox costume, complete with a turquoise crown, sitting on a shiny red lacquered throne that was being rolled out on a platform.

"What's happening?" Anna asked two women who were next to her.

"They do this every Friday!" one of them yelled over the roar of the throng.

"The Fox King is here! Get in line fast because he'll only answer a few questions."

As the Fox King passed, the crowd of revelers reached out to touch his paws. Remembering what the woman told her, Anna followed the throne until it was placed in one corner of the dance floor. A line was forming, and Anna found herself third from the front. She watched as the girl at the head of the line went up and sat on the Fox King's lap and whispered something into his orange-and-white triangular ear. The Fox King rubbed his chin, as if deep in thought, then whispered something back to the woman, who smiled and kissed him on the cheek. Next up was a man who looked to be in his forties, decked out in head-to-toe Gucci couture.

After him it was Anna's turn. He beckoned her with his paw. She didn't move right away, suddenly shy. Again, the Fox King waved her over, and Anna took a deep breath, stepped up on the platform, and sat on his lap. The Fox King wrapped his furry arms around her.

"*Americana?*" he asked in a low and raspy voice. Anna nodded. "Don't be afraid, my little duckie."

"I'm not sure what I'm supposed to do, Mr. Fox. I mean, Fox King," Anna said.

"You ask me question and I will give you the answer."

Anna sat up so she could aim her voice into the velvety blackness of the Fox King's ear. "I'm so lost these days. I don't know who I am." It felt good to finally say the truth out loud, even if it was to a stranger in an elaborate fox costume.

The Fox King growled softly. "Duckie, I cannot answer you if you don't ask a question. Ask me the question that keeps you up at night."

Anna's eyes went wide and she didn't even have to think about it. "Will my broken heart ever heal, or will I feel this sad forever?" she asked.

The Fox King rubbed his chin and scratched his head. Then he turned his snout toward Anna and whispered in her ear.

Moments later, Anna was again on the dance floor, moving to the beat as they rolled the Fox King away, waving his paw, bidding the crowd a good night.

By three thirty in the morning, Anna was back at the hotel with color in her cheeks and a lightness in her step. When the desk clerk saw her, he waved her over and asked if she'd had a good time. Anna told him about the masks and the Fox King. The clerk smiled and said he had asked the fox a question once, too.

"Did he answer your question?" Anna asked.

"I already knew the answer to my question, but he got it right."

"I hope he's right about mine. Unfortunately I may not know the answer for a while." Anna yawned, exhausted, and the man wished her a good night's sleep. "*Grazie.* I'm sorry, I don't know your name."

"Nunzio," he told her. "It means messenger. And my message is *mangia bene, ridi spesso, ama molto.* Eat well, laugh often, and love much."

Anna smiled and thanked him for his wise words. "Good night, Nunzio."

Up in the suite, Anna left a note on the table saying she wanted to sleep late so to please not wake her for breakfast. When she entered her bedroom, she decided to read another one of Vronsky's letters. She was trying to save them, but it was so hard. And she felt like she deserved a treat. She opened the beautiful turquoise envelope with red trim, and on the top of the paper was the name *Alexia Vronsky* emblazoned in a raised crimson font.

> *The knock came late,*
> *A search for a mate*
> *A walk across the park,*
> *Up the plank of the ark*

Together in the rain,
Waiting for the sun
A hint of hope
A place to run
Your hand in mine,
Swinging divine
Glittering and gold
A sight to behold
Chandelier in gloom
Only one in the room,
My moon, the stars alight
When we take flight
Riding the waves
For days until graves
I wait for you

After she finished reading the poem, she carefully placed it back in the envelope. Instead of putting it back in the shoebox, she slid it under her pillow, falling asleep in seconds with the posthumous words of her lost love tucked beneath her head as she dreamed of a half man, half fox, beckoning her deeper and deeper into the forest.

Part Two

Maybe a great magnet pulls all souls towards the truth
Or maybe it is life itself that feeds wisdom to its youth

—K. D. LANG

I

Everyone knows the Fourth of July is *the* holiday of the summer, but in the Hamptons, it is *huge*, as all the hoopla of Manhattan migrates to the outskirts of New York. Lolly and Steven had their first Fourth of July in the Hamptons last year, and together they hit up two barbecues and hopped to six different parties, during which Lolly pulled off three complete outfit changes. It was also the first time they were photographed together as a couple, with their pictures appearing in the Sunday Styles section and later in the party pages of *Town & Country*. It was one of Lolly's most favorite memories of the early days of their relationship because it showed her how compatible they were when it came to their attitudes about party-hopping. Steven looked at it like a sport and like any good sport there were certain principles for success. If he was throwing the party, then it had to top all the other parties that day.

But if he was a guest, then he wanted to make an appearance at as many different events as possible. As Steven was a well-known party thrower from his New Year's Eve bashes, he received invitations to everything, and this Fourth of July was no different. He had on his desk fourteen different invites for parties throughout the weekend. He had a few more invites for Monday, but his plan was to take Monday off, since he usually needed a full day to recover after his sixty-plus-hour party marathon.

This year's festivities, however, were complicated. Dustin, Kimmie, and Natalia would also be there for the weekend, and Lolly was none too thrilled about it. In fact, if Steven had bothered to check in with her, she would have vetoed the whole thing. But he hadn't, and now Lolly was upset and keeping it to herself, which usually didn't end well. She couldn't help it. She was in a constant struggle between letting him know her true feelings and keeping up her image of being an agreeable and accommodating girlfriend. And as if things couldn't get more awkward, now Dustin's mother would be staying at the K.s' house for Fourth of July weekend, too.

The text chain reaction had gone as follows: Steven had been thinking about Dustin's virginity issues once Dustin had confessed his anxiety about it at dinner. Steven told him that girls certainly wanted their first sexual experience with a new boyfriend to be memorable, but that first-time experiences rarely met the expectations that went along with them. In Steven's opinion it was better to remember the night as opposed to the act itself.

Dustin wasn't sure what he meant exactly, but Steven had navigated his first time with Lolly only a few months ago, and the whole thing had been a huge headache for him. As this would be Dustin's first time, but not Kimmie's, Steven thought there would be less pressure, but Dustin reminded his friend that Kimmie had told Dustin her first time turned out to be fairly traumatic, so he actually had more pressure on him to give her a "corrective experience." Steven told Dustin he needed to relax. "Sex for guys is like pizza; even bad pizza is still pretty good."

"I'm sure you're right, which is why I only care if it's good for her," Dustin said.

Steven's solution was to invite Dustin and Kimmie to the Hamptons for the Fourth of July. They would all go to the parties together, and then Dustin and Kimmie could slink off and have some time to themselves. Steven's mother would insist on everyone having their own bedroom (their Hamptons beach house slept fourteen comfortably, counting the pool house), but she was also not the type of mom to check up on everyone and keep tabs. Greer's way of dealing with things was to look the other way. When Greer didn't care to know about certain things, her approach was no approach at all.

The snag in the plan, Steven realized, was Dustin himself.

"I don't know if I can get away," Dustin told him.

"Don't tell me you're going to be a nerd and work over a holiday weekend. It's summer, we're supposed to have fun, dude. I'm sure those kids you counsel want a weekend off from you and all your lecturing."

"I don't lecture. I support an open dialogue about any issues they would like to discuss. Look, I know you're Mr. Party-Time all the summertime or whatever, but that's not me. I've worked every summer, like most teenagers." Dustin went on to further reiterate that technically this wasn't a summer vacation for him at all: since he'd deferred his college admission he now had a full-time job for a year working with teens dealing with addiction.

"Okay, okay," Steven said. "So I'm a spoiled rich kid and you're noble and doing good for the world at large. You deserve a little R and R more than anyone I know, and by helping you get it, maybe that checks a box for good ol' me."

Dustin rolled his eyes at his friend's rationalization. "I don't have to work, but my dad and Marcy are going away with the baby and . . ." He trailed off.

"And what?"

"And my mom will be all alone looking at their pictures on Facebook and she'll get sad," Dustin admitted. "I don't want her sitting home alone all weekend thinking about the Fourth of July weekends we used to spend together as a family when I was a kid. Nicholas was a fireworks fiend and we went every year down to the Jersey Shore to watch them. Even after they got divorced, we'd still go watch them every Fourth as a family, up until he met Marcy, that was."

Steven let out a sympathetic sigh. He admired Dustin's selflessness and how he was always looking out for the emotional well-being of those he cared about, but at the same time, he also found it annoying. Being a teenager was your one chance at being completely self-centered. Any grown-ups who had a problem with it were the ones actually being selfish because they had had their time and enjoyed the carefree days of youth. Either that or they never took advantage and now resented anyone and everyone for not being as big a loser as they were.

Steven knew how protective Dustin was of his mom, so he didn't give him any grief. Instead he fixed the problem that was standing in Dustin's way. "I called my mom and talked to her about inviting your mom for the weekend," Steven continued. "They used to be friends back in the day and they can be lonely and unloved together."

"Hey! Easy."

"Bro, I'm just generalizing! Look, my mom's all mopey with my dad being gone, and she's lying about it to all her hoity-toity Hamptons friends, so it'll be good for them to hang out. They can complain about men, or their smile lines, or whatever women their age talk about."

"My mom is never gonna go for that."

"Well, smart guy, maybe you're not as smart as you think! My mom already invited her, and your mom already said yes."

"Really?" Dustin said, unsure how to feel about it. "So, you're suggesting I *lose it* with my mom down the hall?!"

"Like millions of other teenagers probably . . ." Steven started to laugh. "Look, don't sweat it. Our house is humongous, big enough to span two zip codes! I'll make sure that your rooms are totally far away from each other. Maybe I'll put you in the pool house so you guys can go skinny dipping in the middle of the night and then you can tap that ass."

"Dude, don't call it that! This is Kimmie. And I haven't even asked her yet, so don't get too excited."

"In the history of the world, no teenage girl is going to say no to partying in the Hamptons! Though, now that you mention it, I gotta call Lolls. She's gonna be straight minus-ed, but I'll smooth it out."

"Minus-ed?" Dustin asked.

"Nonplussed. Same as minus-ed, no?"

Dustin nodded. "I like it."

The two boys then pulled out their phones and set about texting their girlfriends about the new Fourth of July plans. Soon, Lolly and Kimmie were calling them to discuss. Kimmie was surprised that Lolly had agreed to it because even though the sisters had boyfriends who were close friends, they had yet to go on a double date or hang out as a foursome. Secondly, Kimmie was a little weirded out by the fact that

Dustin's mom would be there. Yes, they had had a nice dinner together two weeks ago, but a meal is far different from spending an entire weekend together. And the last point, which was the real doozy, was that Kimmie wanted to bring Natalia. The girl's actual birthday was the Fourth of July; and if they were away from Natalia on the Fourth, she'd have no one to spend the day with. "You can't abandon a recovering addict on their birthday." Dustin texted Steven while on the phone and asked if they could invite Natalia, explaining the whole birthday thing. Steven had just convinced Lolly that it'd be nice to hang out with her little sister over the holiday weekend because she was graduating next year and now was their chance to bond. Then he had to mention the Natalia thing, which caused Lolly to send back the Memoji of herself with her arms crossed in an X.

Steven texted Dustin back to see how set Kimmie was on inviting Natalia because Lolly wasn't feeling it, so Dustin texted Kimmie back to make sure Natalia could even come. Kimmie texted Natalia about celebrating her birthday in the Hamptons, and Natalia said it sounded "cool AF," but she couldn't leave because she was dog-sitting Edgar for the weekend. But just as Kimmie was texting Dustin back that Natalia was out, she got a text back from Natalia who had just texted Edgar's owner to see if she could bring him to the Hamptons and guess what? "Edgar LOVES the Hamptons!" So now she was asking if she could bring the dog. Kimmie said she was sure it was fine because Anna had two giant dogs, so surely their house was dog friendly, but she would check. Meanwhile, Lolly was texting Kimmie asking if she and Dustin had to come to the Hamptons with them because it was really her last weekend with Steven before she left for theater camp in two weeks, and to sweeten the deal Lolly offered up her Dyson blow-dryer that she knew Kimmie wanted desperately. Kimmie texted her sister back to say that Dustin's mom was now going and so she had already committed to going but she was wondering if Natalia could bring a pug with her, which was when Lolly texted Steven to ask him why he didn't mention the fact that Dustin's mom was going to be coming, too, and why did he pretend he was asking her thoughts on the whole matter when obviously he had already been inviting literally everyone and their mother?

While Steven was smoothing things over with Lolly, Dustin had to call his mom and find out how she felt about Natalia coming and if that was too intense for her, in which case they could just call the whole thing off. But he was surprised to find out that his mother was happy that Natalia would be joining them. She sounded more excited than Dustin had heard her in a long time, which was when it started to sink in that Dustin would now be one of those people who went to the Hamptons, even though he was definitely not one of those people nor did he usually particularly like any of those people.

In the end it was decided that everyone would be going and Lolly would be getting a new bikini, dress, and sandals from Steven as a gift to show his appreciation for her being so understanding and generous when it came to his family's beach house.

There will be fireworks, Steven thought. *Oh yes, there will be fireworks. . . .*

II

When Anna's car arrived at the television studio in Seoul, a young woman dressed in a black skirt suit was waiting to be her guide. Chang-ri was a newly minted assistant producer who had been working her way up over the last two years after interning while at university. She was recently promoted from production assistant, though in reality she was still fetching coffee and babysitting VIPs. When Chang-ri was assigned to greet the American girl who spoke very little Korean, she had stayed up late the night before practicing her English.

Chang-ri was shocked when Anna stepped out of the car alone. She wasn't used to unchaperoned teenagers. It made her wonder what made this American girl so very important.

"Hi, I'm Anna," Anna introduced herself. "*Gamsahabnida*," she murmured softly in Korean. "Thank you" was the first phrase she had learned, her grandmother had made sure of it. Anna continued in English. "I'm excited to be here."

Chang-ri bowed at the waist and noticed Anna's Valentino pink studded sandals and matching hobo bag. "An honor to meet you, Miss K." She held up the visitor's badge and Anna bowed so Chang-ri could place it over her head.

"Call me Anna, please."

Anna looked down at the badge with her name written in Korean. The anonymity of being in a new country thrilled and invigorated her, and she was looking forward to being the spectator instead of the spectacle. She was touched that her father had arranged for her to visit the set of *King of Masked Singers*. He had introduced her to the singing competition when she was eight years old. Watching it together became a favorite activity for them over the years no matter how busy he was. Edward wanted to come with her but he couldn't rearrange his schedule, so it just wasn't possible. He also reminded her that in times of great sorrow, it was okay to be joyful, too. "It is your last summer of high school, after all."

Chang-ri led Anna through a set of double doors and into the *King of Masked Singers* stage area. This wasn't her first time on a television soundstage. She had been a few years ago when she was in Los Angeles with her mother. Greer had been attending a gala at the Getty Museum to honor the Obamas, and a friend of hers had arranged for Anna and Steven to visit the set of Disney Channel's *Shake It Up*, one of Anna's favorite shows at the time. Steven had no interest at all and quickly wandered off to explore the stage where *The Dark Knight* had been filmed earlier that year. But for Anna, it had been a magical day, sitting in a director's chair onstage, visiting the costume and the props departments, and seeing how many people worked together to put on the show. Anna had also toured the set and met the actors, one who became a big movie star and another who now dabbled in racier entertainments.

Anna had once found it hard to believe that two girls who started in the exact same place ended up with such different careers, but now she understood it. People you didn't even know would judge a person for things they knew nothing about. A year ago she was seen as perfect, but now Anna was viewed as anything but perfect in the public eye. She thought back to her brother's advice before he left to go back to New York: "You gotta reframe the game, sis. You've been emancipated from the bonds of being flawless, so now it's time for you to do whatever you want. The haters are always gonna hate, and never forget, everyone loves a good comeback tour."

The vibe on the set of *King of Masked Singers* was quite different from her experience in LA. It was much quieter, and everyone dressed in suits instead of California casual wear, but the energy of the production was still palpable. Chang-ri asked if she wanted to sit with the studio audience. "You will have to sign a non-disclosure agreement and promise not to post about what you see on social media."

"I'd rather not be on camera," Anna said. "Is it possible for me to watch somewhere else?"

"Of course," Chang-ri said, surprised that a teenage girl wouldn't want the chance to be seen on television. She thought all Americans were obsessed with being famous.

Anna was soon sitting in a chair with headphones on, watching the show on video monitors with the directors and producers. Chang-ri served her an iced green tea and kept asking if there was anything else she wanted, but Anna shook her head. She had everything she needed. "If you have to get back to your job, I promise I won't move from this spot."

Chang-ri looked at her and said with a very straight face, "You are my work today, and it's my pleasure to serve you."

Anna reached out and grabbed her hand, the intimacy of which startled Chang-ri so much she squeaked with surprise. "I'm sorry you have to spend your day babysitting me, Chang-ri. I'm sure you have more important things to be doing."

Chang-ri's face flushed from the attention. Most VIPs never bothered to learn her name.

Anna could tell she was making this girl uncomfortable with her lack of formality, but she felt she had been making progress expressing herself since Italy and didn't want to go backward. "Have you seen the American version?" she asked, referring to the now-popular American spinoff, *The Masked Singer*.

Chang-ri had watched it online and marveled at how much bigger and splashier Hollywood made their show. She liked it but, of course, preferred the Korean version, loyal as she was to the best job she had ever had. "Yes, it is also good. We are proud it has become popular in the United States."

"I know I'm American," Anna leaned in and whispered. "But I prefer your version, too, even though I don't know the music as well. Your masks are like works of art."

"Maybe I can take you to see them. Up closer," Chang-ri said. "Would you enjoy that?"

"Seriously?" Anna's eyes lit up. "That would be incredible!"

The buzzer sounded overhead, which meant they were about to start filming again, and everyone on set had to stop talking. Anna put her headphones on and leaned back in her chair to watch. She patted the empty seat beside her, motioning for Chang-ri to sit. Normally Chang-ri would never dare sit in one of the producers' chairs, but if her bosses said anything to her about it later, Chang-ri would tell them that Anna had insisted, which meant she had no other choice.

By lunch, Chang-ri was totally enamored with Anna. She was the warmest and friendliest and sweetest girl Chang-ri had ever met. Anna kept asking questions about Chang-ri's job and her life in Seoul, and even though such personal questions were not seen as polite in Korea, Chang-ri loved it. Like most other young woman in Asia, Chang-ri was obsessed with K-pop. Anna said she was a fan, too, but was only familiar with Blackpink and BTS, the two biggest K-pop groups that had crossed over to America. Chang-ri explained that her favorite thing was to keep track of all the new bands that seemingly formed overnight. K-pop academies that trained future idols were big business these days. Her newest obsession, the latest and greatest six-member boy group The NowNows, was somewhere in the building right now filming their new music video.

"They have a new single called 'I Want You Now, Now, Now!' that is one of ten songs picked for a contest where fans get to vote for Korea's Song of the Summer."

"Do you think they could win?" Anna asked.

Chang-ri shook her head. "Not against the more well-known groups they are competing with, like BTS, EXO, and Stray Kids. But their song is my favorite, so I think it should win. It's the story of a boy who loves a girl so much that when they're apart, she's all he can think of." Chang-ri held her hand to her chest and said, "*Simkung.*"

Anna shook her head to show she wasn't familiar with the word. Chang-ri explained that "*simjang*" meant heart and "*kungkung*" meant the sound that a heart makes, and together . . .

"*Simkung,*" Anna said, holding her own hand to her heart. "I know it well. Hey, don't you want to go and meet them? Can't you ask your boss?"

Chang-ri was taken aback at the sheer audacity of such a suggestion. "I could never ask my bosses for such a thing. It's not proper."

Anna held up her badge. "What does this say? I can read my name, but nothing else."

Chang-ri explained that Anna's VIP pass meant she had all-access throughout the building. Chang-ri's own pass only allowed her on the *King of Masked Singers* soundstage and in the production offices, where she shared a desk with two other assistant producers. "You must know someone very high up in the company because these passes have to come down from the top. Normally they would have never let me be your escort, but I'm assuming because you are young and female, I was selected to make sure you had the most enjoyable of experiences."

Anna smiled, explaining that her father was a man who knew lots of bigwigs. "I'm sure you were also picked because you speak English so well. My Korean is terrible," she said. "I'm thrilled they picked you to show me around. You're my first friend in Seoul. And to celebrate we should go watch the NowNows video shoot."

Chang-ri shook her head so hard her bangs lifted off her forehead and took flight. But then she remembered she was given very strict instructions that everything possible should be done to make sure the VIP had a good time. "If that's what you would enjoy," Chang-ri said nervously. "But I believe you said you didn't know them."

"True, but it's what you want, so now that's what I want. You've been so nice to hang out with me all morning. And if you like them, I bet I will, too. In America most people just ask for stuff all the time. I was not raised to be like that myself, but sometimes I wonder what the harm is in knowing what you want. What's the worst that can happen, they tell us no?"

Three years Chang-ri had worked here and hadn't seen much besides the show she worked on. But one request from Anna K., followed by a flurry of texts, and they were granted permission to the soundstage where The NowNows were shooting their new video. After walking through a maze of hallways, the red light above the door was flashing when they got there, which meant the shoot was in progress and they had to wait before entering. Anna excused herself and asked Chang-ri to point her toward the direction of the ladies' room.

"Let me take you there," Chang-ri said, but Anna shook her head.

"No, you go in since we don't know how much time we'll have." Anna took her VIP pass off and placed it over Chang-ri's head. "You be me for a while."

Chang-ri tried to refuse, but Anna wouldn't hear of it. "Please, it makes me happy." Chang-ri finally acquiesced, but not before deciding that she would no longer believe what many Korean parents told their children who were infatuated with America: that all Westerners were selfish, putting their individual needs ahead of their family and country. Never had she ever met someone so sweet and generous. Chang-ri handed Anna her badge.

Anna found the bathrooms easily, but on her way back to the stage door, she lost her way. She reached for her phone, then remembered it was locked up with security.

She soon found the bathrooms again and hoped that there would be someone in there to ask for help, though Anna knew only a few Korean phrases. Her mother had once accused her of willfully trying not to learn the language because she had issues with her grandmother. "Even Steven's better at it than you, and we all know he's not the scholar in the family." Anna had rolled her eyes; only Anna's mother could insult both of her children in the same sentence.

Just then the supersonic *whoosh* of a toilet flush startled her. She turned to see a skinny, blond Korean teenage boy walk out of the far stall. He was wearing a black Adidas tracksuit and upon seeing Anna the boy yelped in surprise and ran back into the stall and slammed the door shut.

"I'm so sorry," she said, wondering if she entered the wrong bathroom. "Are you okay?" Her question was met with silence, but she figured that might be because he didn't speak any English. "Hello?" Anna repeated, this time in Korean. "Do you speak English?"

"Better than you speak Korean," he replied in English, his voice muffled by the stall door and the poor acoustics of the bathroom.

Anna laughed and then continued in English. "I'm lost. I'm a guest of *King of Masked Singers* but I'm supposed to be at the NowNows video shoot. My friend is there, she's a big fan."

"Are you a fan, too?"

"Honestly, I'm visiting from America and have never heard of them. Do you like them?"

"They're the same as every other K-pop band to me," he said. "Where are you from in America?" the boy asked, opening the door and peeking his head out of the stall. "I prefer American music."

"Really? Lately I prefer the upbeat happy vibe of K-pop. I live in Connecticut. And New York City. I arrived two days ago in Seoul."

"People want things they do not have," the boy said cryptically as he emerged with a mischievous grin on his face. "You are lucky to live in New York City." His English wasn't terrible, but he had a thick accent.

"I'm sorry, am I in the wrong bathroom?" Anna asked gently.

He put his hand over his mouth and nodded. "Oh yes, sorry. The women's bathroom is cleaner. In the men's room everything is always covered with . . . wetness."

If Anna thought his reasoning was odd, she didn't show it.

"Come, I will help you," the boy said as he washed up at the sink. "But first tell me of New York while I smoke a cigarette outside. I have never met anyone who lives there. I want to know all about Brooklyn."

As they exited the bathroom, the boy offered his hand. Anna took it, noticing his nails were painted the palest blue. In fact, his manicure was better than hers. "I like your nail polish."

"Thanks," he said.

Anna held up her left hand. "I painted my nails to look like Zendaya's."

"Do you know Harry Styles?" he asked.

"Not personally, but yes." Anna nodded, and the boy whose name she didn't even know said how much he admired his "styles," then burst out laughing, an infectious giggle that made Anna crack up, too. And just like that a friendship was born.

III

Anna studied the bathroom boy's face in the late afternoon sun as he lit his cigarette. He looked as though he had been airbrushed. Anna was fortunate to be blessed with unblemished skin herself, but she didn't have the pale, poreless look of the boy in front of her.

"I don't know your name," she said.

He looked at her and spoke slowly. "You don't know my name?" He stared at Chang-ri's badge. "You work here, Chang-ri?"

"This is my friend's ID. And no, you didn't tell me," Anna said.

He exhaled a perfect smoke ring and asked, "Why you don't smoke?"

"It's bad for you . . . you know that, right?" Anna tried hard not to sound preachy. She had tried smoking exactly once in her life, and it made her feel ill.

He shrugged her off. "You only live once."

"So don't you want to live as long as you can?" She had no idea how old he was. He could have been her age, or he could have been in his mid-twenties. His youth was mysterious and elusive, almost vampiric.

"Not anymore," he answered cryptically. "I smoke half." He flicked the still-lit cigarette butt onto the pavement. "For you."

Anna wrinkled her nose at his littering. She thought about saying something sarcastic back, but held her tongue. She had to get going soon. Chang-ri would probably be looking for her by now.

He leaned against the wall, in no hurry to go back inside. "How long will you visit here?"

"A few weeks. Maybe longer. My grandmother has a house here, but she lives part-time in the United States. My father wants me to consider finishing high school here."

"Why would you when you live in America? Everyone here wants to be educated there."

It was Anna's turn to shrug.

"I didn't say I wanted to go to school here," she said. Hearing her own words set her true feelings free. Now that she was actually in Seoul, the idea of committing to stay here for a year seemed daunting. She had been flip-flopping daily at the prospect, and had decided to do what her father wanted: tour the schools and make an informed decision afterward. Perhaps it wouldn't feel like she was running away from her problems if she made the choice for herself.

"It's hot, can we go back in?" Anna asked. "I should find Chang-ri."

"She is your friend who likes The NowNows?"

"Yes, I don't want her to worry that I've disappeared."

"Disappearing sounds good. Shall we do that?"

Anna didn't understand what he was asking. But there was something she noticed right then in his eyes, a look of sadness. One that was all too familiar.

"I get the feeling, but I can't right now."

"Another time, maybe? We can go eat ramen together," he said. "I am a ramen-holic."

"I don't have my phone," she said.

"Tell me your Kakao Talk number," he said, referring to the most widely used texting app in Korea. "I'll memorize."

Anna told him her number, doubtful he would retain the information. "I still don't know your name."

"Quentin," he told her. "The same name as my favorite American movie director."

"You and my brother would get along," Anna said. Steven was obsessed with Tarantino, not only because of all the hip, ironic dialogue and cartoonish bloodshed, but because of the honor-amongst-thieves philosophy of many of his characters.

"Is your brother sad and beautiful like you?" Quentin asked with sincerity.

Anna was surprised by his words. She knew she should ignore it, but she felt the need to ask Quentin how he could tell. "Why do you say I am sad?"

"Sadness recognizes sadness," he said. "Don't worry, your sadness is safe with me."

His answer gave Anna a chill despite the intense summer heat. "Quentin, I really must go."

With a polite nod, Quentin opened the door and ushered her back inside. He grabbed her hand, but Anna didn't feel like he was being romantic. It felt more like how Lolly or Steven sometimes grabbed her hand in a crowded bar so they wouldn't lose each other.

He walked her back to the door with the red light, which was once again flashing. Quentin said good-bye and did a little bow. He then turned and skipped off down the hall, finishing with three cartwheels, which made her clap her hands as he disappeared around a corner.

When Anna entered the dimly lit stage, Chang-ri came running up to her, breathless. Anna assumed she was going to be upset with her for going off on her own, but instead Chang-ri threw her arms around her and squeezed her tightly. Then, pulling back, she held out her forearm to show five different signatures in varying colors. "They signed my arm!

I'm never going to wash it off. This is the best day of my life! And it's all because of you."

"You're welcome!" Anna said, smiling. Chang-ri's mirth was contagious.

"To thank you, I have arranged for you to meet the apprentice to the mask designer, but he can only see you now. Will you be sad to not meet The NowNows?" Chang-ri asked.

"Not at all," said Anna. "I just wanted you to meet them." Her father had taught her as a child that even the smallest act of kindness can ripple through the world, which was why good manners and gratitude were so important. Anna had always loved that particular idea. Helping Chang-ri meet her favorite K-pop group had led to Anna's bizarre introduction to Quentin and then to Chang-ri arranging for her to meet the mask designer. This made sense to her: the things we really want are those we get from being selfless toward others.

Anna felt abuzz that her good karma had been reciprocated; it felt as though things were starting to come back into balance.

Beatrice had been in Los Angeles for over a month and she kept a growing shit-list of all the reasons the city annoyed her. How everyone was overly concerned with exercising and eating healthy. That in Brentwood, where her uncle lived, everything closed early. And that her closest West Coast friends Ben and Addison's show was in production so they could never hang out. There were definitely lots of good things about LA: the dry climate, which was giving her the best hair days of her life, the hot people, and the beaches. But right now, the bad was outweighing the good.

Beatrice had known she'd debut in Greenwich and Manhattan society since she was a little girl, based solely on her family name. She had even participated in the International Debutante Ball, known for being the most exclusive in the world, which was held at the Waldorf Astoria hotel every other year during the Christmas holidays. Beatrice didn't let such things rule her world because she found it to be a bunch of antiquated bullshit; however, that didn't stop her from accepting the invitation. She sought out attention rather shamelessly, always had, always would. And this was her number-one problem with Los Angeles: no one here knew who she was and thus no one here cared about her one iota.

In Hollywood, the only last names that really mattered were those belonging to A-list celebrities, actors currently starring in hit movies and on television shows, or any number of famous musicians who lived there, as well as the big-money producers. Even the queen bees of the reality world—the Jenners, the Kardashians, the Vanderpumps—had more clout than her money could buy, a fact that irritated Beatrice to no end because clout was the one commodity she valued above all else. She told her uncle that it wouldn't bother her, that she welcomed being an unknown quantity. But by the end of her first month, she realized it had put her in a funk.

It was Manny, her uncle's beautiful young hubby, who figured it out over dinner one night. "Aww, are you all sad and mopey because you're just another rich-girl Hollywood wannabe?"

Beatrice laughed, appreciating his ruthlessness. "I'm not mad because I'm a wannabe, I'm mad because I've gone from being a somebody to a nobody!" But as she said it, she crinkled her nose, hating the sound of the word "nobody." Every time she met someone and told them she was from Greenwich, no one seemed to care. One Insta-influencer she met actually thought Greenwich was in Europe.

"Seriously?" she had said, "I barely have a pulse in class, but even I'm not that much of a dummy." Bea was just being herself, but it seemed her caustic brand of bitchiness wasn't translating well because the laid-back West Coast influencer had gotten up from the couch and walked off mumbling that Beatrice needed to get her toxic chakra in check. Beatrice then got offended that the girl got offended and left the party early even though she had been hoping to go home with someone. While Beatrice waited for her Uber, she flirted with a hot valet guy who would normally get her engine revving, but when he asked her if he could maybe meet up with her later, she surprised herself by saying she was involved with someone. The funny thing was that when she told this little white lie, she was thinking about Tiare. But there hadn't been any contact since the night at the zoo—no texts, no calls, no nothing. When she arrived back at her uncle's house after cutting her night short, she announced that it was official: LA was making her boring. Later, feeling sorry for herself, Beatrice even answered Claudine's call when it came in around midnight. When she hung up two hours later, Beatrice felt even more alone.

At least she had a job to distract her.

The "job" that Beatrice had decided upon, when given the choice between several options by her uncle, was to intern for a well-known celebrity stylist named Delia H. Bea was fairly self-aware when it came to her natural talents, her sense of humor and always being the wealthiest person in the room, while also knowing she wasn't the most detail oriented. For this reason she had said no to interning at a talent agency, a music management company, or one of the production companies where her uncle had contacts. She knew that fetching coffee and sitting at a desk wasn't anything she could do for eight minutes let alone eight weeks, so interning with a stylist had been an easy decision. She assumed there would be a lot of shopping involved, so her learning curve would not be too steep. The day-to-day she imagined—going to designer showrooms, looking through racks of clothes, saying yes and no, as in *The Devil Wears Prada*—couldn't have been further from what the job actually entailed. Instead, Beatrice was asked to do a lot of research as if she were some kind of nerdy archivist.

In LA there were many different events that needed attending, movie premieres and award shows being the two biggest. But most actors had loads of other events they had to dress for, as well: restaurant openings, celebrity baby showers, and birthday soirees. But that was not the challenging part. The real headache was making sure that whatever the stylist recommended to the client would be worn only by them and not by anyone else, especially someone who was higher on the Hollywood food chain.

For example, one of their clients was the new young wife of an Academy

Award—winning director, which meant she wasn't dressing for herself but more so to represent her well-known husband with class and style. So, when this client was invited to a game night at her famous director husband's agent's mansion in Brentwood, her outfit needed to be just right for the occasion, just right for the crowd, and just right for the fact that she was the "wife of" and not the main attraction. She couldn't look too young, too sexy, too desperate, too extra, and most importantly too-too, which was what this particular stylist told her was the worst of all fashion sins, the sin of trying too hard.

Los Angeles was simply not as formal as New York, so it wasn't as though everyone was expected to be seen in the latest runway styles like the fashionable society women of Manhattan. These West Coasters were trying to blend in and look like they were part of the LA good life. That meant a relaxed version of whatever brand you were trying to cultivate.

Needless to say, all this overanalysis made Bea's head hurt. She liked her boss, though, a self-made iconoclast who had hit overnight success after dressing a young starlet for the Oscars. The starlet actually won and Delia was called out by name during the acceptance speech after a thrilling Best Actress upset. The idea that one dress could launch an entirely new business was the magic of this town. Delia booked five new clients in twenty-four hours, and now, less than two years later, she had a waiting list of people begging her to dress them, three junior stylists, half a dozen assistants on her payroll, and four interns. Bea was the youngest of the bunch.

On her first day, Delia asked Bea how she'd picked out what she was wearing.

Without batting a lash Beatrice asked, "Do you want the truth, or do you want me to lie?"

Delia was hard to surprise, having worked in the business for so long, but she was taken aback by Bea's frankness. One thing that separated New York women from LA women was how they were much more confident and direct in how they communicated.

"I want to hear both, the truth and your lie."

"My lie would be me telling you that I picked out these R13 jeans because they're the expensive-without-looking-it jeans of the moment, that I found this T-shirt at a vintage store on St. Marks, and that this men's Etro button-down tied around my waist pulls everything together—my shoes, the blue in my tee, and the frayed hem of my jeans. Oh, and this itty-bitty Balenciaga Hello Kitty wallet on a chain? Well, I like that it's so teeny tiny because all I really need one moment to the next is my fake ID, Daddy's black card, and somewhere to put my crystal-encrusted twenty-four-karat coke straw and a baggie of Molly."

"And the truth?" Delia tilted her head and gazed at Beatrice vertically.

"I have a personal shopper at Bergdorf's and an astronomical yearly clothing allowance, and they pick out all the shit that I wear, complete with Polaroids of how to assemble the pieces. Sometimes I do what they say and sometimes I grab whatever happens to be on the floor when I get home from one walk of shame or another. As for the mini wallet, well, that's true . . . but don't fret, I only party on the weekends."

Delia clapped her hands with childlike glee. "You're, like, the real motherfuckin' deal! I love you!"

It was an auspicious start to her job, or so Bea thought. What she soon learned was that Delia was rarely in the office, usually calling in and telling her assistants what she needed and where to go while she was at a client's house helping them sort through their outfits.

Bea hoped that Delia would keep her in mind for some plum job in the future, but so far she was tasked with researching what other celebs had worn and were wearing, and recording all the clothes sent over by various stores and designers in a spreadsheet. Data entry was for Beatrice the equivalent of successive bikini waxes; in fact the waxes would have been preferable.

Luckily, Bea had lied when asked if she had a driver's license, which spared her from the terrible job of returning clothes to stores all around LA and being stuck in heinous traffic all day long. Most of her time was spent in the office on Melrose watching the clock while printing out return labels and packaging up boxes while daydreaming about Tiare.

She had started countless texts to Tiare but never sent them. She couldn't figure out why, since she was totally into her, but maybe that *was* why. Was she scared of wanting too much? Usually, Bea's modus operandi was short, intense affairs that burned hot and flamed out quickly, kind of like what happened with her and Claudine. She knew Claudine was still obsessed with her, constantly texting at all hours and sending presents. Beatrice usually returned Claudine's texts not because she wanted to, but because she didn't have much else to do. Beatrice didn't think it was a big deal anyway, since Claudine was nine hours away from her. Though if Beatrice had bothered to do the time zone match, she'd have realized that Claudine certainly wasn't sleeping much, as most of the time she was texting Beatrice throughout the day and it was the middle of the night in Paris.

Plus, she liked the presents.

Just last week Claudine sent a big box from Maine containing all the fixings for lobster rolls. The note had said, "I feel lobster without you! I miss you awfully, crush-stacionly yours, Claudine." Manny and Bea prepared the dinner that night and when Chadwick arrived home they dined outside by the pool and supped on Claudine's savory offerings.

"What's the deal with this Claudine girl?" Chadwick asked, his mouth full of buttery lobster roll.

"She's a Francophonic sex machine who's obsessed with me," Beatrice replied. "*C'est la vie!*"

"And does she know we're seeing other people this summer?"

Bea answered a bit defensively. "We never had the exclusive talk, and if Claudine knows me, she understands that I do whoever I want, whenever I feel like. Monogamy is unnatural."

"How would you know if you've never tried it?" Chadwick asked, refusing to let the subject go.

"Maybe if I find someone with true magic in their pants one day, a long, long time from now, I'll have to consider it," Beatrice mused.

"The real magic is right here," Manny chimed in, and tapped his chest with his finger.

"Okay, boomers. And the lobster roll buzzkill award goes to . . ." Beatrice said, balling up her napkin, giving Manny and Chadwick a quick eenie-meenie-miney-mo, and tossing it in her uncle's direction. "You!"

V

Steven was in a jovial mood on the drive to the Hamptons. To him the Hamptons meant refuge, and he always tried to make the most of his parents' beach house. The week before Fourth of July was the latest he had ever waited to start the Hamptons portion of his summer, and he was dying to get there. He and Lolly would be alone with his mom until Dustin, his mom, Kimmie, Natalia, and Edgar the pug arrived on Thursday evening.

The night Steven and Lolly arrived, they had a subdued dinner with Greer by the pool. They took turns telling her about their time in Italy, but before Steven regaled her with the night he and Anna got busted, Lolly steered the conversation to Greer and inquired about the first month of her summer. Greer hadn't felt like going out that much, she said, and had been staying at the beach and only going into the city once a week to deal with the construction plans for the CPW apartment. When Steven asked if the renovation would be completed in time for school, he had to be reminded he was done with high school in the city and would instead be doing a post-graduate year at Deerfield to fortify his transcript and play an extra year of tennis. Steven had skipped the formal graduation ceremony at Collegiate with the excuse that he needed to be with Anna in Italy. Truthfully though, for once in his life, he wasn't into the pomp and circumstance of it all, probably because he wasn't heading off to college yet like most of his classmates.

"So if Anna decided to come back and finish school in New York, she wouldn't have a place to live?" Lolly asked.

Greer seemed surprised by Lolly's assessment and asked if Anna had mentioned anything about it. Steven quickly shot Lolly a look and said the last time he had spoken with Anna, she told him she wasn't making any decisions until she toured the schools in Korea. Steven, surprisingly, felt like a year abroad might be good for his sister. He didn't like the idea of her back in school without him nearby to protect her from the gossip.

After dessert Greer bid them both good night and retired early. When she was out of earshot Lolly told Steven that she had never seen his mother so depressed. She urged him to go check in with her while she unpacked.

"You have a big heart and I get how you like to check in on everyone's feelings, but my mom's not like that. I've never seen her cry and I don't really want to start now."

"She seems so sad," Lolly said. "I think she's unhappy about your dad."

"I don't want to get involved," Steven said. "And trust me, my dad would definitely not want me to, either."

Normally, Steven invoking his father's wishes ended the conversation, but Lolly was well versed in the ways of her boyfriend's psyche. "Well, now that you and your dad are on the outs, maybe it's the exact right move to show him you can think for yourself. You know there's a lot of stuff I admire about Korean culture, especially their beauty break-throughs, but this whole notion of men being absolute monarchs of their families is ridiculously outdated! I'm convinced your parents could work things out if they tried."

Steven went to go talk to his mother, not because Lolly was right but because he knew he'd never hear the end of it if he didn't. As usual, Lolly's perceptions were astute, and Greer was quite touched that Steven checked in with her. She didn't open up fully to Steven, but she did in-dicate that her summer had been lonely so far. She was glad Steven was in the Hamptons now because she didn't like going to social events on her own. "I went to three parties by myself," Greer said, "but when people heard you were all in Italy without me, it got the tongues wagging."

Later, as Lolly unpacked, Steven snuck in and put his arms around her waist and kissed her neck. She spun around slowly and found Ste-ven's smiling face staring back at her. He thanked her for pushing him to talk to his mother because the result was that she had agreed to let him throw a Summertime Funtime party on Labor Day weekend.

"Really?!" Lolly squealed.

"Yup, and it's gonna be fucking spectacular! I told her what she needed was something to look forward to and it'd keep all her gossipy friends on their best behavior because they would all want an invite."

"You're a genius, babe!"

"Takes one to know one, gorgeous."

Lolly beamed at the word "gorgeous." It was her favorite thing to be called.

She had promised herself she would do everything she could not to worry about her impending departure for theater camp. Instead she would just enjoy every moment she had alone with Steven.

"Naked hot tub?" he asked.

"I thought you'd never ask," she said, and pulled her top off.

VI

After her day at the studio, Anna's father told her he had to make a quick trip to Hong Kong and wouldn't be home until morning. But he promised he'd be back in time to have breakfast with her and Halmeoni. In her father's absence, Anna and her grandmother took a mostly silent dinner alone in the ornate dining room. Anna had invented a word to describe her grandmother's décor. The word was "ugspensive." She wouldn't dare utter it out loud, except to Steven, who rather annoyingly didn't judge their grandmother's taste as harshly as she did. Steven always had the flashier sense of style. Anna, on the other hand, believed fashion should accentuate a person's personality, not be in place of it.

That's how Anna got through these meals. She'd fixate on one ugly trinket in the room and make up a story in her head about it. Last week she asked her grandmother about the green porcelain vase displayed on the top shelf of the curio cabinet, but was disappointed to learn her grandmother didn't even know where it had come from. Anna wanted to leap up from her chair and run over to the cabinet, pull open the glass doors, grab the vase, and smash it on the floor just to see what her grandmother would do, but instead she let her napkin slip to the floor just so she could bend down to pick it up and she let out a silent scream, under the table, only to emerge with her face a blank mask once again.

Her grandmother went to the salon every day, and it was the simplest thing for Anna to ask about, and her halmeoni always responded with "*gwaenchanuhsuh*," the Korean equivalent of a one-word answer: "fine." But without her father present at the table, Anna stayed silent and didn't even bother.

Eventually, Halmeoni asked Anna about her own day. Her grandmother didn't watch "silly reality shows on television," so she couldn't understand why Anna would even want to waste her day doing such a thing when she could spend hours at a salon being primped and preened. Two summers ago, she and her mom and Halmeoni had gone to the salon, and Anna loathed it. She was bored and had forgotten her book, and the only word she recognized was the Korean word *hapa* for "half-Korean," which must have been the word of the day because everyone couldn't stop saying it when she was around. It was times like this that Anna wished she had taken to the Korean language better.

Anna's mother always urged her to find some common ground with her grandmother, but there just didn't seem to be any. Anna liked designer clothes as much as the next girl, but when she tried to talk to Halmeoni about young new designers, her grandmother would just scoff and say the clothes were too masculine or ugly. Also, they'd once had a heated exchange on the topic of fur. Being a lover of animals, Anna abhorred the practice, but for her grandmother, it seemed to be the animal's sacrifice that made the fur desirable. Anna thought it was such a wild notion that two people could love or loathe something for the exact same reason.

Anna had never been jealous that her grandmother preferred Steven to her. She knew it was cultural, because sons in Korea were always valued above daughters. This boggled Anna's mind. She couldn't understand how her eighty-year-old grandmother could still believe this to be true. This cultural attitude was one of the things Anna was most stressed about when considering schools in Korea. How would living there affect her? Would she begin to believe she was inferior? Her other issue was her grandmother's relentless pursuit of beauty. She had never once seen Halmeoni looking anything less than perfect, every hair in place, her makeup flawless—she must have spent hours a day in front of a mirror.

Her grandmother usually retired to her room a quarter before eight every evening, leaving Anna knocking around the big gaudy house on her own. She had never stayed there before without Steven, and her grandmother didn't have televisions in any of the guest rooms, so Anna had been spending her evenings curled up with a book. She was currently reading a novel, one she had noticed on Vronsky's bookshelf the only time she had ever been in his bedroom, *Americana* by Don DeLillo. She liked it so far and admired the first line: *Then we came to the end of another dull and lurid year.* In a dozen words, the author had conveyed a confessional candor and a sense of immediacy by dropping the reader right in medias res, and Anna enjoyed DeLillo's jump-off. She desperately wished she could talk to Alexia about it.

Around 8 P.M. Anna received a text and put the book down. It was from an unknown number with nothing but a *ramen emoji*. Apparently, Quentin had indeed memorized her number. To make sure it was him, she texted back a cheeseburger and "Royale with cheese?" referring to a famous line from *Pulp Fiction* that she only knew about from her brother, who was known to recite entire monologues from the movie at parties. She then received a *laughing emoji* and another *ramen emoji*.

When? she texted.

Quentin texted right back. Now! I'll pick U up. Address?

Anna stared at her phone, unsure how to proceed. She thought about the fact that no one was home to ask if she could go out or not. Better to beg forgiveness than ask permission was what Steven always said when dealing with such situations. Anna had always done the opposite, waiting for permission for everything, unaware of what it would feel like to not care if you disappointed someone. Besides whenever she did ask to do something, she was usually given the OK. She thought about texting her dad, but she knew he would definitely say no because she was meeting up with a strange boy. Or if he didn't say no immediately, he'd certainly ask her more questions about Quentin and Anna probably wouldn't be able to answer them. She didn't know Quentin's last name. She didn't know what he did, though she assumed he worked at the studio like Chang-ri.

She received another *ramen emoji* and then a *prayer hands emoji* followed up with a *cheeseburger emoji*.

Anna looked out the window; it wasn't even dark yet. What was the harm in going out for a little while?

She sent Quentin a pin of her address, and he texted back his ETA, T minus thirty minutes. She sent a Memoji of herself thumbs-upping, and he sent her his Memoji wearing a crown, but with pink hair instead of blond.

Now she had to figure out what to wear. It was hot and sticky out so a dress was her best option, but she didn't want to be overdressed. This was definitely not a date; it was just ramen. But she reminded herself that she was in a foreign country and she couldn't say she was up on the dating patterns of young people in Korea. Suddenly, she was worried. Did Quentin think it was a date? Those certainly weren't the signals he was sending out, but with Koreans being far more reserved than Americans, perhaps she wasn't reading him correctly. He had a certain impish charm, but she wasn't attracted to him physically.

Then she remembered that Lolly's red Goop romper had ended up in her luggage by mistake. Anna had found it while unpacking and hung it up in her closet. It was cool but very casual and definitely implied meaningful friendship as opposed to sexy one-night stand. Staring at herself in the mirror, she gave the outfit a nod of approval.

She added the Gucci sneakers Steven had surprised her with in Italy with the word LOVED emblazoned in gold, and dug through her jewelry box for a pair of chunky gold hoops. They were not her style exactly, but something made her keep them all this time. Perhaps it was for tonight. She quickly ran a brush through her hair, pulled it up into a messy updo because of the summer heat, and decided to keep going. This was what she needed, the reinvention of Anna K. She used a lip kit to paint her mouth to match the red romper. Next, she put on much heavier eyeliner than she had ever worn before, thankful to have spent the last few weeks with Lolly, the all-time, bar-none grandmaster when it came to the fine art of makeup application.

By the time Quentin had gotten to her neighborhood, Anna had transformed herself into a girl she barely recognized in the mirror. She had a brief panicky moment of guilt: What was she doing? But then she relaxed and decided she needed to give herself the opportunity to have a fun, adventurous night. Her night dancing at the Forbidden Forest had done wonders for her mood after moping about for all of June.

And the most recent letter she'd read from Alexia was just a recording of the minutiae of his day, from what he ate for breakfast (he rode his motorcycle downtown for a Balthazar chocolate croissant), to his day at school (he liked English, he hated math), how he'd wandered around Bergdorf Goodman Men like the male version of Holly Golightly (Heathcliff GoSadly bought a buffed Brioni reversible belt in black and taupe), and then met his mother for dinner at 21, where she nagged him to get a haircut and discussed where they should travel this summer (Geneviève was bored of Monaco and had been hearing good things about Hvar, Croatia). Oddly it was these day-in-the-life letters that hurt the most, because they highlighted the fact she would never get to ask, "How was your day, dear?" and he would never get to tell her.

She scrawled a quick note to her grandmother and left it on her pillow. She told the housekeeper that she was going out, though it was unclear how much English the woman understood.

A black SUV was waiting outside. The window rolled down, and a blue manicured hand beckoned her forward. She crossed the street, and the door opened. Quentin stepped out, offering her his hand. He had undergone a transformation, too. He was now dressed in shiny, skinny black jeans, silver high-tops, and an oversized pullover black hoodie that said EAT ME in green neon paint splatter, and sunglasses.

Quentin pointed to her grandmother's fancy house and whistled. "Yo, someone be a VIP!"

Anna took his hand and let him ease her into the backseat. "Yo yourself," she said, feeling giddy with excitement. "Can we get out of here before my halmeoni comes chasing after us?"

"Driver! Go! Go! Go!" Quentin said. "Now now now!"

VII

Usually on the Uber ride to work, Beatrice would check the Insta-stories of her friends back East while texting with Adaka, her best friend in Greenwich. But lately she had been gazing out the window at the crystal blue skies and vertiginous palm trees lining the streets of LA. It was hard to believe she had been here for four weeks already. The days were passing so fast. And since every day in Los Angeles seemed to have near perfect weather, it all just blurred together, except for Tiare. In Bea's mind Tiare's face was as clear as the West Coast sky.

Then there was Claudine. *Bzzt. Bzzt. Bzzt.* Beatrice's phone had been vibrating with her calls all morning. Claudine had learned Bea's schedule, and now nine o'clock Pacific Standard Time was when she usually called. Depending on her mood, Bea would answer and have a quick conversation using work as an excuse to keep the call short. Today she just didn't feel like dealing with Claudine's endless barrage of questions or her latest update of Anna K.'s whereabouts abroad that Claudine managed to glean off of social media. Instead Bea thought about the fun night she had planned. She had scored four tickets to see Billie Eilish at the Greek, one of LA's two major outdoor music venues, the other being the Hollywood Bowl. She had paid an exorbitant sum on StubHub and invited the other interns at Delia's to join her—Rosie, Indira, and Toddie.

Toddie was the only other intern in high school, but he was a year older than Bea. He was repeating his senior year after getting into a car accident with a friend last January. He had to stay home for six months, not because he was badly injured, but because his friend had died and Toddie was the one driving the car. Toddie hadn't offered this information up to her specifically; Bea had found out from Indira, who was the office gossip. Indira and Rosie were both in college: Indira at Parsons studying costume design, and Rosie, who was sweet but a little flakey in that sunbaked LA sort of way, a sophomore at USC. According to Indira she'd only been accepted because her parents donated beaucoup bucks to the university's endowment.

Some of the senior stylists were going, too, and Beatrice was pleased to find out that her seats were superior. She was all too eager to disrupt the whole Hollywood hierarchy system that was so indifferent to her and her independent wealth. It just went to prove that it wasn't always about who you were but, instead, about how much you were willing to spend. Famous or not, rich was still rich.

That night, as they walked toward the front gates of the Greek, Toddie asked Beatrice if she had her eye on anyone out here in Cali, to which Beatrice shrugged, finding it odd that she felt the need to keep Tiare out of the conversation. The thing about Tiare was that Beatrice had been thinking about her every single day. She blamed Uncle Chadwick for her uncharacteristic shyness, having brought up the notion that she might be developing real feelings for Tiare. She didn't know if that were true, but she couldn't deny the fact that she had started at least twenty texts to Tiare but failed to send any of them. Remembering how Tiare said she wasn't into chitchat, Bea feared the crickets of no reply. Not getting a text back would be far worse than never sending the text at all.

"No one in particular, I'm still just browsing," Beatrice said.

"Well you better hurry up as the summer's basically half over and you never want to start a fling at the end, much better to start one early and give yourself enough time to get sick of them so it won't be sad when you leave."

Hmmm, maybe Rosie wasn't as ditzy as she seemed, Bea thought. "Come on, let's go get our Billie on."

Rosie, Indira, and Toddie couldn't believe how good their seats were: second row in the center.

"Billie could sweat on us from here," Rosie opined.

"Who the hell do you know?" Toddie said to Bea, cutting right to the chase. "I don't think Satan himself could get these seats."

"Wait a second," Indira said, her eyes glinting with epiphany. "You're Three-Degrees-of-Bea, aren't you?"

"What's that?" Rosie and Toddie jinxed each other.

"My little brother goes to Andover, and he once said there's some private-school girl in Connecticut who's connected to every other private-school kid in the country by three degrees. . . ."

Bea winked at Indira mysteriously as Finneas walked onstage and the crowd went berserk. He talked about how special it was for him and his little sister to be performing at the Greek. He said they used to come to concerts here when they were kids and always had to sit in the cheap seats. He apologized that their opener was unable to perform this evening but he'd be taking his place, sharing some of his own solo music. He told them it had been an incredible whirlwind, how quickly he and Billie skyrocketed to superstardom and how their success had taken a real toll on his friendships.

Bea was riveted by his words. For her, friendships had always been tricky, too. She wasn't a world-famous singer, but trusting people still didn't come easy for her. She never judged anyone for the gossip they shared with her, although she had to admit learning that most teens had not-so-nice secrets made her wary of who she let in. She stared at Indira, Rosie, and Toddie, their faces aglow in the stage lights, and got a hollow, lonely feeling. This concert was going to be dope, so why was she feeling so shitty? It didn't make any sense. She wanted to be away from home for the summer, meeting new people, and not thinking about the past. She swallowed hard and excused herself to the restroom.

Sitting in the stall, Bea put her head in her hands and gave herself a stern pep talk. "Get your shit together, Beatrice!" She wanted to give her new friends a night they would always remember because of how awesome it had been, not because she had had an emotional breakdown in the bathroom of the Greek. But what did it matter if nothing good ever lasts? That's what her mother used to tell her anyway.

She'd come into Bea's room blackout drunk, sit on her bed, and wake her up for these little drunken talks. These intrusions happened dozens of times, and Beatrice had never told anyone about it, not even Vronsky. The first time it happened it scared her because her mother was crying and Bea thought something had happened to her father. What she quickly realized was that her mother was out of her mind drunk and didn't even know what she was saying. She just talked and talked, slurring her words and repeating things she had said only moments ago. But the one point she kept making over and over was: "Your youth. Enjoy your youngness. Your carefree skin and your unblemished life. Make as many memories as you can write down because it's all you're going to have to read when you get older . . . the last times don't good, sweetie. The last times don't good."

Alcohol was a depressant; they had learned as much in health class. So Beatrice took her mother's morose words with a grain of margarita-rimmed salt. The first two times it had happened Bea tried to carry on a conversation with her, attempting to soothe her, but once she realized her mother had zero recollection of ever coming into her room, Bea gave up. Instead she just listened to her mother ramble, and her mother's slurred refrain was always the same: "The good times don't last; the last times don't good."

Eventually it became the lesson Bea remembered whenever she made new friends, making sure never to get too close to anyone, untangling her mother's drunken words. If nothing good lasts, then what was the point?

The one exception in her life had been Vronsky, but that wasn't exactly the same. He was more than a friend. He was her blood, her first cousin, and they'd spent almost every summer together as children. Vronsky's mother loved to travel and she'd leave Kiril and Alexia for a month at a time, chipping in for an extra nanny, and off she'd go. Beatrice was an only child and welcomed the company. Kiril was three years older and Alexia was one year younger than her, and every wish she got as a little girl, whether it be from birthday candles, the Thanksgiving wishbone, or a shooting star, she wished that she and Vronsky had been born twins.

They were both blond and oftentimes people mistook them for siblings. Before her mother could correct the stranger, Bea would play along and say, "Yes, he's my twin brother. We communicate telepathically." Then she would throw her arm around him, and he'd look up with his startling blue eyes and smile, in cahoots with his cousin's adorable fib.

By the time Beatrice mustered the wherewithal to go back out to their seats, Billie Eilish was onstage, but for some reason she was wearing a large black boot on one foot. Toddie filled her in that Billie had twisted her ankle backstage. Beatrice felt sorry for the singer, who was clearly in pain but trying her best to give the sold-out crowd what they wanted: a chance to be a part of her one-in-a-billion rise to superfame. She turned around to see everyone behind them jumping up and down in excitement, screaming "I love you, Billie!" their voices punctuating the cloudless indigo night.

When Bea heard the song's refrain, she gasped. *No fair. You really know how to make me cry. When you gimme those ocean eyes* . . . It was Billie and Finneas's first hit, and Bea had distinct memories of listening to it on repeat for months. She loved its melancholy beauty and remembered lying next to Vronsky in the sand in Tahiti during Thanksgiving break when they were thirteen years old. She had taken out her left earbud to put it in his right ear. She told him the song must have been written about him. "No one is going to make more girls cry than you will. You'll be drowning in an ocean of tears. I'd bet my life on it. It's your gift and your curse."

He sat up then, squinting in the sun. "You can't bet your life on it. I wouldn't let you! I love you too much." He had said it with such seriousness it made Bea laugh. She couldn't remember what she said back. She probably made fun of him for being so grossly earnest and sincere, two things that made her highly uncomfortable. But she treasured that moment, and "ocean eyes" always made her think of him.

"Bea, are you okay?" Rosie asked. "You're crying." She placed her hand on Bea's shoulder and Beatrice recoiled.

"I don't feel well suddenly. I have to go. You guys stay, I'll text you later." She pushed her way through the crowd and by the time she exited she was crying so hard she could barely stand up straight. Vronsky was her Ocean Eyes and he was gone. She was never going to see him again.

She opened her Uber app and stared at the where-to field. She knew she should go back to her uncle's house and go to sleep, but that wasn't what she was going to do.

She texted Tiare. I really need to see you. Can I come up there? Please. She hit send and regretted it immediately. *Had she gone absolutely mad?*

Almost instantly, she got a text back. Yes. I'm off work in one hour. Come to SYR.

Beatrice had never been the religious sort, but at that moment, she believed in a higher power, some universal law governing the emotional order of things. She felt so horrifyingly alone and sad, so desperate and demented right now, that god only knew what would have happened if she hadn't gotten a response.

She typed in the address for San Ysidro Ranch. It would take an hour and cost over two hundred dollars for an Uber SUV. Without giving it a second thought, she hit confirm and waited on the curb to be picked up. In the distance, the opening bass of "bad guy" thumped behind her, vibrating the ground like a tremor before an earthquake.

VIII

When they arrived at Ramenonymous, there was a long line of people waiting to get in, but Quentin seemed to know the owner somehow, and they were seated right away in a small back room. Thirty minutes later, the two of them were slurping up noodles and drinking green tea ices at the most popular ramen joint in Seoul. Quentin told Anna he had taken his grandmother there and she had praised the food for having *jungsung*, which meant it was made with "heart and devotion." Anna found this sweet but was unable to imagine her own grandmother twirling the long noodles with her chopsticks and slurping them into her mouth. Quentin was clearly a regular as many of the waiters poked their heads in to say hello. Anna asked him if he lived in the neighborhood, but Quentin never gave her straight answers about his personal life. Instead he grilled her about Brooklyn. He wanted to know what people were wearing, if you could find Korean beer easily, and what Jay-Z was like in person.

He told Anna his dream had always been to visit New York City because of the Statue of Liberty snow globe he had as a kid. He also wanted to see Graceland. "My grandfather visited once and told me about a room with carpet on the ceiling," he said.

"Graceland?" Anna asked.

"I loved that idea . . . that Elvis loved dancing so much that if people danced on the ceiling, he wanted them to be comfortable." Quentin knew this was absurd, but that's what he believed as a child.

Anna told Quentin that when he made it to New York, she'd be his personal tour guide and would take him to Liberty Island. He was especially curious about the dance clubs in the city, and Anna admitted that she wasn't a regular on the club scene but that her older brother could hook him up. She did tell him about her night out dancing in Rome. Quentin asked her if she had gotten to ask the Fox King a question, and she shook her head, not wanting to make up a fake answer when he asked what her question had been.

Quentin wondered what the fox got paid because it sounded like a great job to him, sitting on a throne and beckoning pretty girls to sit on his lap. But, Anna explained, it wasn't just girls who sat on his lap, and she knew it sounded goofy, but it was a pretty intense experience to witness. Anna said she heard people were traveling to Rome just to dance at this club.

"Why do you think that is?" Quentin asked.

"Because it's random." She shrugged. "It's hard for people to deal with all the unknowns in their lives, so maybe fun mysteries make it okay to handle uncertainty."

"You're young, but you are wise, Anna," he said.

"I don't know about that," she replied. "These days I'm realizing being booksmart will only get you so far. What I need is more life experience because in that area I feel like I know nothing at all. My goal for the summer is to figure out what I want as opposed to what everyone wants for me."

"Knowing that you don't know and wanting to know, makes you wise."

"Like meeting you," she said. "Normally I wouldn't have gone out with a stranger. The jury's still out on whether or not it's wise."

Quentin gave her a curious look. "Do you want to know what I would ask the Fox King?"

Anna nodded, intrigued by the seriousness of his tone. "Very much, yes."

"I would ask the Fox King to give me advice about a girl I'm in love with because I don't know what to do." He took a sip of his beer and added, "Her name is Minsoo."

Anna was relieved that she wasn't the target of his romantic interest. "If you need someone to listen, you can tell me anything. I've been listening to my older brother's girl problems for years, and trust me, he's had lots of issues with lots of different girls."

"I do not want to burden you with my sad tale. There's nothing to be done anyway."

"Because she's dead?" Anna asked gently.

Quentin's mouth hung open in surprise. "No, no, no!"

Anna covered her face with her hands, suddenly embarrassed by her words, which clearly shocked him. "I'm sorry! I shouldn't have said that." Then to explain, she added, "Someone I loved died recently. . . ."

"I'm so sorry," said Quentin taking her hand in his own.

"Don't apologize. You invite me out to a fun dinner and I'm ruining it. Dead boyfriends are not polite dinner conversation."

"I asked you to dinner because I was hoping for nonpolite conversation," he said, then shook his head. "That is not what I mean to say. I hope to have an American conversation. Like how people talk in American movies and say whatever they are feeling."

Anna understood exactly what he meant by this and realized that kind of openness was what she had been craving as well. "That's why I'm looking at schools here. My father thinks that I will forget my troubles if I just ignore them. A fresh start."

"I have been trying to forget my own, but it's difficult. Is a fresh start possible?"

"I don't know. I haven't spent that much time in Korea. I've visited a lot, but I don't really know what it's like to live here. I'm afraid that moving to a new city where I don't know anyone may just add to my problems. Also, I don't speak Korean, which makes it tough to make new friends."

"You know me now. I am a friend. I will show you around while you are here so you can get to know it . . . like how you'll show me around when I come visit you."

Anna held out her hand and they shook on it, which made Quentin laugh at her formality. "You are a very serious girl, aren't you?"

"Guilty as charged." She sighed. "But I'm trying to loosen up."

When they left, Quentin led her by the hand through the crowded restaurant. As soon as they stepped outside, they walked into the blinding flash of a mob of photographers. Anna froze, not quite comprehending what was going on until she realized that the flashes were coming from a herd of K-paparazzi all aiming their cameras at the two of them while shouting in Korean.

"What's going on? What is this?" Anna pulled her hand away from Quentin's grasp and blocked her face with both hands.

It was then that she understood what the gathering crowd of fans was chanting at them: "Cutie! Cutie!" mixed with "Now, Now! Now, Now!"

"Oh my god," Anna said, turning her head to Quentin, dumbfounded with disbelief. "Are you . . . ?"

Quentin flashed a smile and pulled her in close. "I'm the front man for The NowNows. My fans know me as QT. Kind of a big deal around here . . ."

Anna's first impulse was to bolt, but the crowd around them was too dense.

There was nowhere to run.

IX

The barrage of flashes illuminated them in a strobe-like flicker as a horde of excited onlookers encircled Quentin and Anna. "How could you not tell me you were famous?" she hissed when she had recovered from the initial shock.

Quentin pulled her close like they were dancing the tango. "I'm gonna dip you."

"Don't you . . ." But before she could finish her threat, he dipped her in front of the throng of paparazzi.

Having attended charity galas with her parents, Anna had some experience in front of photographers, but she'd never seen anything as invasive and chaotic as this. She forced a phony smile to the now upside-down crowd, and delighted them by offering up a queen's wave with her right hand.

Quentin pulled her up abruptly, then pointed to his driver who was beckoning them from the car parked across the street. "Run!"

And so she did, appreciating the fact she had chosen to wear sneakers instead of heels. She followed Quentin and they both jumped in the car. Quentin slammed the door shut and Anna punched him in the shoulder. "How could you not tell me who you were?"

Quentin shrugged and looked down at the pocket on his hoodie. "They ripped it! I just got this today, and now the pocket is ripped!"

"Seriously?!" she said. "Who cares about your dumb hoodie! Take me back to my grandmother's. Now."

"Right now? Or right now *now*?" Quentin teased.

"This may be funny to you, but it isn't to me. If you're a NowNow, then why weren't you onstage when they were filming the video?"

Quentin could see that Anna was truly upset with him. He looked at her and sighed. "In the beginning of the video, I descend from above wearing rainbow angel wings. It was done with a green screen and my part was already over. And, I didn't tell you who I was because I liked that you didn't know. You never told me *your* name!"

"Well thank god for that!" Anna said.

"Haven't you ever wanted to be someone else for a while?"

Anna stared into his puppy dog eyes that had no doubt gotten him out of trouble before. But his oh-so-innocent charms weren't going to work on her; she was furious. "Look, I get it. I've seen all the music biopics. You've become so famous you don't have any privacy, everyone wants something from you, and so you feel isolated and alone. Normally,

I'd be very sympathetic to your plight. I've wanted to be someone else plenty of times, more than even you can imagine. Just because you're in the public eye, you feel like everything is all about you, but it's not. You don't know what I've got going on in my own life and now my privacy is in jeopardy! Do you get that? If my dad sees those photos, he'll lose his shit."

A look of shock swept across Quentin's face. Clearly, he wasn't accustomed to being spoken to this way, and certainly not by a teenage girl. Anna was a little surprised at her vitriolic tone, but her heart was pounding and she didn't care if he was offended by her anger. "Are you famous, too?" he finally asked in a small voice.

"No, but my life is complicated. My father is very private. He's not going to be happy tomorrow morning when my face is splashed over all the papers."

Quentin pursed his lips, clearly holding back a laugh.

"Is there something funny?" Anna asked.

"This is Seoul, the most wired city in the world! If he's gonna see you, it won't be tomorrow, it'll be . . ." He pulled out his phone. "Now!" Quentin held out his phone, and Anna saw his messages blowing up. He tapped the screen and enlarged an image with his thumb and forefinger. "Whaaa, you are even more beautiful upside down. Your face is so symmetrical. . . ."

Anna grabbed his phone and gaped at the screen. It was a photo of the dip from just a few minutes ago. He wasn't wrong; it was a great picture. The good news was that with all the makeup she had on, it looked nothing like her, especially the bright red lipstick. She shut her eyes and let out a long sigh of relief. It seemed highly unlikely that her father would recognize her from the photo alone. Also, Edward probably didn't receive K-pop alerts on his iPhone.

She hit the translation button that turned the Korean characters into English, and she read: *QT and the red-lipped mystery girl!*

"They don't know my name," Anna said with relief. "You can't give it out, okay?"

"I don't even know your name! To me you're an American VIP."

"Wait, how did you post that so fast? I didn't even see you. . . ." She looked back at his phone. The picture already had twenty thousand likes.

"K-pop groups live and die by their fans," he told her. "We have a team of people dedicated to managing our social media. This photo's gonna be a beast and break my likes record!"

Unable to stare at it anymore, Anna handed him back his phone. "This is very uncool."

"No one is going to find out about you." Quentin quickly spoke to the driver in Korean. "I told him to drive in circles for a while, in case we're being followed."

"Followed? Are you serious?!"

"K-pop fans are intense, some are also crazy," Quentin said; he explained the term for stalker fans was *sasaeng*, and they were no joke. "It's smart to take precautions."

"If you knew this might happen, why did we have to go out?"

"Ramen doesn't travel well, you must eat it when it's hot. The restaurant knows me and would never . . . how would you put it in gangster speak, drop a dime? Someone else must have called the press. Hey," he said, tapping the window and pointing outside at a line of people waiting on a sidewalk. "Want to go dancing?"

"I don't dance with liars," Anna said simply.

Quentin whistled and shook his head. "Never have I heard a girl talk like you."

Anna felt her face flush at his words. She was breaking Korean etiquette left and right. Her grandmother would disown her if she knew that she was talking this way to someone older than she was, because in Korea it was customary to be respectful of anyone older than you no matter how selfish they were acting. She knew she should apologize for her directness, but she didn't care. "If you don't like it then I'd very much advise you against coming to America because lots of girls speak their mind way more than I do."

"Who said I didn't like it?" Quentin grinned. "And I didn't lie. I just didn't tell you the whole truth. I am sorry for any trouble I caused."

Anna was growing more and more frustrated that what had started out as a fun night had spiraled into disaster. "Tell me the truth about Minsoo and I will maybe forgive you. Maybe!"

"Or we can go and dance your anger away, that might be good, too?"

It was Anna's turn to laugh now, mainly because things had gotten so surreal and absurd that her only two choices were to laugh or cry, and she was sick of crying. "Fine, but I need a fake name."

"Very!" Quentin announced. "Since you're a very important person. And you use that word a lot." It was a ridiculous name, but Anna liked that it started with the letter V, like Vronsky, so she nodded her approval. It was as good a name as any, and right now, very much better than her own.

"Now," she said to Quentin. "Tell me why you're sad."

"For such a simple question," he said, "I'm afraid the answer isn't the same."

When Beatrice's Uber reached the gate of San Ysidro Ranch, the guard informed her that Tiare would be arriving shortly. Before Beatrice could respond, headlights appeared from the opposite direction. Bea got out of the SUV and held up her hand against the glow of the oncoming lights. She had tried to fix her face when she got in her Uber, but she couldn't stop crying and eventually she had given up. She looked like a train wreck, but she didn't care.

Tiare's Subaru Outback pulled up next to San Ysidro Ranch guard gate, and Beatrice climbed into the passenger seat. Before she could say anything, she started crying again. She was annoyed about it but helpless to stop the onslaught of tears.

Tiare gave her a sympathetic look and reached into her backseat and pulled a T-shirt out of a laundry bag and handed it to Beatrice. "Here, it's clean," she said. "I'm not working tonight, but I do have to stop by the zoo to do a few things. It won't take long. And then we can talk, okay?"

Bea wiped her eyes with the tee and sniffled, comforted that they were going back to the place where they'd had their first night together. She couldn't help noticing the two surfboards on the roof of the car and the duffel bag in the back. "Where are you going surfing?" she asked.

"Not sure yet. I usually check online before I go. Either Malibu or Laguna Beach. There are websites that track the reports on waves."

"Cool," was all Beatrice could say as they drove up the Pacific Coast Highway.

When they got to the zoo, Tiare began typing up instructions for the person covering her duties while she was away. While Tiare wrote her email, Beatrice wandered over to the otter nursery to observe Walter and Jesse. The baby otters were much bigger than last time, and she was surprised at her genuine joy that something in the world was growing and fortifying itself, and not falling apart, like she was. Bea felt a bit self-conscious about her red eyes and puffy face under the fluorescent lights, but Tiare was barely paying her any attention, and it's not like this was a booty call.

Tiare finished up and entered the nursery. She grabbed Bea's hand and told her she was taking her to her favorite place in the zoo. "And then you're going to tell me what the hell is going on."

"Is it dark?" Bea muttered.

"Just you wait . . ." said Tiare.

Soon the two girls were sitting on a bench in the big cat house. It was pitch-black save for the glow of the exit signs and the faint moonlight seeping inside from the outdoor habitats.

"Why is this your favorite place?"

"It's so peaceful with all the animals chilling out," Tiare said as she lifted her eyes upward. "Look up." Bea tilted her head back and stared up at a patch of night sky through the canopy of trees. A skylight to the stars. "Now talk."

And so she did. She told Tiare about Vronsky and how he was the only person she felt truly connected to, the one person she loved unconditionally. She couldn't make her brain understand that he was gone. She told Tiare how she didn't go to his memorial service because she couldn't bring herself to say good-bye.

"Denial is a coping mechanism. Your brain knows what you can handle, and denial gives you a chance to handle it in smaller doses. Don't quote me on this, but my aunt gets *Psychology Today* so I've read a bunch of back issues."

"I don't know if this is normal denial," Bea confessed. "Every time a memory of him floats up to the surface, I bury it as fast and as deep as I can."

"Tell me what happened tonight," Tiare prodded her gently.

"I was at the Billie Eilish concert with my friends from work and suddenly I felt like I couldn't breathe. I just started crying and I couldn't stop. I pushed my way through the crowd and left."

After Tiare heard more, she reasoned that witnessing Finneas and Billie's close sibling relationship triggered Beatrice's meltdown. When she heard the song "ocean eyes," all her emotions came bubbling up to the surface. "Your feelings are still raw and painful, even if you bury them. You can't run from the past. Trust me, I've been watching my own mom try to do it her whole life and it hasn't exactly worked out for her."

"I'm not ready to say good-bye to him." Beatrice's voice faltered. "Why can't I just stay in the denial stage forever? I've made it this far."

"But you haven't made it," Tiare said. "You lost your shit and ended up at a zoo in the middle of the night."

"But maybe this is where I'm supposed to be," Bea replied softly, leaning in to kiss.

Tiare leaned toward her, and Bea felt awash in joy as Tiare kissed her back, slipping her tongue into her mouth. But after a moment, Tiare pulled away.

"Don't stop. I'm good," Bea whispered, kissing the side of Tiare's neck. "I'm fine."

Tiare gently pushed Bea's shoulders back. "You, my dear, are not fine."

Bea's anger was quick. "You don't know me. I tell you one sob story and you think you can say whether I'm okay or not?" She jumped to her feet.

Tiare said nothing and instead pulled out her phone, which lit up in her hands.

"What are you doing? Oh, sending me home again? Telling me you can't start something you can't finish? Who's the one in denial now? You can't tell me you don't feel it, too!"

"I'm looking up the best waves because I think you should come with me. Let's go away for the weekend."

Bea was stunned, grateful that Tiare had the good grace to ignore her outburst. "Yeah, of course. I'm down."

Tiare showed her the site that tracked the wave patterns and predicted where the best surfing would be the following morning. Her plan had been to drive tonight and sleep in her car at whatever beach had the best surf. "The best waves are at sunrise. That's when the truly hardcore surfers go."

Bea pointed to a different list above it. "What are those?"

"Those are the best waves around the world. Mine's set for the California coast."

"Mexico's not that far . . ."

"Bea, I know you're having a moment, but we're not driving to Mexico tonight. I only have four days off."

"Tiare, I've been totally honest with you, do you realize that? Like, never once lying to make myself look better or even lying just to lie, which is a bad habit of mine."

"Okay . . . not sure where you're going."

"I know I fucked up when we first met by throwing my money around, but I swear I'm not doing that now." She paused. "Let me take you to Mexico to go surfing."

"Take me how? We don't have tickets or hotel reservations."

"All you need is your passport, then we just have to stop by my uncle's and grab mine. Leave the rest to me and my dad's black card travel concierge person. C'mon, it'll be an adventure. Don't you want to go surf at"—Bea grabbed the phone out of Tiare's hands and looked at the screen—"Sayulita Beach in Mexico?"

"Of course. I've always wanted to, but—"

"I'm a spoiled rich girl in the middle of a Chernobyl-sized meltdown. Please take advantage of me."

Tiare cracked up and rolled her eyes. "Taking advantage of women on the verge of a nervous breakdown isn't really my style, but I like your honesty."

"And I like how you kiss. C'mon. You work your cute little tail off all the time, and I kinda sorta work now. We deserve a treat! Let's just run away together, far, far away."

Tiare looked up at the stars and contemplated the offer. If she was being truthful, Beatrice had popped into her head a lot since they first met, and Tiare had been mad at herself for not getting Bea's number when she'd had the chance. It had really taken her confidence down a few notches when she didn't hear from her after their big night at the zoo. She had just about given up hope when she got Bea's text tonight. She had a few days off and was in desperate need of a little fun, so the timing couldn't have been more perfect. As a surfer, Tiare knew timing was everything and so it would have been a little self-defeating not to take this opportunity and go ride the biggest waves in the northern hemisphere.

"I'm in," she said. "Let's fucking do it!"

#

The Octagon was no longer the most popular club in Gangnam, but in Quentin's opinion, it was still the best. He explained that the owners only cared about the music, which meant bringing in the hottest new DJs week after week. If you were a true music lover, Octagon was the place to be. Plus, Quentin knew people who worked there, so if they ran into any more issues, they would be on friendly turf.

"What kind of issues?" Anna asked.

"Someone posted on social media that I come here often, and last week I barely got off the dance floor in one piece."

"My friend thinks your group is gonna be the next big thing," she said.

Quentin nodded solemnly. "Last year it was all I wanted. To be successful. To be famous. To be recognized. But now . . ."

"Now you understand the true price of fame." Anna finished his thought.

Smoking a cigarette in the back alley behind the club, Quentin had told Anna that he met Minsoo last year right after they both debuted. To debut meant they graduated from their respective K-pop academies and were selected to be members of two new K-pop groups. He had debuted in The NowNows, and Minsoo had been selected to join the newly formed Dream Girlz, a group of seven girls. Both groups were performing at a K-pop fan showcase introducing new acts to potential fans. The NowNows were scheduled to perform last, and Quentin had been nervous, so he snuck up to the roof to smoke a cigarette. And there she was. For Quentin it wasn't love at first sight, but love at first high note. Minsoo was standing at the edge of the roof looking out over the city, singing "Angel of the Morning," a song she had learned from watching Chrissie Hynde sing on an episode of *Friends*, the show all the K-pop trainees watched to learn how to speak like Americans. As she sang, Quentin stayed still, afraid to move because he knew she'd stop singing if she sensed she was no longer alone. After she finished, he ran over to her, clapping and shouting her praises. She was so startled by his enthusiastic clapping that she grabbed her key chain out of her tiny backpack and pepper-sprayed him.

At that point in the story, Anna interrupted to tell him it was a meet-cute funny enough for a rom-com. She then had to explain to him what a meet-cute was as well as what a rom-com was. He said the day he met Minsoo was a day he would never forget even if he lived to be one hundred and eight years old like his great-great-grandfather. Anna thought of the day she met Vronsky and understood what he meant completely.

They began to see each other in secret, he continued, even though both his and Minsoo's contracts had a no-dating clause. Neither of their groups were well known, so their managers weren't monitoring them closely. But when "I Want You Now, Now, Now!" hit the charts in its first week, everything changed. They called Quentin in for a meeting at the corporate headquarters where he was told The NowNows were being assigned a more senior-level manager, a woman named Aileen C. She informed him that his relationship with Minsoo was officially over. Quentin was too shocked to say anything. Instead he only nodded, accepting the fate of a broken heart as the price of his new stardom.

As soon as he left the meeting, he called Minsoo but her phone was no longer in service. It was the only number he had for her, but it was the phone she had been given by her management company. Fearing the worst, he went to the apartment where she lived with her bandmates and found it totally empty. Later he learned that Dream Girlz had been disbanded, a common occurrence for a K-pop group that hadn't debuted well. When he told his fellow NowNows members what had happened, they told him he needed to let it go. No one wanted to jeopardize their own careers over a silly girl. Quentin was devastated not to have had the chance to say good-bye. Also, he felt awful that he might be responsible for the demise of Dream Girlz. Minsoo had trained for seven years at the academy and no one deserved a career more than her. Minsoo's voice was so beautiful he was sure that if she had been born in America, she could have had a solo career.

At first Anna didn't know what to think. The story was a bit preposterous, but wasn't her own recent heartbreak even more so? Also, her gut said he was telling the truth. Anna had heard that the K-pop industry didn't have the most artist-friendly reputation, but she had no idea how restrictive their contracts could be until Quentin told her his story.

Anna followed Quentin to the side door of the club, where they were ushered into the VIP area by one of the security guards. From there they descended a long, steep staircase into the depths of the Octagon.

Anna had never been to a Korean nightclub before, but she could already tell the vibe of the place was different from the clubs she'd been to in New York. Everyone here in Seoul was so tightly wound in their everyday lives, and at night they could finally let loose. Anna could sense it, too. After spending six hours with Chang-ri earlier in the day, she felt constricted by the formality all around her. The politeness, the careful manners, the respect her VIP badge garnered—none of that mattered here. Anna wasn't sure she understood what she was feeling exactly, but there was a joy to being immersed within the crowded dance floor that she craved. She was one of the many, and she blended right in with all the other girls with long dark hair and bright red lips.

Quentin was an interesting dancer, sort of hopping about letting his arms swing wildly, like a marionette puppet controlled by a manic child. He circled Anna, always keeping his distance. She liked how happy he seemed in this setting, a never-ending smile splayed across his face, and she wondered if he and Minsoo had gone dancing together when they'd had the chance. Was he thinking about her now, the same way she was thinking of Alexia? Quentin's story really struck a chord with her. He had been falling hard for Minsoo and then, in an instant, the corporate bungee cord sprung him back up, keeping him from his free fall into love's ocean below. Anna suspected that given the patriarchal culture, female K-pop stars had even stricter codes of conduct than the boys, and she felt empathy for the Dream Girlz, whose real-life dreams had been unfairly cut short.

As the DJ transitioned between songs, Quentin led her over to a roped-off area with plush couches guarded by bouncers—not the typical big burly tough guys, but two very severe-looking women dressed in pantsuits with AirPods plugged into their ears. Security waved them both through, and Anna sank onto a VIP sofa. She checked the time on her phone, pleased to see it wasn't yet eleven o'clock. She noticed several text messages from Chang-ri and opened them to find a series of screengrabs of a Korean news site with the picture of Quentin dipping her outside the ramen place under a large headline she couldn't read.

Is this you? Chang-ri texted.

OMG. WTF! OMG! Anna texted back. What does it say?!!!

It says . . . "Who is QT's new mystery girl?"

Anna quickly typed back: Don't tell anyone it's me. My father thinks I'm at home. I didn't know Quentin was a NowNow when I met him. He doesn't know my name!

Are you his mystery girl? *red heart emoji* *red heart emoji* *red heart emoji*

Anna typed back: No! Friends only! I swear. *prayer hands emoji*

Chang-ri texted back, promising she wouldn't tell anyone. But Anna should know that the picture was everywhere already and QT's fans, who called themselves the QTpies, were already freaking out at the idea of him having a girlfriend.

Anna put away her phone and looked around for Quentin, who had wandered off while she was texting. She spotted him talking to a group of people in the adjacent VIP booth. She stood up to walk over and realized she was a little tipsy, but in a good way. Her buzz kept her from worrying as her picture made the rounds of social media and tabloid websites. They were several floors underground, and she felt tucked away from reality. Anna had a fleeting wish that she could hide here forever.

When it was time to leave, Anna didn't want to have another run-in with the paparazzi and she asked Quentin if she should taxi home on her own. He insisted on making sure she got home safely and promised they would take every precaution not to draw any unwanted attention. One of the waitresses walked them through an employees-only hallway to another staircase that took them up to more steps leading to the back alley. Quentin called for his car and half an hour later, they were outside Anna's grandmother's house.

"I had quite a night," she said.

"Can we do it again?" Quentin asked.

Anna explained that she was going to start looking at schools with her father and in two weeks her aunt and uncle would be arriving from Los Angeles and she'd need to spend time with them so her free time was fairly limited. "Maybe though," she added.

"Next time will you tell me about your own broken heart?" Quentin asked. "Mine still hurts but maybe the tiniest bit less thanks to you. I haven't had anyone to talk about it with."

"I know the feeling," Anna said as she opened the car door and stepped out.

Quentin waved good-bye as the tinted window lifted and the car drove off.

As Anna walked down the dark hallway to her room, the house was quiet and still. After a quick shower she got into bed with wet hair and opened one of the thicker envelopes from Vronsky. It was four pages but on each page he had typed in all caps one line. "I MISS YOU" "I LOVE YOU" "I WANT YOU" "YOU+ME." She wasn't sure if it was his words or her weirdly wonderful evening that had her smiling after she turned off her bedside lamp. Anna was still filled with so much excitement she wondered if she could even sleep, but before she knew it, she was drifting off, her ears still thumping with the bass of the night's music.

XII

They were a motley crew, the seven of them, showing up at Oceanus Bradford's Fourth of July party in Sagaponack on Saturday night—Steven, Lolly, Dustin, Kimmie, Greer, Natalia, and Dustin's mother, Tamar. If the K.s' house was massive, the Bradford home was behemoth, triple the size with over twenty bedrooms, two pools, and a massive fountain in the front installed by the same design firm that had built the Fountains of Bellagio in Las Vegas.

As their Escalade pulled up, the fountain was in mid-show, a choreographed water dance to the strains of Bieber and Sheeran's "I Don't Care." Greer muttered under her breath to Tamar how tacky she found the Bradfords' property. Dustin could tell his mom was biting her tongue. Tamar had a long-standing belief that individuals shouldn't have extreme wealth, and more importantly, that extreme wealth shouldn't be the end for which people strive. "People shouldn't be allowed too much money," she would say in the privacy of their own home. "How do billionaires sleep at night?"

"In very expensive beds," Dustin would answer to get her to laugh.

Before the driver came to a full stop, Natalia jumped out of the back and ran toward the fountain. She leaped up and walked around the stone ledge with her arms over her head, moving to the beat. Greer cleared her throat, her eyes aimed at Steven, who passed the buck to Lolly, who had already taken appalled and horrified notice. "God, she's like extra and basic at the same time!"

"What's the big deal?" Kimmie shrugged, overhearing Lolly's snarky comment. "Last I checked this was a party, right?"

Tamar caught Dustin by the elbow as he made a move to wrangle Natalia. "I'll handle it," she said. Dustin had been nervous about his mom meeting Natalia, but she was actually being pretty chill about it. Granted, Natalia had been on her best behavior during the drive, and she and Tamar had talked almost nonstop in the backseat while Dustin drove and Kimmie rode in the front.

Dustin watched as his mom walked over to Natalia, who was halfway around the fountain. Dustin couldn't hear what she said, but she reached up and Natalia took his mother's outstretched hands and hopped down. Kimmie always noticed Dustin's mother had this great way of parenting without making a person feel like they were being governed. "It's something about her matter-of-factness or like how she talks to everyone the same way," Kimmie mused, which Dustin thought was fairly astute of her to deduce. "Unlike some people"—her eyes darted to Lolly—"who think they're better than everyone and talk down to others."

"Come on, let's go check in while Kimmie waits for Animal Control." Lolly grabbed Steven's hand and pulled him up to an attendant checking names on a clipboard. Kimmie rolled her eyes as Lolly announced Steven's name with excessive pride. Steven explained that they were now Steven K. plus six instead of Steven K. plus one, and a woman with a different clipboard was flagged over. They waited while she radioed someone. "Someone will be right out."

Three minutes later the host's youngest son, Bucky, a rising senior at Collegiate, showed up in full floral Lilly Pulitzer menswear, sipping a martini. He was perfectly tanned with a beautifully swooped hairdo. He and

Steven greeted each other warmly, and Steven demurred, apologizing that he had ended up bringing a few more people than he had planned. "You know how it goes."

"Indeed Bucky does, indeed he does," said Bucky, already three three-thousand-thread-count sheets to the wind. "Any friend of yours is now a friend of Bucky's," he said, leaning over to give Lolly an air kiss. Bucky was going through a phase that all the Bradford men went through in their late adolescence, referring to themselves in the third person. It usually lasted about two to three years, much to the annoyance of everyone around them.

"Thanks," said Steven. "I'll return the favor at my Summertime Fun-time party in August."

"Hold up, you're having a party? Did you tell this to Bucky, but he forgot? Is Steven trying to steal Bucky's party-throwing thunder?"

"Nah, I just decided. Labor Day weekend, but keep it on the low-low, 'kay?" Steven put a friendly arm around Dustin. "Bucky, meet my boy Dustin. . . ."

Bucky already wasn't paying attention, too busy noticing Kimmie in her pink wrap skirt and sleeveless top standing with Natalia by the fountain. "Is that Miss Kimmie?" Bucky gawked. "Bucky'd like to pick her out of his teeth later."

Dustin coughed and looked at Steven, having no idea what to say or do. Was he going to need to defend the honor of his girlfriend by punching this kid's lights out? No, Dustin had never hit anyone in his life and honestly believed violence created more problems than it solved. Before anything else was said, Kimmie came bounding over and grabbed Dustin's hand. "Hi, guys! Hi, Bucky! Awesome party!"

"Why hello, Kimmie," Bucky said in a deep voice, trying to be sexy as he lifted Kimmie's hand to his lips. "Long time, no see."

Dustin leaned over and whispered in Kimmie's ear as Bucky drunkenly stumbled off to mingle. "Why was he talking to you like that?"

Kimmie whispered back, "I may have played spin the bottle with him at a beach bonfire like a million years ago."

"You made out with that kid?"

"Don't make a big thing about it," she said. "We kissed one time. It was nothing."

"If you say so," Dustin said as they all strolled into the party.

Two hours later, the group was scattered throughout the sprawling *Gatsby*-esque soiree. Tamar, Greer, and Steven were sitting on chaise longues by the pool filled with oversize rafts in the shape of American flags and bald eagles, talking about everything they would do differently in terms of décor.

"There's trying too hard, and then there's whatever this is," Greer said quietly. "As my mother used to say, one of the things money can't buy is good taste."

Steven tapped his glass against his mother's and took a sip. "How come we're not having fun?"

"Who said I wasn't?" Greer said without a smile.

"Are you?"

"God no," Greer scoffed.

"We're far too old for something as frivolous as fun," Tamar said, and Greer laughed.

"That doesn't explain why I'm not having fun," Steven said.

"You're not having fun because your girlfriend and her little sister are fighting, and your mother is here so you can't go play King Tut with your little coke buddies," Greer said simply, as if she were commenting on the weather.

"Mom!" Steven said. "I don't mess with that stuff. Anymore."

"Well that's lovely to hear."

"Why are they fighting?" Tamar asked, changing the subject. "I thought Kimmie and Lolly were close."

"They are and they aren't," said Steven. "Natalia's starting to become a source of tension."

"Oh, I think she's harmless. High energy, that's all," Tamar said, and now it was time for Greer to bite her tongue.

Suddenly Lolly pranced over and sat down at the edge of Steven's chair. She blew her long wispy bangs out of her face. "How long are we staying?"

"Not enjoying yourself?" Greer asked.

Lolly flailed her arm, gesturing across the partyscape. "I used to read about these parties in magazines and I would think one day I'll be one of those beautiful people at some incredible party and then my life will be complete. . . . Now the whole scene just seems played out."

"You can't be that jaded already, you're too young!" Tamar exclaimed.

"Oh no, she can be, Mrs. L.," Steven told her.

"I don't mean to sound ungrateful. But all day I've been feeling so stressed out and now that we're here I keep telling myself to relax, but I just can't. Last year on this same weekend Steven and I had the best time ever. Everything seems different now."

"These last few months have been . . . trying." Greer paused. "For everyone."

Just then Tamar got up from her seat, suddenly entranced with something in the distance. "I'm sorry, you'll have to excuse me," she said. "I just saw Jordan Catalano over there, and I need to go check something off my teenage self's bucket list."

They watched as Dustin's mother marched back into the fray of the party.

"Looks like Dustin's mom's got a celeb crush," Greer said as they watched Tamar and Jared Leto clink glasses in cheers.

"She *is* single," Lolly reminded them.

"The social worker and the Oscar winner," said Steven. "How crazy would it be if Tamar bags Jared Leto?"

"Steven!" Greer said. "Don't be crass in front of your mother."

"Oh please," he said. "Like you won't be interrogating her for every detail tomorrow if she does it. . . ."

Greer let out a hearty laugh and chugged the rest of her wine. "I'm going to go see if Tamar needs a wingman."

"Wing woman, Mrs. K.," Lolly called after her as Greer left Lolly and Steven alone.

"I know something that might liven things up a bit without breaking our no-drug-summer pact," Lolly whispered to Steven. "Rumor has it the latest Mrs. Bradford has a gift-wrapping room with a helium tank. Let's go talk like cartoon mice!"

"Weird flex, babe. But count me in."

XIII

Dustin stood in a great room larger than most hotel lobbies waiting in line for Peking duck. He had only recently grown used to the obscene amount of money that Steven's family had so he was having problems comprehending that there were people who had even more money than the K.s. He also knew that if he was feeling weird about it, then his mom (wherever she was) was definitely having a crisis of conscience about attending such a lavish shindig. While Steven's New Year's Eve party had been pretty over-the-top, it was all done with the good time of the guests in mind. This party had a different vibe, the righteousness-of-wealth-above-all-else vibe. But then Dustin reached the front of the line and tasted the Peking duck. It melted in his mouth and sent a tingle up the back of his neck, and he quickly decided that perhaps he was being overly critical of these fine, good, rich people serving up these heavenly morsels.

Like any good boyfriend, he brought Kimmie a plate of Peking duck to sample, as well as a few oysters from the raw bar. He wasn't sure if she liked oysters, but he had read in some cultures they were believed to be aphrodisiacs, so he figured it couldn't hurt. Dustin wasn't a big fan himself, but he decided if she ate one, he'd give them another shot.

He found Kimmie sitting on a round velvet ottoman and plunked down next to her. "They had these cute little forks over there, and I know how you like miniature things, so I got them for us. We can pretend to be giants."

"Thanks," Kimmie said, taking the plate, pouty-faced.

"What's wrong? Do you not like oysters?" Dustin started to stand up. "Let me get you something else. It's like a Vegas buffet over there. They have a guy making waffles."

"What gives her the right to be so judgmental? Did you hear her tone of voice, like she's the queen of the fucking Hamptons or something?"

"What was it she said again?" Dustin asked, knowing the cause of Kimmie's ire was Lolly.

Kimmie launched into her best Lolly impersonation: *"Keep an eye on your friend tonight, capisce? She goes on one Godfather movie tour in Italy and suddenly she can do an accent?"*

"Look, Lolly hasn't spent as much time with Natalia as we have and you have to admit that at first blush Natalia is . . . a lot."

"Why are you taking Lolly's side?"

"What? I'm not. I'm not taking anyone's side."

"You're my boyfriend!" Kimmie wailed. "You should be on my side!"

"Of course, of course, I'm on your side. I'm always on your side."

"Even if I murder Lolly with this tiny fork?"

"I don't think I can condone sororocide, babe."

"I knew you wouldn't be supportive."

"Of killing your sister with a miniature fork? I don't even know if that's possible."

"Trust me, it's possible."

Dustin looked at his girlfriend. "You do understand that I am fully supportive of whatever you want to do."

"Not in this instance."

"And I am totally on your side, but whatever tension there is between you and Lolly about Natalia, it would really benefit the both of you if you talked about it and cleared the air."

"Lolly's pissed that we crashed her Hamptons weekend because she wanted to get it on with Steven before she leaves for camp," Kimmie said. "I heard her on the phone with her friend Miley and she said she needed to make sure he got his fill before she left."

Dustin was always on edge when Kimmie got in one of her surly moods. Not only did it make him feel he wasn't very good at being a boyfriend, but it also put his grand plan for this to be the big night for him and Kimmie in jeopardy.

As Kimmie sulked and Dustin ate the rest of the duck, Natalia rushed over to them from the champagne fountain. "If this is what it's like to be rich, then count me in. I've eaten like twenty oysters and I've been putting this spicy stuff on it, even though I don't know what it is. I watched some rich dude in pink pants do it, so I did it, too. Rich dudes who wear pink pants know all the best stuff! It's my secret to life factoid number six hundred and seventy-nine." Natalia then leaned in close and breathed into Dustin's face.

"That's horseradish," Dustin said.

"You're horseradish." Natalia pretended to be offended, but then softened. "Dude, your mom is like the greatest human being ever, you know that, right? Isn't she the greatest, Kimmie?"

"Yeah. I got lucky," Dustin said. I'm glad you two are getting along so well. I hope it isn't weird for you."

"Oh, we're way past weird. I'm besties with my dead ex-boyfriend's brother's girlfriend, hanging out in the Hamptons with his mom and their rich-ass friends. I thought Steven's house was dope, but these people are on some next-level shit."

"I know. I feel like I'm on a different planet. How much do you think their air-conditioning bill is?"

"If you have to ask . . ." Kimmie started to say, then Natalia joined in. "Then you can't afford it!"

"I bet this place has a bigger carbon footprint than Mar-a-Lago," Dustin quipped.

"Hey, did you hear there's a bowling alley in the house? I'm not great, but Nick taught me, so I like it now. We should totally go bowling up in this bitch!"

"First we'll need to get that bowling pin out of my sister's ass," Kimmie said.

Dustin ignored Kimmie's comment and added, "I'm down. Let me just find my mom and see if she wants in. She loves bowling."

"I know where your mom is. She's stalking some dude named Jordan Catalano."

"Jordan Catalano from *My So-Called Life?*" Dustin asked and got blank stares from Kimmie and Natalia both. "It's a TV show. From the nineties. She always talks about it. Jordan Catalano is Jared Leto. You know, the actor?"

Natalia shrugged. "Don't know him."

"The Joker in *Suicide Squad?*" Kimmie asked, and Dustin nodded.

Now this got Natalia's attention. "No freakin' way! His relationship with Harley Quinn was so romantic. Nick and I were going to be them for Halloween. . . ."

"Uh-oh," Kimmie said, suddenly lowering her voice.

"What's the matter?" Dustin asked.

"Alexander's here."

Natalia crinkled her brow. "Who's Alexander?"

"Steven's sister's ex-boyfriend. It didn't end well," Kimmie said. "We should go warn Steven."

"Cool, you guys go do that," Natalia said. "I'm gonna go fight your mom for Jordan Catalano, though I'm good about sharing if she'd be into a three way." She gave Kimmie a kiss on the cheek and frolicked off.

"Wait, what?" Dustin said, distracted by the sight of Alexander standing on the other side of the room eating oysters in a pale pink shorts suit. He called after Natalia, "Please don't have a ménage à trois with my mom!"

XIV

The first thing that struck Anna about Branksome Hall Asia was the sweeping beauty of the campus. The other campuses she and her father toured together paled in comparison. Located on the volcanic island of Jeju, the all-female international boarding school was known for its academic excellence. While her father spoke with the dean of Admissions, Anna took a tour of the campus with one of the English-speaking music teachers, a millennial named Isabella who had been teaching there for two years after transferring from Branksome Hall's sister school in Canada.

"Do you miss Canada?" Anna asked, not really interested in hearing the stats about the school.

"Yes and no," Isabella replied. "I miss my friends, but I'm loving the adventure of being an expat here in Korea."

"What made you decide to come?" Anna asked, curious as to why a twenty-seven-year-old would choose to live in a foreign country where she didn't know anyone. "I'm sorry, am I being rude? I never thought of myself as a nosy person, but here in Korea I feel like that's how I'm viewed."

Isabella smiled at her gently. "The exact same thing happened to me. It's a bit of a culture shock at first, the extreme politeness, but I think my students like me because I'm respectful of their culture while also being true to my Canadian roots. I've been told by some of my students here that they find my openness refreshing. Now, do you want the party line of how I got here or the dirt?"

"Definitely the dirt. Not that I'm some kind of shameless gossip, but I was talking to a new friend of mine, and we were discussing how if more people would open up about what they were really going through, it would help them know they weren't alone when they were feeling low. Does that make sense?"

"It does. I really try to foster an environment where my students can come talk to me about anything. I'll tell you, but . . ." The woman paused and gazed out the enormous windows looking onto the grassy lawn.

"I'm sure my father is lying to the dean of Admissions right now, but I'm here because of a revenge sex tape. Of me," Anna admitted. It felt good being truthful about her own reason for standing there. "He really thinks I need a fresh start somewhere new where no one knows me, but I feel like I'm running away from a problem that wasn't even my fault."

Isabella stared at the girl before her, surprised at her startling confession. In a million years Isabella would have never guessed that this girl was escaping a sex tape scandal. "I caught my fiancé cheating on me a week before my wedding," she blurted out.

Anna's eyes widened. "Oh no! How awful. I'm so sorry."

"With my sister," Isabella added.

"No," Anna exclaimed, unable to keep the shock out of her voice.

"I was supposed to be at my last fitting for my wedding dress, but I realized I had the wrong bra so I called the store and told them I'd be late and went home to get it. I lived with my sister and we shared an apartment together after university and she was . . . my best friend." Isabella's voice cracked; it had been so long since she'd talked about it, and all the pain came rushing back. "I, uh, wow, haven't told anyone that since I've been here. I apologize. How unprofessional of me."

Anna reached out and grabbed the woman's hand. "Don't be sorry."

"This school, this place really has been a wonderful escape, a refuge. Now I'm almost fluent in Korean and travel all over Asia. My life is so different from what it would have been because my ex was a sit-on-the-couch-and-watch-hockey kind of guy."

"A screw-your-sister kind of guy, too," Anna said. "You're better off."

"I know I am," she said, and told Anna, "I hope you come here in the fall. We could use a straight shooter around here to shake things up."

After the tour, Anna and her father took an express ferry back to Seoul from the island. As they disembarked from the harbor, Edward ordered them tea, and while they sipped their hot drinks, Anna asked her father what he thought about Branksome Hall. He agreed it was the best school they had visited so far, and he was very impressed with how highly the school was ranked for being less than ten years old. He also preferred it because it was an all-girls school.

"Why should that matter?" Anna asked him.

Edward, not used to having to explain himself to his daughter, frowned. "So you can focus on your schoolwork. Fewer distractions."

Without thinking, Anna blurted out, "You think girls stop thinking about boys just because they aren't around? They don't. I'm still pining over a boy and he's dead." Her immediate clapback to her father's statement surprised her as much as it did him. She stood up from the bench, mumbled a quick apology, and excused herself to go outside for some air.

Anna leaned against the ferry railing at the stern of the boat and took a few deep breaths. She used to be so good at keeping her composure and always choosing her words carefully, but lately she was incapable of keeping her opinions to herself. Anna knew she should probably go back inside and apologize again to her father, but instead she stared at the ferry's wake and watched as Jeju Island grew smaller and smaller as they drifted toward Seoul.

Anna reflected on the music teacher's traumatic story and how it had taken Isabella two years to get past it. Maybe Anna needed to accept that mourning could be a slow process and that the clock of grief ran at its own pace. Eventually her thoughts wandered back to Quentin's ex-gf, Minsoo. Anna had never even met her, but that didn't stop her from wondering where she was now. It seemed so unfair to be forced to pick between a career and love at such a young age. What gave these music corporations the right to control the personal lives of their singers, like parents trying to control the love lives of their children?

Anna thought back to Alexia's latest letter, which she'd read last night. He'd written a full page telling her that he refused to let their parents stand in the way of their love. "These are our lives and this is our love story. I'll be damned before I let others decide what's best for us. I know what's best for me and that's for us to be together!!!" His emphatic use of exclamation points brought a smile to her face, and she fantasized what she would have done had she actually received the letter when he wrote it. He had signed it with the declaration "Love is something that can't be stopped!"

Suddenly she had an idea and pulled out her phone. She texted Chang-ri: I need your help to solve a romantic mystery. . . . Are you game? She didn't have to wait long before Chang-ri texted back: Yes!

XV

It wasn't Anna's place to share the intimate details of a K-pop star's life, but she had done it anyway. Once Anna relayed Quentin and Minsoo's love-gone-awry story, Chang-ri looked around the crowded dessert café to make sure no one had been eavesdropping and whispered to Anna that she wasn't surprised. Chang-ri had heard rumors of other K-pop stars getting busted for clandestine relationships in breach of their contracts. But Quentin's story was the first from a verified source.

"Do you think the punishment for breaking the rules is harsher for females?" Anna asked. "Do you think Dream Girlz was canceled because of Minsoo?"

"Not necessarily," Chang-ri answered. "New groups break up all the time. There's a high volume of churn in the music industry. And absolutely female artists have a tougher road than their male counterparts."

"Doesn't that make you angry, as a woman?"

"If I got upset every time a woman got treated unfairly in Korea, I'd be mad all the time!" Chang-ri answered.

"I guess that's how I feel. Lately I've been so emotional about everything, but instead of resigning myself to feeling angry or sad, I want to do something about it. On the ferry looking out over the water I had an idea about how I might help," Anna said. She asked if Chang-ri could use her work connections to track down Minsoo's whereabouts. The *King of Masked Singers* TV show often featured singers from many different K-pop groups, which meant Chang-ri had access to contacts at all the different companies. "Would it be possible for you to track down the ex-members of Dream Girlz?" Anna asked her. "I don't want to jeopardize your job so if you can't get involved I totally understand. My brother always tells me that money doesn't make the world go around. It's connections."

"Speaking as someone who doesn't have much," Chang-ri said, "money is helpful, too!"

"For sure, but your work connections are everything!"

"I heart *kkanoko malhada!*" Chang-ri said with a big smile. "It means 'speak your mind.' I find it *daebak!*"

"Awesome, I know. And thank you for the compliments," Anna said. "So . . . ?"

Chang-ri was open to helping Anna but she needed to know why Anna was getting involved with another couple's love life.

And so Anna spilled her guts about everything that had happened to her: meeting Alexia on the train, sleeping with him when she had a serious boyfriend, the sex tape, all the way up to the last letter she read of his. "I know this is going to make me sound unhinged, but I have this weird feeling that the universe is trying to give me a cosmic lesson about love. Alexia's letters, the Fox King, the music teacher at Branksome Hall, meeting Quentin because of you. It's like a booming voice telling me not to give up on love, which when I left New York City is all I wanted to do. I want to be clear I'm not *actually* hearing voices, though."

Chang-ri stayed quiet for a few moments, and Anna assumed it was because she thought Anna was crazy, but that wasn't the case. Chang-ri didn't respond right away because she was so moved. Here was this teenager who was dealing with heartbreak and tragedy not by getting bitter and feeling sorry for herself, but by wanting to help strangers at every turn. Like how Anna had made it possible for her to meet The NowNows. Chang-ri agreed to help but first they needed to verify Quentin's story, to make sure he was telling the truth about Minsoo and wasn't, in fact, a psycho stalker, or a liar. "I'm not saying Quentin's a bad person, but you haven't known him for very long. We must find Minsoo and get her side of the story. If it turns out she's in the same situation and is lovesick over him but has no way to reach him, then we'll figure out a way to reunite them."

"Thank you so much," Anna said. "Can we call it Project Q-pid?"

"We must!" Chang-ri said. "Now let's go work out the details at 32Parfait, it's a soft-serve ice cream place that gives you thirty-two centimeters of delicious in a cone!"

A week later Anna's father dropped her off at the Apgujeong Rodeo Street Galleria on his way to the office. She told him she was going to spend the Saturday shopping with Chang-ri. Anna was telling him the truth; she was going shopping with her friend. But she was taking a lesson from Quentin and leaving out some vital information, which was that phase one of Project Q-pid was about to be put into action.

It didn't take long for Chang-ri to track down Minsoo. Apparently she was taking a break from singing and was now working at a fancy cosmetics store on Cheongdam Fashion Street, which was Seoul's most high-end shopping district. Chang-ri cautioned Anna about confronting Minsoo in public and upsetting her at work. They decided it would be best if Anna slipped Minsoo a note at work inviting her to meet them at a nearby restaurant for lunch to talk about Quentin. Chang-ri would meet Anna at a sushi shop down the street and together they'd wait to see if Minsoo showed up. Chang-ri wrote the note in Korean and sent a picture of it to Anna who then copied the Korean characters on some of her grandmother's stationery. She included her Kakao Talk number so Minsoo had the option to text.

Before Anna walked into the store, she took a few moments on the street to calm her nerves. This was by far the most blatantly meddlesome thing she had ever done. She felt like a secret agent working undercover in the name of love. Taking a deep breath, Anna pushed open the glass door and entered the store.

She walked around for a while surveying the cosmetics store, basically the Korean version of Sephora. There were six sales associates, two restocking the shelves, two at the registers, and two chatting by the free makeover area. Anna had a picture of Minsoo that Chang-ri had found online, but it was a publicity photo from when Dream Girlz first debuted: seven girls dressed in bubble-gum-colored fur coats with matching wigs and baseball hats with their names emblazoned across the fronts. Minsoo was the one in the middle wearing a bubblegum pink fur jacket with electric turquoise hair. Anna wasn't sure she'd be able to recognize her in civilian attire, especially as she barely recognized herself in the mystery girl photo.

Anna took another lap around the store. When a sales lady walked over and greeted her in Korean, Anna smiled and gave a small shrug. "Sorry, I can't speak Korean."

"I will get you someone who speaks English," the woman said in heavily accented English.

"Is there a Minsoo who works here?" Anna asked.

The woman waved over another sales associate as she didn't understand what Anna was saying. Anna asked the second girl if there was a Minsoo who worked there and the girl slowly shook her head. "No Minsoo." Anna's heart sank.

Like divine intervention, the overhead speakers switched from Blackpink's hit song "Ddu-du Ddu-du" to the NowNows' "I Want You Now, Now, Now!" Anna was now familiar with it because, as Chang-ri mentioned, it was playing everywhere. It was currently in fifth place out of ten for the Song of the Summer contest. Chang-ri said The Now-Nows had been in last place since the contest started, but things were different now thanks to the mystery girl picture trending across every social media platform for the last two weeks. Anna was blissfully ignorant of all the commotion because she had deleted all her social accounts after the sex tape.

"Oooh, can we turn up the music? This is one of my favorite songs," Anna said in a voice she barely recognized, her nervousness kicking it up an octave higher than usual. The music grew louder, and Anna noticed a salesgirl with long blond hair disappear in the back the moment the song started. She went to the back of the store where they had a perfume counter and found the girl with her back turned squatting by an open drawer.

"Minsoo?" Anna said softly to make sure no one else heard her. The blond girl froze for a moment at the sound of Anna's voice and then slowly turned her head.

Anna immediately recognized the look in the girl's eyes. *Yes,* Anna thought, *this is definitely the right girl.* They said the eyes were the window to the soul, and if this girl's eyes were any indication, then this girl's heartbreak had made her soul sick. Just like Quentin had said when he met her, like recognizes like. Speaking softly and quickly she said, "My name is Anna. I'm a friend of Quentin's. Do you speak English?"

The girl stood up quickly. "How is he?"

Anna opened her purse and handed her the envelope.

Two hours later, the three girls were eating sushi together, their heads leaned in close with everyone talking rapidly. Everything Quentin had said was the truth. Minsoo had been equally devastated by the turn of events. She lost her career and the love of her life in a swift one-two punch. In fact, she admitted she was about to throw in the towel and move back to Australia where she had family, but she felt wrong about leaving the country without being able to say good-bye in person.

Anna made clear to her that Quentin knew nothing about her intervention but now that she had verified his story she wanted to help them meet up.

"You're like a fairy godmother," Minsoo said.

Chang-ri concurred. "She really, truly is."

Anna smiled at their flattery. "The world can be a shitty place. I just want to see people happy."

#

When Natalia asked Kimmie if she could stay at her mom's place when they were dropping Lolly off at theater camp in Michigan, Kimmie knew she should say no. And she did. Sort of. Kimmie knew her mom worried about her intense friendship with Natalia, though she never said so outright. Every time Kimmie asked if Natalia could spend the night, her mom always found a reason to say it wasn't a good night. Most of the time when Natalia slept over, it was at Kimmie's dad's place, where most everything flew, as long as it didn't fly in her stepmonster's way.

"It would be better if you could find somewhere else because, you know, my mom's so uptight about stuff like that. She's definitely going to set the alarm and the doormen will totally snitch."

Natalia had no problems asking for what she wanted, and she also had no problem being told no. "All good. I might be doing a dog-sitting gig in Brooklyn with a little black cockapoo named Mia and a crazy French bull puppy named Ragnar. Also, that guy I met at the Hamptons party, the sexy one with the big ears, he said he shares an apartment with his older sister in Nolita and we've been sexting, so maybe I can finagle a bed."

"Finagle?"

"Yeah, you know, finagle, like I finagle you, you finagle me, and now you can sleep here for the weekend as long as we keep up all this finagling."

Kimmie furrowed her brow. It sounded sketchy to her.

"I mean, we're sexting already. He's a dirty dog with a nice-sized bone.

Though it's pretty easy to fake a good dick pic with angles and close-ups and shit. Could even be a deep fake for all we know."

"Omigod. Are you really sexting? I thought you two just flirted at the party."

"We did, but as soon as digits are traded, sexting is on the table. No one catches an STD and no one winds up stuffed in an old basement freezer from sexting, y'know? Don't you and Dustin sext?"

Kimmie considered lying and telling her they did, but she was afraid that Natalia would ask her to read some of them, and there was no way Kimmie was skilled enough to invent fake sexts off-the-cuff. So she told the truth, even though it pained her. "We don't. I figured sexting was something you did after sex. Or for long-distance relationships. I caught Lolly taking sexy selfies to send to Steven while she's away at camp. She's paranoid about him cheating on her when she's away. Hey, are dirty pics the same as sexting, or are they their own thing?"

"Whoa there, pump the brakes for a sec. How did you survive without me? I can't believe you didn't know you can sext before sex. I sext with guys I meet on Tinder that I never even sleep with. It helps me weed out the weirdos. Like if their sexts sound too aggro then I block their number. Thank you, next. If you want to improve your sex life you should totally sext with Dustin."

"How can you improve something that hasn't started?" Kimmie asked, sighing. "God, it's actually getting worse rather than better. After we didn't end up doing it in the Hamptons, things have just gotten more and more awkward."

"You know I like Dustin, but I still gotta say he overreacted a bit to his mom catching you two skinny-dipping. It's not like she saw you both naked—it was dark, right?"

Honestly it had been horribly awkward. It was the first time they had ever been naked in front of each other, but it was dark in the black-bottomed pool, so they couldn't really even see each other's bodies. It had been difficult to do anything other than make out without splashing or slipping underwater. She was almost relieved when the French doors opened and Kimmie had to dive quickly underwater. They probably could have laid low and snuck away undetected, but as soon as Dustin saw that it was his own mother coming outside for some fresh air, he freaked out and started yelling, "Mom! Leave! Mom! No! Go back in the house right now!" For whatever reason, Tamar thought Dustin was in danger when she heard him yelling, and her Mama Bear instincts kicked into gear. She panicked and jumped in the pool, still wearing her pajamas. Kimmie should have scrambled out of the pool then, but she was so shocked she just stayed where she was, treading water in the shadows of the deep end.

Tamar was frantically doggy-paddling toward her skinny-dipping son while Dustin shouted, "Mom, get out of the pool! I'm naked!"

That was when the lights in the main house started flicking on, which was what finally got Kimmie moving. She climbed up the ladder stark naked and darted to the chaise where she'd left her towel. But before she could get there, the floodlights came on. And that was the story of how Dustin's mother got to see Kimmie naked before Dustin did.

Kimmie shook her head, haunted by the memory.

If you ask me," Natalia continued, "you two are putting way too much importance on sex in general. You just gotta do it and get it over with. Stop overthinking it. Sex is like eating or sleeping or breathing, you just do it. I barely remember my first time, and what I do recall wasn't too pretty."

"Yeah, but do you remember your first time with Nick?" Kimmie asked.

Natalia sighed, "Touché Kittykat, you make a good point. But overthinking it isn't sexy!"

"I'm not the one overthinking it," declared Kimmie, which was mostly true. Dustin for sure was the overthinker of the relationship, but now that things were getting more and more awkward, Kimmie couldn't help but overthink it, too.

"Look, I've gotta run. Three dogs to walk this afternoon. Don't worry about me while you're gone. Worst-case scenario, Tamar said I could crash on her couch, but I feel like that's a last resort." Natalia stood up and started putting on her threadbare Converse high-tops.

Natalia and Tamar? This was news to Kimmie. She was pleased that Dustin's mom had taken a liking to Natalia, but she couldn't say she wasn't jealous of the fact they had gotten chummy so fast. They were pretty inseparable over the holiday weekend and even took a long beach walk on the last morning and hadn't bothered asking anyone else if they wanted to come along. What felt weird was that she was Dustin's girl-friend, so shouldn't Tamar be more attentive to their relationship? Did she think Kimmie was just Dustin's hot girl phase? Of course, being busted for skinny-dipping probably hadn't helped endear her to Tamar.

Without really knowing why, Kimmie suddenly felt it was of tanta-mount importance that Natalia did not stay at her boyfriend's mom's house when she was away. She didn't want the three of them hanging out without her, so she told Natalia she should text her first before she called Tamar, and maybe it'd be fine if Natalia stayed one night at her mom's place while they were gone, as long as Natalia was extra careful.

"Cool, you're the best," Natalia said, giving Kimmie a big hug before she left. "Have a great trip and text me. I've never been to Michigan so I don't even know what it's like."

"Hey, Nat?" Kimmie asked. "Can you send me some screenshots of your sexts? Not the pics, but just the words? Maybe you're right and I need to try it with Dustin. I promise I won't plagiarize. I want to see your work, something tells me you're a good sexter."

"No one gives sext like me. I'm the Queen of the Touchscreen. And my dirty texts are your dirty texts! I'll shoot some your way!" With that Natalia was gone, and Kimmie was left in her room now wondering what Dustin would do if she sent him a sext. Would he like it? Would it freak him out? Would it turn him on? Did she turn him on at all?

Suddenly her phone vibrated beside her. She checked her messages and found four screenshots from Natalia, an eye-popping verbal carnival of dirty talk. She decided to hold off on sexting Dustin for now. Know-ing her luck, his mother would be the first to read it.

Instead she texted Dustin a gif of a tiny kitten sitting in a teacup.

XVII

Beatrice wasn't expecting any pushback from her uncle about the impromptu surf trip. She just presumed Chadwick would be cool with it. When she brought Tiare back to Chadwick's house they found three stragglers from her uncle's dinner party vaping THC in the sunken living room, so she figured they were in the clear. She brought Tiare back to her bedroom so she could start to pack.

Moments later, Chadwick was in the doorway, eyeing the Louis Vuitton duffel with a wary half-baked look. "Going somewhere?"

"Flying to Mexico to go surfing," Bea said in such a casual way as to suggest that flying to a foreign country was as commonplace as a trip to the mall. "Hey, when you fly private, who do you use?"

"You surf?" Chadwick asked Tiare, who was sitting on the bed studying Bea's passport photo.

"Yeah," Tiare replied. "You?"

"A few lessons, but I'm a novice. My husband surfs, though, and he's not bad." Chadwick found a bottle of Visine on Bea's dresser and applied it to his stoned eyes. "Beatrice, can I speak to you? Out in the hall." He smiled at Tiare and pinched the air with his thumb and forefinger. "Give us a moment."

Beatrice zipped up her bag and rolled her eyes for Tiare's benefit. "Seriously? Yeah, fine." She followed her uncle into the hallway and leaned against the wall.

"I hate to be this guy," he said. "But I'm not sure your parents would be okay with you jetting off to Mexico for a weekend unsupervised. You're still a teenager, you do remember that, yes?"

"They won't care," she said, then using her best lockjaw voice she imitated her father. "'Darling, if you're happy, I'm happy. Daddy needs to work, now shoo!'"

"You may be reaching on this one. I'd appreciate it if you asked permission."

"Uncle Chadwick, may I go to Mexico on a surf trip?" Bea asked in a sweetly sarcastic tone, looking him directly in the eye.

"I didn't mean me," he answered, a little exasperated.

"What's your deal? You're my guardian this summer, you can give me permission."

At the other end of the hallway, Manny wandered in holding a pack of strawberry Twizzlers that matched the redness of his eyes.

Beatrice turned to Manny and said, "Your hubby is giving me grief about going to Mexico with the hottest surfer girl on the planet. Will you tell him to stop being a thousand years old and say yes?"

Manny looked at Chadwick, not knowing what to do. This sort of parenting was beyond him. He giggled in response, too high to deal or care.

Bea was about to ask them what business two stoners had trying to lay down the law, but weed was now legal in California, so she pivoted and took another tack. "OMG," she exclaimed. "Why don't you two come with? My treat. It'll be a little thank-you for letting me stay here. C'mon, this place is supposed to have the best surfing in the world. We'll stay in a fancy hotel, it'll be so fun. And if you say no, I'm going anyway and I dare either of you to try and stop me."

Chadwick and Manny looked at each other for a long moment.

"Hell, I'd go," Manny said.

"I guess my vitamin D could use a boost," Chadwick concurred.

"That's the spirit! It's called living your best life." Beatrice smiled, relieved that it wasn't going to turn into an embarrassing scene where she got shut down by her uncle. She didn't have the energy for that right now. Who knew emotional breakdowns were so tiring? She leaned in close so that Tiare couldn't hear. "She's the girl from San Ysidro. This is a big deal for me."

Chadwick nodded, all of it making perfect sense now.

"I'm going to go find my tiniest swim trunks," Manny said and walked off down the hall.

"I'll text you the private plane service I use. I'm too stoned to figure out details," said Chadwick, and Bea hugged him, truly grateful for understanding she needed this trip.

When Beatrice walked back into the room, Tiare was lying on her bed with her eyes closed. Beatrice crossed over and kissed her gently on the lips. "Oh, sleeping beauty . . ." she whispered.

Tiare's eyes opened slowly. "We good?"

"Yeah, they're coming with us. Hope you don't mind. We'll have our own room, though, don't you worry."

"You know this is insane, right? Are you sure this is what you need right now?"

"You're what I need right now. So yes, this is exactly what's needed."

One chartered plane from Burbank with four sleepy passengers, three surf boards, seven bottles of sunscreen, and a wide variety of swimwear took off and landed three hours later on a private airstrip in Punta Mita.

"We're heading straight to Sayulita Beach," Beatrice said as they pulled up to the hotel. She had booked two suites on opposite ends of the Four Seasons Hotel.

She told the driver she'd double his rate if he drove them straight to the beach, and he liked that idea a lot. Manny decided to come along, while Chadwick checked them in, after which he planned to get a pool-side pedicure.

As they drove toward the beach, Tiare, who had barely said a word since they had left LA, finally spoke up. "I know it's impolite to ask, but who's paying for all this?"

"I'm the only child of a very rich man who likes to indulge his hearty appetites, whatever they may be, and he sort of raised me to be the same way. Sure, sometimes he'll get cranky when one of his business managers tells him how much I spend in a given month . . . but normally, he just lets it slide. He's conflict-averse and stingy with his emotions, so that makes him feel guilty enough to let me do what I like and not give me any shit for it."

"Though it was sweet how he called Chadwick because he was worried about you," Manny piped up from the front seat.

Bea straightened up and narrowed her eyes at Manny. "What are you talking about?"

"Oh, you didn't know? Oops. I don't know exactly what was said, but apparently Daddykins is stressed out over your unhealthy reaction to your friend's dramatic death."

"Cousin. He was my cousin, Manny. Get your facts straight."

"Dramatic death?" Tiare asked.

"Oh." Beatrice sighed. "Did I not mention that part? He got hit by a train."

"Fuck me, you left that part out," Tiare said. "When?"

"End of May," Bea said. "Can we change the subject, please?"

"Of course we can." Tiare backed off. "But if you ever want to, I'd love to listen."

"Thanks, but I'm all good," Beatrice said, lowering her sunglasses. "That was a big fat lie, I'm not even close to good. But can we talk about it later?"

Tiare nodded, not knowing what to say.

"So, are you gonna teach our little Bea to surf?" Manny changed the subject.

Tiare glanced over at Bea. "Umm . . ."

Beatrice shook her head. "I'm more the lie-on-the-beach-and-people-watch type of girl." She was starting to feel the twinge of a headache. All she wanted to do was lie on a blanket in the sun, forget the bottomless pit of sadness that had prompted this impromptu jaunt, and just enjoy what Mexico had in store for her and Tiare.

XVIII

When Anna arrived back at Halmeoni's house after her surprisingly emotional lunch with Minsoo and Chang-ri she was surprised to be greeted at the door by one of the servants, who ran up to her, took her shopping bags, and handed her a new pair of pretty pink plaid house slippers, which meant that her grandmother was entertaining company.

She put them on and followed a woman named Hayoon, who never spoke to Anna, only communicating with gestures and hand signals, into the formal living room. Anna passed through the arched doorway and stopped cold.

Sitting on a peach-colored love seat having tea with her grandmother was none other than Quentin himself. Halmeoni was using her best silver tea set. Not even Anna herself had ever been served with this particular set. The two of them were speaking Korean so fast they didn't even notice Anna standing in the doorway.

"Quentin?" Anna said softly. "What are you doing here?"

Quentin turned toward the sound of her voice and stood up as she entered the room. "I came by to see if you wanted to lunch with me. Your halmeoni was nice enough to invite me in for tea. You didn't tell me she had such exquisite taste."

"Anna, don't stand there rudely," her grandmother said. "Come sit and greet your guest. Your friend is telling me about the song contest. He showed me how to vote on my phone." She held up her phone, beaming.

Anna was still dazed by the surreal scene before her, but she did as she was told and sat down next to her grandmother.

"Where did you go shopping?" Quentin asked. "Shall I serve you some?" As he leaned forward to reach for the teapot, Halmeoni's eyes widened in horror and she waved her hands for him to stop.

"Anna, how can you let a guest in our home serve themselves?" She turned to Quentin and smiled sweetly. "Anna was raised in America, which is why her manners are not up to our high standards. She is young and still learning the proper way."

"I, uh, sorry . . ." Anna stood up and offered Quentin and her grandmother a refill of hot water before serving herself some tea. It was so humid outside, hot tea was really the last thing she wanted after her afternoon out, but she knew better than to refuse in front of her grandmother. "To answer your question, I went to the Galleria and Cheongdam Street. I was searching for a gift to send my mother." Again, a half-truth. Anna had bought her mother a pair of sunglasses as a thank-you gift for keeping the letters for her.

"I love the Galleria, but I can't go anymore," Quentin told them and made a sad face. "I suppose those are the perils of fame. Not being able to go out in public without being swarmed by your fans."

"Have you ever tried going out in disguise?" Anna asked, half joking.

"I have never tried," Quentin said. "Like I told Anna, we are a new group, and three months ago no one knew our names or recognized us. Everything changed for us when our song became a hit! Then everything became super intense like *that*!" Quentin snapped his fingers to emphasize his point, and Halmeoni laughed and clapped her hands, enthralled. Anna's grandmother was treating Quentin the same way she treated Steven, as if everything he said was the most interesting thing she had ever heard. It was irritating, but Anna much preferred this version of her grandmother to the surly, judgmental one. Halmeoni's excitement was contagious, and soon Anna relaxed and joined in on the good grandma juju Quentin was eliciting.

Halmeoni decided that Quentin would stay for dinner, and he was even allowed to hang out in Anna's bedroom, although she reminded them it was improper for them to be alone with the door closed. Anna was picking up on the fact that her grandmother assumed there was something romantic going on. Once they were in Anna's room and she was sure they were out of Halmeoni's range of hearing, Anna told him she had rarely seen her grandmother so pleasant and easygoing. "I'm not sure if she has a crush on you or whether she wants to adopt you. I have never seen her so giddy over a guest. She's normally . . ." Anna searched for the right words, knowing it was improper Korean etiquette to speak negatively about an elder. "The opposite of how she is with you."

"Adults have always loved me," Quentin said with a grin. "I have a trustworthy chin. Or so I've been told."

"That must be it. My halmeoni believes the shape of a person's chin can reveal their true character."

"I know," he said. "She was the one who told me!"

Quentin sat on Anna's bed and pointed to the shopping bags. "Show me what you bought."

"Okay, but first, tell me why you're here. You should have texted me before coming over here! I'm not sure it's safe. What you don't know is my whole life blew up in New York, so the last thing I need is to have my already blown up life blow up again because of my involvement with you."

"No worries, Anna," Quentin said with a small smile. "That's right, I now know your real name!" Seeing the look on Anna's face Quentin stopped his teasing and reassured her he wasn't seen. He didn't use a driver; he'd taken the bus and walked.

"Thank you for being careful for my sake," Anna said. "Don't think I'm not happy to see you because you were the first person I was going to text when I walked in the door."

"That's good to hear because I need a favor," Quentin said. "Are you aware that everyone has fallen in love with the mystery girl?"

"I'm not on social media, but Chang-ri said that people really liked it."

"Like it? *Yeokdaegeup!* It's the best thing ever. Every K-pop fan in Asia is obsessed with you! We're in fifth place for Song of the Summer now."

"I heard! Congrats."

"Anna, we were total unknowns, just happy to be in the running. But now . . ."

"Now you think you can win?" Anna asked.

"No, no, no. It's doubtful we could beat BTS—their fans are insane and very sophisticated in terms of voting and social media engagement."

Anna knew what he was getting at. "You want another picture with the mystery girl?"

"Do you hate me for asking?" Quentin said. "My managers have been asking me every day this week but I keep saying no. But now my group is asking me, and these guys are my boys, so . . ."

Anna didn't quite understand. "How come it's okay for you to appear with me when your contract says you can't have a girlfriend?"

Quentin said he had the same question, and his manager explained that fans didn't want to see their idols with significant others because it destroyed the fantasy that they could be their girlfriends or boyfriends. But for whatever reason everyone responded to the photo of Quentin and Anna differently. The fact that no one knew Anna's identity and Quentin refused to explain their relationship status made the whole situation mysterious and intriguing.

Anna crinkled her brow. "You don't worry what Minsoo will think when she sees the pictures?" She knew firsthand that Minsoo was very upset about the picture of Quentin and the mystery girl. When it came up, Chang-ri said she knew for a fact that Quentin and the girl were not romantically involved. Minsoo didn't seem like she believed her, even though she wanted to, obviously not recognizing Anna from the photo.

At the mention of Minsoo's name, Quentin let out a big dramatic sigh. "I thought of that, too, but what choice do I have?"

"Well, we could text her and ask," Anna told him coyly.

Quentin, who had been sitting on the chaise by the window, leapt up and rushed over to her. "You have her number?! How? Why? Are you serious?"

"Of course I am."

He looked perplexed and anxious. "Does she want to hear from me?"

Anna took his hand in hers. "Of course she does." She nodded with satisfaction. "That's what I wanted to tell you. I found her. Well, Chang-ri and I found her together."

#

Lolly loved Interlochen Arts Camp so much, she had attended every summer since the sixth grade. It was at this very camp where she really came into her own. Her little sister, Kimmie, had been an ice dancing star since the age of seven, and everyone always commented on how beautiful she was. Though she'd die before admitting it, Lolly had always felt somewhat overshadowed by her younger sister and she hated ever being called "Kimmie's older sister."

But when she showed up at Interlochen, everything changed. The three-week intermediate sleepaway camp had a full day of musical theater activities. On her first day, when her bunkmate, Jenner S., asked if she had any siblings, Lolly said no. She kept up the lie for the entire three weeks, but when she found out Kimmie was going to come to the performance at the end of camp, Lolly had no choice but to admit that she'd been fibbing and that she did have a sister who she didn't want to talk about. To her relief, her new musical theater friends understood completely. They were all quite melodramatic and even applauded her after her tearful confession at the campfire the night before the show.

Indeed Lolly's confidence had gotten a big boost because of the camp. Mr. Fullson, one of the program's teachers, recognized Lolly's singing voice to be worthy of professional training. She still remembered how nervous she was when he asked her to stay after her "Acting a Song" seminar the summer before her freshman year of high school. Mr. Fullson asked if she had ever taken private voice lessons. She shook her head and wiped away her tears. He told her with the right training she may have exactly the kind of voice that could land her on Broadway. He could hear her voice rise above the others. They could all carry a tune, but the difference was that Lolly's voice, he said, could carry an entire show.

Lolly told him that whenever she performed, she felt like another person, someone worthy of the spotlight. Mr. Fullson told her that the trick to commanding the spotlight was working harder than everyone else, practicing longer, and truly inhabiting every role as if it could be her last. After their talk, she floated back to her cabin and wrote her mother a letter telling her that she had found her calling and wanted to pursue singing and dancing.

Mr. Fullson's intuition had been correct. As the summers passed, Lolly got better and better, and soon she was the Interlochen "it girl," which of course she loved every second of. She had done both camp sessions the summers before her freshman and sophomore years, but that changed once she got her first serious boyfriend, Steven. Last summer they had only been dating for a few months, and she knew she couldn't expect to keep him if she was away for the whole summer.

Now, on the plane headed to Michigan, Lolly couldn't help replaying the disaster car ride that had just transpired. She had begged her mom to let Steven fly to Michigan with her for the start of theater camp, but her mom held her ground with a firm no. This was supposed to be a mother-daughter weekend, not a mother-watching-her-daughter-make-out-with-her-boyfriend weekend. It was something her mother had enjoyed for many years, and she wasn't breaking tradition on Lolly's last year. She had allowed Steven and Lolly to take a separate car to the airport so they could be all moony together on the way to JFK, sparing her and Kimmie from having to test their involuntary gag reflexes. And Steven certainly understood her daughter and her insatiable appetite for over-the-top gestures. While she and Kimmie were waiting for their black car to the airport, Steven rolled up in a chauffeured white Rolls-Royce.

Lolly squealed with delight and threw herself into Steven's arms, saying over and over that he was the handsomest, most wonderful boyfriend in the whole wide world. Steven swept her up and spun her around.

"Could they be any more entitled and disgusting?" Kimmie muttered. "It's like a high-key grossfest."

"Stop talking like that. Slang is for the masses," her mom replied, watching Steven and Lolly tumble into the Rolls. "I think it's darling. He's doing whatever it takes to make her happy."

"What he's doing is setting her up to be disappointed for the rest of her life, because most normal people can't afford to take their girlfriends to the fucking airport in a stupid white Rolls-Royce!"

"Someone sounds jealous," Danielle teased.

"Oh my god, I am not. You couldn't get me to ride in that ridiculous car. I'm perfectly happy with our . . ." A Honda CR-V pulled up with disco lights flashing. "That."

Lolly hung out the car window and waved good-bye, telling her mother to take a video so she could post it. Danielle filmed Lolly waving good-bye and then turned the camera toward Kimmie, who was staring after them with an almost comical look of disdain. Lolly could have cut off the Kimmie part, but instead she hashtagged #limegreenjello with lots of JKs following it.

What wasn't seen on Instagram (and what only Lolly and Steven and their chauffeur knew) was that ten minutes later, Lolly was in tears. They weren't tears of despair exactly, but they definitely weren't happy tears. They were the kind that came when you were super anxious about leaving your boyfriend for the next six weeks, even if it was to go to the arts camp that you loved. Lolly had this whole plan of giving Steven an extra special sexy ride on the way to the airport, wanting to make sure he was satisfied before she left, which she hoped would quell her rising anxiety that Steven would be tempted to cheat on her while she was away.

Unfortunately, her plan collided with his trying to make good on his promise to Anna that he would work on putting other people's needs ahead of his own. So when Lolly started making sexy overtures at him in the backseat, he deflected them and kept asking her if she wanted to discuss her feelings about this being her last summer at camp. Lolly misinterpreted and felt like he was rejecting her sexually, which made her lash out and soon the two were in a shouting match that ended with a very confused and frustrated Steven yelling, "See, this is what happens when I try to put someone else's feelings above my own. I don't get a blow job and you get mascara all over my shirt!"

Eventually they both calmed down and got to the bottom of their misunderstanding, but neither of them was feeling great about their pre-departure interaction. So much had happened with the death of Dustin's brother, followed by the whole Anna and Vronsky nightmare, but these tragedies had bonded her and Steven and made them even closer. She really felt like Steven's past infidelity was behind them. It was just that knowing she'd be away for so long was giving her anxiety that he might be reckless with her trust again.

Standing outside in front of the terminal, Steven told her he had learned his lesson, and would never again do anything to jeopardize their relationship. When he said this, she told him that as much as she loved camp, she loved him more. She then asked if it was a bad omen that she'd ruined their last hour together. He told her she didn't ruin anything, and if anyone were to blame, it was Anna for inspiring him to be a better person. This made Lolly laugh and Steven gave her one last kiss and told her he'd be seeing her at the end-of-camp show, which he wouldn't miss for the world. He also reminded her that they'd still have one week in the Hamptons after camp to hang out before they had to part again for school. At his mention of the future, Lolly's lip quivered. "Don't, Lolls," Steven said, intuiting her thoughts. "Let's get through the next six weeks first and then worry about next year, okay?"

Lolly flashed her sweetest smile, thrilled that he had effectively read her mind.

It was no surprise that Lolly became irritated when Kimmie asked her on the plane if she was nervous about Steven's "wandering eye-slash-peen problem," but she brushed off the comment, attributing it to Kimmie's current trend of saltiness. Kimmie had begged to stay home alone, but their mom had insisted Kimmie come with them for camp drop-off. Lolly knew the real reason her mother said no was not because she didn't trust Kimmie, but because she didn't trust "that Natalia girl," as their mother referred to her. "Who wears black combat boots in the summertime?"

Of course, she never said any of this to Kimmie, because Kimmie would call her judge-y and bring up the fact that it was their duty as good humans to support Natalia on her road to recovery. Lolly knew what her mom was thinking without her even saying it: she wished Natalia's road to recovery was a one-way road out of Manhattan.

"Must be nice to have the luxury of not worrying about Dustin cheating," Lolly said to her sister.

"What makes you say that?" Kimmie said defensively.

"Um, because Dustin's probably the most devoted goodie-two-shoes boyfriend I've ever seen," Lolly said. "Why, what did you think I meant?"

Kimmie looked around to make sure no one was listening, and leaned in close to confess that she and Dustin still hadn't had sex and had been stuck between first and second base for weeks now. It was on her mind and she wanted to know what Lolly thought in case she was missing something; they were sisters after all.

"Kissing is the best part, though! Enjoy it," Lolly said. "And like I said, you don't have to worry about him cheating on you."

"Please! He won't even cheat on his right hand with his own girlfriend!" Kimmie quipped and the two girls howled with laughter. "You don't find it weird, though? Because I have to admit it's giving me a head trip. Sometimes I worry that he's not attracted to me, like maybe he doesn't find me sexy enough. Steven looks at you like a hungry wolf. I want Dustin to look that way at me."

Lolly was taken aback by Kimmie's admission. It had never once occurred to her that her gorgeous younger sister could feel insecure like every other girl on the planet. "Kimmie, trust me, it's not that. Dustin loves you and I'm sure he's just nervous. I mean, sex has gotta be scary for boys, too, even though they'd never own up to it, right? You should talk to him about it and let him know how you're feeling. And don't rush into sex, there's plenty of other stuff you two can do until you both feel ready."

"Thanks, Lolly," Kimmie said. "And don't worry about Steven, if he goes all fuckboi again, I'll kick his ass. Now let's sneak up to first class and make Mom give us her warm cookies."

Beatrice had spent her fair share of vacations on some of the best beaches around the world, but she had never really paid much attention to surfers. They were always part of the backdrop for her. It took her a while to become proficient at picking out Tiare from the other surfers, but it helped that she was wearing a neon-green tankini. Beatrice had no clue how surfing etiquette worked, but there had to be some unwritten rules as to who got to go when because not everyone bobbing and waiting out there went for every wave. The first time she saw Tiare catch a big wave, a swell of pride filled her chest and she jumped up and cheered like a regular goofball. Luckily there weren't very many people around to hear her dorky "woo-hoo." It was early still. On most famous surf beaches, the mornings belonged to the surfers.

Bea had gotten a text from Chadwick back at the hotel saying Bea's mom had called to make sure she wasn't lying about taking Chadwick and Manny to Mexico as a thank-you present. Bea knew her mother was only checking up because her father was traveling for business, which meant she had nothing better to do than wander around the Hamptons house alone trying to decide which sofa needed reupholstering. *The one you spilled the Australian Shiraz on, Mom, start with that one,* Beatrice thought, leaning back on her elbows feeling the warmth of the sand rise through the towel as her skin soaked up the sun.

There was something about watching the waves roll in that lulled Bea into a warm breezy nap and she fell asleep for what felt like no more than a few minutes. She awakened to drops of water landing on her face. Tiare was standing over her.

"Shit!" Tiare said. "You didn't put sunscreen on, did you?" The concern in Tiare's voice caused Bea to sit up in alarm. She had no recollection of falling asleep and no clue how much time had passed. And no, she hadn't put on sunscreen yet because she was caught up watching Tiare surf. Tiare riffled around in her backpack and pulled out a bottle of sunscreen, squirting it aggressively on Bea's legs, so cold it made Bea squeal twice. "You don't realize how intense the sun is because of the ocean breeze, but it's no joke. You're so fair, you probably burn hella easy."

Bea couldn't decide whether to enjoy having her hot legs rubbed with cool lotion, or be annoyed at Tiare's bossiness. She decided to enjoy it. By the time they got back to the hotel, Bea was already turning bright pink and a few hours later she was red as a lobster. It hurt way more than she let on, but she was embarrassed at making such a dumb mistake, so she tried to play it off like it was no big deal. Tiare had gone to the store to get aloe and made sure Bea took some Tylenol. When she got back, the two of them ate room service on the balcony of their suite while Chadwick and Manny dined downstairs at the fancy seafood restaurant in the hotel.

During dinner Beatrice brought up the subject of their sexual preferences and proclivities and asked Tiare if she was bi. Tiare shook her head.
"Nope, no men. Now lemme guess you . . ." She thought for a second. "Pan?"

"Welcome to my Labyrinth."

Tiare stared at Bea quizzically. "Thank you, I guess?"

"I forgot, you don't like movies. *Pan's Labyrinth* is a movie."

"Oh right. I've actually seen that one with my ex. Too trippy for me."

"Your ex?" Bea asked. "Was it serious?"

"Not really," Tiare said, then changed the subject. "Look, I'm not big
on opiates, but you might need to take your Uncle Manny's offer and pop
a Vicodin. I don't know how you're going to sleep otherwise."

"Well, to be honest, I was hoping there wouldn't be much sleeping on
our first getaway," Bea replied, her voice wavering. "But look at me. I'm
burnt to a crisp."

"It's my fault. I should have made you put sunscreen on before I hit
the waves. I feel terrible." Tiare's words were so sincere it made Bea feel
like she might tear up. But Tiare had seen her cry way too much as it
was. And it was nice to have someone willingly take the blame for her
mistake, even though it wasn't Tiare's fault at all. It made Bea feel less
alone than she'd felt in a long time.

Tiare noticed Bea's eyes brimming with tears and reached across
the table to squeeze Bea's left hand, her only body part that wasn't sunburned. "Tomorrow's gonna suck, but you'll be better the day after. You
might be a peeling mess, but it won't hurt as bad."

"Why are you being so nice to me?" Bea asked. "I ruined everything."

Tiare frowned. "Are you kidding me? I got to surf these amazing waves
today, and now I'm in a sick hotel room eating the most expensive French
fries on the planet with the coolest chick in Mexico, also the most sunburned. I'm having an incredible time. You're the one who's not."

Bea sniffled a bit. "There are way more expensive French fries than
those."

After dinner, Tiare propped Bea up with pillows in the bed and
started flipping through the pay-per-view movies. Bea had seen most of

them, but Tiare hadn't seen any, so they decided on an action flick to keep Bea's mind off the pain of her scorched skin.

"So were you surprised to get my text?" Bea asked, bored by the opening car chase of *The Fate of the Furious*, which was surprising since she normally loved a good chase sequence.

"Yes and no. Yes because it had been a while, but no because I knew we had a real connection."

"I wanted to text you, but . . ."

"I get it," Tiare said.

"What do you get?"

"That it's hard for you to put yourself out there. And I know this because I'm the same way. I've had many relationships flame out from my lack of effort. But I want you to know I regretted not getting your number when I had the chance. I would have caved sooner than you did."

"Yeah, you missed weeks of me giving good emoji." Beatrice winked and smiled, which made her face crinkle. She let out a pathetic whimper.

"You poor thing. I'm going to talk to the front desk to see if the local pharmacy might have a better remedy." She got up from the bed and started to take off her bathrobe to get changed.

"You can go in your robe," Bea told her.

"You mean traipse around in a robe? You have to be kidding me!"

"Welcome to the lives of the rich and spoiled . . . here you can do pretty much anything you want."

"Except for you," Tiare said with a sly wink.

"Aw, you made a sex joke about me," Bea teased, but secretly it made her really happy since she was feeling about as unsexy as a girl could feel.

By the time Tiare got back to the room, Bea had passed out. Tiare turned off the television and flopped next to her on the king-sized bed.

"Ouch," Bea said, her voice muffled by the pillow.

"Sorry."

"S'okay."

"Good night, Bea."

"Night, T."

XXI

A week after Quentin's visit, Edward came by the house in the middle of the afternoon to tell Anna he had to fly to Hong Kong for business and would be back the next day. Anna told him she already had plans to have dinner out with Chang-ri, which meant her grandmother would have to dine alone. "Please don't make me change my plans. Halmeoni looks right through me. Like I'm a ghost. I thought things would be different after she met Quentin, but she was only being nice to me because there was a boy around."

She made a fair point. Edward, too, had seen a different side of his mother when Quentin joined them for dinner the other night. Neither he nor Anna had had a clue she knew anything about K-pop, but as it turned out, one of Halmeoni's friends was married to the head of one of the largest music companies in Asia so she was familiar with the business. "She's never been very talkative during meals. She thinks it's bad for digestion." Edward always defended his mother, which made him a good son but not necessarily the most understanding father. Edward's expression softened as he continued. "And I'm not sure how I feel about you gallivanting around with someone so much older."

"Please, Dad! Gallivanting?" Anna said. "*Unnie* Chang-ri's only a year out of university." This wasn't exactly true, but it was close enough. *Unnie* was the Korean word used between female friends. A girl would refer to any friend who was older than her as *unnie*, which basically meant sister. By using it Anna was hoping her father would understand that her relationship with Chang-ri was sisterly so he shouldn't worry. "How am I supposed to make such an enormous decision about relocating if I haven't spent any time here on my own?"

Edward pulled his phone out of his pocket, a call from work he had to deal with. "Okay, fine. But don't be too late, and I want you to text me when you get home."

Anna gave him a hug and kissed him on the cheek. "Thank you!"

It was a strange feeling to be relishing this little deception of hers. If her father knew what she was up to, he surely would have grounded her and put an end to it all. It actually made the whole thing extra exciting. The public demand for Quentin's mystery girl to come forward was reaching a fever pitch, especially after the TikTok he and Anna released the night Quentin came over for dinner.

That night they decided to shoot the video. Quentin did Anna's makeup and left her to work on her hair. He came back into her room ten minutes later holding three Chanel jackets from her grandmother's closet. Anna almost fainted over his audacity, but he assured her he hadn't taken them without permission, which Anna found hard to believe. Almost as much as the Stunna Girl TikTok they were about to shoot.

Quentin appeared first with the "Heyyyyyy!" followed by three quick cuts of Anna in oversized sunglasses, wearing each of the three Chanel jackets as if they were dresses. With her tongue out, giving the camera her best snarl, she lip-synched, *"Bitch, I look like I'm fresh off the runway, nyah! Bitch, I go crazy the dumb way!"* When she watched the video play back, she was utterly unrecognizable to herself, not just in how she looked but mostly through the bratty attitude she conveyed. And she found herself fantasizing about what it would be like if she, too, could keep being a bad bitch for a whole day.

The morning after they released the video, Anna panicked when she saw her phone. There were fifteen texts from Chang-ri, who had taken a screenshot and translated what everyone was saying. In short, K-pop fans around the globe were losing their minds.

Quentin had used Anna's phone to text Minsoo the night before and he explained that the "mystery girl" was just a publicity stunt but he wanted to make sure she wouldn't be upset if he released a TikTok with her. Minsoo was so happy to be back in touch with Quentin that she told him it didn't bother her. She certainly understood how important publicity was for Quentin's career, and she had been pleased that he had the courtesy to check in with her first. Quentin wanted to tell Minsoo that Anna was the mystery girl, but Anna insisted on keeping her identity a secret.

Quentin was overwhelmed with emotion by Anna's "gift," which was what he called her reuniting him with Minsoo. When he FaceTimed with Minsoo, Anna watched with fascination as he transformed upon seeing his long-lost boo, acting like they were the only two people on the planet. Everything else receded into the background, including Anna, and it made her chest feel tight and hollow at the same time because she remembered not too long ago what that feeling was like. When she was with Vronsky, nothing else mattered. All she could see was him, and she reveled in every moment. Watching Quentin and Minsoo talking on the phone, Anna was proud to be the one who had brought them back together.

Now the challenge remained to figure out how they could be together as a real-life couple. If the NowNows' fans seemed fine with Quentin being with a secret mystery girl, how come they couldn't let him be with the girl he really loved? She planned to pose this question to Chang-ri over dinner because she was wondering if there was a cultural component she was failing to grasp.

When Anna arrived at the restaurant, Chang-ri was already waiting outside. "Am I late, *Unnie?*"

Chang-ri squealed at Anna calling her *unnie*. "I'm proud of you learning our customs. Are you going to call Quentin *oppa?*" *Oppa* was the same idea as *unnie* but was used for older male friends.

"Nah, I already have a big brother back at home," Anna said, smiling. "I'm so happy to see you. My aunt and uncle are arriving early tomorrow, so this may be my last free time until I'm back for school."

"OMG! Have you decided to stay?" Chang-ri asked.

Anna had already told Chang-ri about the possibility of her staying in Korea for her senior year. Chang-ri had said she had selfishly been hoping that Anna would stay in Seoul, admitting her life had become infinitely more interesting now that they were friends. But Chang-ri also understood that it was a tough choice for Anna to leave everything she knew behind.

"Yes, no, maybe! My dad sort of assumes it's happening. I flip-flop every hour of every day. Seeing you makes me want to stay here.

Though if I go to Branksome Hall we'd only be able to hang out on weekends."

Next Chang-ri showed Anna the #QTmysterygirl hashtag and watched as she scrolled through the hundreds of photos that had been posted by couples sharing a look-alike pose in front of Ramenonymous.

"I can't believe this," Anna said quietly. Chang-ri saw the change in Anna's color and grabbed Anna's arm and pulled her inside the restaurant.

"I'm sorry," Chang-ri whispered, hanging her head. "I thought you would find the pictures amusing. Not upsetting."

"I'm not upset. It's just . . . strange. Am I a meme now?"

"What's a meme?" Chang-ri asked, and Anna showed her a few examples on her phone. "That's what you are," Chang-ri nodded. "In Korean it's *jjal.*"

"I thought it would be over by now," Anna said, sitting with Chang-ri inside the tea and sandwich shop where they had become regulars, drinking green matcha bobas.

"People are desperate to learn the identity of the mystery girl," Chang-ri reminded her.

"But why?" Anna asked, truly baffled.

"QT's being secretive about it, and that's not usually the way with K-pop stars. Here they 'belong' to their fans, so it's hard for them to keep their private lives private. And because the fame is so fleeting, many share everything with fans to keep it going. QT's popularity is booming right now. He has gotten millions more followers on Instagram since it started."

"Who knew a makeover could cause such a commotion," Anna said, more to herself than Chang-ri. Anna's phone buzzed and she showed her screen to Chang-ri. Free tonight? the message read. Chang-ri's jaw went slack. She was with someone who was texting one of The NowNows! Screening party for our new MV, another text came in from Quentin. Come as Very?

Lemme check if Very's avail . . . Anna texted back.

The dance of the three bubbles appeared immediately: everyone is VERY excited to meet her . . .

Anna put her phone down for a second and looked across the table at Chang-ri, who was giddy with excitement at what was going down. "He wants me to come as the mystery girl. You're going to be my plus one and I'm going to make him bring Minsoo."

Very needs a plus one, I'm with Chang-ri, she texted Quentin. Did you invite Minsoo?

Chang-ri squealed loudly, and the other customers turned toward their table and shook their heads.

OK on +1, Quentin wrote. No can do Minsoo.

Very is very sad no Minsoo. *sad face emoji* Anna typed. She slipped her phone back in her purse and looked up at Chang-ri. "I'm assuming you want to come, right?"

Chang-ri was thrilled but filled with dread. She was not normally the girl who got to hang out with beautiful people and go to fancy parties. She lived in a tiny apartment and spent her weekends staring at her phone and reading about the beautiful people who went to such parties. "I have nothing to wear."

Anna shot Chang-ri a knowing smile. "Then I guess we need to go shopping."

XXII

It was the most fun Chang-ri had ever had in her entire life: going to a fancy department store, trying on beautiful dresses, seeing which designer shoes she would best be able to dance in, and having salespeople wait on her like she was royalty. It was a fantasy straight out of the shopping montages she had seen in American movies or the soap operas she watched with her mom. At the end of their whirlwind selection of party outfits, she and Anna were seated beside each other, getting makeovers from the store's two top makeup artists. This store was accustomed to wealthy women waltzing in and dropping thousands of dollars, but what made it so much fun was that Anna was so young and her carefree generosity made the experience that much more special.

"I want you to know this is not how I normally roll," Anna whispered to Chang-ri as a makeup artist applied her sparkly blue eyeshadow. "I hope you don't find it too excessive."

"Not at all. I'm having the best time ever. Is this what it's like to be famous?"

Anna blushed, embarrassed. "I wouldn't know, my family isn't famous, just rich. My big brother is a total clothes horse, so he's paved the road for me to be a little extravagant now and again. Also, I texted my dad that we were going shopping and he told me to have fun, which is code for 'spend away.'"

Both girls had their makeup done. Anna's eyes were heavily lined with black, and she had fake eyelashes with glittered tips and, once again, a very dark red lipstick that had become the key ingredient of her transformation into the mystery girl. They were careful not to say anything about where they were going, and it helped that Anna couldn't speak Korean and the makeup artist knew only a few words of English. Chang-ri just lied, sharing how Anna was a VIP from America who was sent to be a special guest on their TV show, and they wanted to try out different looks before she went on camera. Chang-ri instructed them that Anna wanted to look like the mystery girl that everyone was talking about. Jung, the makeup artist assisting them, told Chang-ri it was the third time today for that particular look. "I bet once they figure out who she is she'll get offered a cosmetics contract to model the perfect red lipstick!"

Anna, unable to help herself, asked, "Why do you think everyone is so into this girl? I mean, I've seen the picture and the TikTok and she looks cool but it's not like we know anything about her." Chang-ri translated Anna's question and then Jung's response.

"She says in the TikTok video the girl has a killer sense of style and a badass attitude. Every girl has a wild streak deep inside her. The mystery girl is brave. She seems free to do as she pleases, which is what everyone longs for."

Anna felt a twinge of pride. *I'm just doing what feels right for me,* she thought.

When they were in a car headed to the party, Chang-ri was still on a shopper's high and was overjoyed to be wearing her first real designer party dress: a Miu Miu sleeveless pale pink silk dress adorned with a ten-inch fabric rose on her shoulder. Never had she felt more glamorous. She thanked Anna profusely for such a lavishly expensive present. Anna made her feel at ease and told Chang-ri she deserved such a treat for being so incredibly sweet to her since the first day they met.

Unable to resist, Chang-ri peppered Anna with questions. Was QT a nice guy or a bad boy? According to the fan sites he was the most popular member of his group and his appeal was that he was the quietest one of them all, offstage. While onstage he definitely had the most charisma. Did he wear makeup when he wasn't onstage? Did he wear eyelash extensions? For a boy he really did have incredible lashes. And did the other members of The NowNows have secret girlfriends, too, or were they available?

Anna said she thought Quentin was overall a good guy, but she did have a few lingering doubts about his character. How hard had he really tried to find Minsoo? She and Chang-ri had managed to track her down without much difficulty, although Chang-ri had some inside information. But if you were truly in love with someone who had disappeared, wouldn't you stop at nothing to find them? Anna decided to give him the benefit of the doubt. After all, he was pretty young and everyone around him was so hyper-focused on his career that perhaps he needed to be given a second chance at love so he could see that living his life was just as important as living his dream.

"I know he loves Minsoo, but that doesn't mean he couldn't still have a crush on you," Chang-ri said. "Love triangles are so romantic."

Anna nodded politely, and they rode on in silence.

Until they turn tragic . . .

When they arrived at the location, a crowd of photographers mobbed the entrance, and Anna stopped Chang-ri from opening the car door. "I have an idea of how to help Minsoo and Quentin." Anna leaned over and whispered something in her ear.

"Are you sure?" Chang-ri asked. "You don't have to do this. Quentin and Minsoo are both older than you and you've done a lot for them already."

"Let me try. If it doesn't work, it doesn't work. What have we got to lose?"

"Judging by the crowd that's out there, it could definitely work." Chang-ri gave Anna a quick hug and exited the car then stopped, turned around, and peered back in. "When it comes time for me to fall in love, I want you in my corner."

Anna smiled and watched Chang-ri walk into the party.

A few minutes later, Chang-ri texted Anna that Quentin and his manager were on their way down to meet her. She was still sitting in the backseat of the car, thankful for the SUV's tinted privacy windows. When Quentin exited the building, it was as though a switch had been flipped on. The group of photographers previously standing around smoking and talking suddenly snapped to attention. They started yelling to Quentin, asking him if the mystery girl was on her way. Quentin stopped, posed for a few photos, and gave a charming shrug of the shoulders, coupled with a squinty duckface. He then continued walking toward the row of cars parked by the curb. Anna had the driver honk to indicate which car was hers.

Alongside Quentin was an older woman in a neon-yellow dress and jacket, and she did not look the least bit pleased. Anna swallowed hard. What the fuck was she doing? Who did she think she was? The last six weeks had all been about escaping the drama in her life, but here she was not only inviting it, but creating it.

Quentin opened the door, and Anna beckoned for them to enter.

"Hey, Very, what's going on?" Quentin said in an overly casual, bad actor-ish voice. "How come you didn't come up with your friend?"

Anna ignored Quentin and squinted at the woman he was with,

giving her a good once-over, a careful assessment from tip to toe. She had learned the look from Beatrice, who deployed it every time she came across an overconfident freshman in the school hallway. "Aren't you going to introduce me to your handler?" Anna asked, trying her best to sound like the VIP Quentin said she was.

"I'm Aileen C., vice president of JGK Music. You do realize we have a party going on upstairs, one that I am throwing. What is this all about?"

This woman did not seem very pleasant, and Quentin was clearly afraid of her. Anna kept her face very still and decided her best chance for success was to channel her grandmother, or better yet, to keep up her Beatrice impression, as she was the one girl Anna knew who never showed fear. "What this is . . . is me offering JGK Music an opportunity. But if you're not interested in hearing it, I have two other parties I could go to. Like my name, I'm *very* popular."

"Very, maybe now's not the best time . . ." Quentin started to say before Anna cut him off.

"Your loss," she said with casual indifference. "Bye now!" She leaned forward and tapped on the glass. "Driver, my guests are ready to go. . . ."

"Let's not be hasty. Of course we want you to stay and join in the fun at my party," Aileen said through a phony smile.

"Don't you mean you want me to exit the car so all those photographers can take pictures of me with your client?" Anna said. "Which as we all know will give The NowNows and JGK Music a huge amount of free publicity. I heard the song just hit number four . . . only three more spots to go to win Song of the Summer."

"How much do you want?" Aileen asked. "We have a very healthy marketing budget."

Anna shook her head. "Do I look like I need money?"

"What do you want then?" Aileen was starting to lose her patience.

"I want an amendment to Quentin's contract striking out the clause that prohibits him from having a girlfriend. If we're going to appear in photos as a couple, I want him protected. Also, it's really a dumb rule. In my opinion."

"No way." Aileen looked at Quentin. "Where'd you find this girl?"

"She's a New Yorker," Quentin said, hoping that was answer enough.

"I can be your best friend or your worst nightmare," Anna said with a sneer. "Now I want the clause stricken from all the NowNows' contracts. What can I say, I'm a romantic."

Aileen smacked her own forehead and swore in Korean. "You're crazy," she said, reaching for the door handle.

"And your job depends on the success of this group, so I'd say you're crazy if you don't give me what I want."

Aileen froze and pulled her hand back from the handle. She studied Anna with her arms crossed. "Fine. The NowNows can date whoever they want, within reason. Any other headaches you want to give me?"

"Just one more tiny one," Anna said with a sincere smile. "Minsoo needs to be let out of her contract so she can continue to pursue her singing career."

Aileen frowned. "I don't know who you're talking about."

"Quentin, was she not in the meeting when you were told to stop seeing her?" Anna asked, and Quentin nodded. "Don't lie to me again, Aileen, okay? I don't like liars."

Aileen's nostrils flared beneath her ice-cold glare. "Whatever."

"And shame on you as a woman for screwing another woman over."

"Who do you think you are, talking to me like that? I'm twice your age," Aileen said.

"I know exactly who I am." Anna replied in a sing-song voice. "I'm the motherfuckin' mystery girl that all of Seoul is clamoring for."

"Fine, I want three more photos for his social, and two more TikTok videos. I pick the song this time. No profanity."

"Okay, but my identity stays a secret, which is non-negotiable," Anna said. "I'm only in Seoul for another two weeks, which is when I'll disappear, leaving Quentin brokenhearted, and I'm sure your marketing department can engineer a PR rebound story for him and Minsoo to get back together."

"You are a real New Yorker."

"That's right." Anna held out her hand. "A gentlewoman's agreement then?"

Aileen shook it, then turned to Quentin, who gave her a sheepish smirk. "I like this one." Then, to Anna: "I see bright things in your future. Very, very bright things."

"Like your party," Anna said, opening the car door. "Shall we?"

XXIII

When Tiare's alarm went off at 4:30 A.M., she found the bed empty. Beatrice was sitting outside on the veranda. It was still dark out, so Tiare wasn't able to judge the severity of Bea's sunburn. "Hey," Tiare asked gently. "You okay?"

Bea leveled her gaze at Tiare. "Not really."

Tiare sat down at the edge of the chaise. Now that her eyes had adjusted to the darkness, she was able to see that Bea was naked, but not in a good way.

Beatrice explained that when she woke up she felt like her skin was on fire. She decided to take a cold shower, which helped for a bit, but soon her teeth were chattering, and so she put on one of the plush terrycloth bathrobes. But that turned out to be rather painful, so she dropped it on the bathroom floor and slathered herself in aloe. "I'm out here sans clothes because it's cool and dark," Bea said, careful not to gesticulate too much for fear of the excruciating sting such movement would cause. "And because I'm hideous."

"No you're not," Tiare said sympathetically. "You look like you fell asleep in the sun. It could have been much worse."

"Really?" Bea said. "Because I was just trying to think of how this could be worse, and I couldn't come up with a single thing."

"You don't have any blisters, do you?" Tiare asked and Bea shook her head. "I've seen some really terrible sunburns in my day and yours isn't good, but it's not as bad as it could be."

"So what I'm hearing is I'm mediocre at being sunburned," Bea said.

"Ugh, ignore me. I feel like crap. When are you getting back from surfing?"

"I'm not going."

"What? Of course, you are." Bea sat up and winced in pain. "That's the whole reason we're here."

"No," Tiare said firmly. "The whole reason we're here is to be together. I can surf anytime, but what I can't always do is spend the day lounging in the most comfortable bed I've ever slept in while watching movies with a human lobstergirl that can't be touched."

Beatrice laughed and tried to convince Tiare she should surf for a few hours, but Tiare refused. She'd surf tomorrow when Bea would be well enough to revisit the scene of her fun-in-the-sun faux pas, under an umbrella. This unexpected development improved Bea's mood greatly. She couldn't remember anyone except Vronsky choosing her over something else that they wanted to do. It felt good knowing there were other selfless people in the world besides the ones who were never coming back. Tiare was unlike anyone Bea had ever met before. She knew her generation used the word "authentic" too much, but that was the best way to describe her. She seemed so totally real and self-confident, open and honest, yet also mysterious, not like a lot of the people she knew back East.

"Everyone always talks about my self-confidence, but I feel like mine is a kind of manufactured Machiavellian style while yours is the real deal," Bea opined as they lounged in the still-dark suite. Tiare had closed all the shades with the touch of one button on a console by the bed. They were in bed sharing a club sandwich and a massive basket of French fries. "What's your secret?"

"No secrets—maybe that's what it takes." Tiare smiled. "Ask me anything and I'll tell you the truth."

"Have you ever been in love before?" Bea asked, wanting to know but also not.

"Wow. No lead-up questions, no easy one like are you a cat person or a dog person?" Tiare sopped up the last of the ketchup with her French fry. "I'm assuming you mean the biggie?"

Bea nodded, unsure what she wanted to hear. Would it be better if she had been in love before, or if she hadn't?" "Never mind! I withdraw the question." Bea lay back, putting a pillow over her sunburned face. "Ow."

Tiare pulled the pillow away. "Hey now, you gotta be kind to your poor pink face." She studied Bea's face, shiny with the aloe cream they had slathered on it before lunch. "It's getting better. The key is . . ."

"Moisturizing, constantly. I know, I know," Bea responded playfully.

"Nope, I was gonna say . . . baby air kisses." Tiare kissed the tip of Bea's nose without touching it, then the space right above her cheeks, and then did the same above her chin, both eyelids, and across her forehead. Normally Tiare wasn't this cutesy with any girl she dated, but she knew the stony fortress that Bea constructed around her true feelings could only be breached by uncharacteristic and disarming displays of affection.

As odd as this was for Tiare, it was more so for Beatrice, who now found herself rapidly spiraling into an even more vulnerable position with this girl. Rarely did she lay herself so bare with someone else, at least in the figurative sense. In the literal sense, Beatrice had no problem getting naked with any number of combinations of people. She had been sexually active from an early age, sometimes to get what she wanted, other times to make herself feel less lonely, and most of the time because she liked having outrageous stories to impress her friends with. But whose attention was she trying to get, really? Her friends'? Her parents'? Or was it her own? The sex, the drugs, the parties, her constant need for pushing boundaries—was any of it making her happy? These thoughts had been floating about for a while, unspoken thoughts she wouldn't dare share with anyone. But oddly she wanted to share them with Tiare. What would her friends think if she told them that she had met someone and fallen in love? Would they believe her if she said she wanted to be different . . . nicer, better, and perhaps even a little happier? If she wasn't a cynical rich bitch, then who was she?

"Hey, where'd you go?" Tiare whispered. "Do you need a nap?"

Bea's eyes flicked open and she sat up so fast Tiare flinched. "I need to know this is real. What's happening here. Because if it's not, like if you're just out to have a little fun, taking a spin with a bitchy rich girl, I need to know. I'd be fine with all this if we were just fucking, but we're not. I don't understand these feelings if they're not wrapped up in lust, booze, or drugs."

"Beatrice, baby. I feel something with you, definitely. I do. You're not the only one whose head is spinning. But it's gonna be okay, you're not jumping into the deep end alone. We're together. And I can't make any predictions for the future or what's going to happen. It's like waiting for the big one, the big wave. You gotta just follow your gut to tell you when it's the right wave to go for. As soon as you're up on your board and riding it there's no sense in worrying anymore. You gotta just relax into it and ride the wave. So what I can tell you is we're up. We're riding the wave . . . so no more questions. There's nowhere else I want to be right now, except right here with you."

Bea would have smiled if it didn't sting. Tiare sounded right and smart and true, but Bea had never surfed before. She had no idea if she could ride this wave without wiping out and drowning.

XXIV

Lolly's favorite aspect of camp was the intensity of the schedule. There was never a dull moment. They woke up to the sound of the trumpet at six fifteen and walked in their pajamas to the basketball court for morning announcements. Lolly usually held hands with a few friends while they sang an a cappella version of whatever was the big hit on Broadway. Last year it had been *Hamilton,* this year the song was "Better Be Good to Me" from *Tina: The Tina Turner Musical.* Next they did their chores, then ate breakfast, then took acting technique class at ten, to which Lolly always arrived early for a quick warm-up. After that they had dance class, then lunch, followed by afternoon rehearsal. After dinner, Lolly would have another rehearsal to attend, assuming that she was cast as a lead. By ten o'clock, everyone had to be back in their cabins, and at that point staff members would show up to collect all of their cell phones for the night. Lights-out was at ten fifteen, and while most campers fell right asleep, Lolly would often be wide awake, going over every detail of her day, recording it in her memory, filing it away under "best days of my life." An uncontrollably dorky smile stretched across her face in the dark until she fell asleep, hoping to fast-forward through her dreams as quickly as possible so she could wake up and start the next day.

These drama-filled weeks of summer were when she blossomed, always returning home feeling like a more complete person than when she arrived, more poised and self-assured. Camp relationships were intense, potentially lifelong friendships and rivalries that could impact their future careers. There were so many dramatically inclined teenagers together in one place that everything was magnified by a factor of a googolplex multiplied by infinity. Emotions ran sky-high, the competition was cutthroat, and the rumor mill was powered by the endless current of well-rehearsed gossipers flowing against the giant wooden spinning wheel of curiosity and intrigue. Lolly tried to stay above it, but that was because she was a hardcore regular, which meant she knew everyone, and everyone knew her. Her reasons for staying out of all the shit-talk and backstabbery were mostly diplomatic. It also helped that she had the talent and drive necessary to succeed and usually earned a leading role in the end-of-camp production.

This summer's end-of-camp show was *Oklahoma!* and auditions would be held the whole first week. It was a bit demanding for anyone who had never been there before. Not only were the first-timers trying to get used to the schedule, they had to get used to their new cabin, their new cabinmates, the terrible cafeteria gruel they passed off as food. They also had to be mentally prepared to audition bright and early the next morning.

The first two sessions of camp Lolly attended, she barely held it together through "hell week," as it was affectionately called. She once asked who had decided to do things this particular way, and she was informed by her instructor that the campers at Interlochen were seriously considering careers in the performing arts, and if they couldn't handle week-one auditions, they might as well give up any hope of making it in show business.

For Lolly, audition week got easier each time, and now she barely even got nervous, let alone nauseous like some of the others. Admittedly it was easy for Lolly to be confident when she knew she was one of the most talented of the bunch. She had been training for this her entire life. Kimmie had been an immediate breakout star in ice skating at a young age, but Lolly was the one with the stamina and the determination to keep her head down and continue her dance lessons: ballet, jazz, tap; her voice lessons: technique, classical training, musical theater; as well as working on her stage presence constantly. She worked harder than everyone else and never stopped striving to become the best actor she could possibly be.

The first two days of auditions saw the musical theater campers divided alphabetically into groups of fifteen, which put Lolly in the last section.

"When your smaller group is called into the main audition, you will have the chance to do your monologue and the song you prepared before the director of the show, the musical director, the choreographer, and myself," one of the younger counselors announced.

Lolly's monologue was from Oscar Wilde's *Lady Windermere's Fan*, and her song was "On the Steps of the Palace" from *Into the Woods*. She had practiced both with her private teachers the week before and felt very good about her choices, though her music teacher did question if she should have picked a more classic song for her *Oklahoma!* audition. Lolly was going after the female lead of Laurey, a young woman involved in a love triangle with the two male leads.

It never occurred to Lolly she would have any real competition, but at breakfast on the second day she heard murmurings of a late arrival to camp who'd had travel delays due to an issue with her visa. Lolly didn't pay much attention until she heard this girl had already been accepted at Yale, which was Lolly's dream school to study theater. The oldest campers, like Lolly, were rising seniors, so it didn't make sense to have a girl who was about to enter college. She really did her best not to engage in the camp gossip, preferring to rise above and stay positive. But nobody was perfect. There was only one person at camp who she got catty with, and that was her gay BFF Jamieson T., who, like Lolly, had been coming to Interlochen since he was eleven years old. He was easily the most talented of the boys, and the two of them had been the leads playing opposite each other in one of the sessions for the last three years. There was no one she trusted more than Jamieson.

"I already know what you want to know," he said breezily as she approached him outside his cabin on their way to lunch.

"So you're a mind reader now?" Lolly asked playfully.

"Only yours, because great minds think alike," he quipped. "But you've heard correctly. Her name is Siobhan M., and she's basically what you get if you cross Emma Stone with Saoirse Ronan, digitally erase the freckles, and leave yourself with a reddish-blond alabaster goddess. And she has an Irish accent, Lolly. A real one."

"But is she as good as everyone's saying?" Lolly said, trying to keep her voice even.

"She can't be better than you, Lolls. I mean, that's obvi. But she'll make it to callbacks for sure. And I want you to know you're not alone in this."

Lolly took his hand and gave it an appreciative squeeze. "You're the best, sweetie."

"No, I mean you're not alone because the same thing is happening to me. There's some new guy I keep hearing about, and I overheard some little biz-natch saying she thought he was better than me. I don't know his name, but I hear he's from Texas, which makes me nervous that the director might find him more Oklahoma-y than me."

This news was not music to Lolly's perfectly pitched ears. She assumed that she and Jamieson would win the two most coveted roles in the musical, Laurey and Curly. This was their last summer at Interlochen. She couldn't imagine either of them not winning the lead role. "Jamieson, we both need to focus. Are you ready for your audition?"

"I'm done with mine already, so . . ." Jamieson stopped as they arrived at the stone cafeteria. "Holy mother of Regina George," he gasped. "I think I've just seen the fuckboi of my dreams."

Lolly followed Jamieson's gaze across the dining hall. A guy wearing a cowboy hat sauntered through the doorway like he was looking for the barkeep at an old saloon. Lolly had never seen anyone look so good in a Stetson in her entire life, and she had watched every season of *Yellowstone*. He took off his hat and palmed it in one hand. Almost on reflex, Lolly raised her hand and waved at him blankly. He noticed and gave her a wink and a smile as he started to walk toward them.

"What are you doing?" Jamieson asked.

"Keep your friends close and your enemies closer." Lolly turned to the hot cowboy now standing in front of them. "Hi, are you the new guy everyone keeps whispering about?"

"Well I am new," he said in a sexy Texas drawl, "but I'm not sure about the whispering. Name's Dean."

"Your name is Names Dean?" Jamieson asked him.

"No," Dean corrected him. "My name is Dean. Dean J."

"Nice to meet you, Dean. I'm Lolly and this is Jamieson. Please, have a seat."

"I wish I could, but I'm just getting some food for the choreographer, he said he wanted to work with me a little this afternoon."

"That makes two of us," Jamieson mumbled to himself.

Lolly nudged him. "That's nice. Gary's the best," she said quickly. "Well, have fun!"

Dean tipped his hat and headed for the sandwich station. "Later, gators . . ."

"This is a disaster." Jamieson leaned over the table, bug-eyed. "If Gary's already singled him out, then . . ."

"Stop! It doesn't mean a thing," Lolly lied and rubbed her now sweaty palms on her shorts. "Gary's always nice to the good-looking newbies." This was true, but Lolly knew that Jamieson probably needed to be worried about Dean, and if he needed to be worried about him, then maybe she needed to be worried about the pretty redhead from Ireland.

XXV

When Anna opened her eyes the morning after the NowNows' music video premier party, she felt different. She stretched her arms above her head and took note of what had changed.

She didn't feel sad. She didn't feel numb. She felt normal, meaning she wasn't suppressing the desire to scream. But these days waking up to a baseline of okayness was a big win. She marveled over the relativity of her emotions, how not feeling depressed translated into hope. Perhaps the dark clouds hovering over her life were beginning to lift.

The timing couldn't have been better since her Aunt Jules and Uncle Wilson had arrived from Los Angeles yesterday and they were all meeting for lunch in a few short hours. The next week was going to be packed with sightseeing and family time. She was excited to tell her aunt about her crazy adventures in Seoul, knowing she could be trusted to keep Anna's secrets. It even occurred to her that her aunt might see her mystery-girl adventure as a fun movie idea. Anna knew the whole thing was a little silly, but wasn't that the magic of Hollywood? Writers taking zany real-life stories that they lived through firsthand or heard about from friends and turning them into actual movies?

Anna slipped her feet into her worn pink bunny slippers, crossed the room with purpose, and opened her closet door. She opened her suitcase and pulled out the shoebox. She had been so busy playing Cupid to Quentin and Minsoo, she hadn't read any more of Vronsky's letters. There were not many left, and she had decided she needed to savor the last ones, waiting until she was in the right state of mind to enjoy them.

She picked up a creamy yellow envelope with her name written in calligraphy. Using a mother-of-pearl letter opener she had borrowed from her halmeoni's desk, Anna carefully opened the envelope. As she pulled the letter out, the faintest hint of his cologne wafted up to her nose. She closed her eyes and held the paper up to her face and inhaled again. Yes, she would know that smell anywhere.

Goose bumps sprung up immediately on her arms, and she quickly told herself, "Don't be sad. Be happy you get to smell him again, for at least this moment." She pulled out the letter and began to read:

My Dearest Anna,
Guess who watched a "the lost art of calligraphy" video on YouTube last night when I couldn't sleep? Now you know what I do when I can't sleep, a common occurrence for me these days. First, I watched ski jump videos, then I moved on to watching Newfies leaping out of helicopters to do water rescues (I had no idea they were such powerful swimmers!), and then I ended up trying to teach myself calligraphy. What do you think of my handiwork? Capital letters are known as "majuscules"! Are you impressed? I hope so. Everything I do lately is driven by my thoughts of you. Your doormen now know me by name, and they swear they have been giving my letters to your housekeeper, but now it's been so long without a response I'm pretty sure you haven't read them. The alternative is just too awful to consider, that you have them and don't want to reach out. I don't believe that's the case.

I want you to know that I went to see your father yesterday. I skipped school and rode my bike to his office and told his secretary I didn't have an appointment, but that I needed to see him; I was quite desperate. She told me he had a full day and didn't have time to meet with me, but I told her I didn't mind waiting and I sat down on the couch. I brought a book with me, but I was nervous and kept reading the same page over and over.

After two hours he emerged from his office and waved me in. It was clear from the look on his face that he was not happy to see me. . . .

Anna continued reading, and she did not like what she found out. How was it that her father never told her about Alexia's visit? About their conversation? About what they both said to each other?

By the end of the letter, her pleasant mood had dissipated. If she confronted her father with what she'd just learned, he would want to know why she was bringing this up months later, and she'd have to admit to him that her mother had given her the letters and that might make him angry at Greer. Would he also get angry at Marta, their housekeeper, for accepting the letters and not mentioning it to him?

How torturous it was to read about events that if known to her could have altered the course of Fate. How awful to think that the things that had been kept from her were the very things that could have reset her and Vronsky on a less tragic path.

Anna placed the letter back in the envelope and decided she needed to seal it in a Ziploc bag to try to preserve the smell of his cologne for as long as she could. She placed the envelope in the box, stood up, and took a deep breath. She then walked back to the bed, flopped facedown, and screamed into her pillow.

XXVI

Anna stared out the window of the car on the way to the hotel where her aunt and uncle were staying. She tried to imagine her future self walking about on the streets, wearing Branksome Hall's green plaid skirt and blazer, a senior in high school here in Korea. She liked that it gave her a tingle of new-new, a nervous expectation, like how she felt when she used to perform for crowds playing the violin when she was younger. But then the image of her walking on the sidewalk with a backpack slung over her shoulder began to fade, and she wondered if it was what she wanted. To be half a world away from everyone she knew except her father and her grandmother. And she wasn't exactly thrilled with either of them at the moment.

Her father noticed she was unusually quiet. "Anna," he asked. "Did you not sleep well?"

"Are you accusing me of something?" Anna asked.

"Not at all," Edward replied. "Is there something you need to tell me?"

"No," Anna said. Then, unable to help herself, she added, "Is there something you need to tell me?"

This gave him pause, and Anna felt like she could hear the gears in his head spinning, trying to decide the best and most efficient way forward. They weren't far from the hotel. Perhaps whatever this was should be discussed at a later time.

"Do you want to talk now?" Edward asked. "I'm not sure what you're upset about. I thought you would be excited to hang out with your aunt and uncle. They're here because of you."

It was true. Anna was pleased that through her influence there would be a reunion of estranged loved ones. The last time they had all been together was Anna's *Baek-il*, a traditional Korean party held on the hundredth day after the birth of a child. The *Doljanchi*, a child's first birthday, was a bigger deal now, but Anna's grandmother was stubbornly old-school and had demanded a lavish *Baek-il* for Anna.

Anna had seen the pictures of herself dressed in a tiny Korean *han-bok*, a bit over-the-top for a three-and-a-half-month-old sitting next to a cake three times the size of her in the ballroom of their Greenwich house. In the family photos, Aunt Jules was there with her first husband, whom she left shortly thereafter and moved to Los Angeles. Halmeoni didn't believe in divorce, so it caused a major rift in the family. Aunt Jules, feeling unsupported in her decision to leave a failing marriage, couldn't fathom her own mother icing her out the way she had. After that, Aunt Jules was largely absent from the family, a phantom aunt sending gifts on birthdays and Christmas intermittently throughout the past seventeen years.

She had no idea what to expect when they were all together, but that seemed to be how her life was unspooling these days, not knowing what to expect from day to day. All she knew was that Aunt Jules had had her back after the Coachella debacle, and Anna had every intention of having her back in the same way if necessary.

The car pulled up to the Signiel Hotel, where Jules and Wilson were staying. It was the third highest hotel on the planet, located in the Lotte World Tower, and the restaurant on the 107th floor had a spectacular view of the hazy Seoul summer day. When Anna saw they would be dining in their own private room, she thought of the Valentine's Day lunch she and Vronsky had together in one of Keens Steakhouse's private rooms and how nervous yet thrilled she had been to be alone with him.

Anna and Edward met Halmeoni in the lobby, and the three of them arrived at the restaurant to find Jules and Wilson sitting at the bar, chatting with the bartender and one of the waiters. Anna beelined straight for them and hugged her aunt and uncle warmly, taking a bit of pleasure in the scowl that was surely present on her grandmother's face. Halmeoni looked down on loud public displays of affection, and there were only a handful of times in her entire life Anna could remember being hugged by her.

Once they were seated in the small private room, Jules made a joke about how they'd tucked them away in case of a food fight. Anna started to giggle at the thought of her grandmother participating in such a thing but stopped when her father gave her a look. When they chose seats, Anna quickly picked a chair between Jules and Wilson, an impolite move. As the youngest person present, she should have waited to be directed where to sit by the grown-ups.

After they all sat down, Jules and Wilson told them how amazing their suite was and they thanked Edward, who had upgraded their room for them. Anna knew these were the small overtures he made to show he cared without having to be demonstrative in other ways.

"I want to see it after lunch," Anna said, then quickly added, "Please."

"Of course," Aunt Jules said, "wait until you see the size of the bathtub."

"We could all fit in there together!" Wilson added excitedly. "Not naked, I mean, like fully dressed as an example of mass and cubic square feet of . . . quick, Anna! Change the subject, stat!"

"So, what does the rest of the day have in store?" Anna said, stifling a laugh.

Jules jumped in and said they had a whole list of off-the-beaten-path tourist attractions: a trick eye museum that only had trompe l'oeil paintings, a kimchi museum, an owl museum that was the life's work of one man obsessed with owls, and, if they had time, an abandoned amusement park from the 1980s. "Some people think it's haunted."

"Count me in for everything. They all sound cool. Too bad Steven isn't here . . . he had this stuffed owl he loved when he was a kid. He made little glasses out of tinfoil to match the ones Dad used to wear."

"I don't remember that," Edward said quietly, taking a sip of his hot green tea.

Anna looked at her father with annoyance. "What are you talking about? You have that picture in your office of me wearing Mickey ears, and Steven's holding Einstein. Must be nice to remember only the things you want to."

"Anna!" Halmeoni said. "Don't talk back to your father. Respect!"

Edward stared at his daughter, trying to interpret the subtext of his daughter's words. "Eoma, it's fine," Edward said. "She's right, I remember now."

"Apologize to your father, Anna," Halmeoni demanded.

"Mom, Edds just said it was . . ."

"Julia," she snapped. "I wasn't speaking to you. Though perhaps her behavior is your influence."

"Excuse me?" Anna asked. "My behavior? You mean speaking during a meal?"

"Anna," her father grumbled in warning.

"You know," Anna continued, even though she knew better. "Some families actually converse during mealtime."

Halmeoni slapped the table with a bang. "No more talking!"

Their waiter arrived with a sizzling hot plate of *bulgogi*, and everyone went silent. Then two more waiters showed up and soon the table was filled with Korean dishes: fried *mandu, japchae, bulgogi, soondubu jigae,* and sizzling scallion pancakes. When the waiters left, the silence continued for a few more moments. Anna knew she should apologize, but she resisted. She just sat there staring at the steaming bowls of food in front of her and, without thinking, picked up her chopsticks to grab a fried *mandu.* As she reached out, her grandmother stood up from her chair and grabbed the chopsticks out of Anna's hand. It happened so fast, they all froze. Anna's face flushed, but she didn't utter a sound. Instead she pulled her hand back, unable to meet anyone's eyes.

Jules stood up and tossed her napkin down on her seat. "Okay, so much for lunch. Hey, Anna, the owl museum is by the modern art museum. You, me, and your uncle can eat lunch at the café there."

Wilson stood up, too, though visibly bummed they wouldn't first be partaking in the feast before them. Anna stood up and grabbed her purse off the back of the chair.

"Anna, sit," Edward commanded.

"Not unless she apologizes for doing that and you apologize for not standing up for me. I'm not a child anymore. You can't just snatch chopsticks out of someone's hands and then pretend like nothing happened."

A waiter rushed over and asked if there was a problem, and Jules told him that unfortunately they had to leave. Anna looked at her father to see what he would do, but he didn't say anything, even though his eyes were dark with annoyance.

As Anna, Jules, and Wilson exited the private dining room, Jules put her arm around Anna's shoulders and pulled her in close. "Holy shit. Holy shit. Holy shit."

"That was freakin' crazy!" Uncle Wilson wheezed under his breath as they hustled out of the restaurant, leaving Halmeoni and Edward behind. As soon as they were out of sight, Wilson held up his hand and Anna smacked his palm a high-five.

Jules looked at her niece with materterine pride. "Anna, you just became my personal hero."

XXVII

On the third day of audition week Lolly and Jamieson met five minutes before the list for callbacks was posted so they could do their usual ritual of nervous clutching, sweaty hand squeezing, and barely contained squeaks of anticipation. Lolly got called back for Laurey and Annie, the two female leads, and Jamieson got called back for Curly and Jud, the two male leads. Normally they'd be ecstatic and jumping up and down, but this time they played it close to the vest because there were two worrisome names along with theirs in both places: Dean J. and Siobhan M.

Checking the other list, which matched up scene partners for the callbacks, they discovered they had not been paired together. Instead Lolly was to rehearse with Dean, and Jamieson with Siobhan. Lolly was not pleased about it. She already knew she and Jamieson had great chemistry. Having to audition with a stranger was always a crapshoot. Jamieson, however, was thrilled.

"It's like we can be spies. We need to see what's what with these two. Plus, maybe you could work on a kissing scene with Dean and then you can tell me all about it. I bet he tastes like warm jalapeño cornbread!"

Later on, Lolly showed up to the assigned practice room early and was surprised to find Dean already there reading a book. "Hey, you," she said.

Dean held up a finger and didn't look up from reading, which made Lolly wrinkle her nose in displeasure. She had no intention of being put on hold by a cocky boy she barely knew. "Is this the first time you've been to theater camp?"

Dean let the question linger for a moment or two, still not looking up from his book, *Cat's Cradle* by Kurt Vonnegut, which he then dog-eared and closed. "I'm sorry, I didn't mean to be an ass. I have this kind of tic where I have to get to the end of a page before I stop reading."

"What if the page ends in the middle of a sentence?" Lolly asked.

"That doesn't bother me. Weird, I know," Dean said. "But yeah, this is my first theater camp, is it that obvious?"

"Actually, yes." Lolly let out a small laugh. "You don't exactly exude musical theater."

"That's because every summer before this one I was playing summer league baseball."

Lolly's mouth dropped open at this revelation of jockdom and he noticed. "Well shucks, ma'am, I reckon you're just now realizing I'm a rootin' tootin' straight dude," he said in an exaggerated Texan accent. He laughed, but Lolly only gave him a polite smile. She wasn't used to acting out love scenes with straight boys. Her male scene partners were usually gay and she preferred it that way. She had zero interest in singing one of her favorite romantic duets of all time with a real cowboy. Also, there were several kisses in the play, which of course was no big deal for anyone serious about acting, but usually she was kissing a gay guy whose lips were softer than hers. For some reason the thought of kissing a straight boy onstage made her extremely nervous.

"I have a boyfriend," Lolly said. "Back in New York. I know you didn't ask, and maybe you don't care, but I want you to know that I take theater very seriously, and I really want to get the part of Laurey . . ."

"So you're saying that when you're giving me moony looks and batty-eyed glances it'll just be your superior acting prowess and nothing else," said Dean. "Got it."

Lolly tried to stifle a giggle and failed. This boy was very direct, but there was an ease of grace to his manner that was at odds with his masculinity. He just seemed so Texas, not that Lolly even fully knew what that implied. "Thank you for understanding. And I'll offer you the same courtesy, of course, if you have a girlfriend back home."

"Oh, there's no one waiting for me back home, I mean, besides my twin little sisters, but they're happy I'm gone because our dogs sleep in their beds now instead of mine." Dean looked around the empty rehearsal room. "Should we get this rodeo started?"

Without further prompting, Lolly launched into the opening line of "People Will Say We're in Love." Her mellifluous soprano voice filled the room as Dean chimed in with the next lyric When Lolly heard his deep buttery baritone, her heart began to pound. At the end of the song, when she had taken his arm and they were walking across imaginary ranchland, Dean stopped and turned to face Lolly. He pulled her close. She smiled up into his dazzling green eyes, and he stared deeply into hers. Her eyelashes fluttered so fast; she felt light-headed.

"Goddamn, girl! You are one hell of an actress. I truly felt like you were falling in love with me."

Lolly shrugged, struggling to keep her composure, because at the end of the song she had felt it, too. And she wasn't sure it was acting.

XXVIII

Anna asked if they could stop at the mall in the hotel so she could buy some different clothes for their outing. She had no desire to spend the day sightseeing in the stuffy floral Prada dress she had picked out to please her grandmother. Wilson went to the bar in the hotel lobby to get a wagyu hamburger while Anna and her aunt went shopping. Anna was still in shock over her walkout at lunch, while Jules seemed completely herself, as if nothing had happened at all.

"Was she mean to you, too?" Anna asked, looking through a towering stack of jeans at the Lotte department store. "Is that why you two don't see each other anymore?"

"We don't see each other anymore because we have never seen eye to eye on a wide array of topics, and there came a point in my life when I grew tired of pretending to be something I'm not."

"When you were a rebellious teenager like me?" Anna asked.

"I wish I'd had the courage when I was your age!" Jules said with a short laugh. "But for me it was when she didn't support me during my divorce." Jules explained her mother had forbid her to leave her marriage, telling her it would ruin her life.

"But you did it anyway?" Anna asked, knowing the answer already but wanting to hear about it firsthand.

"Sure did," Jules replied. "Though I was too scared to tell her for the first six months after I left him. I finally called her when I was at the Santa Monica Pier watching the carousel. She promptly hung up on me, and then I got on a blue horse and rode off into a metaphorical sunset, happy to be on my own. We didn't speak for a year."

"Whoa!" Anna exclaimed. "Were you scared?"

"I wouldn't say scared. But when I got off the ride I did feel like I was stepping into a whole new life. It's hard to explain."

"I understand," Anna said. "That's how my whole summer has been. I feel like I keep trying on different versions of myself, trying to see which one fits best."

"Be patient," Jules said. "It might take longer than you think."

After shopping they went back up to the hotel to pick up Wilson, only to find him still at the bar, talking to Edward. Anna froze, unsure of what to do. She wanted to make a run for it, but Jules told her she would have to face him eventually, and it would be better to do it now when she wasn't alone. "He won't get all shouty in a public place," Jules whispered.

"My dad has never shouted at me," Anna admitted. "I mean, of course I've seen him angry plenty of times, but he only yells at Steven. With me, he shuts down and ices me out."

But that wasn't what Edward was here to do at all. When she and Jules approached them, Anna was surprised to hear that her father had cleared his schedule so he could spend the day with them. She suppressed the urge to ask whether he was feeling okay but decided that would sound ungracious. All Anna managed was a half-hearted "great."

"All right then," Aunt Jules said. "Everybody ready to have some fun at an abandoned amusement park that may or may not be haunted?" She asked in the tone of a kindergarten teacher trying to engage a room full of bored, surly children.

"I am," Wilson said, pounding the rest of his beer and clunking the empty glass on the bar.

They took a private car from the hotel and rode in silence, everyone blank-staring out the windows. When they arrived at the amusement park, there weren't many people and the place had a post-apocalyptic feel to it. It was obvious right away that Edward regretted coming along. Anna told Jules and Wilson to go ahead and once they were out of earshot turned to her father. "Why did you come if you don't want to be here?"

"What are we doing here in the first place?" Edward asked. "Why anyone would find this entertaining, I haven't the faintest idea."

"That's the whole point!" Anna cried, unable to control her volume. "It's kitschy and cool. Aren't you interested in seeing new things?"

Edward gestured toward a dilapidated fence. "This seems the opposite of new. Anna, can't we go to a museum? Someplace normal . . . and clean."

"If that's what you want, then go!" Anna said. "But don't expect me to follow you anymore."

"Lower your voice!" Edward said.

"No!" Anna shouted. "I don't take orders from you anymore!"

"Orders?" Edward asked, his face showing he was truly confused by his daughter's growing fury. "What's going on here?"

"Why would you send him away with no hope?" Anna asked with a voice barely above a whisper.

"Who?" Edward asked. "Is this about my fight with Steven?"

"No," Anna said flatly. "This is about the fact that Alexia came to you on his hands and knees and begged you to see me, and you said no."

Edward pinched the top of his nose, a tic he passed down to Steven that indicated he was on the verge of an outburst. But he remained silent.

"Don't try to deny it," Anna said.

"I'm not," Edward said. "How do you even know about this?"

"I read it in a letter this morning!" Anna yelled. "A letter he wrote to me!"

If Edward was surprised over her mention of letters, he didn't show it. "How could I have known what was going to happen?"

"Maybe everything would be different!" Anna cried. "Maybe he'd still be alive."

"Maybe he would," Edward responded. "But that's not what happened."

"No, it's not," Anna said. Not feeling satisfied, she put her hands on her hips and tossed a grenade. "I want to go with Aunt Jules and Wilson on the *Orient-Express* in a few weeks. She told me this morning that I was welcome to join them. She invited me."

"She did?" Her father's brow crinkled in annoyance.

"After they leave Seoul, they're flying to London and then taking the train to Paris, Venice, and Verona. It's a week total and once we arrive back in London, I can fly to New York."

"New York? What are you talking about?"

"I'm spending Labor Day in the Hamptons with Mom and Steven. I know I'm not riding in the Hampton Classic this year, but I want to go."

Edward raised his hand. "You're in no position to dictate your plans to me."

"If you expect me to start some all-girls school here in a country where I don't even speak the language or have any friends, then why can't I spend my summer vacation doing things that I want to do?" Anna could count the number of fights she'd had with her father on one hand. She had been close to him, a true daddy's girl, and the only time they ever disagreed when she was younger was when he stopped her from competing in puissance high jumping, deeming it too dangerous. But even then she didn't dare talk to him as she did now.

Edward spoke calmly but firmly. "We decided time away would be good for you."

Anna shook her head. "Not we, *you* decided." No one ever really talked to her about what she wanted, the same way no one ever talked to her about anything in her life. "I'm going to be eighteen soon, which means . . ."

"You're still a minor who needs adult supervision."

"Aunt Jules is an adult."

"Hardly."

"How can you say that? What time have you spent with her in the last seventeen years? You're just as bad as Halmeoni, judging her so harshly when you don't even know her!" Anna's voice rose, and a couple walking out of the park glanced at them curiously.

"Stop, right now," Edward demanded. "I raised you better than this."

"Apparently not. Oh, and by the way, this has nothing to do with Steven, so don't blame him like you usually do. I know you blamed him for that night we snuck out in Italy, but it was my idea. I'm the one who wanted to go dancing."

"I highly doubt it was your idea to get drunk."

"Don't you see what you're doing? Repeating history, unfairly blaming him like your mother unfairly blames Aunt Jules. I'm my own person whether you like it or not, and when I make a decision it's not because someone else made me, so if I have to respect you then you should have to respect me, too."

Anna's eyes were fiery with anger as she ran into the abandoned amusement park to go find her aunt and uncle.

XXIX

By the end of the week, the Interlochen auditions had reached a fever pitch, and it was all anyone could talk about. It turned out that Siobhan's talents were on a par with Lolly's, but as Lolly was the old guard most everyone was Team Lolly, while Siobhan was being unfairly cast as the villain. Lolly was not a fan of pitting girls against each other and tried to tamp down the talk whenever she could, but she was totally distracted by two things. First, she was scared that Siobhan might actually win the lead role of Laurey. Secondly, and even worse, Siobhan would be the one caught in a love triangle with Dean and Jamieson.

Dean and Jamieson were both being considered for the two top male roles, but everyone predicted that Dean was going to be chosen for Curly. He couldn't be more perfect for the part and, whenever Dean sang, he had every girl in camp starry-eyed and thirsting for him.

Lolly and Jamieson walked over to wait for the posting of the roles and were surprised to find everyone already there. Every girl Lolly passed reached out to touch her and wish her good luck, which she appreciated, but it also made her feel for Siobhan, who was currently getting the cold shoulder. Lolly whispered something in Jamieson's ear, and the two of them crossed over to Siobhan, who was sitting alone in the grass.

"Hey, Siobhan, just wanted to say good luck," Lolly said. "And no matter what happens I think you're really talented and I'd love to hear about the Yale admissions process sometime."

Siobhan looked up at Lolly, shielding her eyes from the morning sun. "Thanks. I know I should say the same to you, but I don't think you need luck today. You and Dean have great chemistry, so it's probably for the good of the show . . ." Her words came out in a matter-of-fact manner, and Lolly was floored by the other girl's frankness and maturity. Lolly didn't love Siobhan's implication that she might get the part because of her and Dean's attraction for each other, but before she could unpack all that, she heard people clapping behind her and turned to see the director walking toward the door with the cast list. Everyone rose to their feet all at once, and Jamieson squeezed Lolly's hand so hard she felt her knuckles crunch. The other campers waited to rush the list so she and Jamieson could check first. Lolly looked around to see if Dean was there but she couldn't spot him. Dean had proven himself to be a bit of a loner and could often be found reading by himself, but perhaps it was because everyone at camp had been talking about him incessantly. It was like every day he got more and more mysterious and more and more handsome as his legend grew. And now that the show was cast, he would be even more revered and respected as the first-year phenom who'd landed the lead.

Dean had won the role of Curly, and Lolly won the role of Laurey. Jamieson was awarded the part of Jud, and Siobhan was cast as Annie, the second female lead. But in an odd turn of events, Siobhan was cast as Lolly's understudy as well, while the boys each had their own understudy. Lolly was relieved at getting the part she wanted and thought her anxiety would dissipate, but instead it seemed to be increasing. Still, she wasn't going to let a little latent dread get in the way of her good mood.

Another thing Lolly liked about camp was that it gave her a break from her normally arduous beauty routine. Here, she barely wore makeup except for a little bit to the Monday night dances. Those were the only moments when they actually had time to post on social media. But when it was time to meet Dean for their first night of rehearsal, she found herself putting on mascara, lipstick, and perfume, rationalizing that she was getting into character as a girl who was caught in a love triangle between two men. Who cared if she was going a little more Method than usual? She arrived early to warm up, only to find Dean already there, tipping his cowboy hat at her once again. Before she could say hello, the show's student director, Taleen M., burst through the door with bloodshot eyes saying they were on their own for rehearsal because she had to deal with some personal drama back home in Jersey. When Lolly asked her if everything was okay, the girl threw herself into Lolly's arms and said that her boyfriend back home had sent her a care package, but the note inside was addressed to her best friend, who was currently at soccer camp.

"Do you think it means what I think it means?" she asked pitifully, and Lolly hugged her a little tighter.

"Probably, but you need to confront him and find out the truth. Just know this has nothing to do with you and everything to do with him. And you may possibly need a new bestie." Lolly told her not to worry about rehearsal; she was an old pro and could help Dean with the choreography. When Taleen left, Dean started to blow smoke rings around the room with a vape. One sniff and Lolly knew it was pot, and she let out a yelp like a puppy whose tail just got stepped on. Getting caught with drugs was grounds for immediate expulsion, and though Lolly liked to party as much as the next person, she was squeaky clean when it came to camp and would never under any circumstances do drugs at Interlochen.

Dean said he had a doctor's note that gave him a get-out-of-jail-free pass, but Lolly didn't believe him. He gave her a wry smile and assured her it was the truth. "It's medicinal," he said. "I swear." He went on to tell her he had never been to an artsy-fartsy camp like this before because all he'd ever wanted to be was a professional baseball player. But three summers ago, a week before he was about to leave for baseball camp in Nevada, he fractured his leg on an early morning run before school. It turned out Dean had telangiectatic osteosarcoma, a rare type of bone cancer. So, after six months of chemotherapy and two surgeries to put titanium rods in his leg, his baseball dreams were dead and he had no choice but to utilize his secondary talent: a rich baritone singing voice.

Lolly stared at him, unsure if he was telling the truth. He looked perfectly healthy, but why would anyone lie about such a terrible thing? Finally finding her words, she said the only thing that popped into her head: "I always thought Ansel Elgort was miscast in *The Fault in Our*

Stars because he was way too hot and hearty to play someone with cancer, but I guess I was mistaken." By the time she realized how flirty it sounded, Dean was laughing, telling her that was hands down the best response he'd ever gotten. He thanked her for not getting all weird about it like most girls. He was not a guy who was interested in pity sex, though he'd be willing to accept it from her if she was offering.

Lolly told him pity sex with her was not on the table, though there were few things she enjoyed more than matchmaking if he needed any introductions. Dean declined the offer. He could do all right on his own, though he appreciated her willingness to help him find a camp romance.

"Should we get to work?" Dean asked, holding out his hand for Lolly. Dean's hand was strong and lightly calloused and felt very different from Steven's hands, which were smooth and soft like expensive leather.

"Do you have to work with your hands a lot down in Texas?" she asked.

"These hands have lifted many, many things." He grabbed Lolly by her waist and lifted her up like she was lighter than air.

Lolly squealed, laughing and flapping her arms, batting at Dean's shoulders. "Put me down!"

He lowered her to the ground, and she smacked his arm, laughing.

"Ow!" He grabbed his shoulder and winced in pain.

"Oh my god, did I hurt you?"

He waited a moment and smiled at her, his eyes twinkling. "Darlin', it'd take more than a little pip like you to take me down, though finding out you had a boyfriend sure did sting a little."

"You faker! Don't you dare scare me like that." Lolly swatted him again for good measure. She could sense she was in dangerous territory, so she delivered her first line: "Why do they think up stories that link my name with yours?"

And Dean answered, "Why do the neighbors gossip all day behind their doors?"

And then, Lolly began to sing. They had now performed this song several times during auditions, and she assumed she'd get used to him holding her close at the end, their faces only inches apart. But by the end of the song she still felt a little dizzy. Dean wasn't as tall as Steven, but

Lolly could feel the strength in his arms as he held her, the arms that had lifted her up with such ease.

If it weren't for the sound of someone whistling behind them, Lolly didn't know what might have happened. She whipped around to find Jamieson standing in the doorway, two fingers in his mouth, blowing another high-pitched whistle like he was catcalling. "Daaaaamn, y'all! This is like week one of rehearsals and you're already looking like Brad and Angelina on the set of *Mr. and Mrs. Smith*!"

Lolly blushed and stepped away. "Yeah, it wasn't bad."

"Wasn't bad? Girl, that was Broadway ticket price of admission spectacular! I'm gonna have to up my game or I'm gonna be in trouble."

"Well, get over here and practice with us then." Lolly's voice had a giddiness in it that was unfamiliar to her. And right then she knew it.

She was the one who was in trouble.

Part Three

I'll go up beyond the sky
하늘을 넘어서 올라갈 거야
I want to run fast without knowing the end
끝을 모르게 빨리 달리고 싶어

—BLACKPINK

I

It was almost two in the morning when Anna returned home after sneaking out. Tonight she had gone to Club Arena, a nightclub known for having a well-dressed crowd. Anna had worn a metallic Saint Laurent minidress with chandelier earrings that she now regretted because they made her earlobes ache from all the dancing. As she tiptoed through the marble foyer toward her room, her father called out her name. In the darkness, she stopped and wiped her lipstick off on the inside of her wrist. She quickly pulled off her dramatic fake eyelashes and stuck them to the back of her cross-body Chloé bag.

Edward was sitting at the dining room table waiting for her in the dark. Anna wasn't sure if she should turn on the light or not. She decided dark was better so he wouldn't be able to see her makeup. She stood in the doorway and tried to keep her voice light and casual. "Hey, Dad, I thought you were staying at work late tonight."

"I did. It's two in the morning."

"Is it?" she said, trying to sound as innocent as possible. "I thought it was earlier. I'm sorry, I should have texted you I was going out."

"Who were you with?" he asked. "Quentin?"

Anna debated telling her father the truth about Quentin and Minsoo, but she wasn't sure if she could manage it without confessing that she had agreed to do PR on behalf of The NowNows. She'd spent most of the afternoon filming a new TikTok with Quentin under Aileen's supervision.

Now in the wee hours of the night, staring at her father, who seemed a bit red in the face and bleary-eyed, Anna ran through a few different lies in her head before realizing she was too tired to make things up for his benefit and told him the truth. "I was out by myself. I couldn't sleep so I went out to a club to dance for a while, which usually tires me out. I take a car there and back so it's safe." Anna wanted to pull out a chair and sit down. She had at least three blisters from her new heels, and her feet were killing her, but she couldn't see Edward's face so she wasn't sure how mad he was at the moment.

Anna had managed to avoid being alone with her father since their argument at the amusement park. It hadn't proved too difficult with her aunt and uncle in town. Anna would have a quick breakfast with her grandmother and father then head over to the hotel, where she and Jules and Wilson would plan out their day together. They usually started with a random weird activity, then lunch, and then they'd spend the afternoon indoors at a museum or movie theater to escape the humidity. At the end of the day, the trio would meet up with Halmeoni and Edward for dinner somewhere with everyone sticking to a few safe topics of conversation: the weather, the food, and how everyone's day had gone.

Now coming home from a club, Anna was forced to confront him alone. "You know I trust you," Edward said. "But I would prefer if you would at least let me know where you're going."

"You would have let me go?" Anna asked, a note of incredulity in her voice.

"I don't know. Probably."

"So you're not upset?"

Edward sighed. "I am upset, but not for the reason you think. I've just been sitting here in my mother's dining room, alone, in the dark, separated from a wife I love, and on the verge of losing one of the most important relationships I have." His voice was wavering; his voice never wavered.

"Oh, Dad," Anna said, pulling out the chair at the head of the table, the chair he usually sat in when they ate. "You're not losing me. I'm not going out trying to meet boys or anything like that." She had a fleeting thought that while she wasn't going out to meet any flesh-and-blood boys, she was reaching out to meet Vronsky's spirit somehow. "I go out dancing because I miss him, which may sound stupid to you, but . . ."

"It doesn't sound stupid," Edward said softly. "After my father died, I took golf lessons for a few months."

"Really?" Anna asked. "You hate golf."

"Exactly. But my father loved it, so I thought if I learned how to play, I'd feel closer to him."

"Did it work?"

"My heart was in the right place I suppose. But I didn't have the patience to keep playing. Also I wasn't very good. Anna, my responsibility as your father is to protect you. That's why I want you to go to school here. And if I'm being honest, part of the reason may be a selfish one. I need a change of scenery myself, and I thought it would be good for both of us."

"You may be right," she began. "But isn't that what we've been doing this entire summer? Being away has been good for me, for sure. But I change my mind every day about what I want to do with school. Half of me thinks I'm being a coward by not going back. The other half of me never wants to go back because I feel like all of Manhattan will be haunted by the ghosts of boyfriends past, but then I think, why should I let myself be defined by my relationships with men: Alexander, Alexia, and you. It's like I know what all of you wanted for me, but wouldn't it be the braver choice to go back and figure out what I want . . . for myself?"

"So you think I'm pressuring you about staying here for school?"

"Not exactly, but I know it's what you prefer. I have a hard time separating out my own preferences from yours. Like violin. I played because you liked it."

"You played because you were excellent."

"No, I was excellent because I practiced all the time. Just because I was good at it doesn't mean I liked it. I'm good at calculus, but I'm not a fan."

"So now you're only interested in pleasing yourself?"

"Dad," Anna said with a touch of exasperation. "You know that's not what I'm saying." They sat in silence for a tense moment. "I'm just hoping you'll support me making choices for myself."

"What choices are we talking about . . . ?"

"I am going on the *Orient-Express* with Aunt Jules and Wilson. I know this isn't the real one, but it's close enough, and they are so much fun to sightsee with. They don't just look at art, they talk about it. It's a real shame you and Aunt Jules aren't close. I worry the same thing could happen to Steven and me, even though I know we won't let it. That's how people stay close, someone has to try to keep the connection alive. Aunt Jules told me she's made overtures over the years, but you never reciprocated. You put so much work into your . . . work. I wish . . ." Anna trailed off.

"You wish . . . what?"

"I wish you would choose to put more energy into your relationships," Anna said. "And I'm not talking about ours. I know you try hard with me. But with Steven . . ."

"What about him?"

"You have to cut him some slack. I know you two have always locked horns, but he's an amazing brother and I love him. My mistakes are my mistakes. They don't have anything to do with him. You hurt his feelings when you always assume the worst. He's really grown up a lot lately."

"And if I agree to all your demands?" Edward asked.

"I'll go to Branksome Hall on Jeju. It had the best view, and I liked that teacher I met, Isabella," Anna said. "But if after one semester I'm miserable, then I get to go back home and finish school in the city. Also, I'm only boarding during the week. I want to be free on the weekends to see you and my dogs in Seoul, or wherever you are. I don't want to feel like you're locking me away as a punishment."

"Is that what you think I'm doing?"

"Kinda. I know I disappointed you with how things ended between me and Alexander. I wish I had made better choices. But I don't regret falling in love. Alexia was a wonderful person, and it wasn't just some childish crush. It was the real thing. And he saved my life, you know . . . it could have been me who got hit by that train."

"Stop!" Edward barked, then softened. "Sorry, I don't mean to yell. Anna, please, the thought of losing you makes me ill. I owe him my full respect for saving you. But I've thought a lot about my meeting with him, and I'm sorry to say, but I wouldn't have done things differently. That's the truth. I did what I thought was best for you at the time."

"But—" Anna began to speak.

"Let me finish," Edward said. "But if things had turned out differently, I'd like to believe that I would have liked him once I got to know him better."

"Thanks, Dad," Anna said, wondering why it took a shouting match in an abandoned amusement park to get them to where they could speak thoughtfully to each another.

"Actually, I already booked your train tickets," Edward said. "I was going to tell you tomorrow. Lucky you, the only room left was the grand suite, so you'll be traveling in style. Though the nice thing to do would be to trade rooms with your aunt and uncle."

"Really, are you serious?"

"I'm always serious," her father said.

"That's amazing! Thank you. Of course I'll give them the bigger room. Uncle Wilson is a big dude, he'll need the extra space."

"I tried to change my schedule so I could go on one of the legs with you, but I don't think I can swing it. Maybe I can meet you in Venice on the return trip, we'll see. But as you keep reminding me, it's your summer and you should have some fun."

Anna crossed over to her dad and sat on his lap. "I love you. I'm sorry we fought. I don't like fighting with you."

"Me neither," Edward agreed. "Let's not make a habit of it."

"What are you going to do about Mom?" Anna asked.

"Sharing time is over," Edward said as he stood up from the table. "You worry about you, and let me worry about everything else, okay?"

"Deal," Anna said.

II

Bea had learned a lesson from her Mexico sunburn fiasco and spent a good ten minutes slathering on SPF 50 all over her body before putting on her bikini. She put on sweatpants and a hoodie in the A.M. darkness, and by four fifteen, she was in an Uber, dozing off for the eighty-two-mile trip to Santa Barbara. Normally Bea wasn't an early riser, but she hadn't given the early morning wake-up a second thought. For the first time in her life, Bea was completely, achingly, triumphantly in love. *So this was what all the fuss was about,* she thought, *why pop stars wrote love songs, or why rock stars wrote power ballads.* She was catching herself smiling all the time, like right now walking down the hill toward the beach looking at Tiare in the distance with surfboard under her arm, Bea couldn't wipe the stupid grin off her face if she tried.

She checked her Apple Watch. They still had a little time to hang out before the sun came up and Tiare headed off to her other love, the ocean.

In order to get up at this ungodly hour, Bea had gone to bed early on Friday night. Her new goal was to spend as much time with Tiare as she could before summer was over.

Bea asked if she could come up the night before, but Tiare said she had to work. Tiare didn't take risks when it came to her job, but she admired Bea's unrelenting drive to corrupt her work ethic, while Bea admired her new girlfriend's ability to tell her no.

Last night, when Chadwick had knocked on her door to see if she wanted to join him and Manny for a late movie, he was surprised to find her in bed with a face mask on, scrolling through TikTok. "I'm meeting Tiare at Harbor Beach super early."

"When are you coming back?"

"Sunday." It was the first time Tiare wasn't working since getting back from Mexico, and it would be their first chance to really hook up since

Sayulita Beach had been a bust in that respect. Bea wanted to take advantage of every second of the summer she had left.

Chadwick smiled and sat down on the edge of her bed. "If I told your mother you were in bed before ten on a Friday night . . ."

"She'd think I was terminal."

"So what's next for you and your surf goddess?" Chadwick asked.

"Look at you, always the manager. Can't help but look toward the future, always needing a plan."

"What's the plan?" he said. "You're only here another two weeks."

"My plan is to spend as much time with her as I possibly can and then . . . fuck if I know. Maybe I won't go back East. Maybe I'll just stay out here with you and Manny."

"We've got good schools out here."

"You're serious?" Bea asked.

Chadwick raised his eyebrows. "If you are."

"Let's just all stay in the moment and be grateful for this time right now . . ." Then after a moment she added, "Look, I'm only confiding in you because you're the one who called it from the jump-off. This is all new for me, so I can't really talk about it yet. Does that make sense?"

"It does, sorry. I didn't mean to be pushy."

"It's okay, boomer," Bea said with a laugh. "Go ahead. Tell me about the ways of love."

Chadwick put his arm around his niece's shoulder. "When you find love, the kind that makes you feel like you won the lottery because you didn't think it was possible to feel this good without the help of controlled substances . . . well, you gotta enjoy it, you know. Really take it in. Because you don't know how long it'll last."

"What goes up, must come down? Yeah, I give the same speech to friends trying Molly for the first time. It's fun for a while, but the comedown is always nipping at your heels."

"Yeah, that's true. But what I'm saying is I wish someone told me about embracing big love when I had the chance, because I think I let a lot of opportunities drift away."

Bea stayed silent during her uncle's speech though she felt her phone vibrating next to her. She knew who it was without looking: Claudine. Bea had basically ghosted her by going radio silent, which caused Claudine to call Bea's mom, who told her Beatrice was in Mexico. When she got back, Bea lied and said she'd lost her phone. She did feel a smidgen of guilt that Claudine was climbing the walls wondering why Bea was suddenly becoming more elusive, but Claudine had been calling her at odd hours to check in with her. She was getting more and more clingy, and Bea just couldn't deal with telling her about Tiare. She would protect what she had with Tiare at all costs and didn't want to discuss it with anyone. She hadn't even told Adaka, her most trusted friend back in Connecticut.

She knew this was special, what was happening right now, how she and Tiare had fallen in love during a weekend when they literally had no cares in the world, except what to order from room service and what to tell housekeeping when they flooded the bathroom by pouring a whole bottle of shower gel into the tub and turning on the Jacuzzi jets.

It had worked, that impromptu summer getaway, even though she had gotten sunburned and peeled like a snake sloughing off its skin. LA was supposed to have been her escape, but her sadness over Vronsky's death haunted her wherever she went. Thanks to Tiare, it was like her heart had been patched, it could expand and bear weight again after being punctured, no, slashed, by her cousin's untimely death. After flooding the bathroom, she and Tiare had stayed up late into the night talking about Vronsky. Tiare's opinion was that Beatrice was stuck in the denial part of the Kübler-Ross stages of grief, and if she ever hoped to get over it, she needed to push through the other stages, no matter how painful it turned out to be.

"But maybe I don't want to get over it. He was the person I loved most in the world and now I'm supposed to move on like he never existed? I could never. He deserves better than that," Bea said with a bit more venom than she intended. "Sorry, I'm not angry at you, I'm pissed at Kübler and Ross acting like they know my fucking life."

"Actually," Tiare had said as she rubbed lotion all over Bea's pink back, "maybe you're in the middle of the denial *and* the anger phase."

"Oh, I'm angry all right. I couldn't go to the memorial in Italy because that bitch was going to be there. If I went, I would have tackled her to the ground and made her eat dirt."

"Violence is not one of the stages, FYI," Tiare said gently. "Besides, it's not like she pushed him in front of the train."

"Are you kidding me? She *was* the train!" Bea said. "He was perfectly happy flitting about from girl to girl, and there was a long list waiting patiently for their turn. But as soon as he laid eyes on her, it was game over. All Anna, all the time. It's all he could talk about. She made him obsessed."

"You mean like how you're now obsessed with me?" Tiare asked in a teasing tone, her shadow falling across Bea as she dried herself off with a towel. "Am I your train? Are you happier flitting about from boy to girl? Is that really better? All these random hookups, never really getting to know anyone in a deep or meaningful way?"

Bea knew what Tiare was getting at, but she wasn't quite ready to be rational yet. "We're not talking about me, we're talking about him. This is a totally different situation."

Tiare changed the subject and started telling her how she'd spent her teen years being angry at her dad, a father she never knew because he had abandoned her before she was born. Her mother had struggled to support the two of them. Ultimately she left Tahiti so she could come to America and care for someone else's children. She would send money home to her mother, Tiare's grandmother, who was caring for Tiare on the island. All because some guy was looking for a quick lay and was fine with lying to get it. Tiare was born out of a one-night stand between a liar and a woman who was just trying to escape her life for one night.

Tiare was finally able to join her mother in the United States for middle school, and during her first week, she got into a fight and was suspended. Her mother was irate and told her she was sick and tired of her temper. She made Tiare spend her days writing letters to the father she'd never met, to her mother for getting taken in by a handsome tourist, to the teachers she felt were mean. And then they went to the beach at midnight. In a small boat her mother had borrowed from a friend, they went out into the dark water using only the stars and moon for a guide. Her mom rolled up Tiare's letters and put them in a bottle. She made Tiare fling the bottle out into the water as an offering to the Māori god of the sea, Tangaroa. Her mother told her Tangaroa's mythological son, Punga, would find them. Punga was the ancestral god of sharks, sting rays, and all deformed and ugly things. Punga would read the letters, delight in them, and gobble up the anger for his meal.

Tiare knew it was a silly fable, but it made her feel better. Her mother told her that holding on to anger didn't make a person stronger, even though it felt like fuel for strength. She would only get stronger if she could understand that letting go was the best way to move forward.

Beatrice thanked Tiare for sharing her story and promised to consider her perspective, but she just wasn't ready to let go of Vronsky yet. Tiare told her she'd know when it was the right time, then gave her a quick smooch before putting on a robe and announcing they should order a banana split from room service. Bea remembered thinking how different Tiare's and Claudine's reactions were to her anger over Anna's part in Vronsky's death. Tiare worked to calm Bea down, while Claudine stirred up Bea's feelings into a frenzy and talked about all the ways they could get revenge on Anna for what she did.

At the time Bea had appreciated Claudine's willingness to hate what she hated, but now she saw how much more she needed Tiare's perspective. Tiare wasn't all about the cancel culture, instead she looked for ways to heal. She was a mender, as opposed to Claudine, who reveled in takedowns and destruction. Perhaps that was why Bea no longer felt the same way about Claudine. She no longer wanted to invite chaos into her life.

"Morning, beautiful!" Tiare called out when she spotted Bea walking toward her on Harbor Beach.

"Just catching some worms!" Bea shouted back and Tiare gave her a puzzled look. "'Cuz I'm the early bird."

"Aha! I get it," said Tiare. "Now get your corny ass over here and give me a kiss."

Bea broke into a run.

III

Bea had always been proud of her sexual conquests. She was a firm believer that women shouldn't be penalized for having a strong libido. She used her sexuality like a weapon, and it made her feel powerful when people wanted her. But what she hadn't realized with Tiare was that there was a whole new level of intimacy that she never knew existed. Kissing someone you truly loved was just different, and Beatrice couldn't quite figure out why. What made Tiare's lips softer and sweeter than any lips she had ever kissed before? Why did it feel like rockets were launching in her head every time Tiare's tongue met hers? She wasn't even drunk or high, she had been sober for all of it.

In fact Bea was hardly drinking or doing any drugs these days, and she had to admit she felt healthier. She didn't know if it was the whole California lifestyle rubbing off on her or if she no longer needed the usual rush of chemicals because she was getting all the endorphins she needed from Tiare.

Because of her sunburn, she and Tiare hadn't done much more than make out in Mexico. She'd tried to convince Tiare she was totally fine to roll around in the sack, but Tiare insisted they wait. Their first night of lovemaking should be when Bea was feeling 100 percent. At first she was bummed, but now Bea was happy they waited because she had never experienced this incredible build-up of anticipation. Bea rarely ever delayed gratification for anything. Great wealth and permissive absentee parents had given Bea seventeen years of not only getting pretty much everything she wanted whenever she wanted it but the freedom to go after it however she wanted as well. It was, she had naively thought, how anyone would want to live their lives, but now Tiare was opening her eyes to an entirely new outlook.

Beatrice was hoping that tonight was going to be the night that they would go all the way. When she found out that Tiare had the day and night off she said she'd book them a hotel room, but Tiare said she wanted to plan their day, and so Bea handed her the reins. Tiare was the first girl, or boy for that matter, who didn't want Bea to buy her presents and take her to fancy restaurants, although Bea finally convinced Tiare that she had to let her get her at least one present. Tiare agreed, but said it was unnecessary. She was not someone who cared about material objects and she didn't need gifts to know that Bea cared about her.

"Totally!" Bea said and immediately grilled her friends at work to find out the best surfboard maker on the West Coast. She was going to buy Tiare a new board, the best that money could buy.

Bea spent the morning watching Tiare surf the Sandspit, a surfing area that was accidentally created when a group of engineers were tasked with protecting a boat harbor in 1929 and added a breakwater, which created some pretty awesome waves in a shallow area. Tiare told Beatrice it was a place that surfers went when the other spots were overcrowded. Sandspit kept newbies away because if you got tossed there, it really hurt. Also, seven years before, a surfer got chased by a fourteen-foot great white. Bea liked that she and Tiare both courted danger in different ways. It was a fearlessness they both respected and understood in the other. Beatrice had never been in a committed relationship before and neither had Tiare, because she was never living in one place for long. But today even though there were plenty of beautiful California girls and boys strutting about, there was only one surfer Bea wanted to watch, and that was the girl in the neon-green bikini.

After surfing, Tiare drove them to her favorite breakfast burrito spot, Lito's. Bea pointed to a sign saying that Lito's was featured in *Diners, Drive-Ins and Dives*. "My cousin loved that show. He used to talk about us driving cross-country and visiting places from his favorite episodes. I thought he was nuts. Roughing it across the country. Me and him? They don't even have Four Seasons in most of those cities."

"You know there are good things that don't cost a lot," Tiare said.

"I know that," Bea replied.

Tiare smiled at her. "Do you?"

"Fine, maybe I don't, but I will if this burrito is as good as you say it is," Beatrice said.

Tiare ate two in the time it took Beatrice to eat one, and afterward Beatrice admitted it was the best breakfast burrito she had ever had, definitely better than the thirty-dollar one at the Four Seasons in Mexico.

"See, money isn't everything," Tiare said. "And by the way, I'm paying for our date today. My way of saying thank you for Mexico. Now on to the next surprise."

When they pulled up to the zoo, Bea exchanged a quizzical look with Tiare. They walked to the ticket booth, holding hands, and Tiare flashed her ID card. She introduced Bea as her girlfriend to one of her coworkers, which gave Bea an unexpected thrill. Then Tiare led her through the zoo, and they ended up at the otter enclosure. "Recognize any of them?" She pointed at some of the sleepy rascals floating on their backs.

Bea peered through the glass and saw two small otters sunbathing on a rock. "Jesse and Walter?" She nearly cooed.

"Today's their very first day out here in the big leagues."

Bea was unexpectedly moved by this gesture. That very first night, when they'd fed the baby otters bottles, really was one of the most magical nights of her life, and now she knew it had been for Tiare as well.

"I love them," Bea said, pressing her face up to the glass.

"I love you," said Tiare.

Bea turned to stare at Tiare. "What did you say?"

"You heard me."

"I did, but can you say it again?"

"I love you, Bea."

Bea's heart pounded, and she felt a head rush that left her a little dizzy. Before she could stop them, her eyes welled up with tears. "I super fucking love you, too!"

IV

Jamieson and Lolly spent a lot of their free time talking about Dean. In fact, it was more than a lot. It was pretty much all of it.

Dean had asked Lolly not to share his medical condition with anyone, as he had no interest in whipping up a frenzy of girls wanting to be the Hazel to his Augustus. She swore she wouldn't tell a soul except for Jamieson because he would put a curse on her to turn her hair frizzy if she got caught withholding information from him. "Frizzy hair is my kryptonite."

She explained that Jamieson's frizzy hair curse was legendary and not to be put to the test. "If it be your will, darlin'," Dean said. "Just tell him not to blow all that hay around the barn."

"I will tell him that, but with a metaphor he can understand."

When Lolly told Jamieson the next day during their walk after breakfast, he immediately said, "Oh my god, I'll be his Hazel if he'll be my Augustus." Lolly giggled, though she didn't tell Jamieson why. Dean had sworn to Lolly that he wasn't dying and had been in good health for over a year. He didn't want special treatment anymore, which to him was the worst part of being sick. Lolly declared herself Dean's love guru and said she would help him choose the right girl from the many clamoring for his attention.

"He always finds the dumbest reasons not to like a girl," Lolly complained, lying on a blanket outside with Jamieson after lunch. "Today when I told him he should totally date Annabel B. because she's the best dancer and also super bendy, he said he couldn't because she was from Brooklyn. Apparently, he hated Brooklyn because Brooklyn beat his team from Texas in the Little League World Series when he was ten years old. I thought he was making it up, but 'enemy of Brooklyn' is actually in his bio on Insta."

"Oh Lolls, methinks you've been leaving your hair masks in for too long. The chemicals are making you clueless," Jamieson said. "The real reason why he keeps rejecting everyone . . ." Jamieson handed Lolly a bottle of sky-blue nail polish so she could paint his nails. " . . . is because he only has eyes for Siobhan!" he said in a pretty damn good Irish accent. "He wants to have these perfect strawberry-blond babies with her."

Lolly's eyes flew open in surprise. "What? Did he tell you he's into her? I swear if one more person tells me how she was a wildling extra on *Game of Thrones*, I'm going to scream."

Jamieson blew on his nails to help them dry faster. "I knew it! The look on your face! If looks could kill, I'd be deader than Jackson Maine!" Jamieson held out his right hand for Lolly.

"I know I seemed jealous right then, but I'm not. I have a boyfriend who I'm madly in love with. She's just wrong for Dean, that's all," Lolly said, hoping she didn't sound too defensive.

"And why is that? Is it because her skin is actually too poreless? Or maybe her eyes are too cerulean blue?"

"Ugh, I hate her." Lolly sighed dramatically. "Fine, so maybe I have the tiniest little itty-bitty camp crush on Dean, but it's only because he's such a good singer and actor. I mean he's only been a theater geek for a year, so it seems unfair he should have such natural talent without working at it."

"It is sickening," Jamieson agreed.

"Revolting! And that dumb Texas cowboy thing!"

"Like nails on a chalkboard." Jamieson sat up and tipped a fake cowboy hat. "*'Scuse me, darlin'.* Like that would work on anyone!"

"And his dumb handsome face with only one dimple on the left side. Totally weird and asymmetrical."

"I know! And the way his hair smells like strawberry jam on toast. Could he be any more hetero and manly? Such a phony!"

"You know he's probably the worst kisser. And what girl would want his firm, leathery hands all over her body? Not me."

Jamieson burst out laughing, which made Lolly yell at him for moving his hand and smudging a nail. "So, I was thinking. Shouldn't you have a free Cheatie-McCheat pass since Steven boned that hoebag last January?"

"It doesn't work that way." Lolly finished painting Jamieson's pinky nail and began to blow on his fingertips. "But it does seem like he likes me, right?" Lolly hated herself for asking, but she couldn't help it.

"He's so into you. The way he stares at you when you sing, it's like he wants to make a s'more out of you and munch on you by the campfire. And don't say he's just acting, because if that's him acting, then he's the next Jake Gyllenhaal." Jamieson, always the troublemaker, told her that camp was like Vegas: "What happens at Interlochen, stays at Interlochen." His argument was that camp life wasn't reality; it was a respite from the rest of the world, where campers were free to do whatever they wanted with whoever they wanted. It was the same loophole that all the Hollywood actors used, having torrid affairs on movie sets with their costars and then going back to LA to their significant others like nothing happened. "It's good for your art. You need to expose yourself to a wide array of sexual experiences in order to create a rich emotional palette from which to draw during your performances. At least that's what they said in my new favorite acting podcast."

"I can't. Steven would kill me, or worse, kill Dean."

Jamieson's eyes lit up. "Who'd win in a bar fight, Dean or Steven?"

"Dean's shorter than Steven, but he's got those red-state, I-can-chop-wood-real-good muscles, where Steven's more wiry but really strong, too. Though if Steven didn't think he could kill him with his bare hands, he'd just pay someone to do it for him."

"Ah, to be in a love triangle." Jamieson shivered with envy. "How glam! You know I was just teasing about Dean liking Siobhan. It's totally obvious he'd like to sauce you up and work you like a rib!"

Lolly admitted how fun it was to have someone crushing on her. All her life, she'd been the girl who did the crushing, so it was flattering to be on the receiving end. It was especially refreshing that Dean liked her without her makeup or fancy clothes.

"I'm only gonna say this once: you're a total knockout with makeup or without and you're the only one who doesn't think so. Instead of body dysmorphia issues, you have beauty dysmorphia issues, and I find it super sexy that Dean appreciates you for the natural beauty that you are . . . can you say the same about the great Steven K.?"

Lolly frowned at Jamieson's question. Not because it offended her, but because she honestly didn't know the answer.

It was Anna's last day in Seoul before she headed to London, where she would spend some time with her two Newfoundland dogs, Gemma and Jon Snow. She had missed them every day and couldn't wait for them to charge and tackle her to the ground. After visiting with the pooches in London, she would leave for her trip on the *Venice Simplon-Orient-Express*. Then she'd head to the Hamptons for Labor Day weekend.

Before Anna left Seoul, she needed have a good-bye lunch with Chang-ri, then one more dinner with her grandmother. Over dinner she and her father were going to announce that Anna had decided to go to Branksome Hall. Edward would explain that he and Anna were getting their own place in Seoul. Halmeoni would absolutely not welcome Anna's dogs in her home, so they would need their own space anyway. It was the perfect excuse.

"But what are we going to say when she asks why I'm not finishing school in Greenwich?" Anna asked.

"I'm going to tell her the truth, which is that with all your AP credits, you're basically done with high school anyway so you want to stay in Korea and get proficient in the language before college as you plan to major in international business studies."

"For the truth, that sounds pretty made up," she said. "I don't think I've ever said the words 'international,' 'business,' or 'studies' in that particular order. Like ever."

"Well, if you're going to join the family business one day, you might want to put it on your radar. Your negotiating skills are already impressive."

Anna let her father's words hang in the air. She wasn't sure whether he was being serious or joking. "Dad, remember our little talk the other night? No more men dictating my future. It's time for me to figure out what I want to do. I promise we can have whatever family business discussions you want after I go to college. But I need to survive high school first. Deal?"

"Deal," her father said, smiling. "Though I thought you'd at least commend me for being open to letting a woman run the show."

"Maybe we should start with you teaching me how to drive. Have you told Mom yet about my school decision?" Anna asked. "If you haven't I was thinking we should both fly back home for Labor Day and we can tell her in person. Steven's throwing a Summertime Funtime party and technically I'm a cohost so I really should be there. And don't you want to see Mom?"

Edward rubbed his chin. "I'll talk to my assistant about my schedule and see what I can do. You should go even if I can't. I'm sure your mother will be happy to see you. She asks about you all the time."

"Really? That's a surprise."

"I know you two have had your differences of late, but she's your mother and she's been worried about you. Before we left, she told me to expect a lot of ups and downs from you this summer, urging me to pay close attention to your emotions. Not my strong suit, I'll admit."

"I was a mess the past two months and not getting any sleep only made everything worse. Sometimes I wonder if I have a hard time sleeping because I miss the sound of Jon Snow snoring."

"And sometimes I wonder if I can handle you growing up so fast and demanding to make your own decisions. My parents planned out my whole life for me, and I resented the hell out of it. I promised myself I wouldn't do the same with my own children. I guess I've been breaking my own promise to myself."

"Better later than never," Anna said in a teasing voice. She hugged her father and told him she felt they both had grown up a lot this summer.

Anna met Chang-ri for lunch in Itaewon at a restaurant called Si.Wha. Dam, known for its modern Korean cuisine. It was far nicer than the places they normally met, and when Chang-ri arrived she explained to

Anna the reason she had chosen it. As an intern, she had once had to bring her boss something he had accidently left at the office. He was dining at this restaurant. It was so beautiful and elegant Chang-ri vowed that she would one day eat at a place like this. Today was that day, and she wanted it to be with Anna. "You inspire me to take charge of my life and speak up for the things I want. So I marched into my boss's office and told him I was long overdue for a promotion and if I wasn't going to get it, then I was going to look for a new job. I know this is something that people do all the time in America, but here I could have easily been fired for not knowing my place."

"Don't keep me in suspense!" Anna cried.

"He promoted me to associate producer, which comes with my own desk! This lunch, here, is my thank-you to you."

"Oh, that's amazing!" Anna exclaimed. "I'm so happy for you! And I fully expect you to be running the whole show one day!"

Chang-ri threw her arms around Anna. "I'm going to miss you when you leave."

"Does your new job come with more vacation days?" Anna asked.

Chang-ri let go of her and gave Anna a confused look. "I don't know, why do you ask?"

"I was hoping you'd meet me in London in a few weeks and from there we'll fly to New York together. You don't have to worry about travel expenses. My dad has his own plane."

"Me come to New York City?" Chang-ri gasped. "With you? On a private plane?"

"Well, technically, we'll be in the Hamptons. But it's close enough. My brother's having a big party, and I'll have a chance to see my mom. Then we can fly back here together."

"You've decided to attend school here?"

"I'll be at Branksome Hall in the fall. I only have to board there during the week so we can hang out on weekends."

Before Chang-ri had a chance to respond she pointed to a television mounted on the wall behind the bar. Anna turned around to see a news report announcing that The NowNows were currently in second place for the Song of the Summer. Photos of the mystery girl were flashing on the screen. Anna stared at the photos of herself and couldn't help but giggle at how bizarre her life had become.

Once they were seated Chang-ri leaned in close and whispered, "Aren't you afraid someone is going to figure out it's you?"

"Not really." Anna shrugged. "I've been listening to a podcast that said worrying about the things you can't control is a waste of time. Also, I've fulfilled my end of the bargain with JGK Music, so the mystery girl is gone and never to be seen again."

"Cheers to that!" Chang-ri held up her bubble tea. "And I would be honored to be your guest. I can't believe I'm going to visit America!"

When Anna entered the vestibule back at her grandmother's house, she was overcome with a peculiar sense of déjà vu. Listening a moment more, she confirmed her suspicion. She could hear Quentin's voice inside. He had once again invited himself over to her grandmother's house. Anna rolled her eyes, a little annoyed that he couldn't be a normal person and give her some advance warning.

Anna walked into the living room and found Quentin sitting next to her halmeoni with a tea set Anna had never seen before. It turned out Quentin had stopped by to drop off a gift for Anna and her grandmother. The tea set was a gift from him and once Halmeoni opened it, she insisted he join her for tea.

"Your halmeoni wouldn't take no for an answer," Quentin said as Anna's grandmother rose from her seat and excused herself from the room.

"I understand," said Anna. "How very thoughtful of you."

"Not nearly as thoughtful as you are. I sang your praises to your grandmother and she agrees you are a very special girl."

Anna smiled at the compliment, wishing she had been there to hear her grandmother say such a nice thing about her.

Quentin reached behind the sofa and pulled out a guitar case. "This is my present for you."

"No gift necessary," Anna said. "I'm just happy I could get you and Minsoo back together. Besides, I don't even play the guitar."

"Not the guitar," Quentin said. "A song to show you my gratitude for all that you have done for me. It's inspired by something we talked about and I wanted to play it for you. If I may." He started to strum. "It's a work in progress. And I know you can't understand Korean, but it's about a sad-eyed girl who traveled the wide and wild world." He started to sing.

Without all the electronica of K-pop music, Anna could hear how melodious Quentin's voice was. At the end of the song, Halmeoni appeared, standing in the doorway, clapping her hands telling him the song would be a hit.

Anna walked Quentin to the door, and he gave her a friendly hug. "Minsoo wishes she could have come to say good-bye and thank you for everything."

"It's okay," said Anna. "I know she has to lay low until you guys make the announcement. You know you shouldn't even be here yourself."

Just then his phone buzzed in his pocket and he took it out. Anna watched his face change from sincere gratitude to outright jubilation. "We did it!" he cried. "We really did it!"

"Did what?" Anna asked, surprised by his joyful outburst.

"We're number one!" he shouted. "Song of the Summer!"

"Wow! Congratulations!" Anna said, laughing as Quentin twirled her around on the front steps. Then he stopped and looked her dead in the eye.

"Anna, this is all because of you," he told her. "If you ever need anything from us, your wish will be our command. We owe you everything."

Anna was happy, not because The NowNows had their number-one song, but because Quentin was no longer the same sad-eyed boy she had met only a few weeks ago.

"Can I send you a poem a friend of mine wrote?" Anna asked. "I really think it has the potential to be a good song and now that I know what a talented songwriter you are, perhaps you could set it to music."

"Please do. Any friend of Very's is a friend of mine."

VI

When Tiare first mentioned the hike, Bea was not all that excited about it. She could tolerate the beach, but other than that, she wasn't much for outdoor activities. She had tried one famous hike in Los Angeles, Runyun Canyon, with her fellow intern, Toddie, who swore he walked behind Channing Tatum's cute derriere for an hour just last weekend. But on the day they went, it was hot and crowded and much harder than it looked. Bea hated pretty much every second of it. When they were on the way down, Toddie pointed out a girl who he claimed was Vanessa Hudgens even though she was wearing a giant hat and humongous sunglasses. Bea was so red-faced and cranky she didn't care and went on a seven-minute rant about the freefall of popular culture into the bottomless chasm of Insta-worship and pseudo-celebrities' lifestyle brands and makeup lines. "Because if walking up and down a hot-ass canyon with a bunch of losers is the lifestyle, you can count me out."

But despite her feelings about the outdoors, Bea didn't want to come off as a whiney brat on their day date. She wasn't going to say anything but reconsidered. "I despise hiking," she told Tiare in a fit of honesty.

"We can skip the hike," Tiare said as chill as chill can be. "But it wasn't the hike so much as the hot spring I wanted to show you."

"Do we have to wear clothes in the hot spring?"

"I believe clothing is optional."

"I'll go," she said. "Maybe I won't hate it as much walking behind your bouncy ass as opposed to Toddie's flat one."

"I was going to take you on the Seven Falls and Three Pools hike, but I know a shorter one to the Gaviota Hot Springs," Tiare said. "It's probably better because I don't want you to get too tired before tonight."

"What's tonight?"

"It's a surprise. Or do you hate those, too?"

Bea had never been a girl who appreciated being teased. She was very good at dishing it out, but not so good at taking it; however, when Tiare did it, Bea didn't mind in the least. "No, it's cool. I trust you."

The surprise was very much to Bea's liking.

After their afternoon at the hot springs, an incredibly relaxing soak and make-out session, they made a pit stop at the hotel and picked up a box from the guard gate. Tiare explained that she'd traded a few surf lessons for the kid of one of the sous chefs in exchange for a special picnic dinner. "Before there was money, there was the barter system," she said, and Bea was touched at all the thought and planning Tiare had put into their day together. Bea was the classic rich girl, who relied on her ability to throw money at any situation to achieve a certain effect, but so far, her day with Tiare was better than anything the concierge at some fancy hotel could plan.

After a scenic drive, they reached a private road with a large sign warning that trespassers would be prosecuted. Tiare looked at her phone, punched in a code, and the gates started to swing open. "Oh shit. Is this when you tell me you're secretly a rich girl posing as a poor girl to make sure I like you for you, and not your money?" Bea asked.

"'Fraid not, babe. I've got maybe two hundred bucks in my bank account right now. One of my surfing buddies is paid, though, and he hosted a few of us at his place last summer and said we were welcome to come back anytime on our own. This is the first time I've taken him up on it." They drove into the hills of Montecito and eventually Tiare pulled the car over. "C'mon, we gotta hurry, we only have a half hour before sunset, and the tent takes fifteen minutes to put up."

"Tent?" Bea asked, getting out of the car.

"You didn't think I was going to tell you I loved you and then not give you a night of wild sex in the great outdoors, did you?" Tiare threw back her head and laughed. "The look on your face! Finally, I shocked you with sex talk! Woo-hoo!"

Thirty minutes later the two girls were sitting on a cliff overlooking the ocean as the sun went down. They shared a bottle of white wine and savored an incredible roasted peach salad on organic greens. Also in the box from the indebted sous chef was a loaf of fresh-baked bread, burrata with cold-pressed olive oil, a warm asparagus salad with figs and yellow tomatoes, and a main course of ricotta and lobster ravioli in a brown butter sauce they fed to each other with their fingers. There were also cookies and butterscotch pudding for dessert, but they decided to save those for later. It was one of the best meals Beatrice had ever had.

Tiare had rigged the tent so they could open the front flaps and roll down a sheer netting to keep the bugs out and let the ocean breeze in. She even strung some battery-operated twinkle lights around the inside.

"Before you get stressed out about peeing al fresco, I want you to know there's a little path to the right that'll lead you to a fancy outhouse, a cedar outdoor shower, and a hot tub."

"I'm not stressed at all. I've had to pee in plenty of parking lots outside of clubs before. In fact, this is the most relaxed I have been in . . . god, I can't even remember. I'm starting to get this whole California lifestyle!"

"For me to be relaxed, I need to be unencumbered. Whenever I start collecting too much stuff or stay in one place for too long, I go crazy. This has been one of my favorite summers crashing with my aunt yet."

"Because of the surfing?" Bea asked.

"Because I met you." Tiare stared deep into Bea's eyes.

In the rare moments when people in her life were vulnerable with her, Bea relished the delicious feeling of their sincerity without having to feel anything herself. But with Tiare this wasn't the case. Tiare wasn't like other girls. Bea's experiences with other girls had always been satisfying because she was more confident in her ability to manipulate them emotionally. She knew what girls liked and she knew how to properly excite them. The common denominator in all her interactions, even with her dalliances with adults who should have known better, was that she was the one in control.

But not this time. This time was different. This time she was nervous as hell because when Tiare kissed her lips, she was enveloped in an inky sea of warm endorphins, and it made her tingle. She felt weak but not in a bad way, which was how she would normally categorize weakness of any sort. Before she could dissect what was going on, Tiare had taken her hand and was leading Bea into the tent.

It was nice to be the one who followed for a change. She made a feeble attempt to regain control of the situation by slipping her fingers over the waistband of Tiare's underwear, but Tiare was having none of it. Tiare climbed on top of Bea, who was supine on the sleeping bag, and began to kiss her neck. Bea heard a low moan and it took her a few seconds to realize that the noise had emanated from her own throat.

Tiare continued to kiss Bea and then began to undress her.

"The ground is more comfortable than I thought it would be," Bea whispered, staring up at the twinkling lights adorning the tent. She was surprised at how giddy she felt. The anticipation of what was to come caused her to take nervous shallow breaths.

"After this you'll be begging me to go camping every weekend," Tiare murmured, her mouth now kissing Bea's breasts, sucking one nipple and then moving over to flick the other one with her warm tongue. "God, you're so beautiful."

Bea was a good liar, so she always assumed others were lying too, especially when it came to compliments, but she could feel the truth in Tiare's words. Tiare really saw her for who she was and loved her anyway, flaws and all.

Bea clutched at Tiare's T-shirt, trying to pull it off. She needed to feel Tiare's skin pressed against her own. Tiare sat up and pulled off her tee. She reached behind her back and her bikini fell away. Bea reached her hands toward Tiare, beckoning her closer, but Tiare instead unbuttoned Bea's cut-offs. She pulled Bea's shorts and her hot pink thong off in one motion and cast them aside.

Bea quivered, suddenly shy. "What are you doing?" she whispered.

"I'm taking you in. I love your body and I can't believe you're mine. Are you mine?" Tiare asked, her voice firm and gentle at once.

Bea wouldn't have believed her own answer had she not heard herself say it. From the time she was a little girl, Bea wanted to be in charge of every person she met. But with Tiare she didn't need to be in charge. And she didn't want to be. "I'm yours," she said.

Tiare smiled and lowered her lips to Bea's bare belly and reached up to caress Bea's breasts. Bea writhed underneath her, blind with lust, losing herself in the bliss of having someone you love show you their feelings through touch. Tiare kissed a path down to the hinge of Bea's thighs, and Bea sucked in her breath. She almost pulled back, but instead she opened her legs wider, and at the first touch of Tiare's tongue, lost herself in a void of oblivious pleasure.

A cascade of intense feelings flooded through Bea as Tiare drank from her, not just the physical sensation of being kissed and licked, but something more. And in a moment of epiphany, Bea knew exactly what it was. This was sex with love.

And it was the best fucking feeling in the world.

VII

On the way to the train station in London, Anna asked Aunt Jules why she and Wilson had decided to take this particular trip. Jules explained she'd always found train trips wildly romantic, and one of her favorite books had a famous "meet-cute" on a train. Anna's heart jumped a bit as that was how she had met Vronsky. Perhaps this was why she'd wanted to go so bad. It was the perfect trip to honor their love and, through his letters, she felt like she was meeting him all over again.

Anna asked Wilson what he thought about riding the *Orient-Express* and he said he wasn't thrilled that he had to wear a suit to dinner every night, but if Jules was happy, that made him happy. Because of their Malibu beach-town lifestyle he rarely dressed formally so he brought all his fanciest clothes to wear on the train.

Anna imagined she'd be one of the youngest passengers, but she was okay with that; she was looking forward to the adventure of it all.

"Thank you so much for inviting me along," Anna said. "I really needed this trip. I'm just going to read books and eat scones with clotted cream!"

She texted her brother to tell them she and Chang-ri would be there for the Summertime Funtime party. Steven texted Anna back almost immediately that he was deep into planning the party and if she had any special requests, she needed to send them right away. Anna's only request would be to add some K-pop songs to the playlists. She then sent him a link to the NowNows' summer jam.

Summer had never gone by so fast. It felt like just the other day that she'd watched Lolly and Steven board the plane in Italy, even though it had been over six weeks ago. She was still unsure if she'd made the right decision about school, but she was relieved not to have to think about it. After a whirlwind summer of new people and new experiences she was leaning toward staying the course and seeing what the future had in store for her abroad.

After boarding the train in London, Anna, her aunt, and her uncle first went to the Istanbul grand suite. All three of them were speechless at the sheer beauty of the room. "It's like living in a storybook," Anna remarked, touching a beautiful crystal vase on the table in the cabin's sitting area. "Who knew a train could be so gorgeously decorated?"

"Are you going to be okay by yourself?" Jules asked as Anna went off to check out her suite two cars down.

"I'll be fine," said Anna, excited to be alone and get settled in.

"If any bandits show up, know that I'll be able to handle them, okay?" Wilson added, which made Anna laugh.

"Don't forget we have reservations at seven in the dining car," Jules said. "The reservation is under Shelby Eatenton. Don't ask."

When Anna reached her suite, she remembered she had promised to call her mom before they departed. Her mother picked up on the first ring. Greer had been surprised that Edward agreed to let her go on this trip and said if she wasn't hosting a fundraising dinner this weekend she might have come along since traveling on the *Orient-Express* had always been on her wish list. Anna asked her mother if she was having a good summer, and Greer paused and said there were good weeks and not so good ones. "The chic sunglasses you sent me have been very helpful in covering my dark circles."

"Yes," Anna said. "They do come in handy for that."

Greer then asked about Anna's father, and admitted she missed Edward far more than she had expected to, being so used to him traveling for business. "I guess it was a different feeling in the past, because I knew he'd be coming home to me . . . but this time, I'm not so sure."

Anna told her she believed they could work it out if they wanted and said she knew Dad missed her, too. "Perhaps we could all be a family again by the end of the year," she said. "We could meet up in Hawaii for the holidays." Her mother offered up a noncommittal maybe, and after Anna got off the phone, she was in a somber mood. She knew enough to know it wasn't wise for her to meddle in her own parents' relationship. She decided to explore the rest of the train to get her mind off her parents' faltering marriage.

There were four cars with sleeper cabins on the train, one car with open seating where passengers could mingle, three dining cars, and a bar car. The last car had a sitting room with extra-large windows and beautiful inlaid bookcases filled with leather-bound editions of classic novels. As the train disembarked, Anna returned to her room and was lulled asleep within minutes by the rhythmic motion of the wheels on the tracks.

She awoke with barely enough time to dress for dinner and hustled to the dining car.

She'd never seen her aunt and uncle dressed up before, and she barely recognized them as the elegant couple in the bar car, only realizing it was them when the bartender burst out laughing at whatever joke Jules or Wilson made. *They are such a good couple*, Anna thought, wishing she and Vronsky had been given a chance to find out what kind of couple they could have been.

After dinner the three of them decided to have their dessert in the bar car, and Anna had a toffee bread pudding so delicious her eyes shut involuntarily every time she took a bite. Even though she had napped, Anna was soon yawning and declared that she was ready to turn in. She wished Jules and Wilson a good night and told them she'd meet them for breakfast in the morning before they arrived in Venice.

Back in her room, she went into her closet, unzipped her travel duffel, and pulled out the shoebox containing Vronsky's letters. She knew this train trip was the perfect time to read another letter. She hadn't read one since the letter in which Vronsky mentioned the visit to her father. She felt a tightness in her chest, knowing that there would come a time for her to read his last letter, but she pushed away such thoughts and opened the envelope carefully, ready to savor the next installment of her lover's posthumous words.

> *Dear Anna,*
> *I made a mistake. I Googled famous love letters and read a bunch online and now I feel great pressure to make this one especially good. It seems to me that those who really lay their whole heart out on the page, fears of sounding foolish be damned, the ones who sound a bit unhinged, they are the ones who make me feel less alone. I feel their pain as I read their words, and I believe they in turn understand me.*
>
> > *That's it, right? Love is the most exquisite pain. Rapturous torture. A two-sided coin of heads-you're-happy and tails-you're-miserable. When we're together I feel alive, panting and drooling (like your dogs) with anticipation and joy, but when we're apart the days seem like months, the hours like days, and every minute lasts an eternity. . . .*

Overwhelmed with emotion, she finished the rest of letter. She got ready for bed thinking every girl should be lucky enough to read a love letter on a midnight train to Paris.

VIII

When Bea woke up, she was alone in the tent. She and Tiare had stayed up late into the night alternating between eating their picnic desserts and then going back into the tent for more hot and heavy petting. Bea had never felt so close to another person before, in mind or in body. She felt like they were the only two people in the world, and she was completely okay with it. Maybe she even preferred it. She poked her head out of the tent as Tiare was coming back from the outdoor shower, wrapped in a towel.

"How long have you been awake?" Bea asked.

"Only a little while. You looked so peaceful, I wanted to let you sleep." Tiare opened her mouth to say something else, but then shut up.

"What?" Bea asked.

"Your phone was kinda going crazy, just vibrating nonstop and I wondered if there was an emergency so I grabbed it out of your bag. I probably shouldn't have, I should have just woken you up, but . . ." Tiare looked down at her flip-flops.

"I don't care if you looked at my phone. Sorry it woke you up."

"Some girl named Claudine kept calling you over and over. You had like twenty missed calls from her. I was about to wake you up because I assumed it had to be an emergency but then . . ."

Bea took a deep breath and sighed. "Let me guess? She sent a tit pic?"

"Something like that," Tiare said coyly. "It's none of my business and I know you and I haven't talked about . . ."

Bea cut her off. "Tiare, first of all, Claudine means nothing to me. Not like that. I mean, we're friends and we had a fling before I came out to LA, but it's very over. She lives in Paris and her mother is best friends with my aunt so I couldn't just ghost her completely, you know. There is nothing going on between us anymore. I'll take care of it. I'm sorry if she made you feel bizarre."

"It's no biggie. It was just a little bizarre."

"Oh, you know those French girls . . ."

"I know you say it's over, but it doesn't seem like she knows it, or wants it to be."

"Look, I've never been monogamous, like ever. I'm a free spirit and the idea of being tied down to one person seemed totally ridiculous to me." Bea paused as she watched Tiare's eyebrows raise slightly. "Let me finish . . . that was until I met you. You're different. Hell, I'm different with you. In a good way. I don't want to be with anyone but you. I love you."

"I love you, too, but we haven't exactly discussed the future. You're going back to Connecticut and I'm going to Hawaii . . ."

"You're going to Hawaii?" Bea asked. "When?" Before Tiare could answer, Bea closed the gap between them and kissed her. "Let's not do this now. Last night was so great and can we just not have a heavy talk right now? I want to enjoy our morning together."

"You're right," Tiare concurred. "You read my mind. Hot tub?"

Bea gave her an enthusiastic head nod. "God, yes."

On the way back to Los Angeles Monday morning, Beatrice called Claudine to tell her the truth: she had met someone else, she was in love, and she hoped Claudine would be happy for her.

But Beatrice was wrong.

From the moment she picked up the phone Claudine was all over Bea's case, asking where she had been for the past few days and why she wasn't answering any of her texts. Why did it not occur to her that Claudine would freak out? Did Beatrice know how worried she'd been? Apparently Claudine had become convinced that Bea had been in a terrible accident, and was lying unconscious in a hospital somewhere, fighting for her life.

Beatrice kept trying to get a word in, but Claudine carried on. She wanted Bea to take in fully the mental anguish she had caused her. By the time Claudine finally let her say something, the truth—*I met this super-hot surfer chick who I'm now unabashedly, totally, and completely in love with*—was out of the question.

Instead Bea apologized for making Claudine so worried. It wasn't anything personal. But she wasn't going to beg for forgiveness. She said she needed some time away, and some friends had invited her to go camping in Santa Barbara and so she went. She'd had no idea there wouldn't be cell service, but to be honest she was sort of craving some time away from screens. "Look, losing V. was the worst thing that has ever happened to me and maybe it's causing me to act a little impulsively, because god knows camping is normally something I'd scoff at, but I wanted to try it. Also, who says I have to report my every move to you, anyway?"

The phone was silent for a moment and then Claudine quickly switched gears. "I'm sorry, I've been so miserable without you this summer. You're all I think about. I overreacted; forgive me. The good news is I'm planning you the best surprise present of all time . . ."

Then, before Bea could even respond, Claudine dropped a big bomb.

"My mom is so tired of me moping about the house that she finally agreed to let me come back and visit you before school starts! Isn't that amazing? She already talked to your mom who invited us to your Hamptons house for Labor Day weekend. In less than two weeks, we'll be together again!"

Bea was stunned by the news and could only manage to say, "Wow, really? Wow, okay," all the while cursing herself for not texting Claudine back. She might have circumvented this upcoming shit show. Bea quickly told Claudine she had to get off the phone because she had just arrived to work and was running late. This, of course, was a lie. Bea had already called in sick to work and was currently lying by Uncle Chadwick's pool, missing Tiare.

After Bea hung up the phone, she made sure the call was disconnected before screaming, "Fuuuuuuuuuck!" She had no idea how she was going to handle Labor Day with Claudine there, since, that morning, she had invited Tiare to come for the very same weekend.

IX

Dustin picked Kimmie up in an Uber Black and asked her permission to blindfold her for their surprise date. She nodded happily, enjoying this more playful side of her boyfriend. She had been so relieved when Dustin called her up in the morning and apologized for being distant lately. He had been having a hard time navigating all of his responsibilities. Working with high-risk kids at a community center in Harlem, babysitting his half sister, and helping his mother paint her apartment were all important, but none of them were as important as Kimmie, and he knew he hadn't been doing his best to show how much he treasured her.

He brought it up again as she sat blindfolded next to him in the backseat, how he had been distracted and feeling ashamed for not giving her the attention she deserved. When she tried to object, he silenced her with a kiss. "You're so beautiful that sometimes I feel like it's all a dream, that a girl like you would ever be with a guy like me."

Kimmie laughed then quickly assured him she wasn't laughing at him, but rather she sometimes felt the same way except the reverse: "That a guy so smart and kind would ever love a girl like me who barely knows who she is or what she wants to do with her life."

"That's awesome," Dustin said. "Beyond getting my PhD in robotics I have no idea what I'm going to do with my life, either."

The Uber arrived at their destination, and Dustin carefully led Kimmie out of the backseat, guiding her with both hands onto the sidewalk. He guided her up some steps and then through a revolving door, both of them squeezing into one compartment wedge, taking baby steps until they got inside. She was laughing hysterically as they spilled out.

"Please let me take off my blindfold now."

He told her she needed to wait a little longer, asking for her patience as he guided her into the elevator. On the way up, she heard Dustin talking to the other passengers, explaining that he was treating his girlfriend to a very special date night. Kimmie heard a woman's voice tell her that she'd found herself a keeper, and she nodded happily behind the blindfold. "I know." The elevator stopped on various floors, but Dustin kept telling her not yet. Finally, she heard the door open, and Dustin gently led her out into the hall.

Kimmie heard a familiar sound she couldn't quite place, followed by a door opening. Dustin stood behind her and wrapped his arms around her, holding her close. "I love you, Kimmie, from the first time I saw you." He turned her slowly, so they were facing each other and kissed her softly while reaching to untie the blindfold. "Now . . ." he said.

Kimmie opened her eyes the first thing she saw was the vase of beautiful pale pink roses resting on a low coffee table in front of a blue couch. She looked around, trying to get her bearings. "Are we in a hotel room?"

"We're in the St. Regis."

"What? But, how? Dustin, this place is so expensive . . ." Her words trailed off as it dawned on her where they were. "Is this Steven's father's hotel suite?"

"It is. Have you been here?"

"No, but I've heard about it."

Something about Kimmie's voice gave Dustin pause, and his face fell. "Oh no, you're unhappy. Did I make a mistake bringing you here?"

Kimmie felt terrible. "Sorry, it's not you. It's just . . . I don't know." She sat on the pretty blue couch, fearful she had just ruined another night. "Why is this so hard?"

Dustin walked over and sat down next to her. He grabbed her hand. "I don't know."

Kimmie thought he was going to say more, but he didn't. The two of them just sat in silence until she spoke. "I guess I just want our first time to be . . ." She hesitated, gathering the right words. "To not be here. It doesn't feel right. I can't explain it."

"You don't have to, I get it." Dustin sighed. "This wasn't even my idea. I've been at a loss how to go about this."

"Don't you want to be with me?" Kimmie asked in a small voice.

Dustin turned toward her and took her face in his hands. "More than anything, but . . ." He stopped, unsure whether admitting his fears would bring them closer together or push her further away.

"But what?" she gently prodded, resting her head on his shoulder.

"I just don't know how I'm supposed to live up to the guy who made you want . . ."

"Want to what?"

"Want to die."

Kimmie was so surprised by his words that she leapt from the couch. "Is that what you think happened to me?"

"I don't know, I'm not sure. We weren't exactly speaking then, and I guess I just put two and two together when you went to the desert."

"You couldn't be more wrong, Dustin. I was depressed, yes, but I wasn't suicidal. I was depressed over Vronsky not loving me, I was depressed over how I treated you and then how he treated me. My first time was terrible. It was awkward and horrible, and I deeply regret ever caving in to what I thought he wanted."

Dustin looked alarmed. "Not to speak ill of the dead, but if you're saying he took advantage of you, then I hope he's currently getting sodomized by the Devil himself."

Kimmie threw her arms around Dustin, not knowing whether to laugh or cry. "You're so sweet. Unfortunately for the Devil, it was consensual, but it was also a huge mistake. I don't want to lie. I thought I loved him, he seemed like everything I should want. He was popular and charming."

"You left out handsome enough to be a Disney prince," Dustin added. "I know he had lots of experience with women whereas I have none. I've been scared I'll disappoint you. And that's the honest to goodness truth."

"You've been scared? All this time I felt like you weren't attracted to me."

"Are you kidding me? You're all I think about."

"Do you think about me when you, you know?" Kimmie asked softly.

"When I . . ." Dustin began but then stopped once he'd figured out what she was implying. "Yes, all the time."

"What do you think about?" Kimmie whispered.

Dustin wasn't sure where this was going. The blood was pounding in his ears. "I think about touching you," he told her.

"Where?" Kimmie whispered, taking his hand and bringing it to her breast. A little moan escaped her lips when he grasped her, and he tensed up before leaning in and pressing his lips to hers. They fell back onto the couch, Kimmie lying underneath him. He started to grind his hip between her legs lightly.

"You're all I think about. I get turned on just imagining the smell of your lilac shampoo . . ."

Dustin exhaled as she started to unbuckle his belt. She unbuttoned the top button and then walked her fingers under his waistband. Sensing his excitement made her excited, too. She felt a surge of power ripple through her. She knew he loved her; she could feel it in everything he said to her, how he asked what she was thinking about and expressed real interest in her opinions and concerns. But this was different. This wasn't her brain thinking he loved her; this was her body knowing it.

"If you don't stop," he whispered, "I'm not going to be able to control it."

"I don't want you to."

A minute later Dustin erupted with pleasure and cried out her name. Kimmie smiled up at the ceiling, feeling intense satisfaction. When he came back from the bathroom Dustin was wearing a hotel bathrobe. He held a second robe in his hand.

"Is that for me?" she asked.

"Yes, but for after," he said. "Now it's your turn to tell me what you like."

"What if I don't know what I like?" she asked, because truthfully, she didn't.

"Then we'll find out together," he said, holding out his hand to her.

"Okay, but I don't want to go all the way. I thought I did, but I want to keep going slow. Just not too slow."

"I'm fine with going slow. I just want to make you happy, and if you don't know what that is exactly, we'll figure it out together." She took his hand and stood up, crossing with him to the bed, where he enveloped her in his arms.

As the *Orient-Express* hurtled toward Paris, Anna was planning to soak up whatever nightlife the train had to offer.

They had an entire day to spend in Venice before they needed to be back at the train station and she, Aunt Jules, and Uncle Wilson spent the morning walking the streets of San Marco looking for Scala Contarini del Bovolo, a historic palazzo with a famous spiral staircase built by one of the founding families of Venice. Anna had been to Venice a few times before and always loved exploring the city. It took them a while to find it as none of them had a working knowledge of Italian, and they kept making fun of each other's terrible accents, which caused lots of annoyed looks by the locals, shaking their heads at the silly Americans. But it was worth the effort once they finally found it and walked up the eighty steps to the top. Seeing Venice from such a high vantage point was nothing short of majestic. They stayed at the top for a while, taking in the panoramic view before heading back down to catch the train.

On the platform, Anna insisted that Jules and Wilson should have a romantic dinner to themselves. Anna was going to eat alone and read her book. Her grandmother always said a lady should never dine alone in public, and that made Anna want to try it all the more. Jules agreed, not because she felt like Anna was a third wheel, but more that they had hit Venice hard, so they were looking forward to an early dinner before they collapsed for the day.

Getting ready for her solo dinner, Anna decided to wear a red dress she had bought at Harrods, a very fitted number fishtailed at the bottom. It seemed like something the "mystery girl" would wear if she were on a train traveling through the French countryside. She was ready twenty minutes before her eight thirty reservation and decided to go spend some time in the bar car.

Strutting through the dining cars in her dress and high heels, Anna cut a striking figure. She could feel people noticing her, but she didn't mind the attention since she'd put so much effort into dolling herself up.

Entering the last car, she found it relatively unoccupied except for two elderly men playing chess in the corner and two younger men looking out the back window, talking. A waiter entered behind her carrying a tray with two martini shakers and frosted glasses. He served the younger men and then came over and handed Anna a cocktail menu. She smiled and thanked him.

The more boisterous of the two young men turned around first, and Anna was surprised that he was even younger than she had guessed. There was something about a tuxedo that aged a person up, she supposed. He was probably in college or maybe just out, but definitely in his early twenties. He made eye contact with her and smiled, commenting, "Kiril, my man, I no longer think you're an idiot for making us take the train. Talent everywhere, it seems."

Kiril turned at the word "talent," glancing back at Anna, who was just registering the name "Kiril."

"Anna?" He addressed her as if he needed to verify that she was more than a hallucination.

"Bloody hell, you know this girl? Kiril, I swear to god, it's like fucking spooky, mate. You know every girl in the northern hemisphere." Kiril's cohort scanned Anna up and down. "What are the odds? It must be a trick of destiny, mate, now stop standing there like an arse and introduce me to the future Mrs. Ashton Harris the Third, and proud mother of Ashton Harris the Fourth . . ."

Kiril smacked his friend sharply on the arm. "Bring it down a notch, Ash, she's jailbait. And we both know if you end up in the clinker again, your papa said he'd lock up your trust fund for a decade."

"Can we keep the jailbait talk down, please, I haven't even ordered a drink yet." Anna smirked as Kiril stepped forward and gave her a warm hug. Anna breathed in and gasped a little at his scent. He was wearing Alexia's cologne.

"My turn, my turn," Ashton slurred drunkenly. Anna offered him her hand, but he pulled her in for a hug, and she could smell the whisky on his breath. "Enchanted to meet you, enchanted, enchanted . . ."

"Ignore him, he's my idiot college roommate," Kiril said. "Ash, this is Anna K. A very dear family friend."

At the mention of her name, Ashton's posture changed ever so slightly. He gave her face a good close look and then pointed at her. "You do look familiar, though . . ." His eyes brightened with recognition. "I've seen you before!"

Anna knew immediately that her name had triggered an image in this boy's head, an image from the sex tape. She felt trapped suddenly and took a step back. "Sorry. I . . . I forgot my purse. I need to go and get it. Um, it was nice to meet you. Kiril, always a pleasure."

And with that she turned and walked rapidly out of the skylight car, clutching the purse she'd just lied about not having to her chest. She walked through the dining cars with her eyes cast downward, going as fast as her tight dress would allow. She was flustered, her thoughts and pulse racing so quickly that she didn't even notice someone was following her until she dropped the key to her room and Kiril picked it up for her. "Anna, I'm sorry about my friend. May I please come in so we can talk?"

Before she could respond, Kiril unlocked her door and walked into her suite. He took a seat on the bed. "I'm so sorry, Anna. Besides having the biggest feet in our dorm, Ash also has the biggest mouth in which to insert his big foot."

"It's okay, Kiril. It just caught me off guard, that's all. It was already so strange to run into you on a train in the middle of Italy, but to know that a stranger knew me because of that . . . is scary. I know I look ridiculous in this dress. I don't know what I was thinking, you must think I'm so immature."

"Stop, you look beautiful, you are beautiful. That dress is gorgeous, I didn't even recognize you for a split second but then . . . I mean, you're one of a kind."

Just then the train jolted, and Anna lost her balance. Kiril leapt up and caught her, steadying her in his arms. Again she smelled the cologne and felt light-headed. She wobbled and Kiril led her to the bed. She sat down, and he brought her a ginger ale from the minibar. "Are you all right?"

Anna took a long drink and nodded. "I am. Thank you."

"What are you doing on this train?" Kiril asked.

"You first," she replied softly, not quite ready to talk.

"We were just in Venice with some other college friends and got all fucked up on opium and got bored and just sort of decided we should go to Paris. Ashton's parents have a house there."

"You mean there are more of you?" Anna asked in a shaky voice.

"They wanted to fly but for some reason I insisted on the train. I don't even remember why, though I'm glad we did." Kiril was stalling; he knew that what Anna really wanted to know was how many more boys on this train had seen her having sex with Alexia on their phones. "Just one more. His name is Jordy. The fucker drew the short straw, so he gets the single room, and I got stuck rooming with Ash. Jordy is gay, if that makes you feel better, so if he did see the video, he was probably looking at my brother instead of you."

"So you saw it then," Anna said, looking at her hands since she was having trouble looking him in the eye.

"Only once," Kiril said quickly. "Let's change the subject. How is it that you're on this train? You can't be traveling alone, can you?"

Anna shook her head and explained how she wound up crashing her aunt and uncle's vacation, how they were all on the train from London two nights ago and that she was planning on having a solo dinner so her aunt and uncle could have some alone time. She was babbling, but she couldn't help it. Even though Kiril had heterochromia iridum of the iris—one blue eye, one green—his eyes still had the same intensity as Alexia's, and though his summer tan distorted it, Kiril shared the same cheekbones with his younger brother as well.

"You can't have dinner alone. You should eat with us!"

"No way. Knowing your friend Ash has seen me . . . how could I?"

"Anna, you can't let that episode with my brother define your whole life or make you run and hide. Alexia would hate that."

"Just so you know, I loved your brother," Anna said. "It wasn't some 'episode,' it was the one where my true love dies and my heart fucking shatters."

"I know, I know," Kiril said, hugging her. "He loved you, too. I loved him, too. So, so much."

"So fucking much." Anna sighed helplessly in Kiril's arms. Part of her wanted to forget everything that had just happened, to just take dinner in her room and go to bed early. But the other part of her wanted to be brave and do exactly what Kiril had advised. "Okay, I'll come to dinner."

"Wonderful!" Kiril's face lit up. "If it makes you feel any better, I have at least six or seven different videos of Ash running around naked at college."

"Maybe after we eat," Anna said, getting up from the bed and moving toward the door.

XI

As soon as they arrived back in the dining car, Kiril took Ash aside and warned him to behave. Once he learned that Anna had been in love with Kiril's dearly departed younger brother, it wasn't hard, even for him, to grasp that making a pass at a bereaved teenager was wrong. And as Anna got to know Ashton, it was obvious his obnoxious mannerisms stemmed from having a father who was not only one of the wealthiest landowners in the UK, but also one of the surliest. There were only a few families wealthier, and besides the royal family and J. K. Rowling's kids, Ashton was one of the richest Brits under the age of twenty-five. (Adele knocked him out of the top ten a few years back.) And Ashton's hard partying and boisterous nature were coping mechanisms for constantly being berated by a father who couldn't be pleased.

Jordan Q., known as Jordy to his good friends, was very dapper in his Varvatos midnight-blue tux, and he and Anna got along famously from the moment they were introduced. They were both readers, and it turned out they had read and loved many of the same authors. Jordy's parents were diplomats, and he had lived all over the globe, moving every other year from country to country, which according to him sounded more fun than it actually was.

"So did the three of you end up as roommates by pure chance?" Anna asked, eager to hear about their college experience.

The guys looked at each other and began to laugh heartily. "Not exactly," said Kiril.

Jordy and Ashton roomed their freshman year at Wesleyan in a quad along with Denzel the Dangerous and a guy they called WTF Wyatt. Denzel the Dangerous had been with them in Venice but had met a girl he wanted to spend one more night with, so he was going to fly to Paris and meet them for lunch tomorrow.

Anna was suddenly curious about every detail of these boys' lives. College sounded so much cooler than high school. "Why do you call him Denzel the Dangerous?"

"Because he was named after Denzel Washington and was fortunate enough to grow up just as handsome. The 'Dangerous' came from how treacherous it was to bring a girl you like around him," Ashton told her. "He wound up making out with two of my high school girlfriends, can you bloody believe that?"

"Okay, and how does Kiril fit into the picture?" Anna asked.

It turned out that their fourth roommate, WTF Wyatt, was a shy southerner from South Carolina, a chemistry whiz on full scholarship, and the first of his family to go to college. Their school had its fair share of wealthy kids, and the pressure to keep up could be intense, so WTF Wyatt "broke bad" and started making MDMA with his lab partner. What started out as a small side hustle supplying a few frats and dorms soon grew big enough for the real drug dealers in town to find out and express their displeasure at the duo's entrepreneurial spirit. Long story short, the lab partner got shot in the leg and transferred to BU, and WTF Wyatt didn't get shot because Kiril saved his ass by sheer dumb luck. Kiril being Kiril, he was cocky enough to believe he could negotiate Wyatt's safety and went to talk to the pissed-off dealers on his behalf.

"Kiril basically thinks he's Vince Vaughn in the movie *Swingers*, able to talk anyone into anything. And the smooth motherfucker actually pulls it off most of the time. WTF Wyatt had to become their supplier for a short while to make peace, but who could argue with a few more batches of MDMA when the alternative was getting shot?" Jordy said.

"Look at you, Mr. Hero!" Anna said to Kiril, impressed.

"Not exactly . . ." Ashton said. "WTF Wyatt ended up becoming a coke addict and wound up in rehab. He's now studying theology and wants to be a minister, so there's always a dark side to any good drama."

"Giving up drugs and finding religion is the dark side?" Kiril asked.

"Yes," said Ashton. "It is."

"You sound like my brother," Anna said before changing the subject. "So, Kiril, you moved in with them after Wyatt left?"

"Not exactly . . ." Kiril went on to explain how he'd utilized his big mouth and winning personality to become a party promoter at the two local off-campus clubs and unwisely decided to drop out of college, which prompted his mother, Geneviève, to cut him off as soon as she got wind of it. Kiril went crawling back after a few weeks to apologize and admitted he had made a terrible mistake and wanted to go back to school. He was, it turned out, someone too acclimated to the finer things in life to forego his ample allowance. "Now the four of us live in the off-campus house Ash's dad just bought him."

"Our fifth roommate is whatever girl Kiril happens to be dating," Ash said. "It's a revolving door of little honeybabies, basically."

"I had to change the locks at least eight different times that first year," said Jordy.

"Kiril's skills with the ladies were legendary."

"Present tense please," Kiril said with a wink.

The conversation then turned to Anna and her summer abroad. She regaled the boys with her adventures club-hopping around Seoul with a K-pop star. The boys looked up the "mystery girl" pics immediately. Plenty of people were still obsessed with finding out the girl's true identity, and Jordy dished on all the gossip blogs, having lived in Korea for two years and being able to read a little Korean.

"The top five rumors about you are . . ." Jordy said in his best M.C. voice. "One: QT broke up with you, and you drowned in a river of your own tears. Two: you were lured to America to be in Bieber's new music video. Three: you had to get plastic surgery to change your face so no one would learn your real identity. Four: you had to go into hiding because you will be a contestant on the next season of *King of Masked Singers*. And five: you are actually an American socialite who . . ." Jordy stopped reading abruptly. "Wow, those crazy Koreans and their ridiculous gossip. They're as bad as the tabloid reporters in London."

"What did it say?" Anna pressed him. "It's okay, I want to know."

Jordy looked at Kiril, who nodded him an okay. "Anna's a big girl, she can take it."

"It says you killed your last boyfriend and you were on the run looking for your next victim."

"Well, it's partially true," Anna said, feeling the familiar mix of rage and anguish burble up inside of her, although now for the first time, she was able to quell it. "The part about me being on the run, of course . . ."

Just then, Uncle Wilson walked up to the table, and Anna introduced him to the boys. He said he was picking up some extra desserts. "You know the problem with this train is, the dessert portions are too damn small. I'd toss all three of you pretentious sadboys off this moving train for a couple Klondike bars."

The boys all roared with laughter, and Anna excused herself for a moment. She took a seat at the bar with Wilson and explained who Kiril was, so he didn't think she had picked up a table full of college boys all on her own.

"Even if you did pick them up, I wouldn't care. Remember, you're a teenager and supposed to be having fun. God knows your aunt got into plenty of trouble when she was your age, precocious jezebel that she was."

"So you think it's okay if I stay with them? I don't want to give them the wrong idea about me."

"I'm pretty sure they're all harmless. Well, the good-looking one with the Bowie eyes could be a super villain in a Marvel movie, but I'm only two train cars away if you need me. I'd be happy to kick the living crap out of any of them if you say the word. But I know you're smart enough to handle those knuckleheads. If you're having fun, stay up. If you're not, remember you can leave at any time. And if your drink tastes funny, stop drinking it, go back to your room, and lock the door and call me."

Anna laughed and thanked Wilson for his advice. "That won't be necessary," she said. "I think hanging out with some boys who have been around the block a few times will be good for me."

XII

Mondays were free days at Interlochen, so Monday nights were usually reserved for cabins to do bonding activities on their own. Occasionally there would be an all-camp evening scheduled: a dance, a movie night, or possibly a trivia contest with prizes. That morning at breakfast, the head of the camp stood at the podium and rang a cowbell to get everyone's attention. One of the campers in the back yelled, "More cowbell!" to which his buddies laughed until they got shushed by some of the more serious theater campers.

All of a sudden, the camp director and the counselors started clapping their hands and chanting Lolly's name. Soon everyone joined in, and Lolly, who was sitting with her bunkmate, Juliet B., looked around, perplexed. She had no clue what was going on. Juliet told her to stand up, which she did, and soon all eyes were on her.

"Tonight is going to be extra special," the camp director proclaimed. "Thanks to Lolly, and her very generous boyfriend, tonight we will be having a surprise concert given by the very popular Michigan band Delvin and the Yellowjackets. Actually, it was Lolly's boyfriend who hired them to celebrate her birthday. And he sent over a cake and ice cream food truck for the show!"

The entire camp went insane, cheering and stomping their feet, which soon turned into people chanting, "Speech! Speech! Speech!" Lolly really had no other choice but to stand up on her chair and say a few words.

Before she began, she caught Dean's eye. He smiled at her and she smiled back. "As many of you know, this place, this camp is my happy place," Lolly said. "It's so special to me and I really feel like I've grown up here over the past six summers that I've attended. I've always had such a special birthday every summer, getting to spend it with so many talented people who love the arts the way I love them. You guys really get me. And if I were to have one birthday wish for everyone here, it's that you will be lucky enough to find someone to love you the way I am lucky enough to be loved by my boyfriend, Steven . . . who will be here for the end-of-camp show, so you can thank him in person. I am as surprised by this as all of you. Thanks, and see you on the dance floor!"

She took a low bow and was soon surrounded by her cabinmates, who were already chattering about what they were going to wear for the dance, since this was definitely going to be a night to remember.

"You really have the coolest boyfriend ever," Juliet sighed, as they walked back to their cabin. "He treats you like a fairy princess."

Lolly smiled and said she should give him a call now to thank him for the gift. When Steven didn't pick up, Lolly called Kimmie instead, who picked up on the first ring.

"What's wrong?" Kimmie asked without bothering to say hello.

"What makes you think something's wrong? Can't I just be calling to say what's up?"

"Bullshit," Kimmie said. "You would have just texted. Plus, you never call me to ask me about my life. I'm not complaining, I'm just stating facts."

"Fine, smart ass. Is there anything I need to know about?" The pause at the other end of the line was a moment longer than it should have been, which made Lolly clench her jaw. "Spill it, Kimmie. What the hell is going on?"

"I don't know what you're talking about," Kimmie said.

"Steven hired a band for our Monday night camp dance tonight. And a food truck."

"Aww, for your birthday? That's nice."

"Cut the shit, Kimmie. Steven blows through money like water but dropping thousands of dollars to hire a band and a food truck for my entire camp seems a little much."

"Really? It sounds exactly like him to me . . . being extra by showing off his money and wanting people he doesn't even know to worship him. Did he send a banner over that says: 'Brought to you by . . . Steven K., Super Rich Impressive Fun Dude of the People'?"

"And you wonder why I never talk to you about anything. Forget I even asked!"

"I'm sorry! I'm sorry. You're right, that was super bitchy of me. Look, maybe he's just sad he's not there for your birthday and wanted to reassure you that he's on his best behavior here at home."

"Or he's cheating on me and feels so guilty that he needs to rid himself of his guilt." Lolly sounded very intense, and Kimmie recognized something different in her sister's tone.

"Okay," Kimmie said. "What's his name?"

Lolly was totally taken aback. "Shut up! You don't know what you're talking about." Lolly paused and then looked around to make sure she was alone. "Dean. From Texas."

"You and a red-stater, I can't believe it," she said.

"Kimmie, it's nothing. It's just that he's got the lead opposite of me and so we're rehearsing a lot together and I do feel guilty even though I haven't done anything. I told him I had a boyfriend from day one."

"Then you should stop feeling guilty."

"I know. It's just that before I left I was all over Steven, so convinced he'd cheat and now . . ."

"Lolly, you're allowed to think another guy is cute."

"You're right," Lolly said. "So how are things with Dustin?"

"Better."

"That's good . . ." Lolly said.

"Let's go back to your hot cowboy costar. He is hot, right?"

"Crazy hot."

"Hotter than Steven?" Kimmie questioned.

"No, different hot," Lolly said truthfully. "Kimmie, you can't tell anyone about this. Not Dustin and definitely not Natalia."

"I won't."

Lolly said, "And Kimmie?"

"Yeah?"

"Thanks for listening. I feel better."

"You're welcome, Lolls," Kimmie said. "Happy birthday in advance."

"Thanks, Kims."

After talking to her sister, Lolly left a message for Steven thanking him for his surprise gift and telling him she'd talk to him on her actual birthday in two days. She figured this simple appreciative acknowledgement would buy her some time to unpack how she was feeling, which was complicated. It was hard to admit this to herself, but one of the emotions she felt was relief.

Lolly knew for a fact that she loved and was *in* love with Steven. He was the guy she wanted to marry and have a family with, and she had a secret wedding wish book in the back of her closet to prove it. But what she didn't understand was why she got nervous walking to her morning classes when she knew she was going to see Dean. And now that she would be attending this Monday night camp dance with Dean instead of her boyfriend, who was throwing the party from afar, she was getting especially nervous.

The Delvin and the Yellowjackets concert was a huge hit, not just because they played lots of famous covers but also because the male lead singer was a total babe and the female bass guitarist wore a super-tight white Rolling Stones T-shirt and no bra, which meant there was someone in the band for every hormonally charged camper to lust over during the three-hour show. The dance floor was packed all night, and it was just what they all needed: a chance to let loose. It was two weeks until the big end-of-camp musical, and stress levels were sky high. The time was ripe for every camp crush to reach full bloom, and this impromptu bash was the perfect event to launch everyone out of the friend zone and into the end zone.

That night Lolly decided to pull out all the stops. When she walked into the dance wearing her favorite romper, high heels, and full makeup, everyone was turning their heads. She was the prettiest girl at the dance. That is until Siobhan showed up wearing a pale, peach-colored slip dress that should have clashed with her hair but only served to bring out the blue in her eyes and the natural glow of her alabaster skin. For her, makeup was not only unnecessary, it would have diluted her beauty, like setting fireworks off at high noon.

Lolly had been on the lookout for Dean but hadn't seen him yet, and when Siobhan walked in, Lolly had the overwhelming urge to make sure Dean saw her before he saw Siobhan. She left the dance to look outside but couldn't find him on the trail to the boys' cabins. On a hunch, she went to the studio where they rehearsed most evenings. When she looked in the window, she saw Dean lying on the couch of the *Oklahoma!* set. He was reading a book by flashlight in the dark rehearsal space. She opened the door, and he quickly shined the light on her.

"Hey," she said, blocking the glare from her eyes.

"Hay is for horses, better for cows, pigs don't eat it because they don't know how," was his response, which was so random and odd that she just stood there in silence. "It's something my mom always used to say because she hated when we said hey instead of hello. So you need to remember that when you meet my mom." After a pause he added, "At the show, I mean. Not because we're going to get married or anything."

"I will definitely remember to greet your mother with a proper hello." Lolly walked over and tapped his feet so she could sit down on the couch, but instead he just lifted up his legs. Lolly sat down, and he plopped his legs down on her lap.

"So, no dance for you?" Lolly asked.

Dean shook his head from side to side in an exaggerated manner. "No, ma'am. Bum leg, remember?"

"You seem to dance just fine with me onstage."

"True, true. But that's for the sake of art, which is worth the effort. I don't have the luxury of dancing for fun. Well, I do, but I don't like it."

"I'm pretty sure you're going to disappoint a lot of girls if you don't show up."

"Are you one of those girls?" he asked softly.

"Dean," Lolly said. "I have a boyfriend."

"Real fancy one, it seems," Dean said with a slight edge. "Though I can't blame him. If you were my girl, I'd want to spoil you, too."

"You know the first thing I thought when I heard Steven was doing this?"

"What?"

"I hoped it was a nice gesture for my birthday, but I wondered if it was because he cheated on me again and felt guilty. I shouldn't have to wonder that, should I?"

"That dickhead cheated on you?"

"Yeah, a while ago but we worked it out. But that's not my point. Want to know the second thing I thought about?"

"That you wanted to dance with me?" he asked.

Lolly nodded.

"That was my first thought, too. Which was why I decided not to go. I didn't want to put you in a weird position."

Lolly could think of about ten weird positions she'd like Dean to put her in, but instead she took his legs off her lap and plopped them on the floor. "C'mon," she said. "Dancing isn't cheating. Let's go shake that one good leg of yours."

XIII

After dinner and dessert, there was a question of what to do for the rest of the evening, but being on a train to Paris limited their options. The boys wanted to keep drinking, which was when Anna decided to make her exit. She thanked them all for a lovely evening, wished them a good night, and was met with unanimous protests as the boys gallantly offered to do anything Anna wished if she wasn't up for getting blind drunk. Anna thought for a moment and suggested they play Hearts, a card game she learned while traveling for equestrian competitions in her tweens.

Anna, Kiril, Ashton, and Jordy couldn't be more different but somehow, they all worked together. Anna was nicknamed the Queen of Hearts, and Jordy was the One-Eyed Jack of Spades because he had the best profile. Kiril was ordained the King of Clubs, for his penchant for nightclubs, which left Ashton as the Jack of Diamonds, because he was the wealthiest of the bunch as far as they all knew. "It's too bad there's not a Jack of Asses for you, Ash," Kiril quipped.

"Or a Jack o' Napes for you, my dear boy toy," retorted Ash.

During the hours of card play, everyone shared stories from their childhoods in a made-up game called Firsts: first swear word, first time they got grounded, first time they ever got into a fight. There were a few firsts Anna hadn't experienced, like first time you sent a dick pic or first time you got kicked in the balls, which Anna had no idea was such a memorable event in a boy's life. For a long time, topics like first kiss, or first sexual experience were avoided because of mixed company, but as the night wore on and the merry foursome bonded, even those subjects were broached.

When it came to first loves, Anna gave that honor to her ex-boyfriend, Alexander, but after she met Alexia, her definition of love changed completely. "I thought I knew what love was, but I was mistaken." Jordy's first love was a beautiful boy named Ricardo, whom he'd met in Argentina his junior year of high school. Sadly, they had met a few months before his family moved to Finland, so their love affair was short and sweet. "He's the only guy who still makes my heart pound when I think about him." Ashton's first love was a girl named Meredith, who'd worked on the crew of his father's yacht, and though they only shared one drunken kiss after a night of spin the bottle, he claimed it was true love because, to this day, it was the memory of her that he revisited more than any other girl. "The girl who will forever hold the top spot of my wank bank . . ." Lastly, Kiril said he wasn't sure he'd ever been in love the way they had. "I love all women, shouldn't that count?" Anna told him of course his fondness for women counted, but that's not the emotion they were discussing.

"Perhaps," Anna said, "you haven't fallen in love yet. Pardon my use of a cliché, and I'm certainly no expert in the matter as I can only speak from recent experience, but when you're in love, trust me, you'll know."

The early morning sun was starting to shine through the skylight, and they could hear the bustle and clatter of the dining car staff prepping for the early risers. They all agreed to meet for lunch at 1 P.M. after everyone got some shut-eye. Kiril insisted on walking Anna to her cabin, even though it was only one car over. When they arrived at her door, Kiril asked if he could come in and talk to her about something. She asked if it could wait until later, suddenly aware of how sleepy she was, but he told her it would only take a moment. Anna invited him in, and with a brief thought that her grandmother would be pleased, she purposely left the door ajar.

"Did you know Alexia kept a journal?" he asked.

"I know he sketched and wrote poetry. Your mom was kind enough to give me copies of some of them." Anna debated telling Kiril about the letters, but she wasn't sure if she wanted him to know about them.

"I found it hidden in his closet under a stack of sweaters. I didn't read it because it didn't feel right to invade his privacy. I threw it in my bag in case, thinking I would bury it with him in Italy. But the night before his memorial service when I couldn't sleep, I read it. Was that terrible of me?"

"Only if he was still with us. You're his brother, so of course it's your right."

"Yeah, I guess. Alexia and I were close, but I have big regrets. I wish . . . I wish we had spent more time together before . . ." he trailed off.

Anna was starting to feel uneasy, uncertain where Kiril was going.

"I don't know if you know this, but after the whole horse race accident, our mother demanded Alexia stop seeing you. He refused of course, but she called me and implored me to get involved. I didn't want to, but my mother is not an easy woman to say no to." He paused. "Do you know about this? Did he tell you?"

"No," she said. "He didn't." Kiril coming back from college to visit was mentioned in a letter or two, but no details were given.

"I drove down and had dinner with him and told him he should stop seeing you. He knew our mom had put me up to it, but he was angry at me just the same. I told him no girl was worth this amount of trouble. It didn't make any sense to me. I thought he was being irrational. I said a lot of things I now regret. It was one of our worst fights, and it ended with me calling him a fucking baby, and he called me gutless and weak for taking our mom's side without bothering to meet you. He kept saying how much he loved you and that if I met you, I'd understand."

Kiril cast his eyes down, and Anna moved a little closer to him.

"What got me was the way he talked about you, like he wasn't a boy anymore but a man. More of a man than I am, that's for sure. Eventually I came to my senses after a good drunken heart-to-heart with Jordy, who elucidated the same notion you expressed earlier, that perhaps it wasn't my place to know what was in another's heart. I called him and apologized for being an asshole. I told him I wanted to meet you, but by then, you two were on 'a break.' He was so miserable during that time, and I wasn't there for him like I should have been. I often wonder what would have happened if Jordy and I hadn't talked and I didn't make that call. . . . If he had died before we resolved it, I would have never forgiven myself."

Anna said nothing, waiting for him to continue. Clearly Kiril had to get this off his chest.

"After the accident I blamed you. Totally unfair, but I was hurting. Bea got me all riled up about how his death was your fault."

"What?" The mention of Beatrice made Anna sit upright. "Bea blames me for Alexia's death? Oh my god, is that why she wasn't at his memorial service? I've texted her a few times but she never answered."

"I don't know why she wasn't there," Kiril said. "I came to my senses, of course. It wasn't your fault. It was a terrible and tragic accident."

Kiril put his face in his hands and Anna, not knowing what else to do, leaned in and rubbed his back to offer him some comfort. "You're wearing his cologne," Anna said barely above a whisper.

"We were in Paris for Christmas last year and as a present I took him to Maison Kurkdjian, one of the most famous Parisian perfume creators alive. Kurkdjian helped Alexia design a custom scent all his own."

"I would know it anywhere. His smell."

"I'll send you a bottle when I get back to the city," Kiril said, rubbing his face. "Anna, the way he wrote about you in his journal, so full of love and passion. It was heart wrenching to read. I feel so god-fucking-awful that I let him down. I did exactly what he accused me of, twice, judging you without bothering to meet you. I want to say I'm sorry. I had planned to visit you in New York, to apologize. Meeting you on the train feels like fate. Like he wanted us to meet so I would finally understand. And I do. I get it. And I'm truly happy that my baby brother had a chance to experience something real with someone like you before he died."

The tears cut through Anna's makeup, leaving her face streaked with mascara. Kiril put his arm around her. "It's okay, Kiril. You don't owe me an apology. I understand how complicated families are. I found out recently that my father had turned Alexia away when Alexia begged him to see me."

"He was so in love with you," Kiril said. "I was a little jealous, reading his journals. I've never felt anything for a girl the way he felt about you."

"I loved him with my whole heart," Anna said. "I still do." Kiril reached out to wipe away Anna's tears. She closed her eyes at his smell as their foreheads touched.

And then Kiril kissed her.

Anna kissed him back for a moment before realizing what was happening. "No, wait," she said pushing him away.

Kiril leaped up so fast he almost stumbled, apologizing to Anna with tears in his eyes, in shock over the kiss as much as she was. Anna pointed to the door. "You should go."

And with one sad glance back at her, he left.

XIV

Dustin felt guilty about riding on Steven's father's G5 to Michigan to watch Lolly's end-of-camp show, but Kimmie wasn't taking no for an answer.

"Why wouldn't you want to fly private if given the choice?"

"Hmm, let's see. Air pollution. Global warming. Climate change."

"Flying commercial can't be that much better," Kimmie retorted, not really knowing if her statement was true or not.

"It is better, think about it. Having two hundred–plus people on a plane as opposed to each of those two hundred people flying private . . ."

"Those two hundred people who are flying commercial can't afford to fly private, so your logic is faulty."

Dustin was about to explain how his logic wasn't faulty in the least, but then Kimmie leaned in and kissed him, and he promptly forgot what they were talking about. It seemed unfair of her to employ such a tactic to win debates, but he certainly wasn't complaining.

The plan was to watch Interlochen's production of *Oklahoma!*, spend one night hanging out with Lolly and her fellow thespians, load up Lolly's trunk in the morning, and head home together. Kimmie and Dustin had not anticipated making the trip. It had been Lolly and Kimmie's dad's responsibility to pick up Lolly from camp since her mother had dropped her off, but he called at the last minute to say he'd double-booked a wedding that he couldn't get out of. After their mom yelled at their dad for twenty minutes, it was decided Lolly wouldn't be as upset if they sent other loved ones in his absence. Steven had always planned on going, but he was more than happy to have Kimmie and Dustin along for the ride. Kimmie casually mentioned to Dustin that it would be fun if Natalia came along, too, but Dustin nixed that idea. This weekend was about Lolly, and there was no way she would want Natalia there.

Kimmie admired how Dustin gave her honest advice and didn't kowtow to her just because she was his girlfriend. She found his forthrightness sexy. They had been getting along incredibly well ever since their date night at the St. Regis. They still hadn't gone all the way or anything, but they had been doing plenty of experimenting, and now she felt much closer to him. It was like fooling around was a totally different language they were learning to speak with each other. She loved how his breathy moans made her feel full of confidence. She only wished she had talked to him more directly about sex earlier. As soon as they talked openly, all of her paranoid thoughts just disappeared into thin air. It was annoying; they had wasted so much time! Now they were much more relaxed around each other, and their kisses hello were no longer perfunctory pecks, but full-on smooches that could lead to anything at any moment. Her mom had even noticed the change and gave her the same sex talk she had given Lolly when she first started dating Steven: "Always use condoms!"

Her mom had booked two hotel rooms for their trip with the intention that she and Lolly would sleep in one and Dustin and Steven would share the second room, but all parties involved assumed different sleeping arrangements would be made. "I'm excited about tonight," she told him.

Dustin's face lit up and he smiled so sweetly. "Me, too! I love you."

"I love you, too." She sighed as he pulled her into his arms and kissed her.

Watching Dustin and Kimmie cooing at each other, Steven felt a twinge of pride that their relationship had turned around after his idea that Dustin take Kimmie to the St. Regis. Dustin was not the guy to kiss and tell, but when Steven "popped" a bottle of vintage Veuve in honor of his boy popping his cherry, Dustin felt he had to tell the truth, which was that he and Kimmie had decided to continue to take it slow, so there was no need for bubbly yet. But by the looks of their canoodling, Steven was pretty sure that his friend would be arriving in Michigan a boy and leaving as a man. The only person Steven was happier for was himself. He was stoked that these six weeks of long-distance chastity were coming to an end. Lately Lolly had been so busy with the show that he was barely getting any sexts from her. He could not wait for this play to be over so he could pick her up, sling her over his shoulder, and march her back to their hotel room. He had called ahead and ordered a few dozen roses to be waiting in the room for them.

He had also bought Lolly an antique locket necklace and spent last night using an X-Acto knife to cut out two perfect tiny pictures of himself to put inside it. He figured it was a good gift since they only had two weeks left together before he was heading off to Deerfield. He was normally a guy who scoffed at couples attempting long-distance relationships, but he now felt confident they could handle it. During the last six weeks, he wasn't once tempted by another girl. He had learned his lesson and was ready to reap the rewards for being such a good boy all these weeks. And if he was being totally honest, he was really looking forward to telling her with full faith that she could trust him completely once again.

Meanwhile over at Interlochen, Lolly was a wreck. And not the harmless fender-bender kind of wreck, she was more like one of those zero-visibility-multiple-car-disasters-on-a-snowy-Midwestern-road-where-unsuspecting-drivers-keep-skidding-on-black-ice-and-slamming-into-the-back-of-an-ever-increasing-pileup. Lolly had never felt so utterly tortured.

It was as though there had been two totally different people living in her body for the past month. One was the Lolly she'd always been, the one who was madly and devotedly in love with Steven K., the cool boyfriend who checked off every single box on her list: good-looking, popular, rich, fashionable with a non-annoying family, fit, tall enough that she could wear any heel height, good at giving gifts, and talented in the sack. The second Lolly was different, a girl who woke up every morning thinking about a Texas boy named Dean who checked off a totally different set of boxes she had never even known about: calls me darlin', loves theater, says I look just as pretty without makeup, is kind to everyone, knows how to repair a fence, can shear a sheep, and isn't afraid to cry when a baby calf he helped birth walks for the first time.

Somehow these two Lollys had been inhabiting the same body for weeks now with surprisingly little conflict, but not anymore. Right this very second the wheels of Steven's private plane were touching down at an airport thirty miles away. In less than six hours, he'd be sitting in the audience watching Lolly #2 do everything in her power not to break character and rip open the buttons of Dean's shirt and press her face into the first hairy chest she had ever been attracted by. How was it possible to feel two diametrically opposed feelings simultaneously?

Nothing had happened between Lolly and Dean the night of the dance—well, nothing much. They had danced most of the night together along with all the other campers to the so-uncool-they-were-cool boomer band Delvin and the Yellowjackets. They had shown up at the outdoor pavilion right as Bon Jovi's "You Give Love a Bad Name" began, which Lolly learned right then and there that Dean proudly knew all the words to, because he brought her to the center of the dance floor and sang it to her. "*Your very first kiss was your first kiss good-bye!*" Lolly shrieked with humiliation and rolled her eyes while secretly loving every second of it. But what really got a lot of tongues wagging was when Lolly performed Sammy Hagar's "This Girl Gets Around" from *Footloose* and was invited up on stage midway through it to sing with Delvin himself.

There was a faction of campers, mainly the younger ones, who believed Lolly was totally in the wrong to have been dancing like that with Dean when her own boyfriend was the one who paid for the band and not one, but two food trucks, which were both delicious by the way. There was another faction who believed that any girl, including Lolly, should be allowed to dance with whomever she wanted, even if she did have a boyfriend at home. Besides, dancing, even slow dancing, wasn't technically cheating anyway, so who actually gave a shit? And a third faction of campers, who speculated that maybe Lolly was polyamorous (or as one of the campers dad-joked, Lollyamorous), thought it was wrong to vilify anyone for their own personal choices when it came to love. And finally there were those who fully believed that the whole purpose of life and drama camp was the drama, and it was their duty to fan the flames of any wayward spark, for better or for worse.

Lolly really wasn't sure what she was doing, how she felt, what she believed, or what she should do next. But that night dancing with Dean and her friends, she had decided not to worry about it and just live her best life in the moment. She knew people were whispering about her, but she also remembered one of her favorite Oscar Wilde quotes: "*The only thing worse than being talked about is not being talked about.*" This was her last dance of her last summer at theater camp, the place that had shaped some of the best parts of herself.

Right before Delvin and the Yellowjackets ended their set, Dean had whispered in her ear that he'd like to walk her back to her cabin before curfew, and she agreed. On the walk to her cabin Dean grabbed for her hand, and Lolly let him take it as they walked quietly in the dark. There was so much unspoken tension between them that it was almost too much to take.

After that, their rehearsals became hot and heavy, so much so that Jamieson complained that their crazy chemistry was actually making the play worse, not better. Lolly was playing the role of a woman torn between two men, and the dramatic tension of the play depended on her not knowing who to choose. But the scenes between Lolly and Dean were so electric that it was difficult for Jamieson to compete. In his opinion, they should just go ahead and bang already, which he thought would dampen their allure for each other.

"You think I'm kidding," Jamieson said, his hands on his hips. "Don't think of it as cheating on Steven. Think of it as honing your craft and doing what's necessary to make sure we kill on opening night. I need a smash hit because I want to use this tape on my college apps. Also, I need a detailed account from a trusted wildlife sexpert as to the habits and behaviors of the trouser snake slithering around in Dean's jeans.

Trust me when I say it looks large and dangerous in the best possible way."

Lolly knew Jamieson was kidding, but she also knew there was a nugget of truth in everything he said. She was worried too that her chemistry with Dean would be glaringly obvious to the audience. Would Steven notice it? And if he didn't, then what would that mean?

What she couldn't stop obsessing about lately was how different Dean was from Steven. They were like night and day, chunky peanut butter versus smooth, Kim Kardashian versus Michelle Obama, granny panties versus Hanky Panky thongs; it was almost laughable. She didn't mean it as an insult, but one of Steven's most defining characteristics was the way he flaunted his wealth. He looked rich, he dressed rich, and it was obvious he liked all the things inherent in being rich. And if Lolly was being truthful, she liked that Steven was super wealthy. It wasn't why she loved him, but it certainly made being his girlfriend a lot of fun. Dean, on the other hand, seemed not to care about money at all. His priorities just weren't materialistic. Dean was very close to his parents, and he wasn't embarrassed to talk about it. In fact, he didn't shy away from his feelings at all. This openness could have been the result of his brush with terminal illness.

But he wasn't open all the time. He knew others thought he seemed aloof, and it was partially on purpose. There were many times he would be friendly to a girl, strictly on a platonic level, and then suddenly, she'd be into him romantically and he'd be in the uncomfortable place of having to reject her, which really made him feel awful. "Don't act like you don't have the exact same problem, Lolly. I don't have a big head. I'm just telling you how it is. Don't you feel bad when you have to beat off all the boys with the I'm-just-not-that-into-you stick?"

But he was mistaken. For Lolly, that was not how things were. All her life everyone had gawked at her little sister instead of her. And once she met Steven, she stopped noticing if other men looked her way. She was Steven's girl and only had eyes for him. Lolly never hid the fact that she had a boyfriend in front of new acquaintances, like some girls; she always let people know right away. She talked about Steven all the time because she loved him and because he was constantly on her mind. "It's never been a problem for me."

"Really?" Dean asked with a small smile. "So you don't feel sorry for me at all that you don't like me back?"

And boom, just like that, Dean took all their unspoken chemistry, wrapped it up in a bow, and set it down right in front of her. Lolly stopped walking, pulling her hand from his.

"Dean, we can't do this. The show is in less than a week."

Dean's smile faded away. "Which means your big-city boyfriend will be here, and he'll be whisking you away from me. What am I supposed to do then?"

Lolly was saved from answering his question by Juliet running up behind them with the major news that Garrison J., the first chair oboist, had just declared his love for Taleen in the middle of the dance floor. Taleen, who had been moping around since the early weeks of camp about her boyfriend back home cheating on her with her best friend, had been pouring her heart out to Garrison, who she thought was gay but who identified as bi. Taleen, totally shocked by Garrison's confession, grabbed the collar of his polo and pulled him in for a smooch that ended up lasting so long that it took both Ms. Sullivan and Mr. Brant to pry them apart.

Lolly, seeing her chance to escape a situation she had no idea how to handle, grabbed Juliet's hand like it was a life preserver. With pleading eyes she whispered, "Toto," Cabin Eight's safe word, to let Juliet know she was lost in Oz and needed help finding her way home. Juliet dutifully sprang into action, pulling Lolly away from Dean, post haste.

When they got inside Lolly whispered, "What the hell am I going to do?"

"You're going to remember every stinking second of having the hottest boy at camp thirsting for you while giving hope to the rest of us hopeless romantics."

But now that it was five hours from curtain call, who was going to save her? Jamieson had just handed her a note from Dean saying he needed to see her immediately at rehearsal studio B. Lolly thought about standing him up, telling herself now that Steven was in town that any non-play-related activities with another guy were definitely wrong. Instead, she ran all the way to rehearsal studio B, knowing they didn't have much time together.

When she walked in, Dean was sitting on the edge of the stage. He looked up at her. "I want you to know I tried to let it go. It's not that I relish being a dick and bringing this up at the worst possible time, but the thought of leaving tomorrow without telling you how I feel about you is driving me crazy. You're amazing. And even though you have told me pretty much every day since we met that you love your boyfriend and I should be respectful of your feelings, your loyalty and strength of character has only made me want you that much more."

"Dean, I don't know what to say. Actually, that's not true, I do know what I want to say. I want to be the person you think I am, but right now I feel . . . I feel . . ." Lolly ran toward him and threw herself in his arms, reciting her character Laurey's line from the play: "Curly, I'm afraid, afraid for my life, don't you leave me!"

"Gosh almighty, are you crying?" Dean said without missing a beat.

"I don't know what to do!" Lolly wailed with real tears starting to fall.

"Well, here, let me show you," Dean said, wiping her tears with his thumbs and bringing his face slowly to hers as their lips came together.

When the curtain closed on *Oklahoma!*, the whole crowd ripped up in applause and rose to their feet. Dustin and Kimmie stomped and clapped and gave little whoops of approval while Steven stewed, the only one in the theater to remain seated. Steven was no fool, he could see the heat between Lolly and Dean better than anyone. And even though Lolly always said most guys at theater camp were gay, Steven knew right away that the guy onstage with his girlfriend was as hetero as they came. It had taken all his strength not to jump up when that cowboy-hat-wearing idiot grabbed her hand and pulled her in for a kiss that was much too long to be deemed tasteful. *Who the hell was directing this piece of crap anyway?* Steven thought.

He was currently trying to keep calm, telling himself that it was a show, it was theater, and Lolly was nothing more than a convincing actress. But there was a playfulness between their characters that lacked all artifice, an ease that seemed intimate, and he wasn't pleased about it.

"You feeling okay?" Dustin asked, sitting down next to his friend.

"I don't think 'okay' is the right word for a guy whose girlfriend is kissing another man right in front of him. Did I just get cucked?"

"Dude, it's a play. That wasn't Lolly up there with some guy, it was Laurey and Curly."

"If you say so," Steven said, his voice flat and monotone.

"I do say so," Dustin said. "Listen, I'm sure it doesn't feel good to watch her in the arms of another guy, but you know Lolly is only crazy about one guy. And that guy is you, buddy."

"You guys ready?" Kimmie asked. "Let's go backstage and congratulate Lolly. Wasn't she great . . . wait, what's the matter?"

"Steven's a little jelly right now," Dustin filled her in.

"Am not," Steven said firmly. "And don't say jelly."

"I wouldn't worry," Kimmie said. "That Dean kid's way too hot to be straight anyway. Did you see his arm muscles? I thought they were going to rip through his shirt like the Hulk."

"Whatever." Steven was getting more irked by the second.

"Dude, you gotta get it together." Dustin chuckled, though Steven's foul mood was starting to make him uncomfortable.

Steven stared at Dustin and Kimmie for a moment without saying a word, without blinking even, and after a few worrisome seconds, he exhaled. "You're right, it's probably nothing."

When they showed up backstage, the crowd had already thinned out. All the cast members and their parents were heading over to the cast party at the grand pavilion. They spotted Lolly, still in costume, standing at the front of a semicircle of people. Dean had his arm casually draped around her shoulders while they talked to what were likely his parents and grandparents, if the cowboy hats were any clue. Lolly's back was to Steven, Kimmie, and Dustin, so they watched unnoticed for a moment.

The three of them all held a collective breath as Dean took off his cowboy hat and placed it on top of Lolly's head and she did a cute little curtsy. They stood in silence while Dean's elders filed out of the backstage area. Kimmie started to walk toward them when Dean pulled Lolly in close. He was about to plant a kiss on her lips, but Lolly ducked at the last second, and Dean smooched the air.

Kimmie squeaked like a mouse.

Dustin's eyes bugged out of his head. "Oh shit."

Steven wasted no time leaping forward, yelling, "What the actual fuck?!"

Lolly shrieked and pushed Dean away. "Hey guys, did you like the show?"

"The one I just saw, or are we talking about the play?" Steven asked.

"Technically it's a musical," Dean said.

"Fuck you and the horse you rode up on, bruh!" Steven said.

"Lolls, I'm gonna head to the party. I'll see ya there," Dean said, taking his hat off of her head and putting it back on his own.

"Do not call her Lolls," Steven said.

"Do not tell me what to do, rich boy."

The two boys moved in toward one another until their chests were almost touching. Neither of them said anything but it was clear they were both hoping the other would say something to warrant a good punch in the face.

Dustin quickly squeezed in between them and ushered Dean out, with Kimmie following close behind. When they were alone Lolly looked at Steven and said, "There's nothing going on between us."

"That's not what I saw onstage," he told her.

Lolly hung her head, unable to meet Steven's eyes. "That was acting."

"Don't bullshit a bullshitter," he said.

"Okay fine, I don't want to lie to you. Me and Dean have chemistry but we haven't acted on it, not really," Lolly said. "I don't know how to put it into words."

"Well," Steven replied, looking at his watch. "You've got an hour to think about it because I'm heading back to the airport now and the plane's leaving at midnight with or without you."

XVI

The next leg of Anna's train trip was from Paris to Verona instead of back to Venice. This was Anna's first time visiting Verona, and she asked her aunt and uncle what off-the-beaten-path sight they were going to explore together this time. Jules and Wilson told her they weren't going the obscure route and instead were taking her to a popular tourist destination. They said it seemed like the exact right place for her to visit, but they refused to tell her much more than that.

An hour later, the three of them arrived at a small courtyard where Anna found a crowd of people taking pictures next to a statue of a young woman. Anna noticed the majority of people in line were women, and Jules told Anna she should get in line and await her turn. "Are you going to wait in line, too?" Anna asked.

Her aunt shook her head. "I have no need for it," she said cryptically. "For once."

Anna, unable to wait, asked the woman in front of her what they were in line for. The woman told her that those who rub the breast of the statue will no longer be unlucky in love. Anna learned she was at the house of Juliet, the fictional character of Shakespeare's tragic love story. Although there was no real historical connection from this particular palazzo to *Romeo and Juliet*, there was a stone balcony overlooking the courtyard. When it was Anna's turn at the head of the line, she stared at the statue of the girl with the gold dress, and it gave her a chill in spite of the sweltering heat. She reached her hand up to the breast as she had seen everyone do ahead of her and stopped an inch away from it, suddenly scared that doing so would somehow erase all the highs and lows of love she had experienced.

Yes, she was unlucky in love, and even though things couldn't have ended worse between her and Alexia, she still considered herself lucky to have met him. Anna closed her eyes, reached out her hand, and rubbed the statue anyway.

She found Wilson and Jules at the wall where thousands of people had graffitied the stones with the names of loved ones, and Jules had just finished writing her and Wilson's names with a silver paint pen, which she then handed to Anna. She took the pen from her aunt and wrote her initials along with Vronsky's: A.K. + A.V.

Once inside the museum, they were able to see the original statue that once stood in the courtyard. It now had a slight concavity in the right breast from all the people who had rubbed the supposedly lucky spot. It comforted Anna to know that she was not alone when it came to heartbreak. There were so many others who were survivors like her and stayed open to all that love could offer.

During lunch Anna opened up to her aunt and uncle about Vronsky's letters and explained she only had two more left, which was causing her anxiety. "I'm afraid that when I get to the last letter, I'll feel like I'm losing him all over again."

Jules offered up her own perspective. "You may feel like that, but don't forget you'll always have the letters to remember him by, so when you miss him, you can read them again and again."

"I wish I'd had the chance to say a proper good-bye to him at the memorial service. I was so numb it didn't feel real to me. It was hard for me to take everything in while I was there and now that he shared so much with me in his letters, I feel like I've left things unsaid. I wish I could go and visit his grave site again. I'm in a much better headspace now than I was in June."

"Maybe you should go," Jules said. "Take it from a writer. There's nothing worse than things left unsaid."

"You're right. I should go!" Anna said, thrilled to be continuing her streak of bold choices.

Jules said Anna needed to ask her father first. "And when you talk to him, maybe leave out that it was my idea." Anna would have to take a ninety-minute flight to Sicily, and Jules didn't want to jeopardize the progress she was making with Edward by granting Anna permission for something that might annoy him. So Anna called her dad and told him that she needed to visit Vronsky's grave again, and that she could leave tomorrow morning and return to Verona by early evening, so she'd have more than enough time to get back on the train for London.

Edward agreed, and Anna was pleased that she and her father had finally reached a place of trust again. She thanked him for letting her go, and he thanked her for having the courtesy to ask. Unlike Steven, who had just spent twenty grand on eight high-end drones for the Summertime Funtime party that was already costing him an astronomical amount of money.

The next morning, Anna woke up early, took a car to the airport, and boarded a small plane to Sicily. By noon she was sitting by the plot where Alexia had been laid to rest two and a half months ago. She told him everything: about the sleepless nights and the Fox King at the dance club in Italy; meeting the lead singer of The NowNows and how helping him with his broken heart helped hers feel a bit better; how she ran into Kiril and his college friends, and they had stayed up all night playing Hearts. She left out the part about Kiril kissing her and the fact that she was too afraid to face him the next day, so she slid a note under his door saying good-bye and invited him, Jordy, Ashton and Denzel to the Summertime Funtime party.

She told Alexia she was trying to get used to the idea of going to a new school in Seoul, and that she no longer wanted to go to college on the East Coast. She was thinking of Stanford. She had never considered herself a California girl, but her worldview was expanding, and she was pushing herself to try things that took her out of her comfort zone. At the beginning of the summer she was truly lost, not knowing who she was without all the expectations that defined her life. But now, unburdened by the constraints of perfection, she felt confident to blaze her own trail into the future.

She then opened her purse and pulled out a small velvet bag that held a charm in the shape of a heart, a little smaller than the one Vronsky had given her. She had found a store on Notting Hill that sold antique watches and fountain pens and had had it engraved with the same message—ME AND YOU. As she dug into the soft ground to bury it, she told him that she would love him forever. "I know this sounds crazy, but when I sat on the Fox King's lap and asked him how I could get over a broken heart, he told me that the only way was to pick up the pieces, take in their value and meaning in your life, and then bury all of them but one, which you must keep as a talisman to guide your heart for the next time. So, this charm is me burying the pieces of my heart with you, and the charm you gave me will guide my heart forever."

XVII

Labor Day weekend, the last hurrah of summer, when teenagers all over the country and especially the Hamptons act like it's the end of the world. In high school, summer break always seems to have a different flow of time, a different set of rules, and even the most buttoned-up girls and boys loosen their belts and go for a skinny-dip or two. So as the summer draws to a close, we are here to mourn the freedoms given up in the name of Academia. And with the spirit of summertime funtime in our hearts and minds, Steven K., we beseech you . . .

A few weeks ago, Steven decided the theme for his Summertime Funtime party would be the End of the World, but then he found out a nightclub in Montauk was already throwing an End of the World Labor Day beach barbecue, an unwelcome development that vexed him to no end. And so at the last minute he had to pivot and find another concept, something even better. Having once been written up in Page Six as the kid who had his finger on the pulse of teenage debauchery, he had been feeling a lot of pressure. He also wanted to make sure that his party topped Bucky Bradford's Fourth of July bash not only because he was competitive as hell but more that he felt Bucky disrespected Dustin with his lecherous eye-licking of Kimmie.

Now in the Hamptons less than a week before the party and still without a theme, Steven had been lying by the pool for the last twelve hours barely speaking to anyone. Dustin was starting to get worried. He stood in the living room staring out the French doors at his friend in a catatonic state, which reminded him of Cameron in the scene at the end of *Ferris Bueller's Day Off* after his father's Ferrari was taken for a joyride. "Did he take anything?" he asked Lolly, who had just entered the room wearing a pink bikini with a camo scarf tied around her waist, a yoga mat under her arm.

Lolly walked over and joined Dustin by the window. "Not that I know of. Though I don't know if he'd tell me anyway. He's still barely speaking to me. Like he's said maybe seven whole sentences since we got back from Michigan. I'm keeping track on my phone. Every time I say we need to talk he says, 'Babe, no can do. After the party.' Did he tell you something different? Has he said anything about me?"

"Not really," said Dustin. "Though every now and again I hear him mutter the words 'emotional affair' under his breath and scoff."

"I'm so mad at myself for saying that. That whole plane ride home he kept hounding me over and over asking me whether I'd found the words to tell him what happened between me and Dean. I don't even know where I got the words 'emotional affair,' I think it was something I heard my mom talking about with her friends."

"He'll get over it . . . eventually."

"How long will the ice storm last, do you think? It was one lousy kiss. Don't I get any credit for not having sex when I could have?!"

"I'm the wrong person to ask."

"Because you're his friend and you have to be on his side?"

"No, because I have never felt comfortable commenting on things I have no knowledge of."

"But what if Kimmie came to you and said she'd had an emotional affair with someone, would you break up with her?"

Dustin gave Lolly a side-eyed glance. "This is purely a hypothetical, right?"

"A million percent."

"Honestly, I'd be pretty devastated. Emotions are the foundation of any strong relationship. Is there some emotional need that Steven wasn't able to fulfill for you that this guy could? Actually, don't answer that. Lolly, I'm the wrong person to talk to about this. Only you know what you did or didn't do to betray Steven's trust."

Just then Kimmie entered the room. "I heard there were waffles somewhere," she said. "What's with the faces? Are there no more waffles?"

"Lolly and I were discussing the Steven situation," Dustin said.

"You mean how Lolly's emotional betrayal has turned Steven into a sunglass-wearing zombie by the pool?"

"Shut up, Kimmie!" Lolly said. "You need to be on my side."

"I'm Team Lolly always. But Natalia said your fatal mistake was telling him you had any thoughts about another guy at all. Guys don't want to hear about it. Ever. They would rather you lie to them," Kimmie said. "I know you don't like her, but she knows her shit when it comes to D."

Dustin shot Kimmie a confused look.

"D meaning dick, not you, hon," Kimmie said to him. "But since you're here, is that true? Would you want to know if I think some other guy is hot?"

"Not really," Dustin said quickly. "But I'm going to excuse myself from this conversation and go check on Steven." He went outside through the French doors and walked across the immaculate lawn to the pool.

Lolly waited until Dustin was out of earshot before she turned to face her sister. Kimmie winced, waiting for Lolly to yell at her for telling Natalia about her love life. "What else did she say?" Lolly asked. "At this point I'm desperate enough to hear anyone's advice who might help, even her."

Dustin sat down next to Steven, who was lying perfectly still in turquoise swim trunks and gold-rimmed aviators.

"Dude, you okay?" Dustin asked.

Steven didn't answer Dustin, and Dustin didn't prod him. He knew his friend would talk when he was ready, so Dustin reclined on the chaise and put his hands behind his head.

They sat in sun-drenched silence for forty-five minutes before Steven sat up, lifted his shades, and smiled at Dustin. "I've got it." Then he said nothing.

Dustin waited in Steven's long suspenseful pause. "What is it?"

"You ready?" Steven asked.

"I'm so ready."

"Sexy. Steampunk. Mermaid. Shambala."

"Shambala," Dustin repeated. "As in the mythological Tibetan hidden land where everyone has achieved spiritual enlightenment?"

"Yeah, some shit like that. I saw it in a video game once," Steven said. "It's gonna be fucking dope." He bolted out of his seat and sprinted into the house, leaving Dustin behind in the pool chair. Dustin closed his eyes in the warmth of the sun and heard a splash. When he looked up Kimmie was breaststroking in the deep end.

"C'mon, hot stuff, the water's wet, and I'm feeling fine."

Dustin sat up. "I'm feeling enlightened already," he muttered under his breath.

XVIII

Beatrice understood the yin and yang of New York City and Los Angeles much better after her summer in LA. New York City had the best and worst of everything. It was a playground of extremes that had always appealed to Beatrice, who chased extremes as a way of life. But LA was a totally different vibe. Instead of extremes there was a kind of constancy: the constant sun, the sameness of one blue-skied day to the next. She had lured Tiare east to Montauk, which had the best surfing in the Hamptons. Tiare was going to compete in a regional surfing competition that would hopefully get her enough points to qualify for a national competition in Hawaii in the fall, where she could find sponsorship to support her pro surfing aspirations.

Tiare had arrived a few days earlier with Chadwick and Manny, who had also decided to compete just for kicks. Claudine and her mother were arriving from France the day the competition started, which meant Tiare would be gone all day, giving Bea a solid chunk of time to deal with Claudine before they had to dress for dinner.

Bea's best friend from Greenwich, Adaka, had also come down for the Labor Day festivities and was helping Bea with the logistical nightmare of keeping her current girlfriend away from her former girlfriend. "I don't know how you got yourself into this sitch, but I do know you need a bitch like me to help you get out of it."

When Bea told Tiare how her mom had accidentally invited Claudine and her mother for Labor Day weekend, Tiare took the news in stride. "It's all good, babe. We both have pasts, and I'm confident you'll handle it." Then she added, "I'm still friends with all my exes."

Bea thanked her now exclusive girlfriend for trusting her, and she bought Adaka a new limited-edition Christian Dior tote for her wise counsel. It was Adaka who advised against telling Claudine about Tiare ahead of time. They needed to deal with the situation in person, as Claudine had all the hallmarks of a psychopath and may need to "get handled," as Adaka put it.

In fact, when Adaka arrived she had shared some news of her own. "Remember how at the beginning of the summer Murf was all, 'Just so you know, I don't do the boyfriend thing'? And I was like, 'Yeah, I'm only in the market for a fuckboi myself, so don't get ahead of yourself, sport.'"

"Yeah?"

"Well, there must be something in the stars because last night he asked me to be his girlfriend! So now we're exclusive, too!"

Bea smiled and offered her bestie her sincerest congratulations. "It's like the end of an era with the two of us off the market."

"Or it's like a sign of the coming apocalypse. And the end of the world is a French girl with double Ds who's all like if-I-can't-have-you-no-one-will!" Adaka lifted an invisible knife and made screeching noises. "Kidding!

Don't worry, my big handsome boyfriend will be on hand in case Claudine goes all stalkeriffic and needs to be handcuffed to the radiator when she finds out about your new surfer sweetie."

Bea exhaled a long, exasperated sigh, and Adaka reminded Bea that she had dealt with plenty of upset girls and boys over the years when she had gotten bored of them, or got the Ick, which everyone knew couldn't be recovered from. They just had to give Claudine enough time to air her feelings out and process the breakup without feeling abandoned. Then they'd roll through a few parties where a gorgeous girl like Claudine would have no trouble finding someone to turn her frown upside down.

"Exactly," Bea concurred, more upbeat now. "It's going to be fine, right?" This was new for Beatrice, the neuroses of desperately wanting things to go smoothly. Normally she sowed chaos just for fun. For her, a party wasn't memorable without some mess-in-a-dress wiggin' the F out, but right now all she wanted was a super-chill week hanging out with friends and family.

Adaka was loving this new, optimistic, and in-love version of her BFF. She had never seen Bea this happy, which gave her hope that her own summer fling could be the real thing and not just a way to piss off her uptight parents, which was definitely how it started. Murf was so different from the boys Adaka typically dated, but what he lacked in cash and social status, he more than made up for in terms of being a real human being. He texted when he said he would text, he showed up on time, and he was always good for a roll in the hay, literally and figuratively. Most important, Murf was chill, almost as chill as Bea's new girlfriend.

When Tiare arrived, Adaka was immediately impressed by her no-bullshit surfer girl attitude. Most people who came from Tiare's modest means found the money on display in the Hamptons either repulsive or overwhelming, but Tiare seemed to pay it no mind. She was focused solely on two things: Bea and surfing.

And she was dying to get some waves in with her new surfboard that Bea had given her the night she arrived. "You didn't!" Tiare had said when Bea sat her down by their infinity pool under the stars. She kissed Tiare and then used a remote control to turn on the pool lights, revealing the bright orange custom-made board floating in the water.

"I did," Bea said. "I know you're not into material possessions, but I really needed you to have something from me that will remind you every day how much I care about you."

Tiare dove into the pool fully clothed to check out her new board up close. "It's incredible, babe. Thank you so much. It's the sweetest gift I've ever gotten, everyone's going to flip out when they see it."

"Well that is the whole point of gifts, is it not?" Bea joked. "I measured your board and talked to one of your surfer buddies to make sure I got all the details right. And no pressure, if it's not right for any reason, we can get you a different one."

Tiare faked like she was casting a fishing line and slowly began to reel Bea toward her. "C'mere, you." Bea played along, kicking off her sandals and pretending to get pulled into the pool. Soon they were face-to-face with the rotating pool lights dissolving from red to blue to green to purple. "Thank you," Tiare said. "I love it, and I love you."

"I feel like you should go to bed early," Bea said. "To make sure you're rested for tomorrow."

"I was thinking the same thing," said Tiare. "Want to tuck me in? Which guest room am I in?"

"Guest room?" Bea scoffed. "My bed is your bed."

"Your parents cool with that?"

"My parents are fine with anything that keeps me happy and out of trouble. My dad's always working and my mom's usually bombed out of her mind and in bed by nine every night, probably earlier in the summer because she starts her mornings with Bellinis while the peaches are still in season."

"You're a peach," Tiare said.

"You are . . ." Bea closed her eyes and kissed Tiare.

Three days later, Murf, Adaka, and Bea were in the Mercedes G wagon waiting for Claudine's plane at the East Hampton Airport. They planned to whisk Claudine away to a crowded restaurant where Bea would deliver the news after brunch while Murf and Adaka did their own thing. They had another car and driver waiting to take Claudine's mother back to the house where the grown-ups were heading over to watch the Hampton Classic in Bridgehampton. Bea was avoiding the Classic this year as the last horse event she'd attended was the Greenwich charity event where Vronsky had had his accident and her mother's horse, Frou Frou, had died. Since her return, Bea had hardly brought up her cousin, which Adaka thought was a good sign even though Murf did not. In fact, Murf decided to bring him up now, while they waited.

"So, how was the memorial service for Vronsky?" Murf asked from the backseat. "I felt bad not being there, but it was in Italy. And I wasn't invited."

Adaka jumped in while Bea stiffened. "My mother told me Geneviève said it was small and lovely."

Adaka tried to catch Murf's eyes in the rearview mirror to warn him off the subject, but he continued. "Wait . . . you didn't go?"

"It was a timing thing, my internship in LA . . ." Bea began, but then stopped midsentence. Tiare had really been pushing her to deal with her feelings about it, saying how unhealthy it was to stay in denial. She turned around to face Murf. "I couldn't go, is that OK with you? I couldn't see him buried in the ground and I certainly couldn't deal with seeing Anna there. Geneviève actually invited her. Can you believe it? After all she did."

Murf frowned. "It was an accident."

"One that wouldn't have happened if it weren't for her. And don't tell me I'm being irrational, because I know I am. But ask me if I care."

"Hey, I think that's her plane!" Adaka said, thrilled to be cutting the excruciating conversation short. Still, for Bea, admitting that she was being irrational was progress from a few months ago when Adaka was harangued for bringing up Anna's name in her presence. Perhaps love really did heal all wounds. "I'm scared," Adaka said, watching the plane touch down. "But in a good horror-movie sort of way."

"And thanks to Jordan Peele," Murf said, "all the Black people won't have to die."

"Okay, okay," Bea said. "Now I'm freaking out."

"You ladies need to relax," Murf said. "I remember Claudine from Coachella and I'm pretty sure her fine French booty will be attracting all sorts of people this weekend who can help her get over you, Bea. No offense."

"Oh, offense taken," Bea said with a smile. "No one gets over this that easily."

Adaka gave Murf a playful smack in the shoulder. "And don't comment on how fine her booty is."

"I said 'fine French booty,'" he said. "Now if I said finest booty in all the land we'd know I was talking about your booty."

"Better." Adaka kissed him on the cheek.

Claudine was the first one off the plane. She hardly waited for the flight crew to finish opening the door before she squeezed past them and ran down the steps in a pair of gold gladiator sandals wrapped all the way up to her knees.

Bea rolled down the window and waved from the passenger seat as Claudine raced over and practically dove through the open window to throw her arms around Bea, who had to exert an extreme amount of effort to extricate herself from the embrace. "We have two cars," she explained. "One for your bags and your mother, and one for the four of us to go to brunch. You must be hungry."

"I am famished," Claudine said in her delightful accent. "But not for food. If we were alone, I'd gobble you up right now."

Adaka had to look away from Murf to keep from laughing.

"Come sit in the backseat with me," Claudine said to Bea, trying to open her car door from the outside.

"Claude, I can't. I got some water in my ear yesterday and when my ear is fucked up I get carsick and your new sandals are much too sexy to puke on." Bea was glad her lying skills were still tip-top.

"God! I missed your sense of humor, my brilliant hilarious darling!" Claudine leaned in to give Bea a kiss, but Bea managed to turn her head just in time, and caught only the side of Claudine's mouth.

"Adaka has a thing about PDA," Bea said quickly. "She's that girl who's always screaming at strangers to get a room."

"Oh, sorry. I'm just so excited to be here," said Claudine, glaring at

Adaka as Murf opened the door and invited Claudine to join him in the back.

"Murf!" Claudine exclaimed as she climbed in and threw her arms around him, pressing her ample chest into him in a way that made Adaka's nostrils flare. And any sympathy she had for what was about to happen to this vivacious French nymphette over lobster omelets completely evaporated.

XIX

Anna was in London packing for the long weekend in the Hamptons when she received her brother's call. She knew that when he called instead of texted it wasn't good news, and she was right. Steven had booked the singer Sia as a surprise performance for the party's big wow moment. She was going to be introduced when a dozen men dressed as Tibetan monks would appear in the crowd and begin to play their lutes, leading all the guests down to the beach where a stage would be ready and waiting. "Then on some bullshit, her manager, Bobby M., calls me up and says he double booked her and now we know that Ryan Seacrest's birthday is a bigger deal than Summertime Funtime. How am I supposed to find a worthy replacement with two days' notice? Anyone that's any good will already be booked."

"Ryan is dead to me from this day forth," Anna said.

"I don't need sarcasm, sis," said Steven. "I need a band."

"I may have an idea for a replacement." Anna put the phone on speaker and started texting Quentin.

"I've got three DJs booked so I could manage, but who is it?"

"It's that K-pop group I told you about. The NowNows. Their new single won Seoul's Song of the Summer. And one of the guys owes me a favor."

"Sweet. Let me know," Steven said. "Anna, I gotta jet. Dustin's waving at me and he's looking stressed."

"Oh Dustin? Tell him I said hi. FYI I'm meeting Chang-ri at the airport in an hour and we'll see you late tonight! And as soon as we see each other, we're sitting down and discussing this Lolly cowboy business. She texted me that you're giving her the deep freeze. I can't tell if you're overreacting."

"That makes two of us." Steven wished his sister safe travels and hung up as Dustin made his way over to him. "Anna says hi."

"Hi, Anna," Dustin said perfunctorily. "Dude, we need to talk . . ."

"Yo, have you had a chance to test out the new floating pool lights? Can you be in charge of the remote control? Where's Lolly? Oh right, she and Kimmie went to buy squirt guns. We're gonna fill them with vodka and ginger beer. Moscow pistols, I'm calling them. Dude, tell me the truth. Is the theme too random? What's that word for a lot of disparate ideas all smushed together in one place? Sounds like hedgehog, maybe?"

"Steven, shut up for a second and listen!" Dustin said. "We've got a problem."

"What now?"

"Bea's crazy ex-girlfriend put a hit out on Anna!" Dustin shouted in a whisper.

"Look, I can only deal with party stuff right now," Steven said.

"Murf called Lolly and told her, and then Lolly told him to call me so I could tell you."

"Why couldn't she tell me? Or why wouldn't Murf call me himself? You don't even know Murf."

"They both tried you, but you didn't pick up."

"This sounds passive-aggressive to me. God, is she still pissed that I yelled at her yesterday? What does she expect? This whole new age of 'total honesty' is bullshit; what am I supposed to do with this information?"

"Steven, did you hear what I said?" Dustin asked.

"Yeah, you said that Bea's crazy ex-girlfriend wants to hit on Anna. I wish her luck, but I doubt Anna will be into it."

"Not hit on. Put a hit on. Like she hired someone to rough her up. Break her legs. Cap her ass. Whack her. Sleep with the fishes."

"Why would someone want to put a hit on my sister?"

"It was like a gift for Beatrice. Some sort of retribution for Vronsky.

And she did it with my help. Obviously if I knew what she was doing I would have never helped her."

"You helped her?"

"Remember when you had me talk to one of Lolly's friends about the dark net?"

"Nope."

"We ate big steaks downtown and you had too much to drink." Dustin did his best to jog his friend's memory. "Lolly started texting you that Bea's French girlfriend called her with some computer question but you were too drunk to deal with it so you made me call Lolly back for you and then she got all suspicious that I was calling instead of you, so you got on the phone and you two had that big fight, and then we had to make a pit stop at her place because she was crying?"

"Oh yeah, that was the night when she first started freaking out that I was going to cheat on her while she went to camp. Ironic, eh? She's the one who was so convinced that I was up to no good and then she's the one who cheated on me!" Steven shouted. "Wait, was that the right usage of the word 'ironic'?"

Dustin grabbed Steven by the shoulders and shook him. "What drugs are you on?"

"I'm not on anything besides two Red Bulls and a triple espresso," Steven said. "And an Adderall. But only five milligrams. I've got a fuck-ton to get done today."

"Follow me," Dustin barked, and Steven followed him to the edge of the pool, the pool that now had two hundred LED lights shaped like flowers floating in it.

"Whoa, the flowers were an inspired choice, if I do say so myself, hella Shambala-ish, right?" Steven opened up his phone and checked pool lights off his list. Dustin snatched the phone out of Steven's hands and pushed him into the pool.

Steven came up sputtering. "What the fuck, bro!" he said, wiping his face.

"You need to focus on what I'm saying. This isn't a joke. Some chick I don't even know went on the dark net and paid ten thousand dollars to some random dude to hurt Anna. Anna, your sister," he said, as he tossed

Steven's phone on the chaise longue. "And I'm an accomplice because I'm the one who told her how to do it. She said she was looking for drugs and I told her it was dangerous and that she'd probably get hacked or get a virus or get ripped off, but she insisted I tell her how to do it. Why did I get involved? What are we going to do? This is not something I can live with."

"First things first . . ." Steven reached up for help getting out of the pool. As Dustin lent him his hand, bracing to lift him up, Steven yanked him forward into the pool.

"What the hell?! I'm just the messenger!"

Steven was laughing hysterically. "I can't believe you fell for that."

Ten minutes later the two guys were still in the pool trying to decide how best to handle the situation. "So what's the likelihood that this will pan out?" asked Steven. "I mean, is anything on the dark web legit?"

"How the hell should I know?" Dustin said. "I'm not an expert. Also, you keep saying 'dark web,' which I know is what most people call it, but it's technically wrong. It's the deep web, and the dark net lives on the deep web. Okay, I can tell by your expression that this is an unnecessary thing for me to point out at the moment. All we have to go on is the facts. Claudine told Murf who told Lolly that she paid ten grand in LiteCoin to some unknown party to hurt Anna. I'm pretty sure that's not enough to kill someone, but we don't know exactly what was arranged. The good news is the dark net is monitored by all kinds of law enforcement, so for all we know it was some undercover FBI agent who took the money and they're building a case against Claudine because soliciting such a service is illegal."

"Who else knows about this again?" Steven asked.

"Murf, Beatrice, you, me. And Lolly, of course."

"Which means everyone knows," Steven said in a not-so-nice way. "She probably posted it on her fuckin' Insta-story."

"No, she didn't," Dustin said. "And not that I'm defending her, but Lolly didn't technically cheat. She could've slept with that Dean guy, but she didn't."

"She made out with him though."

"It's not uncommon for actors to develop feelings for their costars in situations like that."

"Is that supposed to make me feel better?" Steven asked glumly.

"I don't understand why you're not freaking out more about this Claudine thing," Dustin said. "You don't think we should cancel the party?"

"Dude, no way we're canceling. If there's no party then I have to deal with my relationship and I do not want to deal with my relationship."

"Selfish!" Dustin fake coughed the words into his hand. "Real talk, though, we have to do something."

"I didn't say I wasn't going to do anything," Steven said. "I'll call Nehorai and let him know what's what. He's the head of security for my dad. Maybe he can double up on security for the party."

"Nehorai? Is he Israeli?"

"Ex-Mossad. Definitely killed people in not so nice ways. I've never seen him smile, like ever."

"I know this party is a big deal for you, but it's a mistake not to talk to your parents about this. Steven, I'm a part of this now, and if something happens to Anna because of my involvement . . ."

"Nothing is going to happen to Anna. You said so yourself. Claudine probably got ripped off. Also, if we canceled a party every time a girl spazzes out over a relationship, there would be no parties! Rich crazy girls talk a lot of shit and for all we know she could be making this whole thing up to get Bea's attention. If it makes you feel better, you can come with me when we talk to Nehorai, and if he says we should call my dad, then we will. But my dad will for sure make me call the whole thing off. And no one wants that."

When Bea came clean to Tiare about the full extent of Claudine's insanity, Tiare thought she was joking. But once Bea explained she was serious, Tiare was appalled. "Man, you rich kids are fucked in the head! Why would she think that was a good gift for you? It's disgusting."

"I mean, I *am* hard to buy for . . ."

Tiare stared at her. "Bea, now's the time to tell me if there's more to this story."

"What is that supposed to mean?"

"It means if you're involved in taking down this Anna girl for revenge, I need to know."

"And what, you're gonna break up with me?" Bea asked, suddenly defensive.

"Don't put words in my mouth, this is some serious shit. It's totally mental that this girl did this in the first place but doing it as a deranged gesture of love for you makes it beyond. This girl clearly needs help. Did you tell your parents?"

"Are you high? Of course not. Let me explain how it works around here. My parents don't want to deal with this kind of shit. I had two nannies growing up! Two of them . . . for one of me. That's how much they didn't want to deal with raising me."

Tiare walked up to Bea and hugged her. "Babe, it's okay. I'm gonna help you figure this out."

"I talked a lot of shit about Anna K. after Vronsky died. A lot. But I was never going to act on it. I hate lots of people. It was just venting," Bea said. "I'm not an idiot, and orange is definitely not my new color."

"You weren't kidding when you said you were trouble, huh?"

"Nope."

"So where is Claudine now?"

"With Adaka and Murf."

"Maybe it's time I met her," Tiare said.

"I don't think that's a good idea. She didn't take the news about us well," Bea told her. "I barely got the words 'I met someone in LA' out before she stood up and started swearing at me in French. Then she climbed over the little fence and took off running down the street. Like she was literally running away from the news. I sent Murf after her because Adaka and I were in flip-flops."

"So how did you find out about the dark web thing?"

"Murf caught up with her, and she let it slip when she was ranting and raving like a lunatic on the beach."

"Any chance she was making the whole thing up, you know, in the it's-the-thought-of-hiring-a-hitman-that-counts kind of way?" Tiare asked. "Have you tried talking to her again?"

"God no."

Tiare stood up. "Let's go talk to her. We need to know if this is legit or some fake news shit."

"Do we have to?" Bea whined.

"Didn't you just rail against your parents for letting other people handle their responsibilities?"

Bea stared up at her girlfriend and was suddenly hit with a swell of emotion. "Well if you're going to put all my psychological ducks in a row and make me keep my contradictory impulses in check, then I guess I have no choice! Okay, okay. I'm in. They have her locked in the guesthouse."

"What?!"

"I'm kidding! But she is staying there with her mom. I'm a hundred percent setting the alarm for the main house tonight so she can't sneak in and kill us in our sleep later."

"More jokes?" Tiare asked.

"Oh no, that was serious."

Bea and Tiare headed outside where all the adults were lying by the pool drinking cocktails and waiting to be called in for dinner. They stopped and made small talk, and Bea bragged about Tiare being ranked second place at the end of day one of her surfing competition. It turned out Tiare's job of schmoozing with wealthy hotel guests gave her the ability to handle bourgeois small talk with grace and aplomb. As they headed down the stone path leading to the guesthouse, Tiare asked Bea if her parents had said anything about her.

"My mom asked who your personal trainer was in Santa Barbara, which means she thinks you have a good body. And you haven't met my dad yet. That guy always next to my mom is the guy my dad hired to make sure that when she falls down drunk later there will be someone to pick her up and put her to bed. He's on twenty-four/seven duty during all major holidays. My dad will make an appearance at some point . . . you'll know it's him because he'll bring up how his new yacht is bigger than the prince of Brunei's by six whole inches in the first five minutes of conversation."

"I've never been interested in having money before, but now I know for certain I don't want it."

"I get it. I can't complain about it because it makes me sound even more like an ungrateful bitch than I already do, but everyone who thinks being rich solves everything is wrong. At least ten girls from my school are in rehab this summer for either drugs or eating disorders, though some might just be getting plastic surgery."

When they entered the guesthouse, they interrupted Adaka and Murf on the couch in a passionate embrace so intense Bea had to clear her throat three times before they disentangled. "Sorry for the interruption. But where's Claudine le Fou?"

Adaka pointed toward the closed bedroom door then turned and looked at Murf. "Baby, will you go with them in case . . ."

"That won't be necessary," Tiare said. She walked to the door, rapped twice, and then opened it, Bea following close behind her.

They stood and stared at the empty room, bed perfectly made, curtain flapping in a warm breeze coming through the open window, Claudine nowhere to be found.

XXI

Steven's Summertime Funtime party was a success before it even started. Taking a page out of the rise of prom-posals in recent years, Steven decided the best way to build excitement was through the invitations. So when Aaron O. was playing in the men's singles semifinal at the Maidstone Round Robin tennis tournament, the spectators started pointing to the sky at a drone that looked like a flying saucer with spinning lights, hovering above the court until the point ended on a drop shot. Everyone's collective jaw dropped as the UFO drone descended, following Aaron as he walked to the bench to towel off before changing sides. His girlfriend, Darcy L., was in on it, filming the whole thing. A trap door opened up beneath it, and an envelope fluttered down. Aaron caught the invite on his racket as the drone took off.

The invite itself was an impressive, unauthorized drawing of Rick and Morty both in aviator sunglasses lying on the beach and watching three suns set over a pink alien ocean. Morty was asking Rick what his Saturday night plans were, and Rick was answering: "I'm going to a Summertime (burp) Funtime party." Aaron looked up after opening the invitation, raised it over his head and yelled to the crowd, "Fuck yeah! Steven K.'s having a party!" Then he went on to win his match in three sets.

Drones showed up in four other such locations, one being in the VIP tent of the Hampton Classic. All the videos were posted across social media, and within the hour every teenager in the Hamptons was craning their necks and looking up, hoping for a party invite.

The morning of the party was hot and muggy, but the forecast said it should cool down by eventide. The adults were encouraged to come in the late afternoon for classic barbecue fare: hamburgers, hot dogs, lobster rolls, crab cakes, veggie burgers, and a French fry bar that featured ten different types of French fries: regular skinny fries, steak fries, truffle fries, curly fries, waffle fries, cheese fries, chili fries, sweet potato fries, avocado fries, purple potato fries, and tater tots.

Steven had wanted to bag all phones upon entry, so people couldn't post videos of all he had in store for them, ruining the surprise for those arriving later, but Lolly was adamantly opposed unless she would be allowed to have her phone. Steven agreed, but then Kimmie wanted her phone, and Natalia said no way was she going be the only basic bitch without a phone. Steven gave up because he just couldn't handle everyone sniping at each other.

He had thrown enough parties to know that if everyone was in too good of a mood going in, then the party was jinxed and likely to end in disaster, which didn't necessarily make for a bad party in his book.

Parties needed to be memorable; this was his only requirement for success. What he didn't totally know was if everyone was fighting before a party, would it make an already bad situation worse, or could the party, if it was planned just so, undo the tension and unleash the good times he believed everyone had within them at any given moment?

These were just some of the things Steven thought about when he was in party-planning mode, but inevitably the day of the party brought its own unique challenges. For instance, the six model mermaids he had hired were now infighting because one of them was refusing to take her turn in a go-go dancer's cage that was suspended above the pool where they were to wave at party guests and blow bubbles that would slowly waft down over the floating flower lights. The other mermaids didn't think it was fair that Steven had agreed to let one mermaid opt out of her turn in the cage just because she didn't like confined spaces. Steven, unable to deal with mermaid politics, assigned Dustin to solve the problem. Dustin gathered the mermaids around for a pep talk but he made the mistake of letting them know how crucial they were to the party's theme. The mermaids soon realized if they banded together as a group, they'd have more collective bargaining power and soon the mermaids were Googling things like "how to unionize," "entertainment lawyers," and "Sun Tzu's art of war." Seeing her boyfriend surrounded by a half-dozen newly empowered mermaids, Kimmie grew jealous and got involved. Right as the mermaids were threatening to "swim off the job," Natalia arrived on the scene and said she'd be more than happy to be the night's only mermaid-for-hire and pocket the time-and-half holiday pay all six of them stood to earn. And just like that the fledgling mermaid union dissolved as quickly as it had been established and it was agreed that Natalia would take the claustrophobic mermaid's shift in the go-go cage.

During that time, Steven caught Lolly on her phone giggling and asked her who she was texting. He thought she was acting cagey so he snagged her phone out of her hands and saw that Dean had texted her a photo of a baby goat wearing pajamas. To say all hell broke loose was an understatement. Steven FaceTimed Dean, who answered immediately thinking it was Lolly and got an earful from Steven, who told Dean that using baby animal pics to seduce another guy's girl was a total pussy move. Meanwhile, Dustin was carrying a crystal pitcher filled with his own superior version of home-made bubble mixture for the mermaids (two teaspoons Palmolive, water, a teaspoon of suntan oil in place of liquid glycerin, and copious amounts of glitter). Lolly, who was now chasing Steven through the house, collided with Dustin, causing the pitcher of glitter water to slosh all over his face and shirt. Seeing his friend now sparkling like a *Twilight* vampire, Steven was unable to contain his schadenfreude, which gave Lolly the opening she needed to grab her phone back and announce to Steven that jealousy was an ugly color on him. In retaliation (and without thinking) Steven replied, "Oh yeah, well that dress is an ugly color on you!"

Lolly could handle a lot of snarkiness and had battled with her share of mean girls over the years, but the one thing she could not deal with was her boyfriend criticizing her appearance. She went ballistic, and the two of them got into a shouting match so loud that both of Anna's dogs heard the com-motion and came thundering down the hallway and burst into the room.

Anna and Chang-ri had been sleeping late due to jetlag, and when Anna appeared in the doorway to find out what Gemma and Jon Snow were barking at, Lolly screamed, "Maybe you shouldn't worry about who I'm texting or what I'm wearing and should worry about protecting your own sister's life!"

Which was when Steven said, "Oh yeah?! Maybe you should call your redneck drama boy to come pick you up on his tractor for the square dance because I'm getting pretty sick of your shit."

"Maybe I will!" she yelled back at him. "A hayride with Dean sounds pretty fucking fun compared to your dumb party!"

Anna knew better than to insert herself into their spat, so she lured her dogs away with promises of cookies and found Dustin in the laun-dry room, trying, with little luck, to wash the glitter off his face. She told Dustin what was happening between her brother and Lolly, and Dustin said an epic fight was probably what was needed because the cold war tension between them had become unbearable. "You're prob-ably right," Anna said. "Steven's like my dad. He shuts down when he's upset."

"What do you do when you're upset?" Dustin asked, always curious to hear how others dealt with their emotions.

"I sneak out and go dancing at clubs," Anna said. "And you?"

"When Kimmie accused me of mermaid lust, twenty minutes ago, I told her that 'mermaid lust' implied I wanted to be a mermaid as opposed to wanting to have sex with one."

Anna made an ouch face, and Dustin laughed. "I know! It doesn't even make sense," he cried. "I have spent the last eighteen years trying to learn how to process my own feelings but I'm at a loss at how to navigate hers."

"This is the first major relationship for both of you. You have to be patient. In a lot of ways, falling in love is the easy part." She told Dustin he was probably just overthinking everything, then asked him what the hell was going on with everyone. She hadn't expected to arrive back home to this much drama. "I spent the whole plane ride telling Chang-ri how cool and chill everyone is, and we get here and it's total mayhem."

"*I never fall apart, because I never fall together,*" Dustin said. "It's a Warhol quote that's embroidered on a pillow in my therapist's office."

"So that's why I haven't fallen apart yet!" Anna said. She started to giggle. "I've been on the cusp all summer."

Dustin joined in her laughter. "I've been on the cusp my whole life!"

"And what did Lolly mean about protecting my life?" Anna asked. "What's that about?" Steven had made Dustin swear that he wouldn't tell Anna about the Claudine situation, but Dustin found himself unable to lie to her face. Instead he just stopped laughing and stared at her dumbly. "Dustin, tell me what's going on."

"Okay, okay," he said. "Allegedly . . . Claudine . . ."

"Wait, Bea's Claudine?"

"Yeah, Bea's ex-Claudine. She went on the dark net and hired someone to hurt you as a romantic gesture for Beatrice because she thought that Beatrice blamed you for Vronsky's death. But now Beatrice has a new girlfriend from LA, and when Claudine found out about it, she took off and is now running loose somewhere in the Hamptons so we have no way to verify if Claudine was being serious or just talking shit. Steven doubled the security for the party just in case."

After Dustin finished the two of them stared at each other for a moment and then they began to howl with laughter. "It's official, I am living in a Korean soap opera," said Anna. "Thanks for telling me."

"Do you want to talk about it?" Dustin asked, wiping the tears out of his eyes. "It's not funny. We shouldn't be laughing."

"Are you kidding me? What else is there to do but laugh? I think the only person I need to talk to right now is Beatrice," Anna said. "Honestly, she can hate me if she wants, but I'd rather hear it from her. Or have it embroidered on a pillow."

Anna helped Dustin remove most of the glitter with toner and told him he needed to go and find Kimmie and hold on to her tight. "Let your heart take the lead instead of your head, for once."

After Dustin went to find Kimmie, Anna checked in on Chang-ri to make sure she was fine on her own for a bit. Chang-ri said she was perfectly self-reliant and that she and Natalia were going to take a walk on the beach and look for celebs. Chang-ri had also gotten a text from Minsoo who was traveling separately from The NowNows and, if anyone asked, the cover story was that Minsoo was Chang-ri's cousin. The plan was to introduce Minsoo as QT's girlfriend after he gained enough sympathy from fans for being ghosted by the mystery girl who had basically disappeared off the face of the earth.

As Anna headed out, she ran into Bucky Bradford's mother on the outside steps, who had just arrived to see if Greer needed any help for tonight's festivities. Knowing her brother wouldn't be happy with anyone getting a glimpse of the party layout before tonight, she ran interference.

"So kind of you to stop by, Mrs. B.," Anna said. "But my mom's getting a blowout in town. I'll let her know you stopped by."

"Maybe I'll run in and leave a note," Mrs. B. said, taking a step toward the house.

Anna stood her ground. "I'm sorry, but it's really not the best time."

"Are you refusing me entry?" Mrs. B. said, employing her best how-dare-you tone.

"Did Bucky send you over to see what you could find out?" Anna asked.

If Mrs. B. was shocked by Anna's forthright manner, it didn't show.

Instead she switched her tactic and used a conspiratorial tone. "My Bucky really wanted to start his senior year with a nice feather in his cap, so he's just been a nightmare worrying about your brother's party topping his own. He begged me to stop by the house to make sure the rumors of elephants and hot air balloon rides weren't true."

"I promise," Anna said holding up her hand. "No elephants. And last I heard the hot air balloon thing didn't work out."

"Aren't you a doll," she cooed. "All this one-upmanship is a waste of time. I told my Bucky if he wants to be big man on campus all he needs to do is make that French gal pal of his his girlfriend. I still remember the first time Alexander appeared with you on his arm at little Sammy L's bar mitzvah, you were the crown jewel . . . then."

Anna's ears perked up at her mention of Bucky's French gal pal, but unable to ignore the slight, she couldn't help but ask, "And what am I now?"

"A lucky duck who doesn't have to go to Alexander's annual barbecue today," Mrs. B. said, proving she didn't get to be the third wife of one of the world's richest men by getting flustered.

"I had no idea that Bucky and Claudine even knew each other."

"The Hamptons is high school; everyone knows everyone," Mrs. B. said. "They're at Alexander's right now."

Anna quickly said good-bye, leaving Mrs. B. to snoop on her own, and hurried down to the garage. She surveyed the cars and landed on her dad's convertible Aston Martin DB5, figuring since she was on a James Bond–type mission, she would need an appropriate whip.

XXII

Driving to Alexander's Southampton house on Meadow Lane brought back a slew of old feelings for Anna. A year ago, she had been competing in the Hampton Classic, and Alexander, her boyfriend at the time, was in the stands, cheering her on. As she pulled up to the valet in the driveway, she told the parking attendant that she wouldn't be there long and asked if he would keep her car up front for a quick getaway.

Anna bypassed the front entrance and walked around the side of the house. Hopefully she could avoid a run-in with Alexander or his father, but she was most concerned with avoiding Eleanor, Alexander's half sister, who was responsible for recording and disseminating the video of her and Vronsky in the throes of passion. But Anna heard she might not be in attendance because according to Lolly's mother, who was on the fundraising committee for the Met Opera with Eleanor's mother, Alexander's father and stepmother were headed toward divorce.

Anna needed to find Bucky and Claudine, which was pretty much the extent of her plan. She texted Lolly, knowing she would have the fastest response time: Found Claudine w Bucky at Alexander's, fyi. I'll be hiding in the shrubbery if u need me. Anna stared at her text, hardly believing the situation, and hit send. She took a deep breath and entered the kitchen through the side door.

It was bustling with waitstaff, some she recognized and some she did not. Jimela, Alexander's family's longtime housekeeper, was midconversation with a sour-faced server when she noticed Anna. Jimela's face lit up and she opened her arms. "Anna?"

Anna went over to her quickly. "I'm so sorry, it's been too long. And I didn't get to say good-bye to you properly."

"I was starting to think I'd never see you again," Jimela said. "Is Alexander expecting you?"

Anna shook her head. "I'm sorta crashing. I need to find a friend who's here. Claudine, a French girl . . ." Anna paused and pulled out a phone. She scrolled through Lolly's Instagram for a Coachella photo of Claudine. "Her."

"Ah yes, she and the Bradford boy have been floating about . . ." She tapped her nose with her finger. "Check the guesthouse bathroom."

"Thanks."

"I'm sure Alexander would be happy to see you," Jimela said.

"I don't know if that's true."

"Ahh, I'm going to tell you the same thing I told him. Life is long and lovers come into your life for three things: a reason, a season, or a lifetime, and no one knows which one it is until later," Jimela said.

Anna gave Jimela another hug, and then froze at the sound of Eleanor's voice growing in volume over the din of the party. "Is that . . . ?"

Jimela nodded, and seeing the panic on Anna's face, she quickly led her to the pantry. Putting her inside, she told her to give her a minute while she ran interference on Eleanor, who was no doubt coming to lodge a complaint about the waitstaff.

Anna spotted a stack of gray uniforms and white aprons on the shelf and, knowing there was no better way to become invisible around rich people than dressing like the help, she slipped out of her dress and into the server's outfit. Now in the starched gray uniform, her hair in a tight bun and holding a tray with two empty champagne flutes as she made her way through the party, Anna walked right by Eleanor, who didn't even give her a second glance.

Anna hurried toward the pool area. She spotted Bucky's madras shorts and lime-green sweater, but no Claudine. As she scanned the crowd milling around the vast lawn, a woman approached her and asked for directions to the bathroom. Anna said there was a ladies' room in the pool house, but the woman said that was where she had been waiting. "The door has been locked for quite some time." Anna lowered her head and directed the woman back into the main house and then beelined for the pool house.

Anna knocked gently on the locked bathroom door. "Claudine? Are you in there? Open the door." There was no answer, so Anna tried again. "Claudine? I need you to open the door, please!"

"Anna?" a voice behind her said. Anna grimaced and turned her head to see Alexander standing there. It was bizarre to see him, this person she had dated for years. He now seemed like a stranger, a very familiar stranger. He looked good, healthy. It was actually good to see him, not because she had any romantic inklings left for him, but exactly the opposite; she felt nothing for him at all. Except perhaps a vague nostalgic fondness for the ancient history they shared.

"Hey. So is there a master key to this bathroom? It's a long story that

I promise I'll tell you another time, like when I'm not in disguise at your dad's party."

Alexander reached above the door frame, pulled down a small key and handed it to her.

"Thanks," Anna said, opening the door. "I'll be back out in just a minute."

Inside the bathroom Anna found exactly what she expected, a very drunk Claudine on her knees in front of the toilet, retching. "Are you okay?"

"*Mais non, je suis horrible*," Claudine said into the toilet bowl. "My heart. It has been flushed away."

Anna replied in flawless French. "I am sorry things did not work out between you and Beatrice."

At the mention of Beatrice's name, Claudine lifted her head and looked up to see it was Anna who was talking to her. "You know Beatrice?" she asked, this time in English.

"I do," Anna replied. "We've met before. I'm Anna K."

"*Merde!*" Claudine cried and scrambled up off the floor. "Why are you here, you hateful twat-waffle?!"

Anna laughed out loud at her reaction. "Did you really hire someone to whack me?"

Alexander knocked at the door and asked if everything was okay in there.

"We're fine, thank you!" Anna said cheerily through the door. "Claudine, focus."

"Yes, whack you, like with a stick, not to kill you, but maybe break your pretty nose," Claudine said, casting her eyes to the floor. "For this I was willing to pay ten thousand American dollars."

"Was?" Anna asked. "So did you do it or not?"

"I intended to, but I didn't know what I was doing, so I had to trick the smart boy into helping me by telling him I wanted to buy illicit narcotics, but then they did bamboozle me, the evil little hacker trolls who live deep down in the dark networks."

"So there's probably not a hit on me?" Anna asked, growing impatient.

"I don't think so." Claudine shook her head miserably. "But I cannot be sure. It wasn't about you, it was a gift for Bea. But she doesn't love me anymore. No one loves poor Claudine."

"We should go find Bea so we can all talk," Anna said. "You'll feel better afterward."

"Why are you helping me after what I just tell you?"

"I'm here, Claudine, because running away from a broken heart doesn't work. And neither does blaming other people for things out of their control. We girls have it hard enough, it seems wrong to turn on each other."

"*Qui n'avance pas, recule,*" Claudine said.

"Who does not move forward, recedes," Anna said, translating the French proverb.

When Anna and Claudine exited the bathroom, she found the shades drawn and the door closed. Alexander was sitting on the couch, looking at his phone, waiting.

"Can you help get her to my car?"

"Of course," Alexander said, standing up.

After Anna and Alexander loaded Claudine into Edward's Aston Martin they stood in an awkward silence, each waiting for the other to speak.

"Did you hear that Steven is having a party tonight?" Anna spoke first.

"You'd have to be dead not to have heard about Sexy. Steampunk. Mermaid. Shambala," Alexander said. "I'm assuming it's supposed to be nonsensical?"

"You know Steven, some things change, some things never do," Anna said with a smile. "You should come. We have a K-pop band performing on the beach. They arrived last night from Seoul."

"My distaste for parties hasn't changed, so I'm going to pass. But if you have time this weekend, maybe we could go out for coffee? As friends."

"Let's play it by ear," Anna said. "Can you tell Bucky that Claudine will meet him at the party later? I'm going to take her back to the house to sleep it off."

"Oh, before I forget," he said and produced Anna's dress from the jacket he had draped over his arm. "Jimela brought this to the pool house while you were in the bathroom with Claudine." Anna glanced down the front of her gray uniform. She had almost forgotten she had it on.

"Thanks for being cool about all the hijinks," Anna said.

"I've been trying to be less uptight these days. And for what it's worth. I'd say the hijinks suit you well."

XXIII

Anna texted Beatrice that she had Claudine and that they needed to talk. Beatrice's reply came right back, saying she'd be at the party in a couple of hours and they could talk then. "She hates me and yet still wants to come to my party. Only in the Hamptons on Labor Day," Anna said and then started to laugh.

Claudine, who was resting her chin on the side of the car, letting the salty ocean air blow in her face, started to laugh, too.

When they arrived back at the house, Anna called Dustin and requested his presence in the garage. When he showed up and saw Anna in the servant's uniform, he did a double-take. "Should I ask?"

"Please don't," Anna said. "Dustin, I'm pretty sure Claudine got scammed before she could actually hire someone to hurt me. Can you help her into one of the guest rooms for now? She needs to sleep. I'm pretty sure a nap will fix her right up."

"Are you sure you know what you're doing?" Dustin asked.

"I'm not sure. But I'm okay with that."

After Dustin whisked Claudine away, Anna changed out of the uniform and back into her dress, now a little crumpled. She headed into the house and as she passed through the living room toward her bedroom, she stopped short. In the dining room her father sat at the head of the long table, talking to her mother. Anna was about to run over and ask him why he had told her he wasn't coming back for the party, but she could see that he hadn't even noticed her. He was so focused on what he was telling Greer. Anna saw the smile on her mother's face and decided to leave them alone. She could always act surprised to see him later.

As she walked down the hall, she heard the sounds of a girl crying and stopped by a closed door. She briefly thought about continuing to her room as if she hadn't heard anything but then she opened the door and found a Lolly-sized shape sobbing under the duvet. Anna lifted up the other side of the covers and crawled under to talk to her.

"I don't know about you," Anna said. "But I'm starting to question whether love is really worth all our tears."

"Oh Anna," Lolly said with a sniffle. "Everything's a mess."

"Tell me something I don't know," Anna replied.

And Lolly did. She told Anna she had never been so confused in her life. She knew from the moment she met Steven that she'd love him forever, and her feelings hadn't changed but somehow at camp she'd developed feelings for a boy named Dean. It just didn't make sense to her how she could feel this way about two different guys. "I know things could never work with Dean. But he's such a good actor and we've only been texting about the different theater programs at colleges, stuff Steven has no interest in."

"I loved Alexia with my whole heart," Anna said. "But that didn't erase all of my feelings for Alexander. I don't think that's how it works."

"Then how does it work?" Lolly asked.

"Nobody knows. It's either working or it's not. It's hard enough to tell if it is or isn't, let alone how!" Anna said, and the girls cracked up laughing. "What I *do* know is moping around all June did nothing. Only when I started doing things, making choices for myself, did I start to feel better."

"But how do I know what's the right choice when it comes to Steven?" Lolly asked.

"You should do what feels best for you. If that's taking time on your own to see if this Dean guy is your Vronsky, then do it."

"So you agree with Steven about taking a break?"

"Taking a break doesn't mean it won't work out. Look at Ross and Rachel. Justin Bieber and Hailey."

"Prince William and Kate!" Lolly said with a small laugh.

"Maybe even my mom and dad," Anna added. "He just showed up to surprise my mom."

"Aw, that's so romantic!" Then remembering something, Lolly sat up suddenly. "Oh no, does Steven know he's here?"

"I don't know, I just got back myself. Why?"

"Your dad nixed the fireworks after the concert, but Steven got them anyway," Lolly said. "I know he hates me right now, but I should go and warn him."

"My brother's lucky to have you, Lolly," Anna said. "Make sure he knows it."

While Lolly went to go find Steven, Anna went to her bedroom and changed into a white strapless Prabal Gurung dress with wildflowers bordering the skirt around the hem. When she undid her bun, her hair fell down in waves. Instead of combing them out, Anna added in some product and left it wild and free. She was tempted to put on her mystery-girl red lipstick but decided to go with a natural lip and smoky eye instead. Chang-ri showed up wearing the pink dress she had worn to the K-pop party and asked if Anna had any earrings she could borrow.

"What's the word on Minsoo?" Anna asked.

"She made it! Yay! This is her first time in America, too. She said that she and Quentin are renting a convertible to drive down to Memphis to see Graceland this week," Chang-ri told her. "It's like the ending of a romantic movie where the happy couple gets to drive off into the sunset together!"

"I'm glad she's having the life she wants," Anna said and opened up her jewelry box to help pick out earrings for Chang-ri. "Someone should."

XXIV

Natalia found Kimmie on the beach, hanging out with a miniature horse and a team of sand sculptors who were putting the finishing touches on a steampunk sand sculpture. They had been explaining their process to Kimmie, who was fascinated, telling Natalia she had already asked them if she could be their intern next summer. Next Kimmie introduced Natalia to her new friend, Julep, a South American Falabella miniature horse who lived in Montauk.

"Can I just say if poor people knew all the dumb ways you rich people spent your money, they'd band together and storm the castle."

"I overheard Steven saying they were getting paid seven grand plus expenses to build this thing, which sounds pretty sweet to me. Just think about it, they get to travel around the world and build fucking sandcastles. Sounds like a life to me."

Natalia conceded it did sound like a pretty good side hustle. "But if they really wanted to make some bucks, they should use their exotic travels to cover up a highly profitable drug- or diamond-smuggling business."

"You'll be a great evil genius one day," Kimmie said.

"Fuck one day, I'm here for world domination now," Natalia said with a grin. "Hey, can we talk about a few things?"

"Sure," Kimmie said. "You sound weirdly serious. Did something happen?"

"Nah, everything is cool. I mean, what do I have to complain about? I'm in the goddamn Hamptons! So, here's the dealio. I first have to say thank you for being a really incredible friend. I honestly don't even know where I'd be if I hadn't met you."

"You don't have to—" Kimmie began.

"Shush. Lemme finish." Natalia playfully put her finger over Kimmie's lips. "You're awesome. Checked off list. Numero deux, I know you feel weird about me hanging with Tamar and I get it. I don't know what it is about her, she's like the squarest woman alive but she's also such a good person. She's gonna help me get my GED because . . . I lied to you, I never finished high school. And then I'm gonna, I dunno, go to community college. The plan is for me to move in with her."

"What?" Kimmie asked.

"I know it's a lot to take in, but Dustin's gonna get his own place during his gap year before he goes off to brainiac U. I'm gonna take his bedroom. If I live alone, I'll be using again by the first weekend. Dustin wanted to tell you, but I asked him if I could. Because if you think the whole plan is nutso, then I won't do it. You've been too good to me, and you are my first true friend and I want to do right by you. And look on the bright side, you'll be the coolest high school junior ever, having a boyfriend with his own pad." Natalia stopped talking and motioned toward Kimmie. "Okay, now you say something."

"I don't know what to say," Kimmie said. She was feeling all sorts of different emotions. She was happy for Natalia, but she also felt weird that Natalia and Dustin, the two people she was closest to in the world, had been discussing this behind her back for who knew how long. Was that why things with Dustin had been so weird lately? They'd had some good weeks after their night at the St. Regis but since picking up Lolly from camp, she had started to feel disconnected from him again.

"Okay, how 'bout a thumbs-up or thumbs-down? I mean it, Kimmie-Kat, if you're like, screw off, then, I mean, this is your life . . ."

"Nat, you're the best friend I've ever had, and you deserve to have a nice home and someone to look after you. I wish you had told me you were having a tough time staying clean earlier, though."

"I'm always gonna have a tough time. It's just how being an addict works. I know this sounds crazy, but I feel like this is Nicky's doing. He's the first guy who I believed when he said he was gonna take care of me forever and maybe this is his way of doing it. Tamar was practically begging me to let her help me. I think she sees a second chance with Nick in me."

"I'm happy for you, Natalia," Kimmie said. "And it's gonna be so fun to tell Lolly."

"Oh, that's the third thing I wanted to talk to you about. Your sis found me earlier and apologized for being such a bitch and asked if she could get my advice about some boy stuff later. You'd tell me if I'm about to get a bucket of pig's blood dumped on my head, right?"

"Lolly's not really a mean girl. I have no idea what her damage was when it came to you."

"I do," Natalia said. "She was jealous that her little sister was coming to some other girl for advice."

"Jealous?" Kimmie stared at Natalia in amazement. "That thought never crossed my mind. Forget Dustin, you're the genius."

"You won't be thinking that when you're helping me study!" Natalia laughed. "C'mon, let's go back to the house. I got a mermaid tail to wriggle into and a seashell bra to reinforce."

XXV

The sun had set at half past seven on this the last day of August, and when Anna peeked into the guest room at the end of the hall, Claudine was still asleep. Day drinking while jetlagged was definitely a bad idea, which was why Anna was sipping a Diet 7Up and a sugar-free Red Bull as she walked around the house. Lolly had changed into a black backless Rag & Bone dress from the cruise collection, fixed her tearstained face, and asked for a truce on all relationship talk for the night, which Steven was more than happy to grant. The two of them were standing together in the foyer greeting the parade of arriving guests like they owned the place.

After an exhausting day of party prep, Dustin and Kimmie were already over it and snuggled up in the screening room partaking in their favorite Saturday night activity, watching a Criterion Collection movie while eating gummy candy. As she leaned on Dustin's shoulder underneath the projector's glow, any doubts Kimmie was having about Dustin faded and her confidence grew that she was with the right person. They were both the same kind of people, happy to be at the party, while not actually being at the party. After watching the first movie in Kieślowski's *Three Colours* trilogy, they planned to head down to the beach for the NowNows' performance and the fireworks show.

Aunt Jules and Wilson had arrived earlier with Edward, who had invited them to the Hamptons, making good on his deal with Anna. If Anna pressed him she knew he would reluctantly admit he didn't know the last time he'd laughed as much on a transatlantic flight. Her aunt and uncle had also hit it off with Chadwick and Manny, who were also in attendance, one-upping one another with their Hollywood horror stories, much to the amusement of Chang-ri, who was hanging on their every word. Chang-ri had decided she loved the United States within six hours of her arrival and was formulating a plan that would have her working in Los Angeles within the next five years. Both Aunt Jules and Chadwick gave her their contact info.

Adaka and Murf arrived a while ago and when Anna asked them where Beatrice was, they told her that when they left Bea's house, she and Tiare were getting out of the pool, heading to get dressed. "So basically you gotta factor in an extra hour for some sweet, sweet lovin'," Murf said, grinning. "You're not gonna believe it, Anna. Bea's like a totally different chick with this chick."

"It's a little spooky," Adaka agreed. "I hope you live long enough to see it."

Murf busted out in hysterics. "Don't mind her, my girl's a little twisted right now."

Anna brushed it off with a laugh and asked whether she could have a little of whatever they were smoking, which was when Adaka opened up her pink Judith Leiber French fry–shaped purse and held up a tiny joint for her. "I rolled it in twenty-four-karat gold paper."

Anna declined, but Murf insisted. "Vronsky would never want you to stay sad. The best way to honor his life is to find your bliss. This weed is bliss."

Anna nodded graciously, took the joint, and slid it into her pocket.

"No really, this strain is named A Kiss of Bliss," he said. Adaka had already wandered off toward the French fry bar and Murf gave Anna a tight squeeze. "It's good to see you, we'll catch up with you later."

Once outside, Anna stopped to admire the fruits of her brother's labor. Sure he had many people helping, but the vision was all his, and the backyard was unrecognizable from a few hours before. There was a canopy of twinkle lights, a gazebo covered in exotic flowers, and a pair of robot dogs on loan from Boston Dynamics walking about in custom steampunk costumes. The pool area had been transformed into a glittering turquoise oasis of sexiness. The overall effect was breathtaking, especially the spotlit mermaid lying in a cage blowing bubbles above the guests. Anna squinted at the mermaid's face and felt an odd recognition.

"Natalia?" Anna asked, walking to the edge of the pool to get a better look.

"Who's asking?"

"I'm Anna, Steven's sister."

"No shit," Natalia said. "I finally meet the famous Anna K."

"I don't even want to know what you've heard about me," Anna said, waving her hands.

"Not one bad thing," Natalia said. "People talk about you like you're a saint or something. I've been so curious to meet you."

"We've actually met before," Anna said. "At Grand Central." She reached into her pocket and pulled out the heart-shaped charm as proof, which she only had in her possession because Natalia had found it after Vronsky's death.

It wasn't easy to shock Natalia, but this did it. She was struck dumb up in her mermaid cage. Anna quickly told Natalia she had to go to the beach to check on a friend, but she'd find her later and they could meet properly. She then continued following the path, now lit by metal tiki torches, down to the oceanfront. An impressive stage had been constructed, and The NowNows were doing their sound check with extra speakers to make sure it was loud enough over the *whoosh* of the surf. At that moment a test firework lit up the sky with a boom, an upside-down smiley face in bright blue. The barge was anchored five hundred yards out with a crew that consisted of three generations of a local family that had been putting on pyrotechnic shows for the Hamptons for the last fifty years. The plan was to have the fireworks display start as soon as The NowNows finished their encore.

Anna saw her father and mother talking to the head of the fire department, who happened to be the father of seventeen-year-old twins who helped Steven get the last-minute permits lined up. As she got closer she saw her parents were holding hands, an occurrence she hadn't seen for the last two years.

"Well, look who's full of surprises!" Anna said, sidling up to her father.

"Where have you been?" Edward asked. "I've been here for hours."

"Oh you know, just doing a little of this and a little of that," Anna replied. "Mom, on a scale of one to ten how shocked are you that Dad showed up?"

In a rare moment of vulnerability, Greer spoke the truth. "I'd say five, because I didn't want to get my hopes up. So, did you know that Steven ordered fireworks even after your father expressly told him no?"

Here was Anna's chance to finally pay Steven back a little for all the times this year he was unfairly blamed for things that were her fault. "Don't be mad at Steven. He told me Dad said no and I'm the one who said we should do it anyway."

"Anna!" her father said, truly surprised at her admission.

"I just felt that we needed it. Or maybe I needed it. It's been a long and weird summer and I wanted to end it on a high note."

"Do we have a late-blooming rebellious teenager on our hands?" Greer asked.

"I wouldn't worry too much about this one," Edward said. "She's got a good head on her shoulders."

She quickly hugged her dad and told him she was proud of him for inviting Aunt Jules and Wilson, and he replied that he was proud of her for owning up to the fireworks even though he knew she was covering for her brother.

When Quentin saw Anna walk up, he did a flying leap off the stage and landed in the sand in front of her. "How's that for an entrance?"

"Amazing! Just like you coming halfway around the world on such short notice. Thank you so much. You saved the party."

"I love that you call this a party. This is no party . . . this is *paladaisue*," Quentin said, using the Korean word for paradise. "This is our dream, me and my bandmates. As trainees we often talked of how exciting it would be to play in America and now we're here and living the dream."

"And with your very own dream girl, too!" Anna said. "I hear you and Minsoo are taking a road trip to Memphis later this week? Be sure to send me a postcard from Graceland."

Anna's phone vibrated and she pulled it out of her pocket to see a text from Lolly. Beatrice just arrived! Anna texted back, asking Lolly if she could tell Beatrice to meet her in the pool house.

"I've gotta go take care of something important," Anna said, giving Quentin a quick hug. "Good luck and see you after the show!" Anna walked up the path, steeling herself for a show of her own.

XXVI

When Anna stepped into the pool house, Beatrice was sitting on the couch with her back to her, staring at the Apple TV screen saver, the one with all the seals swimming around underwater.

"That one's my favorite," Anna said.

Beatrice didn't turn around to speak to her. "Mine, too. What's your least fave?"

"The jellyfish," Anna said. "I got bit by one when I was eight. Steven was only ten but he had heard something about how people pee on sting-ray bites and he peed on my leg. It's hard to know which part was more traumatic."

"I was stung in Tahiti when I was twelve. My whole foot swelled up and Vronsky said my toes looked like purple potatoes and I screamed, 'I hate you' at him and do you know what he said?"

Anna sat down next to Bea on the couch. "No, what?"

"He said, 'Too bad, you big baby, 'cuz you and your purple potato toes are stuck with me.'"

"He told me that when you were little, people used to think you two were twins and he would always lie and say that you were a rare set of identical twins even though you were a girl and he was a boy. He loved you like a sister, you know that, right?" Anna said softly.

"I don't need you to tell me how much V. loved me," Beatrice snapped. "But that twin story is true, though the way I remember it is that I'm the one who came up with us being twins. He was the person I loved the most in the entire world."

"I'm sorry if you missed his memorial because of me."

"Don't flatter yourself, you didn't stop me from going. I stopped myself from going. I wasn't ready to say good-bye. I'm still not. I'm a girl who's used to having everything I want, but there's no amount of money that can bring him back."

"I'd do anything to bring him back, too. Sometimes I wish it were me."

Beatrice turned to face Anna for the first time since they started talking. "Is that why you're so chill about the whole Claudine debacle?" Bea asked Anna. "You have a death wish or something?"

"Nothing like that," Anna said. "The most disturbing part is not that Claudine may or may not have put a hit on me, it's *why* she might have ordered a hit on me . . . for you."

"You're right, she wanted you to suffer. Because I did," Beatrice said.

"I get it. You were grieving and Claudine was obsessed with you. Desperate to show you how much she cares. People do crazy shit for love."

"Fucking hell," Beatrice muttered. "After Coachella, V. and I got into a fight about you. I was sick of his sulking and was telling him it was time to 'thank u, next' your ass, but he wouldn't hear of it. He told you were the smartest and kindest and most empathetic person on the planet—he talked about you as if you were a goddamn unicorn. But here you are oozing with empathy for Claudine."

"She's here, you know. I found her with Bucky Bradford at Alexander's house."

Beatrice raised an eyebrow. "You went to Alexander's house? For Claudine? You may be as crazy as she is."

"I dressed up in a maid's uniform to get past Eleanor," Anna said. "I guess you could say I've had a time, today. You should really talk to her."

"I know," Beatrice said, and took a deep breath. "Okay, I'm only going to say this once: I was wrong. I blamed you because I needed to point the finger at someone. I kept thinking if he'd never met you, if he never fell in love with you, then I'd still have him."

"I think about that every day," Anna said.

"Well, you should stop, because it's not true. I met someone in LA. Her name's Tiare and she's my girlfriend. My first real girlfriend. I love her. Like I really love her. She's knocked me off my feet and I get it now. I get how Alexia felt about you. Over and over, he told me how you were different, how he'd never felt this way before. That it was like looking out at a field of flowers but only seeing one flower. It made me crazy listening to him jabber on about you. Maybe I was jealous because I was always the most important girl in his life and then all of a sudden, he meets you like one fucking time and it's like he's a completely different person? But I get it now with Tiare. She's my one flower."

"I'm happy for you, Beatrice," Anna said. "Alexia was my first big love, too."

"What the fuck, so I'm Beatrice now?"

"You're the one who said only your friends get to call you Bea," Anna said. "Anyway, did you hear? I'm going to school in Korea. I fly back next week. So you won't have to avoid me in the hallways at school."

"You're switching schools for your senior year? Because of me?"

"Don't flatter yourself," Anna retorted with a smile. "My dad thinks I need a fresh start. He's hoping if I spend a year abroad, everyone will forget about the sex tape."

"Please, everyone has forgotten it. Twenty-four-hour news cycle and short attention spans. No one remembers anything anymore. You should stay."

"So, you don't hate me?" Anna asked.

"Any girl who Alexia loves is okay in my contact list."

"I have a letter from Alexia where he talks about you. That's when he told me the twin story. I have a copy of it for you in my room."

"For fuck's sake, Anna, you need to see a doctor because you're too goddamn nice. It's a little repulsive," Bea said. "I suppose you're going to make me hug, now, right?"

"Damn right I am." Anna threw her arms around Bea. "When can I meet your girlfriend?"

"Now if you want. She's really amazing," Bea said.

Anna smiled. "Alexia would be happy to see you in love." She paused. "Sorry! That was the last sappy thing I'll say." Anna pulled the gold foil joint out of her pocket and held it up. "Any interest?"

"Anna K. offering *moi* a joint?" Bea let out an appreciative whistle. "I never thought I'd see the day."

"It's been a helluva summer."

Bea produced a lighter and handed it to Anna. "Fuck yeah, it has."

XXVII

Had there been a roof over the beach, The NowNows would have blown it straight through the stratosphere. They kicked off their set at 10 P.M. with their hit single, Seoul's Song of the Summer, "I Want You Now, Now, Now!" The Hamptons crowd delighted at their perfectly synchronized dancing skills, known as *kalgunmu* in the K-pop world, and by the end of the show, everyone was jumping up and down.

Anna, still buzzed from the gilded joint, was standing up in the front with Chang-ri, Bea, Tiare, Adaka, and Murf. Lolly and Steven were on the other side of the stage with Edward and Greer.

At the back of the crowd, Claudine stood with Bucky and a group of Collegiate boys who were drunkenly copying the NowNows' dance moves in a way that was only funny to them.

Unbeknownst to Anna, Kiril, Jordy, Ashton, and Denzel the Dangerous had just arrived and were currently passing a blunt back and forth as they hit the beach from the torchlit path.

This was only the third time Anna had ever smoked pot and the first time she actually enjoyed it. She could feel the music reverberating through her brain, the bass thumping to the beat of her heart as each K-pop hook electrified every cell in her body. She turned to Bea and Adaka swaying to the music. "This weed's really good!"

"This band's really good!" Bea said.

"How did you meet them?" Adaka asked.

"Long story," Anna shouted over the boom of the massive speakers blaring into the Hamptons night.

After The NowNows finished their set and left the stage, the crowd was shouting, "Encore! Encore!" and Quentin came running back out on his own. He thanked the audience for their energy and told them he wanted to share a new song he just finished. "It's a duet," said Quentin, and locked eyes with Anna, giving her a wink. "Half this song is in Korean and the other half is in English. The Korean half was written by me. The English half is a poem that a sad-eyed girl I met this summer gave me. It was given to her by a boy she loved. That boy is no longer with us; this song is for him. Now please welcome my very, very, very good friend, who is going to help me sing it for you . . . Minsoo!" Minsoo walked out onstage. The crowd roared. She stood next to Quentin and the two of them launched into the song.

> QUENTIN: Have you seen the sad-eyed girl
>   Do you know how she got that way?
> MINSOO: No longer waiting for love
>   Running straight at it
> QUENTIN: I see her with my own sad eyes
>   Recognizing all the lies

MINSOO: My heart is pounding
　　　　Emotions confounding

As Anna listened to the words, tears streamed down her face. Not the tears of pain and heartache she had cried all summer; these were tears of joy, of hope, of the belief that things could get better. After Quentin and Minsoo finished singing, the rest of The NowNows came running back out and sang a cover, a K-pop remix of the theme song from *Friends*, which ended the show on a random high note.

As the encore ended, Steven texted the pyrotechnic people, who were waiting on a barge to begin the fireworks. The sky lit up with three chrysanthemum fireworks, pink, purple, and red, and Anna looked around the crowd, overjoyed to be standing with her close friends and loved ones. She didn't see Kimmie and Dustin though.

Those two were busy making fireworks of their own. It didn't last long, their first time, but they both knew they would have plenty more practice in the future and of course homework was one of Dustin's specialties.

In the multicolored flash of the pyrotechnics, Anna spotted Kiril, and their eyes locked. She was starting to feel overwhelmed from all the stimuli and being stoned, and all she wanted was to get to Kiril and his friends, who were pushing their way through the crowd past Claudine, Bucky, and his posse of rising seniors. It all happened in slow motion under the burst and flicker of the sparkling night sky: Bucky getting too handsy with Claudine; Claudine slapping him in his drunk rubicund face; Anna clasping her hand over her mouth in disbelief; Bucky flying back wildly into Kiril, Jordy, Ash, and Denzel; Jordy's glass of Shambala cider splashing all over his new white linen shirt; Bucky pointing and laughing hysterically, unapologetically; a sharp shove from Ashton that sent Bucky slamming back into Claudine; Nehorai and two other members of Edward K.'s security detail closing in on the commotion; Anna getting a tap on her shoulder and turning away from the fracas to see a girl she'd never seen before, strangely out of place, wearing black jeans and a red hoodie cinched tightly around her head as she raised the pistol slowly and aimed it at Anna's chest; Anna registering the graphic on the front of the young gunwoman's sweatshirt, a depiction of the mystery girl encircled in red with a slash through it; Kiril pulling Bucky out of the scrum of teens now scrapping with the twentysomethings; the grand finale of the fireworks, a machine-gun burst of supersonic booms; Kiril socking Bucky in the jaw and Bucky sailing through the crowd; Anna learning the difference between the sound of a firework pop and a real gun's sinister report; Bucky stumbling in front of her as Nehorai bum-rushed and tackled the young woman in the red hoodie; and Bucky falling face-down into the sand at Anna's feet.

Trapped in a state of shock, Anna stared down at Bucky. A dark red stain grew on his shirtsleeve and the sky fell silent. A good portion of the crowd ripped up in applause, oblivious to all that had just transpired. Bucky rolled over onto his back and looked up at Anna, clutching his blood-soaked shirt. "Bucky's been shot!" he cried. "Help me, I'm shot."

Kiril stayed close by Anna's side in the aftermath. While Dr. Becker, who was in attendance, bandaged up the flesh wound on Bucky's upper arm, Anna answered all the questions from the authorities. "It happened so fast," she said and told them the girl they had in custody was the girl who fired the shot. She also came clean about her identity as the mystery girl. Anna decided not to bring up the whole Claudine situation, though she assumed that would eventually come to light. Once she and Kiril had finished giving their statements, the grown-ups waved them from the room to discuss how they were going to use their money and influence to keep a lid on the night's events from a public-relations perspective.

As Anna walked to the main house to change out of her bloodstained dress, Kiril followed along and kept asking if she was okay. She repeated to him over and over that she was fine. And she was fine, still a little shell-shocked from the night's unexpected turn of events, but as a person who had endured far worse tragedies, she was oddly composed.

Anna and Kiril stood in front of her open closet in her bedroom, both of them staring at the selection of summer dresses hanging before them. She wanted to tell him she didn't need his help to pick out a dress, but she also didn't want him to leave her side.

"Do all girls have this many dresses?" Kiril asked, reaching out and touching a few of them.

"Do you want to help me pick one out?" Anna asked. "You seem fascinated by them."

"That's probably because I'm rolling right now, but no, Alexia was the one who cared more about such things," Kiril said. "Hell, he picked out most of my clothes for me. Oh god, what am I going to do now?"

Anna knew Kiril was referring to his future wardrobe, but his words really struck a chord with her. *Oh god, what am I going to do now?* That was how she felt at the moment, too, but for a very different reason. Being with Kiril made her feel like her life was opening up in a new and exciting way. She didn't know where this new friendship would lead, but she was interested in finding out.

"Hey, Anna," Lolly said, appearing in the doorway. "You guys okay?"

"All good, Lolls," Anna said, waving her to come in and join them in front of the closet. "I'm trying to pick out something else to wear. Something without Bucky's blood all over it."

"I'll help," Lolly said, entering the room. "Maybe I'll change outfits, too."

"I should go find my friends," Kiril said, taking the hint. "You're coming back out, right?"

"Oh, definitely," Anna said. "This party is just starting to get good." She and Lolly looked at each and giggled. After Kiril exited, Lolly closed the door and leaned up against it.

"Is it me or did things get weird?" Lolly asked, her eyes twinkling, referring to the palpable tension that just left the room in the form of Vronsky's older brother.

"Things have been weird all summer," Anna said. "But, you know what? I'm okay with it. I've decided to embrace the weird."

Just then Anna's ears perked up at the opening strains of her favorite karaoke song, Gloria Gaynor's "I Will Survive," coming in from the party still raging outside. And with that, the girls threw on new dresses and quickly ran downstairs to join their friends on the dance floor. Summer was almost over, and they knew better than to waste a moment of it.

Epilogue

Vronsky's last letter to Anna, written on the morning of his death:

Dearest Anna,

I woke up happy today for the first time in a long time. I'm not sure why . . . well, that's not entirely true. Tonight is the charity concert where Lolly is singing, and I'm hoping you'll be there. The mere thought, the tiniest chance of being near you again, fills me with joy. All I want to do is see you . . . and I have a feeling that tonight is the night.

Indulge my good mood as I take you on a flight of fancy. This summer I would love to take you to my favorite place in the world. When I was four years old, my mother and father rented a house and spent the summer in Sicily near Catania. According to her, it was the happiest time in their marriage, that summer. On the last night of their stay, when my mother was sad about the summer's end, my father told her he bought her the house. To this day she says it was the most romantic moment of her life. We went back every summer for the next few years. Those were the best summers of my life.

It was there where I learned to ride a dirt bike for the first time. Nothing was more fun than zooming around the countryside with Kiril all day, every day. We stopped going there after my parents split, which I found more upsetting than their divorce, if I'm being honest.

*After my father died, my mom brought up selling the property, but
I begged her not to. When she asked me why, I told her that it was
the place where I understood how simple a good life could be. My
happiness felt true there. It was all quite melodramatic, especially
when I announced I wanted to be buried there.*

*I can't wait to bring you to Sicily. You will love it. I swear the sun
shines differently there. Everything is clear and bright, kind of like
the way I see you. If I close my eyes and concentrate, I can almost
feel your arms around my waist as we ride off into the Sicilian sunset
together.*

I hope I see you tonight and then every day for the rest of my life.

Love always,
Alexia

The letter Anna wrote to Alexia on the night before her first day of her
senior year:

Dear Alexia,
*Summer ended with quite a bang in the Hamptons. It's a long, absurd
story involving a crazed K-pop fan who got pissed when her favorite
group didn't win Song of the Summer and she blamed the mystery girl.
The important thing is no one got hurt too badly, and the party was
memorable.*

*Your cousin Bea is doing better. She even has an Instagram-
official girlfriend, Tiare, who is pretty incredible. You would
love the two of them together. They decided to do a long-
distance relationship because Tiare is in Hawaii practicing for
a big surf tournament. The plan is for Bea to go to Hawaii for
Thanksgiving to see her, and I might go, too. Bea and I have
become much closer. We both want to keep you present in our
lives and we have even gone to a few support group meetings for
teens who have lost loved ones.*

My parents and I all went up to Deerfield to get Steven settled for his post-grad year. Lolly wasn't there . . . she and Steven decided to take a break, but I'm not sure how long it will last because I know Lolly is visiting him this weekend. Dustin and Kimmie are doing great. Dustin found a very cool apartment in Harlem close to the community center where he works with high-risk teens.

The biggest news is I decided not to go to Branksome Hall for my senior year after all. But I'm not going back to Greenwich Academy, either. I have decided to live in the city and attend Spence with Lolly. I can't believe I am finally a senior in high school who will be graduating in 2020! I wonder what this new school year is going to bring! My mom and dad are taking me and Steven to tour colleges this fall, a nice normal family activity that will definitely be more fun now that my parents are officially back together. My father is making real efforts to work less and enjoy his life more.

We moved into a temporary apartment downtown on lower Fifth Avenue while our CPW place is getting renovated. I have to say I really believe I'm a downtown girl. There's a different energy below Union Square and I love exploring our new neighborhood. Gemma and Jon Snow seemed to love their new life in the city, and whenever I walk them in Washington Square Park I am soon surrounded by an admiring crowd.

I took your letters to a print shop and made copies of them because I didn't want to damage the originals. They are now in a leather-bound journal that I keep on my bedside table. It comforts me to keep you close. I hope you don't mind, but I shared a few letters with Bea and Kiril. Kiril showed up in the city last week, and took me and Bea over to the apartment and let me take a few items from your room. Bea took your favorite burgundy scarf and your "Count" baby blanket. I took the blazer you were wearing when we first met and your gray cashmere cardigan, the one I called your "dad sweater" when we had Valentine's Day lunch at Keens. Kiril also gave me a bottle of your signature scent, which makes me happy whenever I sniff it, which is often.

I have nowhere to send this letter . . . but that's okay. I know as I write the words that you will find a way to read them. Wherever you may be.

Love always and forever,
Anna K.

Acknowledgments

Writing a sequel was far harder than I expected, and trying to craft it during a global pandemic was damn near impossible. But somehow, with a lot of help from so many people, here we are....

The new people who deserve recognition and my deep gratitude: Jenna Hensel, for being an excellent first reader; Juliet Burks, for sharing your theater camp stories with me; her mother, Lucy Burks, for being such a great cheerleader; Mackenzi Lee, YA author extraordinaire, for letting me pick your big brain; Diana Snyder, for always answering my text questions about all things Greenwich, Connecticut; David Holden, for reminding me "you got this" even when I wasn't sure I did; Tasha Blaine, for your keen editing eye, Jordan Moblo, for all your warm encouragement; Jordan Cerf, my manager, for your enthusiasm; Kristin Dwyer of LEO PR, for all your pitching; my incredible editors, Sarah Barley and Caroline Bleeke, for your patience and wise counsel through the many rough drafts; and to Sally Wofford-Girand, for being my literary agent as well as my good friend. I appreciate you all so much and this book is better for your contributions.

To my wonderful family and loving friends, who were all mentioned in book one, thank you again!

To Flatiron Books, my truly exceptional publishers. I am so grateful for Bob Miller, Megan Lynch, Keith Hayes, Kelly Gatesman, Malati Chavali, Chrisinda Lynch, Cat Kenney, Jordan Forney, Marlena Bittner, Sydney Jeon, Nancy Trypuc, Katherine Turro, Jonathan Bennett, Vincent

Stanley, Emily Walters, Emily Day, Alexandra Quill, Peter Janssen, NaNá Stoelzle, and Kyle Avery.

Lastly, the MVP of this entire process is my husband, my favorite thing, John G. Kloepfer. Thank you for being the best first reader, editor, therapist, friend, and husband of all time. I love you like crazy, and I thank my lucky stars that we had each other (and Gemma!) during this unprecedented time in history.